Chasing Rainbows

Parallel Shades of Normality

PRISQUA CAMIUL

Published by Richter Publishing LLC www.richterpublishing.com

Editors: Jenna Rimensnyder & Mandi Weems

ISBN-10:0692667245
ISBN-13:9780692667248

DISCLAIMER

DEDICATION

To my children, Amanda and Antony, you are the light of my life.

To my besties, HotFish and Mother Hen, you are my inspiration and mentors.

I honestly don't know what I would do without you. I love you all.

TABLE OF CONTENTS

ACKNOWLEDGMENTS

Thank you to David Tyc for your unconditional support along this journey. If it was not for your kind words, I don't think I would have gone through with this book.

Thank you to Jacob Baines and Jarrad Hurley for giving me the words to fill in the blanks when needed. Thank you RedBlackCrusade aka Stephen, for your advice and suggestions.

Being able to talk about my fears, doubts and hopes about the book was of tremendous help. So, my love and gratitude go to Amanda McIntosh, Ellie Ritchie and Ben Vizer. And a huge thank you for listening to my babblings and supporting me in this endeavour.

Thank you to all the wonderful people who were looking forward to reading this book, I hope I don't disappoint.

Thank you all.

Unfinished
"I still want that goodbye kiss."
- Demetra Gregorakis

For some reason, I thought love conquered all.
That when you fell in love destiny would fall into place - that it was
guaranteed your path would cross with this soul you fell for,
time would pass but it was okay because he was going to show up,
he would see someone else for a while,
you would do your own thing and then one day you end up in the
same place at the exact moment.
But I quickly realized that love is not a script in a movie and I had to
endure all the feelings of what it was like to fall in love with
someone whose future just couldn't include me.
- Demetra Gregorakis
Love is not the only thing you need, sometimes love isn't enough.

PROLOGUE

UK. Allanah

In this country, there's no end to the rainbows. Our proud island is at the mercy of every weather system in the world, but thankfully, by the time it all gets to us, it's a subdued version of whatever angry storm it used to be.

That seems to just about sum up my life perfectly. I sit on the edge of a storm, wondering how on earth I'll ever make it out to the clear skies beyond. Then I see the magic. At first, it's just a shimmer of light that I can't quite focus on, the sun tries to break through the clouds, and then, there it is in all of its glory. A huge rainbow spreading across the sky, there's no mistaking its presence and with it comes the warmth of our life giver, the star of our galaxy. Things will be okay, rainbows never lie.

As my youngest sits on my lap, sucking the remnants of his biscuit that he'd dunked in my tea, I know there's a rainbow out there, even if I can't see it. I feel like I haven't slept for more than three hours at any one time in a lifetime, but those soggy fingers tell me that it doesn't matter. I can sleep when I'm dead. We have found our rainbow, I can see the pot of gold, and I'm frantically hoping it's still buried enough so that no one else can steal it away from me.

I've met my soulmate. I found him and I grabbed him even though the world tried to tell me I was already spoken for. There was no way I was giving up my chance for happiness, I fought hard and selfishly, but I think it was what the universe wanted me to do, to put things right and bring my little corner back into balance.

I know he's my soulmate with my entire being, he brings out the best in me, he makes me feel, he makes me live. There's no replacing his sunshine in my life; he chased away the clouds and let

1

me walk that bridge over the rainbow. I know how lucky I am, and to experience life this vividly, you have to have felt the dark days, it's the only way to appreciate the intensity of what we have together now.

Oh we're far from perfect, it's taken us five years to climb out of debt, we've chopped and changed our jobs trying to find the best path forward, and no matter how good we are together, we have a broken family that we glued back together. No matter how hard we try, the cracks still show, but thankfully, the glue is strong and always holds.

Despite that, we are somewhat isolated. The choices we have both made mean we're far from our friends. It seemed like a simple sacrifice in the large scale of things, but the soul is a complex beast that needs filling from all angles. We feed ourselves with each other and the here and now, hoping that will be enough to keep us satisfied. At least our own families have accepted us now.

What will I do when this little treasure has grown and gone to school? I'll build my empire of dirt, I'll make sure our family business is flourishing, and then I'll start my own. A mobile coffee shop, one that sells every type and flavour of luxurious and refreshing sweet tea you can ever imagine. A five-minute pit stop in the daily chaos of life, put your feet up for just one second and unwind, recharge before you head back to the grind. I'll even have a selection of carefully chosen entertainment, quick reads, to accompany your teapot treat. The first ever short story, daily pick, mobile tea house that England has ever seen. Once my little man has started school, I'll work part time in a teashop or cafe, learning the ropes, discovering the secrets, and chasing that rainbow.

I'll never stop chasing rainbows.

I want to get married on the beach, on Fraser Island, Australia to be precise. Rainbow or not, it will be the most magical thing. I want to climb the jungle pathways and discover the world of the ancients, see the pyramids in the sand, watch the stars in an untainted sky, swim in the open ocean with dolphins, run free as the wind and live for every moment.

I hope my children discover the world, strive to succeed so they can have their very own hopes and dreams in the palm of their hands. I want them to see the colours of the rainbow and know everything will be okay, without ever having to feel the fear of the approaching storm. I hope I have done enough to shelter them from the coming winds, I can only keep trying, keep moving, keep giving. Keep learning from my mistakes, after all without the past there would be no future.

Sometimes I wake in the night with a sense of dread and fear. The darkness closes in. That past haunts me, the decisions I've made, the choices forced upon me and the mistakes that always seem larger and uglier in the dark. Thinking about your own life can be worse than any nightmare in those long lonely hours. Did I do my best, am I a good person, do I deserve to be happy? Who would I be if things had happened differently? Would I still have my friends?

Australia. Zéphirine

Today we celebrated Zéphirine's birthday. Birthdays are normally a time for celebration... so why was she crying? Ten minutes earlier, her daughter Allison barged into her bedroom and handed her a pink paper bag that read 'I <3 Mum'. Zéphirine opened it to find a box way too small for that bag, and in that small box was a candle. A $50 candle. She knew the price, because her daughter had bought the same for her own bedroom, and they had joked about how amazing the candle smelled.

It was not the price or the candle itself that had caused Zéphirine to cry. The lack of thought behind the gift and her daughter merely handing it over on what was supposed to be a special day brought on these feelings. Her daughter made her feel worthless. While Allison handed the bag to Zéphirine, she cared enough to add, "You'll get the rest on Mother's Day." She then closed the door and was gone, her good deed done for the day. "Shall I bundle your birthday present in with Christmas?" Zéphirine sneered under her breath. Instead of saying it aloud, she tried to hold back the tears because in less than 10 minutes she had to drive Allison to work.

Zéphirine had moved in with her daughter and her boyfriend through no choice of her own. She had nowhere else to go after she could not renew her lease due to much-needed renovation to the apartment. Initially, she had not expected to stay at her daughter's apartment for long, but after a while, it truly began to feel like home, and she enjoyed being closer to Allison.

Allison, not one to be 'house proud', hated housework and it certainly wasn't a priority. In her own words, "I don't have time, we both work full-time and clean on weekends." The apartment was a mess to put it mildly, her bedroom looked as if a tornado had blown through, and you couldn't even see the timber floor. The dirty dishes piled up on the kitchen sink, as well as on her desk and coffee table; upon which Allison and her boyfriend would eat their dinner. The laundry basket overflowed with clothes waiting to be washed. Everywhere you looked something needed attention.

Even though Zéphirine paid rent, she took it upon herself to help out around the house, because it was her daughter after all. She did the dishes, kept the kitchen tidy, and emptied the ashtrays. She washed and folded the clean clothes ready for her daughter to put away, but the folded clothes would stay on the couch for days, if not weeks. It felt like an endless and unappreciated task, but Zéphirine kept at it.

Allison would also run late or miss the bus most mornings. So, in the end, it was sort of decided that Zéphirine would simply drive her daughter to work every day. This went on until they argued over an electricity bill; it ended with an exchange of harsh words, and it was clear that Zéphirine's daughter failed to appreciate her being around. Zéphirine realised she would never be good enough for her children. After that squabble, they stopped talking to each other for four weeks. Zéphirine decided not to do anything but the bare minimum tasks around the house, making sure she cleaned her own dishes and washed only her own clothes. Allison took the bus to work. Even when they started to talk to each other, the only thing they resumed as normal was the driving to work.

Zéphirine tried hard not to cry. She smiled at the sunshine, which gave her a reason to wear her sunglasses in the hope it would hide her red eyes. A few tears still managed to escape despite her best efforts to hold them back. Maybe Allison knew she was crying, but if she did, she failed to show any acknowledgement. Zéphirine was not in the mood for an argument anyway, especially while driving. As soon as Allison got out of the car, the relief of tension overwhelmed her and the tears finally came in an unstoppable flow.

As she sat there in the car with a flood of anger tying knots inside her stomach, she wondered how she'd manage to carry on with her day. The gym had never seemed so appealing, a hard session lifting dumbbells to channel the emotions churning in her gut. The only problem was that she could not stop the tears; her soul was crying out in pain and anguish.

She drove home and fell into bed with the feeling of both relief and desperation. Nothing was wrong but nothing was right either. She was tired of everything and tired of nothing. "I don't want to be a mother anymore. I'm done! I quit!"

She had not spoken to her 16-year-old son in months because he'd called her a 'cunt' without any remorse or even a hint of an apology. The father, again, failed to see it as a big deal, and said *she* should be the one apologising. She refused. "If he wants to see his mother, he knows where she lives." She'd told him in no uncertain terms. Just 16, and he hadn't been in school in years. He had no job and smoked weed all day, which by the way, his father was cool with. In a fruitless endeavour, she tried to engage professional help. Unless he endangered his life or someone else, no one could or would do anything. Surely that would simply be too late, but who was she to argue? So, she simply gave up on him.

At least she could be proud of her 19-year-old daughter who had a loving boyfriend, a full time job which she earned good money that allowed her to shop like there was no tomorrow. Yet Allison only saw Zéphirine as worth a $50 candle. She couldn't shake the thought from her head. She thought she shared a close relationship with her daughter, and Allison knew her well enough. Sure, that candle smelt good, extremely good even, but so does the $5 candle from the corner store. Zéphirine knew because they had a house full of damn candles. They both liked to burn candles, but only Allison could afford to spend $50 on one candle.

Even if Zéphirine could have afforded it, she wouldn't put that much into one candle. She could think of a million things she would rather spend the money on, like a video game or a day spa voucher. Her daughter should've known that. So why the thoughtless present? That bothered her a lot. Especially when

Allison liked to brag about loving to buy meaningful presents. So what happened there? Her birthday was on the same day every year if you can believe that... Unlucky for Allison maybe, it was only a few weeks away from Mother's day. So she had to buy her mother two presents within a few weeks, how painful could that be?

On top of struggling to fit into this world, fighting to find a reason to get up every morning and stay alive, Zéphirine was now ashamed of being a mother more than ever. In fact, from now on she might tell people she did not have kids, it would be easier. But there was still time. Allison was not a morning person. Maybe she had planned a surprise dinner, flowers, or a birthday cake at least. Zéphirine got out of bed and decided to go for a walk to clear her mind. She thought perhaps she made too much of nothing; birthdays can have that effect on you.

Her phone rang while she was walking on the beach, her daughter's face flashed on the screen smiling in her infectious way. Zéphirine couldn't help but get excited. She thought Allison had something to tell her about what they were doing for her celebrations. Her heart sank with an ever increasing heaviness when all Allison wanted was to let her know that she had been overcharged on her phone bill. Because that is something Zéphirine needed to know NOW. Then came the icing on the cake, she proceeded to tell her that she'd be heading to her father's place after work as he told her she never went to see him. So, on her mother's birthday Allison went to spend time with her father.

Zéphirine stopped by the supermarket and bought a cake. She went home, poured herself a glass of wine, and served a piece of cake. She checked her Facebook account and welcomed the birthday wishes from her friends and strangers alike; it was the first thing that had made her smile that day. She then decided to go to a party on *Second Life* and enjoyed dressing up her avatar. After spending an hour in *Second Life*, she opted to watch a movie. Instead of taking just another piece of cake, she took the remainder along with the rest of the bottle of wine and nestled down on the sofa. It was her birthday after all. She turned on her Xbox and watched Netflix.

Eating a whole cake while drinking wine did not make her feel better. She felt worse. The demons that haunted her about watching what she ate were old, but still screaming as loud as ever. She'd carried them for years and at that moment, they made her want to cry all over again. She couldn't escape the fact that she was worth a thoughtless $50 candle. Her mind drifted and she thought about Dr Oliver Lang. She was still under the spell that was Oliver. He wasn't just the boy next door, he was nonetheless a scientist, and *'way out of my reach'* Zéphirine thought when she'd finally found out who he was. She remembered that night clearly. How long had it been? Almost a year now. But how could she forget? She remembered his smile, his kisses, and his hands brushing her hair from her face with such an overwhelming display of tenderness it had made her heart stop.

She had been minding her own business that night and was there to have fun; a girls' night out. He appeared from nowhere, causing her to jump slightly in surprise. He definitely caught her off-guard, her normal defences lay curled up in the corner, completely oblivious to the danger that approached. Of course, predictably and inevitably, she had not been good enough for him either. She had been meaning to send him an email to ask why. Why? Why did he approach her? Why did he kiss her? Why did he invite her out to then retract his offer after simply proclaiming to be too busy? Why did he disappear? Why didn't he give her a chance? Maybe she didn't want to know the answer. Was she that worthless of a person? It seemed that destiny had other ideas for her: a long, single, and sad existence.

Zéphirine had a whole load of people around that kept telling her how much of a great person she was. Really? Because right now she did not feel so great. She felt insignificant, thanks to daughter dearest, who re-affirmed that feeling. She thought about the guy she was dating, or no longer dating, since she hadn't heard from him in two weeks. Her friends had nicknamed him "Scarface" because half of the disfigurement on his face. Besides the fact he had managed to hide this detail on his dating profile, she knew it was not a serious relationship and would never be. She told Julia from the beginning:

"He is not into me."

"Don't be ridiculous!" Julia replied. "If he wasn't into you, he wouldn't be dating you!"

"I know when a man is into me, okay! And this one is not. I'm not sure why he's still seeing me. Maybe because he has nothing else better to do until he goes back out to sea?"

Of course it was okay not to be into her, she was just hoping for some honesty at the very least. She asked him why he didn't hold her hand and had not even tried to kiss her when they went out to a coffee shop some days earlier on. "We don't know each other that well," he replied. They had slept together a few times by then, so he did know her a little, enough to hold her hand and kiss her in public she thought. Why can't people tell you what they truly think instead of letting you hang in there making all those assumptions?

She was so tired of hearing the clichés, 'you will find him when you stop looking', because she was NOT looking, god dammit! They found her! She was beginning to feel that she was obviously an idiot for thinking that she would ever find love. Apparently everyone else was allowed their Prince Charming but her.

Maybe she was doomed, or was it the so-called karma from a past life? She didn't understand anymore. What was the point of living if it was to be unhappy? She had tried to comprehend life. She had accepted and put up with everything life had thrown at her, but whatever path she took, it seemed the result was always the same.

Okay, let's put things into perspective here. Zéphirine was thankful because nothing dramatic had happened to her, and it could have been a whole lot worse. A friend once told her when she was feeling down, "There are a lot of people dying of hunger or disease, so you really should not be complaining about your life." They were no longer friends after that talk. Then she thought about another friend, Marie. She had come into her life in an unusual way. Zéphirine didn't consider Marie to be her best friend; she was more like a sister to her, the kind of sister she would have liked to have.

Marie was one of the most wonderful people Zéphirine knew. Marie was like Mother Theresa, but Marie was also the unhappiest person she had ever met. Marie lived with a secret. It took a while for Zéphirine to figure it out. She had to put two and two together: Marie was raped on her seventh birthday which happened to be on the seventh of July to make it more coincidental. Zéphirine got confirmation by asking Marie on a text message to which she replied a simple yes. "Is he family?" Zéphirine had to ask, to which she replied no. Not that it mattered but somehow Zéphirine felt a small relief to know it had not happened by the hands of a family member. Either way, it was dreadful. That was all she could ever get out of her.

Zéphirine assumed Marie's boyfriend had come to the same conclusion. That was why they were together, using each other as a front in a loveless relationship. She was young and beautiful. He was an ugly, grumpy old man, and an asshole, but needed a visa to stay in Australia, which their relationship would grant him. Zéphirine could not stand their fake relationship and knew he was cheating on her just because '*he could only get sex once a year.*' Yes, those were the exact words he had told Zéphirine when he got caught; like it was his goddam right to have sex, a gift that she was withholding from him. It nearly destroyed Marie, but she took him back. As much as Zéphirine didn't want to lose her friend who'd meant so much to her, she decided to step back for good and let Marie be. *You cannot help those who do not want to be helped.*

So yes, there were definitely worse cases in the world than her own, and there would always be someone else that was wearing worse shoes. That didn't help how Zéphirine felt. Her emotions were real and valid, and she wondered if this was how you live life, by thinking there was always someone worse off than you? Why couldn't she get a break? She was not asking for a million dollars to miraculously fall into her lap! She just wanted to be happy and live happily, to love and be loved.

Actually what Zéphirine's mind – or heart – was longing for was Oliver. She *just* wanted Oliver. "*Is it too much to ask for?*" Why put him in her path if he'd be gone almost instantly? Not a single day had passed since they first met without her thinking about him. *Not again*, she told herself as she shrugged. And she knew it was crazy, irrational thinking. She tried hard to push those thoughts away, but they were there; he was never far from her mind.

The right person will come along. To be honest, Zéphirine thought she had more chances of a truck hitting her and that she may as well be chasing rainbows. She only had to look at the past

40-odd years of her life to know.

CHAPTER 1: LOCKED AWAY

I kept it in a box. My box, Allanah's box. It was a pretty box, wooden and ornate, with a small amount of gold leaf decorating the edges. A swirling pattern of leaves that was tiny, but there none the less. I kept the box shut tightly. Sealed firmly and wrapped up so the bad couldn't seep out. It was a box that should never be opened.

Sometimes life is taken out of our hands, choices don't exist, and things happen that send us sprawling into chaos. It happened to me when I was 17, so I locked it up in the box. I didn't expect it to ever happen again, so now I was forced to look back inside the box. If I hadn't learned my lesson enough to stop it from ever happening again, what was I to do? Put this inside the box too? Was there room for all of it inside that one pretty little box? Well, I'd have to try, it was the only choice, that or curl up and give in, and I would never give them the satisfaction of knowing they had won.

Maybe if I take it all out of the box, crimp it around the edges, perhaps even smooth it out a bit, then the whole thing, old and new, will fit much more neatly back inside the box, and then I'll never have to open it again. Yes, that seems a good way forward, learn and move on.

When I was younger, I loved the snow. Watching it fall slowly down, a soft, clean blanket enveloping the world and spreading a gentle quiet across the ground. It was soothing and peaceful when I was tucked up in my room with my nose pressed up against the glass. I'd have to keep moving across the window so I could still see when the fog from my breath obscured my view. I especially loved it at night, there was a magic that danced hand in hand with the snow. Perhaps it was the anticipation of playing in it the next day, the promise of no school if it was deep enough, or the pleasure of a new world to explore and shape as my own.

Every year I'd ask for a sled for my birthday. I dreamt of whizzing down hills with my scarf trailing behind me and of the wind biting at my cheeks; making me feel so alive. The answer would be the same each year, there'll be no snow after your birthday, and it'd be a complete waste. Year after year, I'd watch the snow fall after my birthday had been and gone, with an inner smile to myself that I had been right. I knew there would be snow after my birthday, and I had told them so.

The sled wasn't important; I'd probably never have been able to use it, even if they had bought me one. The biggest hill I knew of near where I lived ended in a row of parked cars, one of them being my dad's Capri, and I knew that was the real reason I wasn't allowed one. I was happy to watch from the window and play in the garden, creating my own magic in my mind.

On the year of my 17th birthday, the magic had happened: this time the snow was falling on my actual birthday! Still no sled, but that was all a distant childhood whimsy. This year would be spent being adult in my newly-established teenage delusion. The girls were going out for drinks, and I was excited.

As it turned out, there was just the two of us, the weather was so bad that no one could make it out, and because I was in walking distance, I'd been able to get there fairly unhindered. As always, I thought the snow lying on the ground held an inner peace; all sound was dampened and the glow from the street lights gave everything a feel that was like Christmas—a soft, warm kiss.

A few people were in the bar we'd chosen, but it was pretty much ours for the night. I felt invisible in my scarf and cherry red

Docs, drinking my half a lager (because I was, after all, a lady). I'm not sure if it was the cold air or the invincibility of youth that sealed my fate, but that night after only drinking half lagers, I was the drunkest I had ever been. At 17 years old, it is a scandal, I agree. I wasn't a wild child, I wasn't off the rails, but I did like to go out on a Friday night and drink with my friends. It's something we'd been doing from the age of 16, so I was a dab hand at it by the time 17 knocked on the door. We were friendly with the bouncers, my friend was far friendlier than I was, and as such, we were offered some protection and access to the pubs. We behaved ourselves and stayed out of trouble, we danced the nights away, and loved being carefree and single.

It was all an illusion.

The other people in the bar on that snowy wintry night lived in a flat two doors away. There was a reason they lived so close to the hub of nightlife. I knew who they were, everyone knew who they were; it was part of survival. They're the ones you avoid, the ones you don't upset, and if they talk to you politely, reply without causing offence, but do not do anything to encourage their attention. They made their living from other people's addictions, thriving from making people needy, and they thought the sun shined out of their own arses.

I had no time for them, I'd watched them stand on the edge of the dance floor, smug smiles on their faces, thinking they ruled the world, walking round like peacocks in a mockery of their own self-importance. What really made me angry was the fact that if they clicked their fingers, the girls would flock, positively running to do their bidding, desperate to be in their zone. Personally, I didn't see the attraction, they were all ugly inside and out, and having money to splash around as a result of another person's addictions certainly wasn't attractive to me.

That's how I know that what's in the box wasn't my fault. I didn't ask for it. I didn't give permission. I didn't want it. It should never have happened.

Now as I lay the contents of my pretty little box out bare before me, I can see things differently. Is it time, wisdom, reflection, and maturity or finally, after all of these years, is it love for myself that lets me see things for what they are? What's in the box is so ugly it

13

should never be seen, but sometimes we need the ugly truth to allow us to see the beauty underneath.

The box feels as cold as the snow was that night. It lies open so I can't see the gold leaf on the lid, I can't feel the safety of its clasp firmly shut tight. I can only see the harsh reality laid bare, waiting for me to iron the edges and fold it all back up neatly inside the box.

I can't remember if the other people in the bar brought us a drink that night. I think they did. I can't say they put something in my drink because I don't know if that's true. I can't say if they had planned it all along, because if I hadn't made that one silly mistake, none of it would have happened.

They asked us to go to their flat after the bar had closed, a birthday party in my honour. I remember that. I declined, as I had no interest in them and was ready to go home. To prove that to them, I took out my key and shook it, declaring my intention to go home.

Then, I dropped my key in a mountain of snow. In that one second, I'd shaped my future.

I desperately scrabbled in the snow, searching for that one single key that would mean I could go home. In my frantic search, I remembered my mum's words as I'd headed out that night, "Don't lose that key." It wasn't because I was in the habit of losing keys, it was because it was the first time I'd taken one out with me. Normally she'd wait up for me, but that night, I'd told her there was no need.

I'd lost that key. On my hands and knees, the impossibility of my task hit me full force. I was never going to find it.

I felt a hand on my shoulder, a gentle persuasion—*come upstairs for a drink, and then we'll find your key.*

I never found the key. I didn't make it home that night.

This is where my memory becomes sketchy. Masked by alcohol, pain, humiliation, and maybe something more, I don't know how I got into the flat. I don't know how I ended up in that room. I don't know why I was naked.

I do know that I said no.

I can remember lying on my front and not being able to move. I can remember saying no, over and over again. Maybe I was screaming it in my head, but I know the actual words came from my mouth, too. I know they heard what I said. I know they ignored me. I know they laughed as they took it in turns. I know there was someone else who opened the door and said "You shouldn't do her like that, she'll get pregnant," so they changed how they were doing it, violated in every way, and still I said no.

I know I said no. I know I didn't want any of it. I know I didn't ask for it. I know who that person was that stood in the doorway; I thought she was a friend. I knew who they were, I could identify them in the blink of an eye. I knew I would never ever tell a soul. I knew what they had done would ruin me if I let it, so I locked it away, deep within. I hid the ugly truth of what had happened and pretended I would be ok. It wasn't that big a deal, they'd never say anything, so there'd be no gossip. I'd just pretend it had never happened.

I don't remember going home. I do remember my mum scolding me for not letting her know I wouldn't be home that night. She didn't care about the key; she was happy I was safe. I was sorry that she'd been worried and apologised, telling her it wouldn't happen again.

I washed. I scrubbed. I felt numb. Locked inside the box.

I didn't go out anymore. I pleaded that I was broke, that I couldn't afford to go as I was saving up for my driving test, I was revising for my exams, or I was babysitting that week. The box let me do it. When I did have to go out on errands or with my mum, I ignored their stares, because they were there, and they were looking at me, and now I see why. They were scared I'd told on them. They didn't know if there'd be a knock on their door, if their days of dominance were over.

I did feel guilty for being a coward. How many people had they done this too before? How many more would they use and abuse in the future? I wasn't strong enough, I couldn't stand up against them, who would believe me and after all, I shouldn't have been there, I was drinking under age, I was breaking the law. I also couldn't understand why she had been there, the other girl, she knew what had happened, why didn't she stop it? Why didn't she ask if I was okay? So I locked it inside the box and tried to pretend it had never happened.

15

The problem with wounds is they heal, but the scars remain. I carried scars that gouged deep into my soul. I felt unworthy, tainted, and guilty. I wanted so desperately to forget what had happened that I ran away from the truth. I elbowed my way into university, making desperate calls from a phone box to be given a place so that I could leave the town. If I could start somewhere new, maybe I could pretend it had never happened. Like a pebble thrown into a pond the ripples move on and on.

So as I iron out the edges, I feel a newfound peace. It wasn't my fault and I should have gone to the police. It wouldn't have changed the damage though, or the depth of my scars. If I was labelled a victim and made to share the sordid details over and over it wouldn't have helped me heal. It would be out there for all to see, for everyone to judge or pity. It's much better and safer wrapped up neatly in my pretty little box.

How do I learn to love the snow again? That's my biggest regret.

There is more, it saddens me to admit, it angers me too. This one burns so fresh in my mind that I don't know how to put it in the box, I can't fold it tight enough to fit. I can't forget the taste in my mouth or the shock of how it could be happening. Luckily this time it was just an unwanted grope and fumble, but the fear froze me, the old scars broke free, and the glistening snow on the ground mocked me.

The one thing those men did was make me hate myself. What was wrong with who I was that made them want to hurt me. My university years were a spiral of self-destruction, alcohol became my best friend, my forgiver of sins, my absolution, and my way to forget. I was happy to go out again, that was good, I felt safe with my new friends, but underneath it all I hated myself. I had friends with benefits because I didn't deserve anything else. Who would ever want me as a girlfriend? Damaged goods.

That's why I fell for his charms. A man who paid attention to me, who told me I was pretty and clever. He was in pain himself, his wife had cheated on him so he'd bought a motorbike to prove he could have fun too. To me, it seemed like a good adventure, someone who would take me away from the life that had hurt. I didn't see that he was continuing to hurt me, I missed the signs, I let him manipulate me and control me until he was my whole

16

world.

I dropped out of university, I got pregnant, I got married, I hurt my family, and I lost myself.

For ten years I gave that man everything. I still felt worthless, I had made my choices so it was my penance to deal with the consequences. I loved my children, I gave them my all. I lost myself in alcohol and thought that this was life and the best I could expect.

I had to make the break myself. There are those that would disagree. They see my life now and have judged me for the choices I have made. I cannot at any point disagree that sometimes things were handled badly, but the fact remains I broke free. I did that myself. If that snowy night I'd have kept my key in my pocket where it belonged, I don't think I would have ever met him though, I wouldn't have had to fight him for my life back, I wouldn't ever have to feel the pain I do each time I see my children suffering because I had to have my life back.

I want the snow to be magical again, I want to feel the peace as it blankets the ground and fills the world with its beauty. I want the box firmly closed forever.

CHAPTER 2: LUC

Zéphirine was 17 when she flew the nest. When the decision was finally made, she was counting down the days like it was the end of a jail sentence. She was so happy. She even went to school on her birthday just because she wanted to rub it in their faces that she was actually leaving. She hated school, and she hated the people there, except for her best friend. Zéphirine could not care any less that she was dropping out a few months before her final exams. She'd already been told she wouldn't pass unless she had higher grades. It was unlikely at that time of the year she would get higher grades, especially since she hadn't studied for anything and chose to wag school more times than she could remember.

Zéphirine said *chose*, but it was the others that pushed her away. She didn't fit in, she wasn't like them, and they made damn sure to let her know that. Bullying seems to be an overused term now, the same as racism, but she hated being at school, being subjected to their taunts and prejudice. As if things weren't bad enough at home, her school days were made into a living hell, too. To this day, she can't stand the term 'négresse' or 'nigger', and to some extent, she was glad her sister looked completely different than her as she didn't have to put up with the same level of hatred from everyone. Then again, her sister had not subjected herself to it. While Zéphirine went to holiday camps in a desperate attempt to fit amongst other kids and be liked, her sister hid at their grandmother's farm.

Zéphirine and her sister weren't close enough for her to ask her why she went to their grandmother's every summer. Zéphirine wished they had been able to talk, she really needed an ally that would have understood. It wasn't meant to be though, they looked nothing like sisters and for whatever reason they were both too scared to confide in one another. Zéphirine assumed her sister had her own demons to battle, and for every physical difference that marked them it seemed it accentuated how different they were in personality too.

Zéphirine was at times a little jealous of her sister. Why couldn't she have had some of her 'white' traits to make her fit in a little better? She just wanted to be accepted, but her darker skin and hair (which was black and thick, but not quite an afro) made sure that no one wanted her, or that's what it seemed like to her then and now. Even her name seemed to mock her, proclaiming her to be different and not one of the normal French children.

If she'd had the safety of home, or a hint of acceptance from her parents, Zéphirine may have been more confident out there in the real world where kids can be so cruel. She may have been able to hold her head high when they called her names and let the words wash over her. There was only her sister that understood that need, their parents yelled and disciplined, but never loved them or each other, at least not that they could see. They'd host big parties in the summer, inviting all of their friends, but they didn't hold hands, kiss or dance together; they got what they needed from the attention of their guests. Their father was the life and soul of the party, and their mother was the beauty fashion queen. Zéphirine thought that was how relationships were for the longest time.

And how could she know any different? She had never seen an example of what a good relationship was, certainly not between her parents and family. Most of her father's side lived miles away in Martinique. A few lived in Paris, but they rarely visited because they disapproved of their son marrying a white woman. The generation gap amazed her still, like her parents seemed to be frowned upon while the rest of the family waited for the marriage

19

to fail as it surely would with the white woman and her wanton ways.

Zéphirine thought that for her sister, the farm represented a safe place, somewhere she could be that no one would hurt her, she was happy to lose herself in the work, and Grandmother certainly worked her own fingers to the bone at that place.

So they were the examples of love Zéphirine was given to work with. Perhaps their parents were fighting their own battle as they were a mixed race couple in a world that still stopped to stare and judge. Zéphirine was close to one of their cousins from Paris; they seemed to share some of life's more trying challenges, as he was the only black person in the family to marry a white woman (besides her parents).

***

Her 17th birthday was the best day of her life. She was leaving for London. She had fallen in love with the city on a school trip when she was 12, and she'd decided there and then that she would speak English fluently and live in London. So when she saw the ad in the newspaper, she wasted no time and managed to talk a friend of her mother's into convincing her mother that it was a good idea to let her go. Surprisingly, it was not as much as a fight as she had imagined it would be. *She's probably glad I'm leaving*, Zéphirine thought.

Freedom comes at a price, she knew that now, but she never looked back, and without hesitation she wanted it to happen. Even to this day, she thought it was the best decision she could have ever   made.

And then there was Luc.

Luc came to say goodbye and promised he would write to her. It felt like she was saying goodbye to the love of her life, because as much as she wanted to be as far away as possible from her parents, she was also heartbroken to be tearing herself away from him.

Love. Not that she knew much at 17, or could even understand what she was feeling, but it was there, or something was there. It just happened. Out of nowhere. It's the closest she had ever been to love at first sight. Not that she knew that at the time, she was an innocent passenger along for the ride.

Her parents' had identical houses right beside each other. They lived in one of the houses, but at first only on the ground floor level so that her parents could rent out the upstairs, all four bedrooms. The other house was rented out completely. For the girls it was cool, an adventure, as it meant they were always meeting new people over the years. The town they lived in was small, but there were still quite a few people coming and going for short-term work or whatever else, so they never had a shortage of tenants.

Zéphirine and her sister were eventually moved to a bedroom upstairs when it was decided that their father needed an office. He was taking over his boss' plumbing business, so it made more sense to use the bedroom downstairs, which was also next to the back door, which was actually the front entrance of the house, but was rarely used as such. Just one more thing that was topsy-turvy in their lives.

Zéphirine and her sister had never really gotten along, but thankfully that came without any sense of animosity, they were just never close. They had absolutely nothing in common except for playing Barbie and creating happy families. Now that Zéphirine looked back, she could see they weren't all that different. The world they created together with their dolls was the perfect escape, they just dealt with their own reality in different ways.

Zéphirine decided one day to move out all her stuff to the opposite vacant bedroom which had served as a giant cupboard since the last tenant moved out. She did not bother asking, she just did it, a clear symptom of her impulsive personality. She was always afraid to approach her parents to ask for anything, so it was better to act, plead ignorance, and deal with the consequences later. She thought that since she was not doing anything wrong, this time at least, the worst that could happen was to be told to move back with her sister.

With her shoulders firmly broached for some form of rebuke, Zéphirine awaited the challenge that would surely surface from her parents. They did not say a word, not even 'good idea', or 'you cleaned up that room well' or even a grunt! She was not sure what was more annoying, their apathy over such a big impulsive change that she'd taken upon herself, or the fact that she'd taken so long to come up with the idea and courage in the first place.

Only one room was still being rented out in the main house, and it turned out to be the last one that was ever rented in the house. Hortense Brideau was 17 and doing her hairdressing apprenticeship in town. Hortense was a bit overweight but no one really noticed it because she was tall. She wore glasses but styled them out perfectly like they were an accessory we could all use. She would change her hairstyle and colour every month, but that's all part of the perks of being a hairdresser. She was the kind of girl who would do anything for anyone, but that made her vulnerable, especially where men were concerned. She would fall hard for any man that showed her attention, which was difficult to watch but she was definitely fun to be around.

It also happened that one of Hortense's close friends, Margot Ménard, was in Zéphirine sister's class. Margot blended in so well that they all got along like old friends and spent most of their time in Hortense's bedroom. With average looks, brown hair, always in jeans and t-shirt, with no makeup whatsoever, Margot was always Margot. She was dependable in her predictability and laid-back attitude; they all knew where they stood with her.

Hortense's bedroom became the place to hang out, even when she was away in Dijon for her studies one week per month. They did everything in there when their parents didn't demand them for one chore or another. It felt like they had some kind of freedom and acceptance in their lives at last. Hortense's room became a sanctuary as well as being the one place for fun. A place to giggle and learn all about those things that girls need to understand. A place to grow and become young women, plan nocturnal adventures, and devise the best escape routes. Hortense enjoyed the planning as much as they did. She could just get up and walk right through the back door anytime she wanted, go anywhere and do anything, she was a tenant paying rent and didn't need to explain herself to her parents, but she chose to help them hatch their plans and egged them on every step of the way.

One evening Margot's sister, who owned a shop in the town centre, asked her to pick up something on an errand so they all decided to walk there together.

As it was winter, it was dark already and getting colder even in the early evening. The streets at this time of night seemed unusually quiet compared to the hustle and bustle of a few hours prior. The only break to the solitude was the occasional lone car that would drive past and then disappear into the night.

As they were walking up the bridge, Zéphirine saw *the* car drive by. There was only one in town like it, a black VW Golf GTI, with tinted windows. The driver was legendary, the hottest and most wanted guy in town, or so she was told. She had actually never met or seen this guy up close before, but she'd heard enough from one of her friends who seemed to know everything about the boys of the town, and like she said, he was legendary. What made him so special, or different, was the fact he owned an expensive sports car at 19, in addition to being extremely good-looking.

They were walking down the stairs when she saw the car coming towards them. Zéphirine was quite surprised as they were in a cul-de-sac, so there was no reason for that car to be coming their way at this time of the day. The car stopped. Two of the finest specimens of mankind Zéphirine had ever laid eyes upon got out of the car. Well, one was the finest specimen, the other a close second. She now understood why everybody was talking about him. He actually was drop-dead gorgeous and of course he seemed to know it. He flashed his smile at Margot as she was talking to him. Zéphirine had no idea Margot even knew him. She had never mentioned him, ever! There was a small part of her that felt her failure to disclose her friendship with him was a betrayal; surely she should have thought to mention that she knew a man like this!

Zéphirine was dying for that smile to be directed at her personally. As her heart thumped in her chest, her breathing seemed to strangle in her throat. Is this what love at first sight felt like? Because if it was, right then and there in that split second, she thought she was in love. The way his eyes twinkled when he smiled, the perfect set of teeth in the most perfect mouth that was now and forever on the most perfect face, and that body! What did he eat every day and what did he do to achieve that Greek God image?

Zéphirine couldn't help but stare at his long, lean legs, his quads bulging in his almost skin-tight jeans. The way he stood, towering over them, and so very comfortable in his own skin. Standing tall over everyone, he seemed to ooze confidence and even seemed to be aware of the effect he had over them, mere mortals who worshiped the very ground he walked upon. She saw him look at his friend, and they both seemed to be enjoying the effect they were having on the girls. His friend was almost as perfect as him but not quite, she thought it was the smile; it wasn't as sexy and definitely not as unrestrained or infectious.

They chatted for a little while and Margot decided to invite them back to Hortense's. Hortense wanted Tom, it was transparent to see that much. Zéphirine was still in complete shock of being involved in a conversation with the man who was quite obviously the hottest man in town. More in awe as she thought, he seemed like a God to her at that moment in time. As they walked back to her house, Margot explained she had known Luc for years and that they'd always been good mates. Zéphirine didn't know whether to laugh or cry, why hadn't she mentioned it before?

What happened next? Zéphirine couldn't even recall how it all happened. It was like one minute they were in a room full of people, the next, it was just Luc and her. He played the guitar and the drums, and dared her to play her saxophone.

"I'll play my sax when you play your guitar for me." she said thinking it was obviously not going to happen that night, if ever.

"I'll be right back." he said, and to her surprise, off he went to get his guitar.

Surely he was joking, surely it was his way out or something; but nope, he came back and they both played a piece of music for each other.

He also told her they'd met before. If she had met him, she was pretty sure she would have remembered him, he was after all the sexiest person she had ever come across so far.

"Remember that lingerie modelling show you did last year? At the end of the show, I spotted you next to the bar. I went to tell you how beautiful you looked out there."

How strange life was. She clearly remembered that moment even though she couldn't put a face to the voice. The more she thought about it, the more she could see him now, but she had never made the connection and she certainly hadn't taken it seriously at the time. Even in her young age, she had already mastered the skill of putting up a shield up when men approached her. Compliments did not get her attention.

One thing led to another, still not knowing or even caring what had happened to the rest of the world, Luc was lying on the bed and Zéphirine was on top of him. They were chatting and teasing each other. He told her about his girlfriend, a not so great relationship (which now, come to think of it, men always say that). They joked around, almost egging each other on, with a little bet that even though she was a very attractive girl, he would not get a hard on just because she was on top of him. Well. Okay. That probably lasted all of 10 minutes.

Everyone else had disappeared, not that she knew when or why. They were definitely alone.

He said something about her small frame. He guessed her weight, and he was only off by a few kilos. He snorted at her. "Oh, I was off two kilos. Big deal. You are still petite." They were so close to each other that she was completely intoxicated by the scent of him. She tried to pull away from him slightly and told him not to get any ideas, but it was too late, she was enthralled by him and her body didn't want to resist him.

They woke up in the early hours. She went back to her bedroom. He went home.

As far as firsts go, it was as good as she could ever have imagined or hoped for. Obviously there were no romantic gestures and seduction, but what did she need that for? He was very pleasurable to be around up close and personal. She was uncertain if he found her as pleasurable or attractive. She was left with a whole host of unanswered questions that were confusing for her then, and probably would be still if the same thing were to happen now too. She would have to wait and see if she would ever see him again, to see if he liked her.

Zéphirine felt a little foolish though, like she was waiting for a dream that would never happen; after all, he was so divine and he had a girlfriend already. Why would he ever be interested in her? There was also a part of her that thought she'd bitten off more than she could chew, this was grown-up stuff and she wasn't sure she was ready for it, the whole relationship thing, especially when there was another woman involved!

She didn't think he would ever want to see her again. Little old insignificant her. Why would the most wanted man in town who has – well she didn't think she was the most beautiful woman in town – one of the most popular women in town as his girlfriend want her? Personally, Zéphirine thought his girlfriend was a snobby bitch and because she was tall and slim, she thought she could bully everyone around her when they had to practice on the catwalk. Yes, she was a bitch. Why on earth was he attracted to a bitch? Either way, Zéphirine thought she was no match compared to her, but maybe that's what he had wanted, her innocence.

Surprisingly, he was back at the house by lunchtime that same day. "Hey, fancy seeing you here," she casually called out as he walked into the house. *Oh, god almighty.* Zéphirine inwardly cringed at her own moronic greeting. Is that the way to greet a Greek God?

He remembered she'd said she would make crêpes and he was there to taste them. While they were enjoying the crêpes, he told her he owned a house and asked her if she wanted to see it. She didn't quite believe him, but at this point, she would have done just about anything to stay in his company. At 16, getting the attention of man like him was just incredible, like a dream come true, and impossible to refuse or resist.

They went to his house. His drums were there. As the house was next to the train tracks, it was not really a place you'd want to live, but as a place to practice, it was perfect. They talked about decorating the house and what furniture they would buy. It was all so bizarre but she was devouring the moments. He then wanted to go for a ride.

Luc had been taught to drive rally cars. Being with him in his car was not for the faint-hearted. It was like being on a rollercoaster and he enjoyed every minute of the driving, especially as it was scaring her. He chose a little road on the way up to the top of the *Purgatoire*, with loads of tight turns and rocks that would make the car slide. It was like being at Interlagos, flying through the circuit, or the hair pin bend of Ras Cass at Monaco; he took her breath away. When they got to the top, he stopped the car and asked her if she wanted to drive.

Zéphirine had never driven a car, never even thought of driving one, but she simply couldn't say no to him. They both got out of the car at the same time, walked to the back of the car and as they crossed paths, he kissed her—a long, passionate kiss that left her breathless before they carried on back to their seats as if nothing had happened.

She sat down in the driver's seat, not knowing what to think or say. She looked in front of her because she was too afraid to look at him, it was a straight road for at least 2km, so she should be fine. He guided her on starting the car, undoing the hand break, changing gear, accelerating and braking; he was the perfect tutor. They spent the rest of the afternoon driving around and stopping for a chat. He did not kiss her again.

Luc would randomly pick her up from the school bus stop. Zéphirine was quite surprised because everybody could see them together and he had a well-known girlfriend. Zéphirine lived 500 meters away from the bus stop, so she didn't need a ride either. They would talk in his car for at least an hour. It was nice, but she would always get worried about being in trouble with her mother. As strange as it sounded, her mother never ever said a word about it, and Zéphirine never once got in trouble for it.

If Zéphirine was already at home when Luc wanted to see her, he didn't call; he would drive by and take the first turn. She knew it was him because of the way he drove and the sound of the turbo, no matter where she was in the house, and it was no small house, but she knew it was him, she knew he wanted to see her. Nothing else would matter. She would rush downstairs and go out to wait for him on the street. She would get in his car and off they went, to wherever he felt until he decided to park and chat for hours with only a few awkward silent moments when they ran out of things to say. He never randomly kissed her again, though they did sleep together a few more times.

Life seemed exciting for a while. That was until Zéphirine relapsed again and ended up in the hospital for an attempted suicide. It was not the first time she had tried to harm herself, but this time it was different, it was not an overnight stay. "Put her away, I can't handle her anymore!" She remembered hearing her mother yelling at anyone who would listen.

She was on the psychiatric ward. Her parents were not allowed to see her and she was thankful for that. She had made friends with the other mentally ill patients who were all adults. They would hang out in the lounge area because they were allowed to smoke and they still needed to socialize. She was sharing a room with a woman slightly younger than her mother, who seemed to be permanently spaced out. They were watching a movie in their room when one of the actors got shot and died.

"Tell me Zéphirine, this was not my father that got shot just now?" she asked in a frantic voice.

"No Suzy, it was not your father." Zéphirine replied.

"Okay. Good." an appeased Suzy would say calmly going back to watching the movie.

As strange as it sounded, Zéphirine loved that place, and it became an even better place when Luc was there.

She had called Luc the following day after being admitted to hospital. He was not home, so she left a message with his mother. He called back within 30 minutes.

"My mother said you sounded distressed. What are you doing in hospital?" Before she could answer, Luc said he was on his way.

Luc came to see her every night; he never asked why or how. After a while she'd forgotten why she was there. After seven days, Luc said he would stop visiting her, because she *didn't belong here'*. Zéphirine quickly organised a meeting with her psychiatrist. She was allowed to go home the following day and, of course, Luc picked her up and took her back home.

They remained friends even though they would not see each other as often. Perhaps something had changed in their relationship, her vulnerability was clear, even if she resumed her wild child image for the world to see. Luc knew how fragile she was on the inside, but he never flaunted it.

What else could Zéphirine do? She didn't know how to explain how she felt, so she bottled up her emotions, her frustrations, and carried on with her life. Somehow, she'd find a way to change her destiny.

She still loved Luc but it was time to move on and she was moving to London.

CHAPTER 3: LOST YOUTH

It felt like we were flying. My cheeks were flushed with the glow of alcohol, the music was blasting from the stereo, and I honestly thought we were going so fast we might actually die, so I closed my eyes. A smile spread across my lips. If I died now, I would be happy, I could see it now: "Allanah died happy" on my grave. Oh, the innocence of youth.

I was letting the music take me away, to that other place where nothing matters, where there is only the now, only Axl Rose. There was no need to worry about tomorrow, yesterday, or anyone else in the world ever.

My first true love was in the driving seat. I was smitten with him and the feeling wasn't mutual. He was older than me, more experienced than me, and wanted by every girl in town. I wasn't sure how I had managed to steal this moment in time with him, but I think it was my circumstances rather than me. My house offered him freedom from his life, and if he had to give me some attention to keep that illusion alive, then he seemed happy to do so for now.

I could feel him slipping away. My heart belonged to him, but he never took me out, he never invited me to his house, it was like he didn't want the world to know we were together. He did pick me up from school once. That was the highlight of my school career! The number of times I'd sat on the white double-decker trying to be invisible on the way home from school was embarrassing. In my first year at high school, one of the older boys had yelled at me and I'd never felt like I had a right to exist since then.

"Ugh what's that! Is it a girl or a boy? There's no boobs, it has to be a boy!"

Great.

The school was on top of a hill and spread down a slope with its different blocks, so a multitude of steps led down to the yards and bus stops outside the gates. Parents would park in the bottom yard for pick-up time, it was small, but there were hardly any cars that used it. During the day, jets would fly over the school and use it as a turning point when play fighting with each other. They don't seem to do that anymore, another witness to the passing of time.

I was an awkward child. I didn't feel like I belonged to my body. When I looked into the mirror, the reflection looking back at me didn't match who I felt was in my soul. I wanted my eyes to shine, I wanted people to be able to see the real me trapped inside this nondescript person. I wanted to be funny, clever, and popular. I wanted to be sporty, active, and just good at something. I wanted to escape from the pain of my life. The rejection that I felt from my family, and from the reflection that stared back at me, was a pain that I felt hard to endure. I found a way to cope with the pain, but now I know that was just a way of extending it, of causing harm, and there was no one to blame but myself. All I needed to do was take a step back and love myself, but that's easy to see now.

The most popular girl in the school tapped me on the shoulder as the released pupils flowed down the hill like a swarm of eager ants.

"Isn't that your boyfriend down in the car park?"

My heart soared! It was definitely him. I skipped down the hill and jumped in the car. He even gave me a quick kiss on the lips as I'd sat down. This was amazing, and the whole school would see that he'd come to get me!

I loved how he drove. Fast and dangerous. He was a mechanic, so he was always tinkering with his car, and was absolutely VW Golf potty. To put it simply, he knew everything there was to know about VW Golfs and loved them more than any other car. He'd get pulled over by the police a lot, did he realize that exhaust was illegal? He couldn't have that number plate on. Had he informed the DVLA that the engine had been replaced? This time was a warning, but if they saw him speeding again, he'd definitely have a ticket. He'd always charm his way out of the situation, and I loved hearing him tell his tales of near escapes and evasion, "I wasn't speeding, Mr. Orrifice, I was just moving out of the way." To me, as a 15-year-old girl, he was a small hint of danger; he was reckless, fearless, and exciting.

I drank a lot as a teenager. He was an older working class lad, and his weekends were all about the alcohol. I tried to keep up and for the most part I managed. That day, listening to the music in the car things felt different. He'd bought the Guns 'n Roses CD just for me, he told me he liked listening to it on the way to work as it reminded him of me. We were on our way to his house. This never happened. In the whole nine months we were together, I went to his house twice. I don't know if it was because his next door neighbour broke his heart or that his dad was an alcoholic.

He took me up to his room and we listened to music. His stereo was huge; together with the speakers, it covered the whole one side wall of his tiny box room. He took me home later that day and never came back to see me. I'd lost him—there were rumours he was seeing someone in another town and that he'd been cheating on me. I couldn't see how that was possible, as when he wasn't at work, he was at my house. His visits had trailed off over a period of weeks, but that's not cheating if the decision in his mind had already been made.

Why had he taken me to his house that day? I was devastated and had no idea what I'd done wrong. He popped round to the house one weekend some months later to see how I was, but I was at work. The hurt came rolling back when I found out I'd missed him; the tears stung my eyes and I wanted to know what I'd done to push him away. My mum told me he'd come to check that I was all right. I wasn't and she knew it, but I doubt she told him that. Her motto is *'show no weakness in the presence of men, we don't need them anyway'*. I wish I could have believed her. I'd be lying in bed at night would hear him drive by, it was unmistakably him. The loss seeped deep within my soul and I mourned it. I wanted him to be the one; I'd given him my most prized possession, but I wasn't enough for him.

The next two years were a mix of rebellion and conformity. I helped my mum in the house, cared for my brother and sister, did my homework, went to school, passed my exams, and went to college. I was lucky as I'd spent time away from school—I'd get on the wrong bus in the morning and skip the entire day, forging a note from my mum. I'd skip days from college, spending the day doing absolutely nothing or waiting for a visit from the married gym instructor who managed to use my own infatuation with him against me. I can't blame him, who wouldn't be flattered by the affections of a 16-year-old?

I did have morals however. When my mum's boyfriend climbed into my bed and started whispering in my ear, I told him to leave me alone. His gentle art of seduction definitely left something to be desired. He had one long fingernail on his little finger, and ran it up and down my leg in an attempt to make me succumb to his wishes. It only served to make me more repulsed. He never tried it again, and I certainly didn't tell anyone.

Looking back, I can see the pain I was feeling reflected in my actions. I wanted to be loved and I'd take that offering from whatever source possible; whether they were married or not didn't even enter my sphere of thinking. I hadn't asked them for anything, so I wasn't doing anything wrong. The innocence of youth and ignorance. These were all secrets though. I never told anybody about who I was seeing. I couldn't and wouldn't. Secretly, I mourned the loss of my school days. After my exams, I'd been so eager to explore the world, so hurt about my loss of boyfriend, that I was determined to flex my wings and experience the world. I should have stayed with my friends, and gone out with that boy who asked, explored my sexuality at a slower and gentler pace. I should have maintained my innocence for as long as possible, but in all reality, that wouldn't have changed what was waiting to happen.

Take me back to the freedom of youth, to the day when tomorrow didn't matter and yesterday was a blur. Take me back to before it all went wrong.

CHAPTER 4: FINALLY FREEDOM

Freedom at last. Someone should have explained to Zéphirine what traveling light actually meant. Being very attached to all her things, she left home with the intention of never coming back, but she had seriously under estimated how her few possessions could be so heavy.

She remembered running away at 15; yes, her 15th year of life had been hectic. One particular night, they knew they'd taken a very calculated risk, and almost too predictably, their father had caught them sneaking out. As time went by and the Barbie dolls were cast to one side, Zéphirine and her sister seemed to drift further apart; in fact, it seemed they didn't like each other, and they were like chalk and cheese in every sense.

Her sister was long-legged and sporty, but Zéphirine was more interested in painting her toenails than in actually letting her feet do any work. Her sister was a brilliant runner and Zéphirine was a model. Their physical appearance also couldn't be more different; Zéphirine had black hair and rich dark brown eyes and her sister was blonde with blue eyes. They were a striking contrast. But they did agree on one thing: they were going to go out at night. Her sister had the idea, and Zéphirine found the means to do it.

The first night was experimental and Zéphirine was to be the guinea pig on her own, her sister would stay at home. She thought it would be like in the movies: she made a rope out of sheets and expected to be easily granted her means of escape and freedom. As she stood by the open window and looked down, she felt scared; there were so many factors that could come in to play.

They could easily have been spotted, as they lived right on the busy main street and the window wasn't hidden from view. It felt like there were miles of space to the ground; it was foolish to even try, but she had to do it. She ended up half jumping and half falling. In the end the rope hadn't helped lower her down but knowing it was there had made her feel more secure, giving her that vital piece of Dutch courage. Besides, Fred and Michael were waiting for her, yelling for her to jump, so she did.

They hitchhiked their way to the next village where the mobile disco was. The DJ was one of their tenants, so most of the time she got a free pass, likely one of the reasons they were able to get away with their secret nocturnal habits for so long. There's no way she would have been able to take enough money from their mother's wallet for smoking and partying without raising at least some suspicion!

It was winter and freezing outside. Zéphirine was dressed to go out but not to withstand the cold, a mini-skirt and tiny top with a light jacket, definitely not the kind of outfit you should be wearing at -10 degrees.

That first night, she woke her sister up by throwing stones at the window. Again, Hollywood had deceived her. It looked so easy in the movies to climb up with a rope made of sheets, but in reality, it was impossible, even more so than trying to get down in the first place.

After a few tries, she realised she'd never make it back up. The hallway of their house next door was always open as their father was yet to fix the lock so she waited on the stairs. She was literally freezing as there was no heating, even now as she thought about it, why didn't her sister throw her down some sort of cover or blanket to help her in her vigil? She had gotten home around 3am. They decided to wait until 6am for her sister to open the window in the bathroom downstairs so she could easily climb in, put her pyjamas on, and voila! It was a long, cold three hours, but so worth it.

The next time, Zéphirine decided to try with a real rope. Her sister and her friend, Sonia were sneaking out this time too. It was a little bit easier for Sonia to jump out the window from her house than it was for them. The same thing happened with the real rope;

the ground seemed a million miles away, and panic began to set in. Zéphirine got so scared she ended up jumping. Her sister's attempt was nearly disastrous, she slid down the rope, desperately trying to hold in the pain as the rope dug into her flesh, the resulting burns were bad. The inside of her leg was bleeding, as well as her hands. Determined in their task, they managed to secretly attend to her wounds, but that night, she was rewarded with a scar on her leg that would last her a lifetime.

So sheets and ropes were out of the question. There had to be a better and easier way... such as a ladder! It was perfect. It was a brilliant, although not a simple idea. It was a massive exercise to take it out by the window, hide it in the garden, then come back, set it up and hide it again. They had it hidden in their room behind the bed against the wall. The ladder itself was a double one, which was the only way they could be sure it would reach the ground as the window was too high. Metal scraped against itself as they opened it out, and the whole town must have heard them. In fact, it was something they would never have been able to do themselves, they needed help from the others that were going to the disco with them. It helped the atmosphere of the night, they all felt like they were getting away with something in the name of youth and freedom.

Zéphirine was never sure what drove them to do this every weekend; they did it for a few months until they finally got caught. They should have stayed home, but being out got the better of them. There was a sports event at the local stadium they had to attend with their parents, and they pretended to be tired and told them they wanted to go to bed instead.

Zéphirine was smoking outside the mobile disco when she saw her father's van pull up, white with big red writing emblazoned on the side 'Bernard Castille Plumbing and Heating'.

The van was impossible to not notice and was unmistakeably his. Zéphirine ran back inside to find her sister and told her to run. She then started to run and hide, but where was she going to run and for what? She had no choice but to surrender. She ran towards the back of the truck and quickly slid inside as she didn't want people to see the beating that she would undoubtedly be getting from her father—an added humiliation to being caught. Only their friends needed to know. Her father was mumbling, something as he always did when angry and while beating the shit out of her.

The next day, everything was all as normal. Zéphirine's family wasn't very talkative at the best of times, unless her parents were arguing or giving the girls them the third degree. Their father would use a stick to beat them, and their mother liked to use the martinet. The martinet was cruel. A martinet is a short, scourge-like type of whip made of a wooden handle with 10 leather lashes. The stick was a simple piece of wood that never pretended to be anything else and you knew where it was going to land when their father used it. The martinet was different, an unpredictable weapon, when their mother lashed them with it, the tails would sting wherever they landed. The two sisters would try to hide them whenever they could, but their mother was one step ahead of them and had them dotted all around the house.

After being caught that night, their friends came over to see how they were – they knew. They decided to go for a walk as usual, trying to shrug off the horrors and everything they couldn't explain or understand. They were walking along the main street when they heard the horn of a car angrily demanding their attention: Zéphirine's mother, of course.

"Go back home! You're not allowed to go out!" her mother yelled at her.

Not allowed to go out? Zéphirine's mother was insane if she thought she could trap her inside that house all day on top of stripping her of freedom at night. Come to think of it, her mother did look a bit insane that day, blaring away on the car horn, almost frothing at the mouth while shouting at Zéphirine. Didn't she realise the whole village could hear her?

Zéphirine packed her bags, took a cheque, forged her mother's signature (something she had mastered over the years to wag school), and asked a friend for help. She wanted to take all her possessions with her, which included a little vanity case full of nail polish. She used to do her nails every two days, and she owned every colour that possibly existed. That little case on its own probably weighed at least 4kg. She had to take all her clothes and shoes; there was no way she could leave those behind. Her bags were far too heavy to get down the ladder by herself. In her mind, she was never coming back.

Even though they'd been caught sneaking out, their parents never searched for their means of escape or bothered to ask how they'd been making their fantastic bid for freedom. The ladder was still hidden in Zéphirine's bedroom. That was just another shining example of how much her parents didn't care about her. They cared that she had embarrassed them, not that she'd found a way to get out. Her mind was more than made up: she was leaving, for good.

Zéphirine had no idea what she was going to do once she got to Paris, but she had to take her little priceless possessions. Her friend helped her out and they walked all the way to the outskirts of town. As at this time of night the only train to Paris was at the next station, she had to hitchhike her way there. She would have to buy a ticket on the train as the station itself would be closed. No one wondered what a 15-year-old was doing out alone at 1am, carrying all of her worldly possessions. No one asked questions, and no one seemed to care. She was just another person going on a trip.

Zéphirine arrived in Paris around 5am and was starving. She had absolutely no idea what the hell she was doing; she was an impulsive person, she didn't think; she just acted and did whatever. She put her bags into a locker which was going to cost her a lot of her precious funds, but she had no other choice as she couldn't walk around with all that. She needed to figure out what would be her next move.

She bought a croissant and orange juice for breakfast, and her adventures soon found her outside Gare de Lyon. She had to admit, she was a little scared. Not fearful that something bad would happen to her, but scared as to not knowing what to do. This was Paris, a very big city. They'd come here a few times a year to visit family and friends who lived there, and her mother loved to go on day trips into the beautiful city for shopping, so although this wasn't an alien world, she just had no idea where the rest of her family actually lived.

Then there was the big question of where she was going to sleep that evening. She had already spent an adrenaline-fueled night of travelling with only a few hours of dozing on the train. Yes, she was now forced to admit she had really not thought this through. She wanted to leave because her mother had pissed her off with what she thought were stupid rules. Yes, stupid rules. Her sister and Zéphirine did everything in the house, from cleaning to cooking to gardening. Did they ever get rewarded? Did they ever get a 'thank you'? Of course not. All she wanted was to be allowed to sometimes go out at night—if she could, none of this would have happened in the first place. Eloise and Martine were allowed to go out, their mother would drive them to the club and would pick them up at 4am. Why couldn't her mother be cool like that? She couldn't imagine her mother ever being cool; somehow, it was something you either had or you didn't, and clearly her mother didn't have it and would never be a cool person.

Zéphirine got talking to some random guy off the street. He looked like his hair had never met a brush in his life and there was a definite smell emanating from him, like old crusty socks but worse. Maybe homeless people pick up on others as if it was written on their foreheads.

"Don't worry," he said, "I'll find us a place to crash tonight."

"Okay." was all she could think to say. Perhaps she should have been scared. Did her mother ever tell her not to talk to random strangers off the street? She didn't think so. All she knew was she needed a place to sleep, so this was as good as it was going to get. She followed that guy to an unknown place where she slept on the floor. There was a small part of her that was a little bit worried, but she was also too tired. So if it was going to be the day she died, so be it, she didn't care.

But Zéphirine woke up safe and sound and just left. She was not in the mood to talk to random strangers again, and didn't want to answer a whole heap of questions and be judged or told to go home. She decided to head back to the train station to call an ex-boyfriend, Nicolas. Even though they were no longer seeing each other, they had remained friends. And he was not surprised at all when she called.

"The police came to see me!" Nicolas exclaimed.

The police knew Zéphirine was dating a married guy 15 years older than her? How? This also meant her parents had to know about it! That was a bit of a surprise. Anyway, as much as people would never understand what kind of relationship they had, she considered Nicolas a true friend and his guidance was not just sexual; she was sure it would be the first thing coming to mind from people.

Zéphirine trusted Nicolas. He convinced her to give herself up and come back home. They talked for hours on the phone on and off. Later that night she recognised a friend of her mother whom she guessed was looking for her. Paris couldn't have been that big a city after all. She showed herself.

Zéphirine was sent back to her parents the next day. She had to talk to the police though, they couldn't understand why she would want to run away: after all she had such a nice father. A nice father? Obviously they weren't there when he was beating the hell out of her with his wooden stick! To Zéphirine, her father was a tyrant. The man everyone else saw simply didn't exist in her world. It seems everyone knew and loved her father. Not just because he was the plumber, he was active in the community and also played all sorts of sport at a competitive level. Behind closed doors he was the scariest person she had ever known, the one man you did not want to cross or upset in the slightest.

Spending one night in a room full of strangers in a city far from home was nothing compared to facing her father. She would have rather jumped from an aeroplane with no parachute than face him, but it seemed she had no choice. She hated him. Not as much as she hated her mother but she hated him nonetheless for being black. It was his fault she didn't fit in or belong to society, it was his fault there was no affection in their lives and it was his fault because he never asked her to respect him as a man, as a father. To this day, she can hear a similar voice or see a van that will take her back to that time, the fear that the memory of a father instils can leave her frozen with dread and loathing.

But that was all in the past.

Now Zéphirine was in London. She didn't have to be afraid of anyone. It was going to be her own rules. But to be free she had to learn a few things, she had to learn about life.

Zéphirine hailed a cab, because she couldn't carry her luggage around and she had no idea about the underground. The cab driver was happy to drive her round and never once mentioned that there was a better – and cheaper - way of travelling through the capital. From the airport, he drove her to Piccadilly Square and she paid a hefty £100. That was when she realised she had done something really stupid: Just before leaving France, she'd changed the jacket she was wearing, and left the old one at home, with half of her money in the inside pocket!

Zéphirine's mother had prearranged to sign up at an agency so she could work straight away. Once she got there she had to pay six weeks in advance for her accommodation. She also needed a travel card as she was going to live in a house in Wembley, Greater London. After paying all her dues she was left with just a few pounds. She called her mother to let her know she had run out of money, which meant she could not even feed herself.

Zéphirine went to a job interview the next morning, at a hotel in Bloomsbury Court for a part-time waitressing job. Even though she was top of her class in English and she had studied it for six years at school, she couldn't understand a word of what the restaurant manager asked her. Luckily, one of the waiters was French and came to her rescue. To her absolute relief she was hired and started work the next day.

It turned out that most of the staff were French, so on the first day, she already had friends. One in particular stood out: one of the porters who was tall, with dark hair. His mother was Chinese, so he had the most spectacular eyes she had ever seen. He was into body building so of course his body was like nothing she had ever seen before either. Strong, muscular, and self-assured. The boys took her out the first night to celebrate her new job and her being part of their team. She liked him. He liked her. He was sharing an apartment just behind the hotel, which was very practical compared to her living all the way out in Wembley, which was an hour and a half train ride. The sad part was that he was only staying in London one more month, but he told Zéphirine she could take over his room if she wanted to.

CHAPTER 5: The Wonder Years

The beginning of my teenage years passed by with a nostalgic innocence. I went to school, helped at home, and earned my pocket money, which let me go into town every Saturday afternoon for my choice of chocolate bar. I did want other things, but couldn't afford them. Most of the time I was on my own when I was out, so I perfected the art of shoplifting to keep myself occupied and in supply of lipsticks I would never wear. Perhaps that's why I have an aversion to makeup now, the fear that pulsed through me when the woman tapped me on the shoulder to tell me I hadn't paid for that is still tangible.

I spent a good five hours in a police cell. My mum and dad had been out for the day, my dad cashing in his birthday present of a helicopter flying lesson. He was disappointed in me—I'd tainted his whole day, he was embarrassed, ashamed to be my dad, whatever would he say to the people at work? The barrage of guilt was endless, but as he droned on, telling me what an awful person I was, all I could think was *as if you even care, you're not really my dad*. That same thought made a frequent appearance throughout my childhood. Whenever there was a situation that required his intervention, it seemed he was carrying out the motions of a dad, doing what he thought the role entailed, acting out what the other men at work said they did when their children tested their strength.

"What are you hiding in that wardrobe for? You're acting like a crazy person, get out like a normal child."

As if you even care, Dad.

"Why are you crying? It's not like you didn't know she was poorly; she was always going to die."

Actually, I didn't know, that's the beauty of being a child. I'd hoped beyond all else that my Grandma wouldn't leave me, that she'd get better, that I could keep her in my life.

As if you even care about me, Allanah, your daughter.

When my mum and dad separated, I felt liberated. It was like a cloud had left the house, I didn't need to worry about what I was doing, watch what I said, or pretend to be someone and something I wasn't. Things got hard for my mum and I regret that; I wanted her to be happy, safe, and secure, but too much had happened between them to ever move forward in their lives as a couple. The loss of my grandma and granddad in the space of 6 months nearly broke my mum. She was an only child and they were gone far too soon, only in their 60's, and were devout Catholics. That was when I stopped believing in God; the prayers offered at school screamed at me like lies. I didn't see how God could even pretend to exist in a world that offered so much physical and emotional pain.

The shoplifting probably came at a disastrous time in my parents' relationship. Mum didn't shout at me; she didn't even try to make me feel guilty. She calmly told me that there would have to be some form of punishment but that dad had probably said it all already so she wouldn't keep going on. That's my mum, the one solid person always there, who has always loved me and knew I wasn't a bad person.

My dad was the closest person I had to a dad, he tried in his way to be my father, but there was a barrier between us that just couldn't be broken. My birth father left when I was 3 months old. I felt rejected even though it was never about me, it was about him being unfit to call himself a father.

When I looked at my dad playing with my brother and sister, I felt the rift. I fed the rift myself with my loneliness. *As if you even care, Dad*, but he probably did, he just didn't know how to show it.

So, the shoplifting was the height of my scandalous teenage years. Well, to begin with, at least. In those days, I loved going to the youth club and dancing away to Grease Lightening and Rick Astley, and eating penny sweets until I felt sick. I remember laughing and being care free. I'm not sure when the transition came, probably high school, but I suddenly began feeling very uncomfortable in my own skin, not liking what looked back at me from the mirror, and shying away from any and all attention.

My shell was forced from my back when my mum became one of the most well-known adults amongst the teenage population in the town. With her inheritance, she'd decided to branch out in business. What began as a themed soft play party area for toddlers became an under-18's nightclub, 'The Basement'.

At 15 years old, I was suddenly the focus of everyone; they all knew who I was. In all honesty, I loved those days. I felt important. I worked behind the drinks bar; serving Tango and Pepsi through the Britvic machine with a spray tap was a power trip. I had endless chocolate supplies to fuel myself with, and could watch all of the comings and goings without fear of not belonging, as this was actually my stomping ground. I even got to make burger and chips for the hungry lads, and to this day, I love a good burger.

The atmosphere there was amazing; every Friday and Saturday night the place would be packed, and I'd be kept busy until 11:30pm every night. I really was in my element. There was one room that was kept off limits to the main crowd, and the pool tables were locked away at night to stop the fizzy drinks being spilled all over them. We had bouncers on the door, but most of the time, the kids were drunk on 20/20 or Diamond White before they had even stepped foot in the building. Sometimes a drink slipped its way through the net, and I learned the hard way how not to deal with that. I asked the girl for the bottle, but instead of giving it to me, she smashed it against the wall and held it up against my neck. No harm was done; after a shaky few minutes, the bouncers were hauling her off me, and all calm was restored. Apparently I'd handled the situation well, as everyone seemed to give me a bit more respect after that. The craziest girl in town even apologised to me herself the next week.

We also had a robbery one weekend. Fortunately, not much was stolen, as my mum and her business partner were savvy enough to remove the money when we weren't there. I think a window was smashed and some graffiti sprayed, but the worst thing was they took a dump in the diner. I didn't ever see it, but I remember wondering if that was some kind of revenge thing for something I'd done the weekend before. One of the lads, Eddie, was hassling me to hurry up with his burger. He was a strange-looking boy; a normal sized body with a big head that was accentuated with curly hair down to his chin. To tame his hair, he used wax that made him look like he'd just stepped out of the swimming pool, and he smelt like musky lynx. He knew what deodorant was for, but couldn't be bothered to wash before putting it on. Making burgers was a process that couldn't be rushed. He kept shouting at me through the kitchen hatch, goading me, and never stopping. So, I gave him his burger. It wasn't cooked and he knew it, very raw in the middle he threw the burger away and walked off. The police identified the fingerprints at the break in as being his. I did feel guilty for that, even though he'd seen me get into trouble for serving him a raw burger.

On my break on those club nights, I would bribe Matt, the most gorgeous person in the whole of Redditch to come play pool with me. He was always accompanied by his friend, Paul; they were inseparable, but I'd put up with that just to be in his company for 30 magical minutes. We would play pool, or I would watch them play, they would let me drink their contraband and the laughter would never stop. I loved his smile, his eyes, his hair, his maturity, and the carefree way he approached life. I idolised him, besotted, and embarrassingly so. He tried to put me off—I was too young, I deserved someone better, and he wasn't ready for another relationship.

I wouldn't take no for an answer, and eventually I was at the edge of heaven; popular and Matt's girlfriend. Matt drove a Volkswagen Golf, Matt had a job, Matt stole my heart, Matt taught me what a broken heart feels like and how to mend it.

The Basement didn't last for long. It didn't make enough money to be a viable business, as teenagers don't have a disposable income and can really misbehave when they want to. Those weekends helped me grow in confidence and gave me the saddest love story of my life, but we've all got to have one somewhere.

CHAPTER 6: A THIEF'S END

Freedom, independence, and most importantly, a new life. It's what Zéphirine wanted the most and that's what she got at 17. It came at a price, though. She had to work to earn money and pay the bills to support the cost of living in general. Though working to earn money to buy things felt completely liberating, she hadn't always been so self-sufficient. In fact, if she ever wanted it, she'd take it without fear of consequence. She wasn't soulless, but she did embark on a dangerous path, especially if her father had ever found out.

When Zéphirine was just a child, she wanted a Barbie doll. Every year, it was on her Christmas list. And every year, she got the cheap version because, according to her mother, it was the same thing, just not as expensive. It most definitely was not the same thing! Her mother was firm in her belief that as long as it was cheap or cheaper, it was good enough. "That's how we got what we have today." she would claim. *Blah blah blah Mother, whatever you say*, Zéphirine would respond in her mind, never quite brave enough to air her displeasure. If she had voiced her feelings, it would have been swiftly rewarded with a serious beating.

She loved writing, and took great pride in presenting neat work at school. It was no easy task being left-handed, as smudging was a constant danger. Mother didn't understand that all pens were not created equal, as Zéphirine had preferences. She had her favourite types of pen which were more expensive, and this was unfortunate when her mother only bought the cheapest stuff.

The same went for the type of paper: it wasn't just because a notebook had a fancy cover, although, it should look nice if you were going to put important words in it. She could feel the difference when she wrote on certain pieces of paper. Again, her mother failed to see it her way. She never did and never would. Why should she pay extra just because it had a pretty picture on the cover or that it made the writing from Zéphirine's pen smooth and flawless?

Everybody had cool stuff but Zéphirine.

On a rainy day, Zéphirine was looking for something in the armoire where her mother kept her sewing materials when she stumbled upon a huge bundle of money—$100 notes, and loads of them. She must have been 8 or 9 at the time, and told her sister about the find, as it was too exciting to keep that discovery to herself. She'd never seen so much money all at once! After much deliberation, they both decided that taking one note would go unnoticed.

Off to school they went with a nervous spring in their steps. In primary school, lollies were a form of popularity currency, and for once they had some money to buy a bunch of them. Of course, Zéphirine bought a few fancy pens as well; that was inevitable. And if their mother asked, she would say a friend gave them to her.

They only stole the money a couple of times as they soon found out it was their father's money, and he certainly did count it. It was only a matter of time before he realised some of his money was missing. Of course, they denied having anything to do with what they saw as a petty crime, but they never did it again. Fear or perhaps sense, took over, and by some miracle, they escaped any retribution or punishment. In her heart of hearts, Zéphirine was still not sure if he believed them. But if he did know the truth, it was a rare display of mercy.

That was the end of her short career in theft. Or so Zéphirine thought.

Zéphirine met Dorothée Fleury and Stéphanie Pasteur in her third year of middle school. She'd seen Stéphanie before; her parents used to own the convenience store on the other side of the bridge, which was on their way to primary school. One day as she walked to school, Stéphanie was walking too, but Zéphirine noticed the girl was crying, so she just walked with her in silence. Zéphirine knew she could relate to Stéphanie, even though she didn't know her. Stéphanie's parents would always yell at her in the shop, not caring if customers were there or not. Stéphanie was older than her, so they never hung out together other than walking to school together from time to time.

That was until Stéphanie stayed back one year and ended up in the same class as Zéphirine. Her parents had sold the shop and moved into the new apartment complex five minutes' walk from Zéphirine's house. Living closer to each other was convenient and a blessing.

Stéphanie and Zéphirine became best friends and were inseparable.

Stéphanie Pasteur was a simple girl in an uncomplicated way. She always wore blue skinny jeans with a loose jumper that hid her figure. What was most significant was her shoulder-length wild black hair. It was like she'd given up trying to control it years ago and the untamed mane gave her an edge that she liked in herself. She admired her blue and pink makeup. She thought it made her beautiful brown eyes shine in a way that hers never would.

In the first year of middle school, all students had to choose their first language: English or German. English was the most popular and there was a ratio of 1 class for German to seven classes for English. Zéphirine had chosen English and Stéphanie had chosen German. For two hours of the day, they were in different classes, but for the rest of the time, they were joined at the hip.

That's how Zéphirine befriended Dorothée Fleury. She lived in a village about 15 kilometres away and was taking the bus to school. She would eat at the canteen for lunch before Stephanie and she would walk home. Dorothée was different from Stephanie. Much taller than her and thin to match, she was elegant and feminine. Zéphirine liked being around Dorothée, with her dark hair and deep brown eyes. She didn't feel like so much of an outcast, even though it was obvious that Dorothée's skin was different from hers.

When Dorothée wore jeans, she made them look like they were a thing of sophistication. One of her sisters was a model, so it was either in their blood or she'd observed her and picked up on those nuances that added to a girl's femininity. She always thought Dorothée would become a model herself, as when she dressed up and used makeup, she looked amazing. Maybe she was too smart for that, not that she flaunted her brains. She was always leaving her homework until the last minute, scribbling away in her book at the back of the class, trying to avoid a detention. She could read so quickly and digest everything without effort. Zéphirine admired Dorothée without envy and wished she was more like her, with her neat writing that Zéphirine could never manage to copy.

Zéphirine enjoyed both Stéphanie and Dorothée's company. She loved them both as friends. She didn't think she could have chosen one over the other. But she did know that without Dorothée by her side throughout high school, she would have killed herself. That was not meant to be melodramatic, but the honest truth. Suicide was a part of Zéphirine's thoughts more than what was healthy for any one person, and Dorothée was the force that kept her on the right side of sane for the majority of the time, not that Dorothée knew it.

Dorothée had an infectious sense of humour that would brighten even Zéphirine's darkest moments. With both of them having such different personalities, they were both fun to be around. Together, they were a perfect combination. They shared so many different moments that have left her with precious memories.

No friendship circle would be complete without its own drama queen, Mimi Defraine. She was a short little thing who thought she was *THE* girl everyone loved. She knew everything. She'd been there and done that, and always much better than they had. She also thought that all boys adored her. Mimi seemed to always be here and there. There was no escape from her. When Stéphanie and Zéphirine argued, Mimi would be ready and waiting to take over and be best friends with one or the other.

While Stéphanie didn't talk to her, Zéphirine got to know Dorothée better. She was a pro at stealing, and she'd steal just about anything for the fun of it, so she taught Zéphirine how to do it. They started at the local stationery store just around the corner from the school. Oh, how she loved that shop! They had every type of pen imaginable, ink, notebooks, cute postcards, rubbers, pencil cases. The list was endless. Every Tuesday morning, their first hour lesson was a free period, and they'd go there and wait for the shop to open. The owner began to expect them, and Zéphirine thought she genuinely liked them. They used to have a little gossip and chit-chat with them every time. It left the shop owner blissfully unaware that her pens and cards were stuffed into their pockets.

To keep up appearances, they would buy something cheap from time to time. By some miracle they never got caught. They then moved on to the newsagent to get free magazines. At only 14, she'd gotten into the habit of smoking, thanks to Stéphanie and Mimi. They didn't put a gun to her head, it was just the cool thing to do and Zéphirine wanted to be cool, too. So, she mastered stealing money from her mother's wallet when there were lots of gold coins. It paid for her smoking habits amongst other things. In her mind, her mother was not counting the money in her purse, or if she was, she ignored it.

Life was grand, or as grand as Zéphirine needed it to be for her at the time.

She got caught for the first time when she was in high school, stealing makeup at a supermarket. She was careless, and they knew the staff had spotted them. Dorothée was wise enough to put it back, but Zéphirine thought she could still make it, and course she didn't. She denied that she was stealing while the Revlon eyeshadow palette was itching in her underwear. By law, the security guard was not allowed to touch her, so he threatened to call the police. She couldn't run away; there was no way out. She quickly put her hand inside her panties to grab the makeup and handed it to the security guard with a smirk on her face. She was allowed to go home.

Stealing was not something out of the extraordinary, as she'd realised she had a few friends that were doing it. The ones that were too afraid to do it themselves would just ask others to do it for them instead.

Margot Ménard came by the house one day and told her how she'd stolen heaps of lingerie at a new shop in Dijon, and raving about how easy it was, so Zéphirine decided to try it. They went to Dijon, an hour's train ride, and Zéphirine was wearing her jean jacket as it was the best choice for that purpose. It was thick and made her look fat because it was a winter jacket; therefore, it wouldn't arouse suspicion, or at least it had worked that way so far. But the place today was buzzing with loads of customers and security guards. Zéphirine was still confident she could pull it off and opted to get herself some sexy new underwear. She had the strange feeling, however, that she'd been spotted. She looked around but couldn't see anyone, so she carried on her shopping spree even though her instincts were warning her.

As she was walking towards the cashier, she felt a hand on her shoulder and a voice said: "Please come with me, miss." She was done. The guard took her to a room where she unloaded the goods on the table. She could see from the corner of her eyes the man was looking at all the stuff in astonishment. There was at least $500 worth of merchandise. Yes, when Zéphirine did something, she did it wholeheartedly. "You have fine tastes in your lingerie choices," the security guard told her. "Well, you don't think I would go through all that trouble to steal crap, do you?" she wanted to reply to him, but thought she might be better off keeping her mouth shut at this point. This time around, she was in big trouble. There was no getting out of this one without her parents knowing.

Since it was only a few months since her last relapse, she was assigned to a social worker on her case. So Zéphirine decided to call him instead of her parents, and let him deal with the situation. She waited a few hours for him to get to the shop, sign the paperwork with the security guy, and drive her back home. She looked at the lingerie on the table thinking, then looked up to the security guy who was still staring at her. She winked at him as she turned around and left with her social worker.

She got the angry look from her father and of course her mother wondered 'what they were going to do with her'. Zéphirine did not care what they thought one way or another, but it was enough to make her realise that this wasn't an avenue she wanted to carry on doing. There was not much she needed that she hadn't stolen already. It had become a bad habit that she would do to shy away from boredom and to give herself the pretty things she wanted, but it was time to stop.

In the dizzy lights of London, that world seemed a million miles away. Money was the only thing that was going to get her what she needed to survive now, and for that, she was happy to earn it.

CHAPTER 7: MONEY RULES ALL

We were officially a single-parent family, my mum, my brother, my sister, and I, Allanah. My mum was working full time, I was studying for my exams, and my brother and sister were much younger than me, so as a family we seemed disjointed. I took my responsibilities in the home seriously. I did the housework, although completed through a child's eyes, it probably wasn't to a high standard. I looked after the younger ones when I could, entertained them a bit then skulked in my shared room for the rest of the time.

Occasionally we would have a lodger stay with us. He was a hangover from the Basement days, my mum had taken pity on him as he pleaded homelessness and promised he was entitled to housing benefit which he could then pay to her. He was a stinky teenager on the verge of adulthood and got himself into all sorts of trouble. Black eyes were not unusual, even from his own mates, and normally because he owed them money. I have no doubt drugs were involved, and his later prison sentences would explain some of the things that disappeared from our house during his stay. If it wasn't actually him, then it was definitely one of the unsavoury characters he would occasionally bring home. I'm sure my mum has many regrets from that period in time, one of them being the loss of her mum's wedding rings. I don't judge her though, she was fighting for survival, she was doing what she had to do to pay the bills and keep her sanity.

We did everything we could to keep the money flowing in the house and I was old enough to help. I had part time Saturday jobs as soon as I legally could. I was working in a man's clothing shop, selling ice creams and helping people find their seats at the cinema, serving drinks and burgers at The Basement before finally finding myself working as a carer, someone who looked after people with disabilities. That gave me some freedom. I was given a scooter for my own personal use, they paid for everything, and all I needed to do was be the standby carer for the evenings and weekends. I felt like I'd found my calling, helping other people, something I was good at and I could always earn money doing it too.

I shouldn't dismiss those early working days so easily, on reflection they've shaped me just as much as anything else in my life. I quit, possibly got sacked, from that first Saturday job. If you asked the manager, she'd say she sacked me although I told her I quit first - so in my eyes I win. Subordination can't be allowed to breed; I can see why she'd stretch the truth. It's not as exciting as it sounds, but for me I stood my ground and held onto a sense of what was right. We were paid minimum wage, if memory serves me I'd earn about £15 a weekend if I worked 9am - 5pm on Saturday and 10am - 4pm on Sunday. Not a lot - but better than nothing. The shop sold mediocre clothes. Fosters was one of the first men's clothing shops to lose business and close when the internet market exploded, but I'd been long gone by then. Downstairs was the casual section and upstairs was for nights out on the town and pulling power, some of the shirts were obviously designed by Harry Hill with the most outrageous collars. I never have been a fashionista, but some of those clothes were absolutely horrendous-looking to me. I would have never looked twice at a man wearing them, even if the lights were out and the booze was flowing. I dreaded being asked my opinion from men in the shop, 'does this suit me? Is this the latest fashion? Is lime green too bright?' The best question I was ever asked, 'if you were in the club and saw me wearing this would you try and pull me?' Did I miss an opportunity there? My cheeks would flush every time and I was definitely well beyond my comfort zone. I have no idea what ever made me think I wanted to work there!

There was one thing I loved in that shop, a Levi's denim jacket. I saved up my minimum wage for what felt like forever and bought it for £40 and that included my 20% discount. It was the most expensive thing I owned, but it fitted me like a glove, a little half jacket in a rich deep blue. I hate myself for getting rid of it, discarded to charity without a forward glance, all because it wasn't black!

A soundtrack played in the shop on an endless loop. I didn't mind that, Edwyn Collins, "Girl Like You," made me happy and made the time pass quicker. I didn't really get on with any of the other staff there. We had nothing in common and I certainly didn't aspire to be in the fashion or retail industry - whereas I think they did. The one thing that really got my back up was the fact we were expected to stay behind after the shop closed to clean and restock. As far as I was concerned, work finished at 5pm, and after stewing about it for weeks on end, I let my feet do the talking. The shutters came down at 5pm on that Saturday and I went straight home while the others stared at me slack mouthed with mop in hand.

I turned up for work as normal the next day and the boss was there, highly unusual for a Sunday, I knew I was in trouble. I felt bold, I was right, the wages were low enough without me giving them an extra 4 hours of my time free every month. Of course there was a pang of guilt, if I didn't help to clean after hours it would take them all that little bit longer. There was fear too, I'd never openly defied anyone before, and in my heart I knew that I'd be without a job by the end of the day.

Sure enough, before the shop even opened I was summoned to the office. It was really more of a cupboard, windowless, and stacked full of unused stock. She had a form in front of her and a pen at the ready. The blurb came in the form of, "I have to warn you this is a formal interview and will be documented to be retained on file blah de blah," and it worked, my hands were shaking but my resolve never faltered. I knew what they were doing was wrong and it helped me speak up. I think I did myself proud, I'm sure I was only fifteen at the time, sixteen at most, and to hold on to your beliefs in the face of authority is no small task. She asked me why I left the premises without carrying out all of my duties, so I returned the question with one of my own. "What time was currently stated as my contracted hours of work?"

She seemed angered by my attitude and reeled off a whole load of jargon about the contract not being a factor in this, part of my job was to prepare the shop for the next day and I hadn't done it which was a sack-able offense. The meeting didn't last for more than 5 minutes. I requested an extension of paid hours to cover the time required to clean and restock - which of course was declined. I calmly, even though I was shaking inside and out, told her, that in that case, I would no longer be able to continue to work for her as I was not in the business of giving my time for free. I later heard that she had told the staff she had no option but to fire me, I don't think she did and it certainly isn't what I remember. I wonder what the paperwork actually said, and I wonder if she had any legal standing. Onwards and upwards.

My next job left me with some really happy memories. The bosses were dragons, but the perks were amazing. Working at the cinema was a wonderful experience, even though I dreaded the interval. Standing at the front of the screen with a tray filled with ice cream and a hoard of greedy children was really disconcerting. I still to this day have a phobia of numbers, I'm capable of doing sums, but if you ask me I get really stressed and fumble around with cotton in my brain. The ice creams all had extortionate price tags added to them, and people always bought them in bundles of three or five—which really didn't help my math-scared brain.

Somehow I made it through that trauma and was able to keep my job. Watching the films on the big screen as they were released was an added bonus, and during the promotion of the Disney Lion King release we were visited by an actual lion cub. He was adorable, but had the worst smelling farts I have ever encountered. I also managed to obtain some promotional material, a Radiohead CD and stills from *An Interview with The Vampire*. I absolutely adored Tom Cruise and Brad Pitt at that stage, and I had just begun embarking upon my journey into the alternative. For me that was real treasure.

The only reason I left that job was to become a carer, and I got to feel the wind in my hair as I raced around town on my two wheels. It really wasn't that glamorous, in fact I look back and see myself as a complete geek. The scooter was more suited to a retired old lady and the kit I wore was too embarrassing to even describe. The job was good though, a list of people to go and help get up in the mornings and another list to help get into bed at night. I loved the contact with people, I liked to be needed, and I adored the pay. I have no idea what I spent my money on but I remember thinking I had a well-paid job at last.

My ma never asked for money from me for the house, whatever I earned was mine to keep. I helped her in return, we ironed for hours, and the smell of hot starch filled our house for a good few months. She would work full time in the day and then we would iron other men's shirts in the evening. Baskets and baskets of other people's laundry would be dropped off by the first lesbian couple I had ever had contact with. They both looked like they were trapped inside the 1980s - tight perms and they always wore the same jeans and t-shirts. They were brilliant to us though, always made sure we had a steady supply of clothes to iron for those extra pennies.

I can remember boxes of envelopes being delivered to the house one evening, we spent the rest of the week filling them with carefully folded leaflets. It was therapeutic in a way, and we didn't have to deliver them so I really didn't mind. The paper cuts were an annoyance though. She even joined an Escort Agency at one stage. The money offered was excellent but it wasn't the way out for my mum, she didn't go back again. She was a trier; she'd try anything if it meant we could all have a better life. That included night shifts at the local supermarket, which for some reason later got labelled the 'shag shift' for reasons I wasn't sure of at the time. She regretted her lost and wasted opportunities, she saw her life as having being limited. My mum deserved more and better, but it seems we were destined to merely survive.

It made me want to escape. I was determined to make it to University, I saw it as my way out, away from all that had happened that I couldn't ever share with anyone, and I would be less of a burden to my mum. She wouldn't have to worry about me, I'd work while I was away and loans would cover the rest of my expenses.

I wanted to be a midwife, I thought I'd be good at it, even though I didn't really have a clue what the entirety of the job involved. In my romance, I was a kind and skilled woman, helping mothers deliver their babies into the world with big fluffy slippers on. I also thought that I'd be able to travel after I was qualified, I'd go to Africa and do voluntary service, experience the world, and give a little back in the process. I even toyed with the idea of joining the army, and then do nurse training with them that I could use to later convert to midwifery. I was absolutely convinced helping mums and babies was the future for me.

Only one university offered me an interview, I wasn't surprised.

The number of people applying for midwifery in relation to the spaces available on their courses was ridiculous, 800 applicants for 30 places. The odds were always stacked against me; I wasn't a straight A student, I was exceptionally naïve, and there were thirty people out there better suited for the course. Perhaps they could sense the true nature of my character when I went for interview, this girl just doesn't have the balls to see anything through to the end.

Naturally I was devastated when the letter arrived. There was no university place for me. I had no idea what to do next. My tutors at college tried to reassure me that this was normal and that most places were granted during clearing. All I had to do was work hard and get good A level results, then I'd be able to choose my university, they'd be practically begging me to attend. I'm not sure I completely believed them, but it sounded promising and so I immersed myself back into teenage life.

College opened up a whole new genre of friends for me. My best friend had the same name as me, and we gave ourselves the tag of 'the sexy bastard appreciation society' She was a year older than me but I thought she was as comfortable with herself as a person that I absolutely aspired to be like her. She liked bands that I'd never heard of, like *Soundgarden* and *Faith No More*, she even knew them all by their first names. She also knew the names of all the long haired boys at college. We'd share a portion of over salted chips that we'd bought from the college café, and dream about how fabulous our lives would be if just one of those sexy bastards would acknowledge our existence. We were their biggest fans, idolising them, and trying to see what bands they were following so we could listen to them too.

It was the era of canvas bags, we decorated them with marker pens - stating our allegiance to alternative music, and trying to be one of them. Our efforts were rewarded handsomely; we became the alternative girls. Every time we passed them in the corridor they would nod at us in acknowledgment. I'm sure we squealed in delight when it happened the first time—which was not very hard core of us. We were then invited out to the pub with them at lunchtime. This was it, this was living! I'd never been to a pub at lunchtime, this was being an adult and having freedom. We all stayed at that pub for the whole afternoon, the boys were hilarious and we didn't stop laughing the entire time we were there. One of the lads was a newsreader's son. His mom was really famous, and when he told us how much trouble he'd be in if anyone recognised him, it just added a whole new level of danger to the event.

The time at college was short, we all sat our exams, one of the lads walked out of his math's paper after having only written 'fish' as an answer. We were amazed at his apparent coolness about it all. We had no idea why he'd do that, and it wasn't until we were all at a BBQ later that week that he admitted why he'd done it. He'd said he hadn't done any studying, and when he saw the questions he knew there was no way he'd ever pass - so decided to share his realisation in code.

Fish represented the fact that he should have eaten more fish as brain food. We all thought he was super cool, but he didn't look too pleased with himself. He'd lost his chance to escape from his life. He lived in a tower block in Birmingham. Now he had no chance of going to university, and he was destined to stay on a council estate for the rest of his life. It didn't take him long to recover, a few weeks later he was back to being the life and soul of the party - Crazy Dave was up to his old antics again and being unashamedly outrageous.

We went clubbing too. We did all try to go to a mainstream club one weekend, but it ended before it started. One of the lads was wearing a full length leather jacket and plimsolls. The bouncers took one look at his clothes and his long hair and declared he wasn't allowed in. As one we left the club and demanded our entrance money back. We all took it as a sign, as an intervention from the gods. The lights that were cast into the sky were like a calling beacon were for the hip and trendy people, not the dark wearers like us. After all, what were we thinking, anywhere that had 'Discotheque' on the signage clearly wasn't going to play the music we wanted to hear!

We happily left the beautiful people in their high heels to wait their turn at 'disco the queue', as we renamed it, and headed for the alternative pub. It ended up being the best time, the music, the people, the moshing, and the sense of belonging.

Before I knew it, the exam results were ready, our futures were set even if we didn't know it yet. I have no idea where my best friend is now, what she does or where she is in life. I regret not keeping her close to me. I regret that the last time I spoke to her I questioned her decision to be with an older man who already had children. I lost her forever that day in my pig-headed sense of morality. I search for her on Facebook every now and then, but I can't find her. It feels like a loss, a self-inflicted one. If I could find her, then maybe I could recapture that glimpse of happiness our time together gave me. Without her I wouldn't be the crazy person I am today, she was the best influence.

I didn't have amazing results, but they were good enough to get me a place at university. I thought I was leaving home to study midwifery, the paperwork stated that, the subsequent and immensely stressful telephone conversations also said that I was indeed enrolled in the midwifery course. In my heart of hearts, I knew there was a mistake, but I couldn't ignore the glimmer of hope. After my initial rejection I had asked for feedback following the interview. Apparently I had performed well, it literally was a case of too many good applicants for too few spaces. They had told me at that point that they were applying for extra funding and if they were successful a further 5 places would become available. My name was on the shortlist for those extra places. All I had to do was apply to them during clearing for Adult Nursing - as that would put me back on their system - which would enable me to transfer if the opportunity arose. It was a done deal for me, I believed them.

I arrived at university to enrol for my course, a massive hall full of complete and excited strangers. I waited my turn for what seemed like hours in the right lane and handed over my slip of paper. My name wasn't on their list, there was some mistake. My world shattered. I'd left home and committed to this course of action, I was alone and I had no idea of how to argue my case. I could feel tears stinging my eyes, in anger, frustration and humiliation. 'You can do Adult Nursing instead, we have lots of places available on that course, and it's practically the same thing'. I felt I had no choice. I'd come to university to study after all, there was no point in going home now.

It really wasn't the same thing though, and I should have had more fight in me. It was a complete and categorical disaster, and someone should have been accountable for the mistake. I had spent hours standing in a phone box on the street corner because we couldn't afford to have a phone at home. I was trying to organize my life in a booth with boy-racers beeping their horns every other minute and again tears of frustration threatening when I'd be placed on hold for yet another time to check that yes I was indeed enrolled on the midwifery course. I tried to tell them that it couldn't be right as I'd had the rejection letter after interview, and the endless stream of ten pence pieces kept clinking down into the depths of the phone for them to tell me that it was all fine and to show up for enrolment. It wasn't all fine, and it could only have ever happened to me.

Still it was freedom. I'd made the leap and flown the nest. I was my own person and I was going to enjoy it!

CHAPTER 8: LIFE IN LONDON

The glitz, the glamour, the streets paved with gold! Well maybe not, but to Zéphirine, London was as good as it gets. Although she was used to Paris and its beautiful architecture, along with its rich cultural history, London still felt like a good luck charm to her. Everything was so British, from Buckingham Palace with the Queen to the Marble Arch and Trafalgar square. The irony of the similarities wasn't lost on her, but the atmosphere of the two cities was so different. Instead of side street cafés, there were hotel restaurants for afternoon tea. So refined and sophisticated, it was where she was destined to be. It was the stuff fairy tales were made of and where dreams could come true.

London. She was here and determined to live her life.

Her story of London began at the Kingsley Hotel. It was no Ritz or Savoy, but to her, it was English and grand. Its Victorian persona was everything she wanted from London. She thought she got lucky. For once. She landed her job as a waitress one day after her arrival in London for a starter. What made working at the Kingsley Hotel more fabulous was the fact it was only a five-minute walk to Oxford Street, where the classy shops were.

Even though she was hired to work part-time, she ended up working full-time hours covering for everybody else. She'd do five days on and two days off, randomized every week. Working shifts on the weekend would only be for breakfast service, as the restaurant closed for lunch, but she was still getting paid for a full day's shift.

She was dating the French guy, who worked as one of the porters, for about a month until he had to go back to France to study. That was a real shame — as she liked him a lot. He had the body of an Adonis and embraced the whole raw egg yolk drinking thing, which made Zéphirine queasy to watch. When she looked at him she could imagine him being on the front cover of a magazine, with his muscles tanned and oiled, glistening enticingly.

Zéphirine couldn't actually believe they were dating. When they all went to a pub after work one evening to celebrate her arrival, he was all over her! She was glad to have overcome her shyness and had accepted his advances, even if their relationship was to be short-lived. Unfortunately, his return to France was inevitable. He had planned it before she came into the picture. Their relationship was too new to make those kind of changes to his life plans. Zéphirine was disappointed, but she knew it was for the best. She took over his bedroom in the apartment behind the hotel. It made a massive difference - rather than having to travel in from Wembley every day.

Calling it an apartment was being a bit generous though. The building was old and some of the rooms were packed to the rafters with junk. Their floor had two liveable rooms, and this was what they called their flat. One room was large, shared by a lesbian and a gay guy in their late twenties. The other was a small kitchen, approximately a three meter squared in all, with a fridge, a stove, and a table accompanied by three chairs. There was a lone mattress on the floor hidden by the dining table for a bit of privacy which served as her bed. The bathroom was in the hallway, and she never managed to work out how many people were sharing that tiny washroom. It was the smallest bathroom she had ever seen and there was never enough hot water to go around. It always seemed to run out just as she managed to get her turn. Needless to say she never spent much time in that bathroom.

In reality, the living conditions were terrible, and in hindsight probably completely illegal. That place should never have been rented out to tenants. Beside the near proximity to work, the house only had one other redeeming feature— access to the roof. Which was almost enough to make her forget about how awful everything else was, being that it had an incredible view over the entire city, as well as being a hotspot for their private sunbathing. It was the beginning of summer when she arrived in London and was going to be one of the hottest on record for the UK of all time - so this little perk was going to come in handy.

Even though the accommodation was nothing flashy, it didn't matter. Zéphirine was free to do whatever she wanted and when she wanted. She was in her favourite city learning English—which in itself was a dream. And she loved her job and the people who worked there. For once, she felt at peace. Her demons seemed to have vanished into thin air and she would wake up clear minded. And Luc... well he was still there in her heart and there was not much else she could do about it.

For the first few weeks in London, she was overly excited and out almost every night clubbing or partying. She ate her first hamburger at MacDonald's, drank her first Vodka, and discovered that Malibu on the rocks was her preferred drink of choice.

There was one time that Zéphirine was late for work, they were out on the town until 5am. She knew she had to work the next day but the recklessness of youth dared her to keep going. She was still living in Wembley at the time and somehow had to make it back there for her uniform before making it to work on time. By the time she turned up at the hotel, her shift was over. She thought her days were numbered and that the dream would be over. Thankfully the restaurant manager forgave her, although there were stern words hurled her way, "Please do not do it again!" The fear of losing what seemed like the perfect job made her think twice before she did anything like that again.

They knew Zéphirine was a hard worker. When there were hours to fill, she never turned them down, even though it meant she rarely had two days off together. It was not a highly paid job and London was an expensive place to live. So money was scarce, she had to budget sensibly. It was all worth it though, for the first time she truly felt like she loved her life. It wasn't sunshine all of the time, Luc wrote to her once, so she got the blues and organised to have four days off in a row, Saturday to Tuesday to go back to France. It was stupid but she needed – wanted - to see him. Zéphirine knew nothing serious would ever happen between them. They would spend hours talking in his car, nothing more. But any time with him was better than nothing, even if it hurt.

The people at Zéphirine's work knew each other inside and out.

There was one guy in particular who stood out, Max. Max loved flirting although he never seemed to flirt with her. Maybe she subconsciously emitted a signal declaring the fact that '*I am not interested*' and he got it instantly. Her self-confidence served as a coat of armour, making her seem hard and cold to any onlookers. There was the voice of self-doubt that challenged her: '*why isn't he interested in me? Am I not attractive?*' Either way, she was fine, they were colleagues and good mates. Zéphirine was thankful that the situation was not complicated. Then there was Aaron Adkins.

Aaron looked after the parties in the hotel, so she only came across him in the kitchen when he needed to pick up glasses and plates. Aaron was tall, exceptionally good looking, and charming. She could see why he was in charge of entertainment, when he told a joke it was funny and never at anyone's expense. He had a way of talking that was captivating, you actually wanted to know what he had to say. Everybody loved Aaron. Without fail, he would take the time to make them laugh when he entered the kitchen with the latest joke or a comedy expression, they were enthralled by him.

Gradually, Aaron and Zéphirine became an item until they were *the* couple at the Kingsley Hotel. She could barely understand his Cockney accent. So the first few months of their relationship consisted more of kissing and hand communications than anything else. She didn't know much about him because of the lack of understanding. But she wanted to know him inside and out because she felt it was her first true relationship. Everyone knew about them, they were inseparable, and always walked hand in hand.

Zéphirine had boyfriends in the past. In fact, probably too many of them. But it was mostly one-night stand basis and she would be very lucky if she would be seen with the same guy for more than four weeks - Nicolas being the exception, but he was married, so it was a different situation. And there was never that walking hand in hand stuff, or any kind of public affection to confirm she was indeed in a relationship. Though she had wanted that with Luc, and had hoped it would eventually happen.

She didn't have sex with all the guys of course, because that would have earned the title of 'slut' like some of the girls in town. Zéphirine was spending enough time with the boys to know how and who was considered a slut or not. It was a small town and everybody knew, or at least had heard of each other. Then again, they probably would not have told her what they thought of her. Honesty was not a word associated with those boys. But she didn't like the idea of being called a slut behind her back, so she wouldn't do anything that could jeopardize that. Some guys had lied and said they had sex with her. But she knew better and so did the guys with whom it had actually happened.

Having a guy in her life at all times provided her with a sense of security. If she had a guy by her side, even for a day, then it meant she was not totally unattractive and fat. Silly thinking maybe, but that was how it worked for Zéphirine. It got her out of bed each morning to go through the motions.

Now that Zéphirine was settled, and finding her stride in London, she decided to look for a more decent place to live. She knew it would be difficult to find something as close to work as her current flat, but anything would be better than that disgusting place - it could barely be called living!

She found a room in a shared three-bedroom house, exactly thirty minutes away from work by bus. The place had bus stops directly in front of the house and in front of the hotel, so that was almost perfect. The bedroom was not huge and came furnished. There was a single bed against the wall by the window overlooking the backyard, a chest of drawers with a tiny black and white TV perched on top that only functioned when it felt like it, stood against the opposite wall. She was not much of a TV watcher, so she didn't mind that it was temperamental. But watching TV was good practice for her English skills, besides, she enjoyed watching *Home and Away* from time to time. A coffee table was in the centre of the room, an attempt to make it feel more homey and functional simultaneously. It was small, but it was private, clean and it had a proper bathroom with hot water and a bathtub!

There were only two other people to share the house with. She occasionally saw her housemates, who seemed to want to keep to themselves and she was fine with that. At this point she thought her life was great; she had a hot boyfriend, a job, and a roof over her head - what more could she want?

Aaron stayed at her place most nights, as he lived outside of London. They worked a few shifts together, and even after she was hired as a full-time waitress, she would still not turn down extra shifts. The money was terrible. Once she paid for rent, electricity, and groceries there was not much left over. She even had to reduce her smoking habit. She could no longer afford a packet of 20, which was twice the price they were in France. This made her grateful for England's packs of ten.

She worked long shifts over the Christmas holidays and she was beginning to feel exhausted. It was time to take a week off from work since she had accumulated paid holidays. She called her mother to touch base - one of her occasional calls to say she was fine, and somewhere along the line Zéphirine must have mentioned she was taking a break.

Aaron and Zéphirine were coming back from his parents' house. He parked the car down the street and as they were walking towards the house they both saw a familiar figure.

"It looks like my mother." she told him.

"That's because it is your mother!"

And there she was, completely unannounced! Zéphirine's mother was on her doorstep. She was so excited to tell them about how she made it up here with her not so well-spoken English. It was one huge adventure for her, and Zéphirine could not remember having seen her mother so animated before. Now they had to figure out how they would all fit into her tiny bedroom - as her mother was not the type to spend money on a hotel room.

There was only a single bed which Zéphirine shared with Aaron. And there was no way she was going to give up her bed, on *her* holidays! Nope, not happening! There wasn't even a lounge room or a sofa in the house that Zéphirine could offer her mother as a temporary camp. Her mother had to sleep on the carpeted floor but that didn't seem to deter her.

The next day she told Zéphirine about her plans which involved visiting family friends with her. Immediately Zéphirine felt like her mother was trying to control her. She had Zéphirine's holidays perfectly mapped out, and was to be her mother's trophy to display amongst all of her old acquaintances.

In her new found freedom, Zéphirine rebelled and told her mother she wasn't interested in visiting people she could hardly remember. She saw the disappointment on her mother's face and it hit her like a slap to the face. She didn't like to hurt anyone, even if it was her bitch of a mother. But she refused to back down. This was her first paid holiday holiday and she was going to enjoy it the way she chose to - with her boyfriend. Her mother left as quickly as she had arrived and her life resumed its mundane routine.

She was no longer going out clubbing since dating Aaron. Besides she no longer had the time with her work schedule. Most of their free time was spent at his house or hers. Sometimes they would grab something to eat or go out for drinks with colleagues. Aaron didn't seem to be much of a sociable person outside of work. He had introduced her to only one childhood friend, which was ironic given that he was the life and soul of the hotel. But like her, he was a workaholic.

Zéphirine loved her job because she liked the people she was working with. It felt like they were a big family. They told each other everything, they laughed together and they sweated together when the hotel was busy and the pressure was on. There were also regular customers that visited the hotel, two business men in particular would ask for Zéphirine and only allow her to serve them. She loved hearing their stories about the USA where they were traveling back and forth for business. This is when she decided she wanted to go to the USA next.

After work, she called her mother, "I need a passport so I can go to the USA," she told her. Her mother didn't say anything and just organised the passport. Her mother was bizarre like that, perhaps there was a part of her that wanted to be her mother? Or maybe she wanted her daughter to be as far as possible from her?

Zéphirine loved Aaron, but she wasn't in love with him if that made any sense at all. Despite her feelings for Aaron, Luc's unshakeable presence loomed in the back of her mind. She and Aaron made a good couple. They suited each other. They got along fine. She loved how sometimes the new girls at the hotel would look at him. She felt proud to have a boyfriend that other girls would envy, it was prestigious. Aaron was not the flirty type at all, though he was well aware of the girls demanding his attention. He loved being the centre of attention. He loved making people laugh by acting silly which some women might consider to be flirting.

She recalled the one time a new chef in the kitchen showed a little too much interest in Aaron. She was a petite and delicate girl with blond hair, and it was more than obvious she had a crush on Aaron. Zéphirine was a little confused as to how the new girl didn't seem to know she and Aaron were an item. There were absolutely no secrets in that hotel. So Zéphirine watched her flirt with her boyfriend, trying to get his attention.

After a shift, Zéphirine went downstairs to the canteen to get a late lunch. She was chatting with some of the staff at the table, the cute little blond thing was there with them. Aaron came in and joined them at the table, bursting at the seams with a joke to share. Once everybody had finished laughing, he got up, walked over to Zéphirine, leaned forward to kiss her and said "see you at home gorgeous."

The cute little blond thing's face dropped, her eyes going from him to Zéphirine. Zéphirine pretended not to notice but in her my mind she was laughing hard, proud of herself. *'You can look but you can't touch, because he is mine,'* she wanted to tell her. Perhaps she should have been more abashed, in that one single second the girl's heart had probably been crushed. There was a part of Zéphirine that thought Aaron had orchestrated the whole display for her benefit, which was, she admitted on reflection now, a little cruel.

Zéphirine and Aaron didn't work the same shifts except when she had to do overtime. Her roster was pretty much the same, every day from 7am to 3pm. Some days Aaron started mid-morning, others from mid-afternoon. Their off days did not coincide either so quality time to discover the city around them together was limited. Sometimes, while waiting for Aaron to get off work, she would explore the local shops secretly wishing to one day be able to buy the many luxurious items on display. She would go home and he would come over or choose to go back to his place. There were no specific rules to their relationship, they just went with the flow, or so she thought.

One afternoon, Aaron asked Zéphirine if she could wait for his shift to be over so they could go to her place together. She was rather tired that day after a busy breakfast, so she declined: "I'll meet you at my house." He seemed fine with that so she kissed him on the cheek and turned around to leave waving goodbye to the staff as she was walking toward the door.

"Zéphirine! Wait!" She turned around and saw Max jogging towards her.

"Hey Max, what's up?"

"I need you to come to the shops with me to help me chose a shirt. I'm going on a date tonight." he explained.

Zéphirine really wanted to go home and Max knew it so he made the puppy face she could not resist. She also knew he was really into that new girl at the reception, so scoring a date with her meant a lot to Max. She couldn't let him down and agreed to go shopping with him. The store was just around the corner from the hotel. But this errand would still not take long enough for Aaron to finish his shift.

Aaron didn't drop by that night. And it wasn't unusual. There was no mobile phone back in those days and she did not have a landline either. When she got to work the next day and saw his face, she knew something was wrong. The happy go lucky guy they all knew and loved was replaced by a complete stranger that none of them recognised.

Aaron stormed into the kitchen, in front of all the staff and started shouting at Zéphirine. He was standing so close to her, with his finger raised pointing in her face with wild angry eyes. He was accusing her of cheating on him with Max, and in front of everyone for them all to see her embarrassment and humiliation. How could he even think that? Max and her were friends and always had been. They were shopping for his date, how could that ever be construed as cheating?

From that moment on things had changed, the argument had upset the rest of the staff. Aaron and Zéphirine were *the* couple of the hotel after all. After he left the kitchen they all told her not to worry about it, that it would all blow over soon enough; he must have just been letting off steam. *Letting off steam?* she thought. Unlikely. There had to be more to it than that. But there wasn't.

Max tried to speak to him to allay his fears but even that didn't seem to work. Aaron didn't speak to Zéphirine for a whole week. His attitude had completely changed, and a serious jealous streak was becoming very apparent in him. It had shown its ugly head once before, but in her naivety she had dismissed it without another thought. It started in a shop one day where the salesperson must have been over friendly towards her - because when they stepped outside Aaron made a huge scene, snatching her handbag from her arm so hard he broke it.

After he'd seemingly forgotten all about the scene and they were back to normal—until he'd seen her serving the business men in the hotel. He waited until they got to her place later that evening where he took her umbrella from her hands. A beautiful quintessentially English one made from solid wood that a customer had left behind at the hotel. When the manager gave it to her she instantly loved it and held it like a treasure. Aaron smashed it on the rail of the staircase in front of her, staring at her like he was willing her to challenge him. At that moment, something inside of their relationship broke. He resented her popularity and she resented him. They had pretended it hadn't happened and fell into the neutrality of routine.

He quit his job, after five years of services, just like that without any discussion or warning. What was left of their relationship died the day he quit. It was like what they were, was linked to the hotel, and by leaving he had broken it. His decision hit them hard on other levels. He couldn't find a job that he wanted to do, not that he knew what he wanted to do, and nothing was ever good enough for him.

Aaron was quite a tight ass in regards to money, Zéphirine had to admit. She knew he was saving but what for? He was not a big spender and would easily let her spend her money first. They rarely went out. Never had he offered to pay for half the groceries, even though he was eating at her house most of the time. They would always go to his house on a full stomach. That put a lot of strain on her tiny resources, besides there were things in life she wanted and an unemployed jealous boyfriend had never been on the list.

Their relationship got worse. Zéphirine wanted out. But she didn't quite know how to break up with him. In fact, she had never broken up with anyone before. Her relationships always seemed to end on their own—no big breakup fight, no drama. Just a natural flow away from the old and onto the new.

She was torn. She didn't know what to do. In desperation she decided to quit her job, much to the dismay of her managers, and go back to France. Aaron had refused to learn even a tiny bit of French so she thought she would be safe going back home. When she told him the news he decided to come with her. She felt cornered, she had no idea what to do other than follow through with her plans.

Her mother never liked Aaron. She never liked any man she dated, except for Luc, though Zéphirine doubted she knew her true feelings for the man. Or did she? Aaron had a temper, he never touched her but he would throw things at her when he was angry. He seemed to always miss her by a few inches but it left her wondering what would happen if one day he didn't miss? And what if he used a knife instead of a mug?

Zéphirine found them a job as waiters in a restaurant just outside town. After one week the manager told her she had the job if she wanted it, but not Aaron as he couldn't speak French. They also only paid her for the week which was unfair as if Aaron could not speak French he still had done his job. She had to decline the offer, of course, and that didn't please her mother at all.

She remembered an argument between Aaron and her mother, a silly spat that had obviously been simmering under the surface. It wasn't a big deal, the plates had been stacked wrong on the drainer, but because of the language barrier, in addition to blatantly disliking each other, the sparks were flying. The body language was terrifying, and Aaron stood in such a threatening way that Zéphirine actually thought he was going to hit her mother, she could see the rage building inside him.

To make matters worse, her father was hospitalised the next day for appendicitis. Her mother wasted no time and took it as an opportunity to kick them out of the house. Lucky, Zéphirine had just agreed to a live-in waitressing job in a chateau in the South of France. She went to the hospital to say goodbye to her father. There was no point mentioning that her mother had kicked them out. Would he even care? Whatever her mother said, her father seemed to always go along with it. *Everything would be fine* she told herself.

But things were far from fine. They lasted two weeks at the chateau—which was soul-destroying as the job was perfect, the surroundings beautiful, and the staff was welcoming. The restaurant manager was a good looking guy in his early twenties. He seemed to have a crush on Zéphirine from day one. Or maybe he made a rule to sleep with any new waitresses, she wasn't sure, but her co-workers told her on their last day, "If you had come here single, you would still have a job!"

Zéphirine was disappointed. This seasonal job would have allowed them to save up a lot of money, more than she had ever earned. They did pay both of them, which was a relief. And it was a good pay for just two weeks of work which was a reminder of how much they could have made... but she decided to not dwell on it. At least it would help them survive until they, or rather *she,* found something else.

She picked Nice for their next destination. It was a stab in the dark as she'd never been there before.

They stayed in a caravan park on the outskirts of Nice, and the first week felt like a holiday, but it was expensive and at the rate they were going it wouldn't take long to run out of money. They had to move. They had to find work. She had to find them a job. She went on the search for cheap accommodation as well as a job. She chose to avoid Nice centre and headed for what seemed to be the shadier areas. She stumbled across a little hotel and got talking with the owner who was actually looking for a receptionist. The fact she spoke English fluently was a bonus and it was a live-in job! It was simply perfect for them.

Zéphirine quite liked the room. It was a rectangular shape with one huge window that stretched nearly up to the ceiling, filling the whole room with the glorious sunshine. As it was with most buildings in France, the ceilings were high, making the room feel more spacious and open. Under the mezzanine, where the bed was located on, was a small living area with a couch, TV, and coffee table. This little area was destined to become Aaron's favourite corner.

It was not huge or lavish, but it was a grown up space, a place to live and be independent, and it was clean. Zéphirine loved the way the sun filled the room. She couldn't see the ocean but she could feel its freedom becoming from beyond the walls.

The hotel itself spanned across the whole first floor of the building with 24 rooms in total. It had its own entry point downstairs, with a tiny reception space at the top of the stairs that consisted of a notebook, phone, and calendar. The mother and daughter that ran the hotel were of Italian descent and Zéphirine somehow felt akin to them and admired their desire to run a business. The hotel itself was on Rue d'Angleterre, which reminded her of the happy days back in London so she embraced her new role with tenacity and fervour.

As time went on, Zéphirine's relationship with the business owner was okay, but things with the daughter were strained. Zéphirine thought the daughter was a bitch, plain and simple. She would be nice to her face but as soon as her back was turned would stab her. She thought she was this hot thing, but truth to be told, she was quite plain, an average woman who was a gold digger trying to be something she was clearly not.

Despite her initial enthusiasm Zéphirine didn't like the job as much as she had hoped. She was the receptionist, answering the phone, checking in and checking out guests, the usual expected tasks, but in the mornings she had to clean the empty rooms too. She was given a part-time pay in cash despite working more than full-time and one day off per week.

Aaron had no interest in the job and barely summoned up the energy to help. He wanted to be a model. Being a model had become a dream of his. So one day on her day off, she decided to take him to a model agency, more to appease him and hope he would do something constructive with his time than any real expectation.

Aaron was tall, slim, extremely good looking, and he was photogenic. The only thing he was lacking was he didn't pack the muscles. He really could have done with some weight training. She thought he had some potential but the agency did not share her opinion and for once she was glad Aaron did not understand French.

"We have no work for him, but we can hire you." the guy said.

"Thank you for the ego boost, I always need that." Zéphirine thought to herself, but right now she needed her boyfriend to work. Amazingly her wits were about her and she replied without a blink, "If you hire him, you can hire me. Basically you take us both or no one." The modelling agency managers agreed and told her about a gig that would happened within a few weeks.

Her job provided them a roof over their head but she was working seven days a week. Some of the guests would arrive late at night so Zéphirine had to stay up for them. The owner had given her a day off, but she was expected back to the hotel by 6pm so it was not a complete day off. She knew she was underpaid but the job gave them food and a roof over their head. She had no time going job hunting and could not rely on Aaron. Zéphirine was only eighteen and it was her second job in life so far. She was at the mercy of those around her.

The modelling agency had the gig ready for them. It was going to be a bit of a struggle to be back in time but Zéphirine wanted to do it, especially with the promise of extra cash for both of them. She probably should have talked to the owner of the hotel. She felt a little intimidated and afraid to ask for extra time off, and the rebel in her thought that an hour here or there unaccounted for wouldn't result in the owner firing her. And let's be honest here, right or wrong, Zéphirine knew she was doing more than what she was getting paid for so surely her boss would overlook her coming back late on her day off.

The gig was a modelling show for some local shops. The catwalk was set up along the long stretch of pavement that ran adjacent to the beach adding a sense of exotic glamour to the whole event. The traffic flowed as normal while they modelled the latest bikini's and beach wear in the glorious sunshine. Ferrari's, Lamborghini's, and motorbikes streamed past as they walked the walk, with a few toots to be heard here and there. The crowd wasn't huge but it was a fabulous atmosphere.

The fashion show went well. It was a good thing Zéphirine had enjoyed herself as they never saw a penny from that gig. The agency disappeared without a trace before paying either anyone. Her relationship with Aaron just degraded even more after that, almost as though he held her personally responsible for the agency not employing him. One guy staying at the hotel picked up on the problems Aaron and Zéphirine were having. He was in Nice for work for a week, and they became friends or maybe he was a shoulder to cry on.

Zéphirine couldn't deny that she fancied the guy too. They talked all of the time which of course made Aaron jealous, especially since he couldn't understand a word of what they were discussing. With reckless abandon she took off for a drink one evening with the guy and that made Aaron furious. But she couldn't care less. She did steal a kiss from the guy that night, nothing more, and it felt good. She'd had enough and had probably intentionally provoked Aaron as she was sick of working all day with him not helping. All he ever did was watch TV and mumbling about becoming a model. He still refused to learn any French that at least would have gone a small way towards appeasing her.

No matter which way she looked at her future at the hotel it was in jeopardy. Shortly before she'd met the good looking guy, she had made one of her occasional phone calls to her mother. In her exasperation Zéphirine told her all about her pay, the long hours, and frustration about how they would always come and go in their room like it was part of their own living space. Never mind her mother's personal feelings about Zéphirine, or the obvious shortcomings, when someone was trying to take advantage of her daughter financially all hell broke loose. Her mother called the Ombudsman.

The owner was a bit upset, and understandably, but the fact remained that she was exploiting Zéphirine. So when the inspector came they determined that she was to be paid part-time in exchange for working part-time with set hours and on a seasonal contract, which of course was not going to be renewed. At first both the mother and daughter stopped talking to Zéphirine. The daughter was giving her a look of pure hatred because on Zéphirine's day off she had to clean the rooms herself.

Aaron and Zéphirine were still arguing about the cute guy and her going out without him. He was so angry he punched the door of their room. There was a big hole in the door which Zéphirine had to explain to the owner and that is when she confessed to her about her shambles of a relationship with Aaron. The owner was a mother too so she told Zéphirine she had to let him go and send him home back to the UK.

Finally, Zéphirine and Aaron had the talk. Of course she had no money to pay for his flight. She told him to call his mother and ask her to lend him the money. She promised she would come back to London when she could. But it wasn't really for him she would go back, it was more because she loved living in London and had no intention of staying in France no matter what. Either way she had to save money to be able to go back there and that simply wasn't going to happen with him around.

Aaron didn't argue about it. He knew too it was time to leave. Nothing good could have come out of the situation. And so he left, quietly and calmly.

CHAPTER 9: STEPPING OUT

So my new life started with humiliation and disappointment. I try not to be a negative person, I want to see the best in people and every situation, but this was a bitter pill to swallow. Count me in as Allanah the negative. I needed to embrace my fate and make the most of the opportunity. After all, university was a once in a lifetime experience so I'd best grab it with both hands.

Looking back now my memories are a mixed bag of emotions. I discovered so much about myself during that time, yet was never allowed to truly flourish. I blame myself for not taking the chances that life threw at me and honestly, it's mostly regret that haunts me.

For the first year, I stayed in residence halls, and we were like our own little village of knowledge hungry, experience lacking, borderline adults as our campus was 8 miles outside of the city of Oxford. There was a shop, laundry room, computer suite, dining hall with breakfast and evening meal included in our stay, and, most importantly, a bar. Every night had a theme in that bar, they must have made a killing from us, but it was important to the social dynamics for all of us, and I'm sure it helped us keep tabs on what was socially acceptable. Without the bell for last orders being called, we would never know the rest of the world was going to bed.

The halls were in the form of a quadrant with a huge tower

block on one side that over looked the sports field. My room was in the tower, floor M, room 13. It felt significant, 13th letter of the alphabet, unlucky for some, a perfect allocation for a misfit like me. I had a fabulous view over the sports field although it was completely wasted on me, I played none, participated in even fewer, and observed even less. Before I left home, I had been really active. I'd run all across town, for miles and miles, at least twice a week in addition to kickboxing. There'd be a fitness video at least three times a week too, Step Reebok and Cindy Crawford were my favourite forms of torture. The most exercise I got from my new life was pushing the button for the lift and holding a pint of lager. When my mum picked me up after the first term she laughed, I couldn't understand what was funny, she told me it was because I was fat and had podgy fingers.

Variety is the spice of life, and the students that inhabited Wheatley Campus certainly had that. My direct neighbour was so posh she hardly ever came out of her room, I'm sure she hated every second of being surrounded by us riffraff. We hardly ever spoke, she would pronounce us all to be childish and immature quite often, and I don't remember ever seeing her drunk let alone tipsy. She would have been better placed at the other end of the corridor, they were far more sensible than us. Hannah was to the other side of me, she was a beautiful person, gentle and quiet with an infectious laugh. She moved with grace and never did anything that made me question her character in all of the time I knew her. I liked her that little bit more because her mum made the most delicious lasagne that I to this day have ever tasted and her poshness was never used to judge the rest of us. Her room was directly above the most gorgeous person I had ever seen in the flesh, but she pronounced that to be a bad thing as sound travelled very well through the sink in the room, and he and his girlfriend were not shy in their affections. I did my very best to give that girl the most evil look that could ever be summoned, not out of jealousy, but purely to protect Hannah's delicate soul of course.

My most favourite friend was two doors away and completed our corner of the tower. Nell was an Olympic gymnast, a tiny dot of a woman, and she really was a woman as she was a mature student. I fell in love with her, there was never a time that she wasn't smiling, or tumbling around, or making us all try our own hand at gymnastics. We'd be bridged out and piled up in a tangle of arms and legs to the point that I couldn't be sure what arm belonged to which body. She'd flip her way home after a night out at the bar, I was in awe of her, and the stories she had to tell. I'd spend my time in her room rather than sit by myself and in fact her room became the focal point for all of us even when we moved in to our shared house ready for the next academic year.

There were some truly outstanding characters in those halls, from Jay the 6ft American Punk to Charlie the actual certified poshest man alive. Our university was an old polytechnic that had recently been promoted to university status in Oxford, which was seeped in academic history. The best of the best applied to attend the Oxford University Colleges, from Christ Church and Magdalen to Balliol and The Queen's College, only straight 'A' students need apply. The cost of living in Oxford was as equally prestigious although I didn't find that out until much later, but it attracted the rich and wealthy families, including princes from the Middle East. Oxford Brookes University gave those people a chance to study at Oxford without needing the straight 'A' grades, the old poly had much lower academic standards, but offered the beauty of the spires and shires. It showed with the students that made up the majority of my peers, very affluent, but not necessarily the sharpest tools in the box. It gave for exotic tales of adventure at the bar, and there was always a bottle of Tequila circulating through the halls with a worm in the bottom from the last family holiday to Mexico.

The morning after The Summer Ball the entire quadrant was a mess. It was a ghost town at breakfast, hardly anyone had made it out of their beds in time for the morning service. Outside of the main doors there was a chalk outline of a body and a string of police tape hanging from one of the windows above. One of the lift doors kept opening and closing and we could hear it sliding for the entire time we ate breakfast and had our cheeky cigarette outside.

We'd walked down the stairs that morning. We were feeling full of vitality even though we had been to the ball ourselves, our advantage was a lack of tropical holiday destinations so the bottle of wine we shared hadn't left us with any after effects. We were full of the joys of summer, recalling our high jinks from the night before. Officially we were delinquents, we hadn't paid for our tickets to the ball in the guise of an anti-capitalist protest. The truth was we couldn't afford the tickets let alone the ball gown and shoes.

Dressed in my tie dye mini skirt and cherry red doc martins complete with purple haired pigtails, I was ready to take on the 'poshos'. Luckily the security guards were feeling generous, perhaps they were on a promise from one of us I don't really remember why, but I do know we all had shiny wrist bands that declared our entrance was permitted not long after darkness fell. We didn't waste our good fortune, we danced until I had blisters, we rode the high wheel while singing along to Lesbian Seagull as loud as we could, and we made sure we soaked up the atmosphere to the tips of our toes.

On our way back to our room after our peaceful breakfast, we found the source of the lift doors problem. Charlie was lying on the floor of the lift, full dinner suit on, shiny shoes sticking out of the lift, dickey bow limp in one hand, empty bottle of Tequila with no magic worm in the other, and face down and snoring. It saddens me deeply that we didn't have mobile phones back then, there was no way to permanently record this perfect moment in time.

That year, I discovered that drinking Gin makes me cry. I told the 6ft tall American Punk how amazing I thought he was and would he consider ditching his girlfriend so that I could be the new addition to his arm. He was so gentle with me; it had been the first time I'd ever spoken to him but he must have seen me watching him from a distance. He managed to let me down without humiliating me and for that I fancied him even more. I still cried though, blurbed my eyes out in a darkened corridor asking the world what was so wrong with me. If I was able to listen I would have heard it shouting back at me, 'nothing, you need to live, grow, and flourish is all'. A week later his girlfriend arrived for a visit, she was the most amazing and gorgeous girl I had ever seen. She was the exact image of Gwen Stefani, and I didn't hate her, I wished I knew them all well enough to speak to, as I was convinced they'd have the best adventures to share.

Being online was a foreign concept to me back then. I did venture into the computer suite once or twice as an attempted distraction from alcohol. We'd been shown how to use the online directory to search for resources for our studies, I did actually go to a few lectures here and there. When I logged on to the system there were a whole host of other things you could access too. I'm not a technophobe, but neither am I completely comfortable with new things, I like to know how everything works and feel stupid if I can't understand or utilise things to their full potential. Trying to access the online journals was proving more difficult than I'd initially anticipated and it was late at night, my patience was wearing thin. That was when I noticed the inter campus chat icon. I had no idea what it was but wondered if it would help me understand what I was trying to achieve a bit better. I opened the programme and was dropped into a chat room. This was the very first time I'd ever experienced anything like it.

One of the names stood out like a beacon to me, Machinehead. In my new found superior musical knowledge I recognised it as the title to a Bush song. I didn't stop to think about what I was doing, I plunged straight in, hey, I love your name. They replied immediately, a message addressed to me visible without having to open any mail or click on any tabs. This was magic. I can't remember the exact words, or even what completely unimaginative name I would have used as my online identity. The conversation and my excitement was short lived. They replied with something along the lines of, thanks, do you recognise it? Of course I did, Bush were my new favourite band, and that was even before Gwen Stefani married Gavin.

That was when I discovered that I was in fact musically challenged. They were referring to the hard core band and not the soft song. I felt embarrassed and logged off quickly, for some strange reason I felt like I could be seen and that whoever Machinehead had been would be laughing at my ignorance. As I scanned the room to see if anyone was watching my discomfort, I noticed that my second biggest crush was in the room, busy tapping away on the keyboard. I felt sick, grabbed my bag and ran out of the room. I didn't pluck up the courage to attempt online chat for another 6 years, and even now I can be revisited by that sudden panic of have I just said something completely stupid, take it back, take it back please. If it was him on the other end of the conversation he would have definitely known it was me who had been chatting with him, and I knew he already knew I thought he was the best male option on campus, 6ft American excluded, so who knows how history would have been written if I'd have had the courage to stay online that night.

Regrets, they plague my dreams. Some of them are fanciful what ifs, others are life shattering bad choices.

Despite my initial disappointment, Nursing seemed to be a good path for me to follow. I enjoyed my biology lectures and marvelled at the Human Body. I seemed to be quite good with patients too, my grades were coming back as A's in that first year, I was doing well. I'd found an agency in Oxford that allowed me to work casual hours as a carer, cleaner, and chamber maid. I could stay in Oxford throughout the summer and earn money there, so there were a few of us that remained all year round. We'd moved into a shared house and all seemed to be going well. There were two other girls sharing with our tower corner posse, Talitha and Carmen. Talitha was so charming, she was into trance music and had long flowing beach hair. She did everything with flair, and she was fabulous to be around. I was insanely jealous of Carmen, tall, long black hair, and a gorgeous boyfriend. Not only that, she took the attic room, I had wanted it, thinking it was obviously more suited to my dark soul and after all I'd need to be away from the hustle and bustle of the house when I was on shift. No one else saw it that way and the coin toss awarded her the prize.

We all got on really well in the house, the dynamics were brilliant, and there were enough of us to water down any bitchiness that might have developed. If we were getting catty we'd move to a different room or just pile into the Temple Bar that was literally two doors away. Talitha turned out to be the daughter of a diplomat and she would entertain us with her tales of bodyguards and James Bond type briefcases that she swore were real. Her mother was French and I loved listening to her talk to her on the phone every Sunday evening, her voice was like a melody.

Carmen gave us the naughty stories, her dad was a vicar, and her parents were much older than any of ours. She told us about something her and her boyfriend had done while staying at home during that summer, it involved a courgette from the fridge that they put back after they'd finished with it, and then had to eat when her mum had served it roasted that Sunday for dinner. Her boyfriend would sometimes wear her underwear over the top of his trousers, but hidden under a jacket, when he went out to Tesco just to add a hint of excitement and naughtiness to their day. Apparently he only drank wine that was on the very bottom shelf, forcing him to bend over and expose his antics. At that time to me she was outrageous and worldly wise, and I was still jealous of her. One evening in the house we were all a tad high spirited and in

Nell's room as usual, partly because she had the Nintendo 64 in there and partly because she was a magnet to us all. Carmen was in her penthouse suite locked away with her boyfriend as was normal for them on a weekend. She raced past the door on her way down to the fridge to collect another bottle of wine. As one the rest of us decided that we'd intercept her on her way back up the stairs and hold her hostage, forcing her to spend time with us. Our plan was executed perfectly and we pounced on her, dragged her into Nell's room and declared her ours. She squealed with delight and played her part perfectly, calling for her gallant boyfriend to save her for she had been taken captive.

Her boyfriend emerged from the attic room, wrapped in a double duvet, which at the time I had taken as part of the role play. He declared himself to be his love's champion and that he would indeed save her. He took one step down and slipped on the quilt. A bundle of arms and legs later he was at the bottom of the stairs and completely naked. Luckily for me, I didn't see the undignified part, but the others had seen everything, Talitha screamed and ran away, Carmen stood motionless with her face frozen in shock and Nell just laughed, a deep hearty laugh. I was laughing too, I thought it was the funniest thing I had ever witnessed. I did also have my nurses head on, as always, and moved forwards to ask him if he was ok. He shouted at me and told me to leave him alone as he desperately tried to disentangle himself from the quilt and he scurried back upstairs without a backwards glance. Carmen followed close behind and we didn't see him again for the rest of the weekend.

It wasn't until Talitha had stopped laughing enough to tell me that he had been completely naked underneath that quilt that I understood why everyone was so amused, and why he had been so angry. Hannah looked a little traumatised as she wiped the tears from her face, 'but they were so red, and angry' was all that she could say while Talitha managed to declare that he must shave his balls before she dissolved into another fit of giggles. I guess he really was stark bullock naked underneath that duvet.

Our house dynamics changed shortly after that. Nell decided she was leaving university. I was devastated and begged her to stay, but she had to do what was right for her. She lives in America now, she's lived the most amazing adventure and I'm so happy for her, but when she left everything changed.

That wasn't the only thing to cause us all to drift apart. I was finding my courses harder all of the time. The late nights pretending I could party with no sleep and the lack of finances were starting to take their toll. I would buy cigarettes with a cheque from the local newsagent because I knew there was no money in my account but a cheque was guaranteed. I'd sleep overnight in clients' houses when they were too scared to be by themselves and then go on shift at the hospital the next day. I was starting to think that life was possibly harder and more complicated than I had initially conceived and wondered if this stress was worth it.

It was the worst possible time to meet a man. Especially one that would actively encourage me to stray from the sensible path. I wonder if he saw an opportunity to sway my path, or if it was a cruel fateful coincidence.

Whatever it was, the fun was over and life was about to get serious.

CHAPTER 10: RED AND PINK

Things were kind of going downhill for Zéphirine, as she was jobless and soon-to-be homeless. Add to that she was now single, but there was no way she was going to let that get to her. So she did the only reasonable thing she could do: she found a cheap hotel with monthly rates and took up some paying modelling gigs.

It was a lot of pressure to her self-esteem though. She was still self-conscious and barely ate. Food was a poison to her, so she kept her eating to the bare minimum. When she had something to eat, she could feel the fat going down her thighs and settling there. And whenever she saw herself too fat, she wouldn't eat at all for a day or two. She would do one hundred sit-ups twice a day without fail to keep a flat stomach. She also had a small collection of exercising DVD's that she would use at least three times a week. But she had her sweet tooth to thank for keeping her away from being anorexic as her only meal consisted of a freshly baked chocolate croissant in the morning.

Even after a few modelling shows, Zéphirine still felt like she was the fat ugly duckling. Of course this whole image was all inside her head. The photographer obviously seemed to think she was good enough to be on pictures. She needed the money so she kept at it. In some ways, it did help when she would see herself on the photographs. She would get that split second when she thought she looked amazing, but those thoughts would leave her mind as quickly as they had entered.

It was at this very low point in her life that Bertrand Frassin became a part of her life. He was a plump guy in his early thirties, who was starting to grow bald, but still looked somehow cute. He had been a regular at the hotel and had helped Zéphirine to move out. She was aware of the soft spot he had for her. She also knew it was the only reason he was helping.

Once she had moved out, he started taking her out to the best and fanciest restaurants in town. He bought her expensive perfume and paid for a first class train ticket for her sister to come over. He also drove her to her parents for a weekend, little did he know the only reason she wanted to go home was to see Luc. There seemed to be no end to his generosity, but of course it came with a price: he started to be controlling over her, like she had sold herself to his affections by accepting his help, and thought that money would buy her love. Of course she had never promised him anything.

Zéphirine's heart was way out of his reach. She had decided to call Luc one day and they had stayed in touch ever since. They would spend long hours talking on the phone. She would also call Aaron sometimes to make sure he was okay. The calls created huge phone bills, which would get into Bertrand's nerves. He would come to the hotel, pay her rent, pay her phone bill, and give her the third degree for having such a huge phone bill.

"I didn't ask you to pay for my bills! So back off! I can handle myself." she'd tell him every time.

Bertrand did not understand she could not be bought. He even bought her a monkey. Yes, a real, live, breathing monkey! She was living in a hotel and it was not easy to find a proper apartment when doing cash jobs on an ad hoc basis. She had to give up the monkey which she had always regretted. She didn't even think of calling her parents whom she was sure would have loved to take care of her beloved pet.

One night, Bertrand decided to take her to a nightclub after dinner. Zéphirine had been single for a while now, which was more than she had ever been. She thought maybe it was time to let someone in. And maybe that would get Bertrand to back off. While she was waiting at the bar for her drink, she scanned the room for potential suitors. Bingo! She noticed a dreamy blond guy with long hair, nice blue eyes, and a great smile. She also loved the shoes he was wearing, a snazzy pair of moccasins, as she thought the choice was original.

But she had to get rid of Bertrand. She decided to dance, and dance, and dance some more. She was hoping he would get tired of it and go home before the slow dances at the end of the night. He lasted longer than she wanted. Zéphirine loved dancing but this had been going on for hours and even she was starting to get tired. When Bertrand finally said he had to go her heart jumped with joy and relief. She told him she was having such a good time she wanted to stay. Besides, her hotel was just a block away so there was no need to worry about her getting back home. Bertrand shrugged and left. The slow dances arrived, three guys asked her to dance whom she politely declined, until the blond guy finally came to ask her to dance. He introduced himself as Audric Bouteiller.

This all happened the weekend before her sister was due to arrive in Nice on Bertrand's first class ticket. She was only staying for a few days and they only saw Bertrand on the first day she arrived. Zéphirine thought he was giving her space to spend quality time with her sister.

She was back in her room at the hotel after dropping her sister at the train station when the phone rang.

"Just to let you know I can't stand you!" Bertrand said and promptly hung up.

Zéphirine was a bit surprised by the sudden declaration, but truth to be told, she didn't care. She had never promised him anything, never asked for anything. She could have declined the invites, but she was lonely and had no friends yet. Not that the conversations with Bertrand were the most interesting, but it still beat being at home, sitting on a bed, watching TV. She could have said no to the gifts, but no one had ever bought her nice things so she thought there was no harm in taking them.

Anyway, Zéphirine thought Bertrand was obnoxious. So if it meant he was now out of her life for good, she was happy. The more she thought about it, the better it seemed. It also meant she could enjoy dating Audric freely in the meantime.

All of a sudden, Zéphirine's life seemed to be in some kind of order again. She had a steady job, a roof over her head and a new boyfriend. Audric was a great guy, but he was young, 18. He was actually the first guy she dated of the same age as her. He was more of a physical person making up for few conversations. In fact, she spoke more to his mother than him. Guess she couldn't have it all, but it was fun nevertheless.

Zéphirine started to hang out at the Kodak Store at Nice Etoile, the main shopping centre in town. Her photographer would sometimes lend her the negatives so that she could organise a print of some of the pictures. Grégoire Larousse, the manager, was always there. He was also a big flirt, and not a very subtle one. As he was a very short man, he kept telling her about how big his dick was and how he would love to have sex with her. He was married. His wife was bi, or so he said, which allegedly gave him permission to have extra marital affairs. Besides knowing everything about his sex life, they did have some good conversations and he would always give her good prices for the reprints. She gladly accepted the interactions as she still didn't have many friends in town yet.

"You should check out the fruit juice bar upstairs," he suggested one day, "they are looking for staff."

'*Fruits à Gogo*' it was called, on the first floor, kind of in the middle of the floor plan so that people coming from the escalator would basically stumble onto the stall. They made fresh fruit juices and served ice-cream cones. For extra income, the owners added an espresso coffee machine, a pop-corn maker, and hotdogs cooker. The owners were a couple from Corsica, Silvestre Vanier and Françoise Delarue.

Silvestre was most of the time in Corsica and handled all deliveries. Françoise was the same age as Zéphirine's mother, never had children of her own but she was a happy aunt. In many ways, Zéphirine felt her boss treated her more as a daughter than an employee, or even a friend.

But Françoise could also become a real bitch at times. Twice she accused Zéphirine of stealing money from the tilt to find out both times it was an 'end-of-day' miscalculation. They wouldn't talk for days, until she would finally come to work bearing gifts, usually food she knew Zéphirine loved. Françoise had learned to know her well in such a small period of time.

In many ways, working in a shopping centre was great. Zéphirine got to meet a lot of people who were working in there too. She also had a lot of regulars coming to the stall. One of them was Damien Delage, a married guy who wanted her as a mistress. They would catch up for coffee from time to time. He was a smart man and she thoroughly enjoyed his company, but not enough to sleep with him and certainly not to become a mistress. Before saying goodbye, he would always ask or give her reasons why he wanted her as his mistress and how wonderful it would be. She would always decline.

She kept the friendship because Damien was never pushy and never forced himself on her. She trusted her instincts and they told her to trust him. He would always make sure she was safe - Nice was a pretty safe town in general, but she had had a few scares with people following her home. A few times he had driven her to a casting because it was too far away with no easy way of getting there with public transport. Or he would accompany her to a photo shoot when the assignments felt a bit shady.

Damien was a business man with a lot of connections. When she needed assistance, he was there. Now that she had a full-time job, she could look for a proper place to live that was cheaper than a hotel. Damien organized a real estate agent to find her a studio. In the meantime, her parents helped get a loan to pay for the three months' bond and one month rent in advance.

For the first time in her life, she had her own apartment, on République Avenue. It was a spacious furnished and self-contained studio. The studio was on the third and last floor of the building. She thought it was better to avoid the noise as République Avenue was a main straight road. An avenue loved by motorbikes she later found out, so it was still quite noisy. It had a spacious bathroom and separate kitchen. For just her it was perfect. Located close to the centre of Nice, it was a 20 minutes' walk to work. She did not even bother to take the bus except on rare rainy days.

Zéphirine was pleased. She had a full time job. She had a roof over her head that she could afford and pay herself. She got her first loan. She had friends. What more could she ask for? A boyfriend maybe and Luc came to mind, she thought about the relationship she would never have with him. She sighed.

She got a phone line installed to keep in touch with Aaron and Luc. Françoise hooked her up with one of the guys, Florent Briand, who worked at the optometrist shop.

"You need to get out more and meet mature people." she said. She did not like Audric. Françoise thought he was too young and immature for Zéphirine. She asked Florent what he was doing in his spare time and suggested to include Zéphirine in his plans. He did and they became buddies. They would go out with his mates once a week at least, to the movies, ice-skating, bowling... it was great!

A few months went by. Zéphirine was no longer doing modelling gigs because her job did not allow the time for it. But as she was busy, she didn't have time to think too much about her self-esteem and being self-conscious. At the end of the day, she modelled because she needed the money, but it also gave her that confidence boost she needed to stay alive. Now, working full time and being surrounded by people was an excellent therapy. She would walk home after a long day at work and be too tired to think about herself. After a nice shower, she would relax in bed with a movie and fall asleep, ready to do it all over again the next day, six days out of seven. Sundays she would stay home, have friends over, or go to the beach.

One day, Françoise was at the back of the stall, hidden by a pillar from customers' view smoking her Gitane, while Zéphirine was at the front cleaning the juice machine, when a courier showed up with a bunch of pink and red roses.

"For you," handing her the flowers, "please sign here."

"For me?" Zéphirine asked totally surprised.

"Yes, you are the brunette working at Fruit a Gogo?" he asked her.

Françoise was blond and there was no other staff but her. So the bouquet was definitely meant for her. Françoise and Zéphirine were staring at it like it was something sent out from space.

"Open the card!" Françoise exclaimed.

The card read:

'Red for love, pink for passion.
Dinner?
Marc'

It was nice, it was sweet. The problem was, as far as Zéphirine could think, she didn't know anyone named Marc. So her boss and she made the assumption it was someone who worked in the shopping centre. They asked the head of maintenance and the head of security if they had a staff member named Marc. Zéphirine was a social person and enjoyed talking to everyone even if it was just to say hello. But in no way she would know the name of all the staff working at the shopping centre. Nothing positive came back from the enquiry though.

Françoise thought of a client who came to the shop on a regular basis, one of those awkward characters, but always polite, attempting conversation with Zéphirine each time he would order a juice. Françoise was convinced he had the hots for her. But then again, Françoise thought the same about a lot of people that would come to the stall. Françoise decided to put the bouquet in a prominent position besides the juicing area and they set out to watch people's reactions to it. Nothing came out of it.

By the next day, they were still not even close to figure out who had sent out the flowers and by then the whole shopping centre knew about it. Disappointed Zéphirine couldn't figure out who was the mysterious Marc, she took the bouquet home. It was a nice a touch. She loved roses; she loved receiving flowers, signs of being a hopeless romantic even though she had never truly experienced it.

On the third day, an hour before closing time, she noticed a blond guy waiting for her to take his order. She remembered him. He usually came over in the morning with a tall guy and sometimes a few other guys. They were working at C&A doing the floor tiling and they had been regulars for the past week or so. Not sure why, but Zéphirine got the urge to ask the stranger:

"By any chance, is there anyone on your team called Marc?"

"Yes, that would be me." he replied with a proud smile.

"Oh" is all she could come up with for a response. Then fell the awkward silent while she pretended to be very focused on making those fresh fruit juices. Until he finally broke the silence:

"So, how about that dinner?" Marc asked.

"Sorry, I'm too busy, but thanks for the flowers, they are lovely." Zéphirine replied without hesitation, thinking it was possibly the lamest excuse she had found.

He paid for his juices and went away. Her boss was giving her the look. She looked angry and disappointed in Zéphirine.

"Why on Earth did you say no? Here is a mature man, instead of the babies you have been dating and he has a job and you say no? What is wrong with you?" Françoise asked, stunned.

Yes, what was wrong with her?

CHAPTER 11: ALLANAH THE ADULT

My best friend had left and returned home, it left such a gap in our house, but I knew she was doing what was right for her. Nell needed adventure and movement in her life and sitting in her room with all of us surrounding her day in and day out certainly wasn't either of those things.

That wasn't the only thing that had changed. I'd met someone. I had been beginning to think that it would never happen, all of my friends were either in a long term relationship or had absolutely no problems finding someone to have fun with when their heart desired. They say love finds you when you least expect it, and this was no exception.

Dad phoned me and asked if I fancied camping with him for the weekend as he was on a motorbike rally just outside of Oxford. He said it would be the perfect opportunity to catch up, all I needed was a sleeping bag, a bike jacket and some boots for on the back of his bike, he had a spare helmet I could use, so we were good to go.

This was a surprise, my dad rarely instigated contact, whether it was to meet up or just speak on the phone and now he wanted to spend the whole weekend camping. For the last few years, we'd tried on and off to establish a relationship, I'd flat sit for him while he went on holiday, we tried going to a gig together, but the generation gap was just too much. It was the motorbike that sold it to me, it sounded like an adventure, dangerous fun, I was wholeheartedly on board. He had taken me out on the back of a bike once before and I'd loved the thrill of being on the open road with the wind pushing at you like it was trying to make you fly in the other direction. It felt dangerous, it felt like living, so this was something I was absolutely not going to miss.

I used to have romantic notions about fate. I would personalise it like a great entity that looked down upon us from on high and decided who had been good and deserving, and who could be punished with some mirth for his own entertainment. If that's the case, then Fate has a sick sense of humour. I know I'm a good person, of course I make mistakes, and lots of them, when you add them all up over the years, but that's being human. We try at life, we get things wrong, and we adapt our behaviour, learn, and move on. It's not punishable, it's natural. Now I dislike fate and its entire concept, it's caused me so much pain, cost me so much time, and pushed me in a direction that I can't turn back from.

I have my marriage certificate on the desk next to me, its part of my jobs to be done list. That job has been waiting 5 years and I've no idea why it's taken that long. I have no desire to remain married to that man, I would happily erase the entire historical episode, wake up one morning with none of it having ever happened, because that's how angry and resentful I still am towards him. Perhaps time will change that, maybe one day I'll heal, I'll be able to see the good.

It's so painful to tell you all of this. It's like exposing all of my ugly bits all at once, standing naked before you waiting for those eyes to cast a judgement on the shadow of my soul. I find it hard to smile at the moment, sharing my life accentuates the mistakes, the losses, the dark days. I feel like I've dragged those I love into the madness with me, that I'm stealing their hopes and dreams for my own selfishness. Then again, it may be tiredness. Only time can tell.

I met my husband on that motorbike weekend my dad took me on. The reason behind his invitation became more than apparent as soon as I stepped of the bike. I had never felt so self-conscious before in my life, the picture of Axl Rose emblazoned on the back of my leather jacket burned into me like a beacon shouting 'I'm pretending to know what I'm doing in life'.

The jacket was actually my pride and joy, the most expensive birthday present I'd ever been given, my mum had found it on a weekend away she'd had with her first sensible boyfriend since my dad had left. I don't remember his name, he had a daughter that was a year younger than me called Beckie and she was what I wanted to be, confident with an older boyfriend who knew so much about music. We went to see Bon Jovi together in Sheffield on what must have been the hottest day I'd ever experienced; my shoulders were so burned in the tiny strappy black summer dress. It was so hot people were dropping like flies. The bouncers at the front railings gave up on giving out bottles of water, they just hosed us all down with a huge industrial fire hose. The only other thing I remember about her boyfriend was the pot he used to cook in, he never washed it, said that there were no germs as it was heated to boiling temperature every day and it kept the flavour in his meals. I'm not sure how I feel about that now. They'd gone to Hastings for a seaside treat and had found Axl in a tiny alternative shop, perfect timing for my birthday, with his white cycling shorts on that we used to laugh at every time he jumped up and down. We used to say he was boggling, well that's what he made our eyes do when those tight shorts accentuated his every movement and left nothing to the imagination, a revelation to a 15-year-old!

All eyes were on me, there was no doubt about it. It's not a self-indulgent big headed whimsical fancy that was the way it happened. I desperately fumbled with the straps on my helmet, hoping above all hope that I didn't look like a complete idiot. Thankfully the straps came undone seamlessly and I felt a confidence growing within. I can't remember the exact words being spoken but the general theme was one of my dad being a sly fox. He was loving the attention, and eventually confessed that I was his daughter. That refocused the attention back on me, I was fair game.

The memory of that weekend is blurred, partly through time, alcohol, shame, and regret. What I do remember is the bar, the sunshine, and the endless flow of alcohol that didn't cost me a penny. Once again, alcohol would play a huge part in shaping my life and I still hadn't learned my lesson. Those big boys with their big bikes liked to drink, that's basically what this weekend was all about for them, away from their wives and family, away from the dredge of everyday life, they were here to party and loudly. Being the student, I decided I could match their pace, every time someone offered a drink, I accepted and it was no delicate journey of Malibu and lemonade, it was pints of lager and bottles of Newcastle Brown as each one tried to impress or find a weakness in me. I said no to nothing, accepted all challenges with a smile and answered all of their questions. I was a student nurse, no boyfriend, I did kickboxing when I was at home, yes I loved riding pillion on a bike, I liked any music that had a real band in it, and yes, I did feel sea sick and it wasn't just the drink.

The bar was on a lake, it was the strangest feeling ever, stepping into the bar and gently swaying on the water. The lake itself was calm and peaceful, but the bar reacted to the people on board so the more boisterous they became, the more we swayed. There were some real characters there that day, and only one other female. I loved their free and easy natures, the laughter was free flowing, and the jokes were rude, but never at my expense. The day was hot and sunny and I was faced with an endless table of aviator sunglasses all staring back at me every time I joined in the conversation. I have no idea what I could have possibly contributed that would have been of interest to those men but I was no shy wall flower that day.

The day was deliciously warm, but as the shadows crept in there was a distinct chill in the air. I remember one of the guys suggesting we moved to the front of the bar to shelter from the breeze. A chivalrous gesture, there was only one picnic table there so not everyone would be able to gather around. I think I know what he was trying to achieve now, he wanted to get me on my own. His plans were foiled as there were the three of us sitting on that bench and I'd finally had enough of staring at my own reflection with my bedraggled plat hanging over my shoulder so I asked the two suitors to take their glasses off so I could actually see who I was talking to.

There was a sea of blues eyes looking at me. I like blue eyes. Neither of them was what I'd call good looking, but I had beer goggles on and the attention they were lavishing on me was really flattering. Beside that I've never been good with flirting and the whole dating game, I hadn't even been on dates! My past history consisted of schoolboys, drunken nights, and idolising my first true love. This was a completely new and alien experience. Both men would become a permanent presence in my life. That one day in the sunshine really did have a massive impact on the rest of my life.

Mac and Sean seemed to be in competition with each other, they were asking questions and trying to make themselves look better than the other all of the time and I could feel some animosity brewing. This was Sean's first ride out with the bike crew, it turned out that he'd actually only passed his test that week, so as far as the others were concerned, he was still wet behind the ears and certainly had no right to be getting all of the female attention. It seems that men can be as catty as women, as soon as Mac left the bench to get the next round of drinks, Newcy Brown for him as he was a Newcastle lad at heart, Sean wasted no time in telling me that our companion was married with children.

In my little drunken haze, I wondered why he'd be telling me that, I hadn't asked for any personal information, I didn't find either of them particularly attractive either. If I had to choose between the two then Sean would have the upper hand, his eyes were a brighter blue and he talked about bands I'd never heard of in an animated fashion that made me enthused. It was the flattery that was my downfall, and of course the endless flow of drinks.

As darkness fell, the bar began to rock with more fervour, the music was cranked up, and the party really started. We didn't have exclusive use of the camp site and its facilities, but I certainly don't remember there being room for anyone else in that bar that night. It was a whirlwind of laughter, of dancing, and of drinking. I'm sure my dad started a strip dance at one point, Right Said Fred 'I'm Too Sexy' was the trigger for that little treat, there were pants involved too, but thankfully my memory has blanked that out. The only reason I know is because the next day they were pinned up on display above the bar, and they were certainly no Calvin Klein's!

Now, I think about it that's the reason why I left the party, in my drunken state I proclaimed I had no interest in watching my dad strip naked, so Sean offered the use of his tent. My fate was sealed and history written.

The next morning was a haze; I remember my dad demanding to know where his daughter was while Sean's dad rather sourly stated that I was with his son. What were the odds of that? I was so worried about facing him, and then thought about it hard, I only had two choices, sweat in the tent all day or go out bravely and shrug it all off. I shrugged it off, boldly stepped into the dewy grass and went over to say morning to my dad. He was brilliant, he simply said, what happens on bike weekends stays on bike weekends, and no more was said. I was stunned, but then realised his behaviour had been fairly outrageous too last night. Besides, he was too hung-over to do anything else.

There was a run out on the bikes planned for later that afternoon, followed by another session on the floating bar, the rest of the time was spent rehydrating and filling up on carbs to restore their gusto. I was on a strict diet of tomato soup, much to everyone's disapproval, but there was a good reason for it. Perhaps not a good reason, but a reason, I'd had my tongue pierced the day before the weekend and I couldn't eat anything else! I was a cheap date! Before the ride out, I spent the day sitting with Sean, I thought I could at least try to not seem cheap and get to know him better. He spent the time avoiding questions and reading a book by Terry Pratchett. The quietness of our surroundings was occasionally broken by the odd biker groaning with post swampy headaches and Sean's self-assured outspoken laugh. I kept asking him what he was laughing at, to which he told me he couldn't explain unless I'd read Terry Pratchett. I thought that was rude, arrogant even, and I can remember wondering if I'd made a huge mistake, but all of that was forgotten as soon as I was on the back of his bike.

CHAPTER 12: THE BOY NEXT DOOR

Marc managed to find a door in the thick walls Zéphirine had built around herself. He opened it and took a peek at who she really was behind those walls and he used his knowledge to get to her. In a way, it was a good thing, a lot could come out of it. But she was supposed to be at least smart if nothing else. She should have known he would be the end of her. She should have known that his nicknamed should have been '*Trouble*'.

Zéphirine grew up thinking she was fat and ugly. Other kids made fun of her because of her dark skin. She was half white, half black and didn't seem to fit in this world. She craved the company of others, she loved to have fun, yet her presence did not seem to be well received. She started to hate who she was, feeling ashamed. She resented her father for being black.

Dark hair, dark eyes, and dark skin Zéphirine was. Blond hair, blue eyes and not so dark skin was her sister.

To make her feel even more inadequate in this world, she had to get all the defaults that life had to offer: she was asthmatic, she had a very dry skin which gave her terrible eczema, and she wet the bed until age thirteen – coincidently, even though her mother would insist it stopped because of the drugs she fed her, it stopped the first time a cute boy kissed her on the cheeks to say hello at school, a priceless moment she could never forget. She was also left handed, the only one in her class. She longed for long, straight hair, a stark contrast to the short, tight curls she had inherited from her mixed lineage.

Zéphirine and her sister were never best friends, but tolerated each other because, well, they were sisters and they had to. They had to team up because of all the chores their parents would give them. They understood, they had to help around the house, but to what extant? They were still children. In Zéphirine's mind it was no chores, it was slavery.

The sisters were never looking forward to school holidays because every single one, they would find the piles of boxes waiting for them in the kitchen: cherries or apricots to be pitted, peas, beans, whatever was in season; their parents had three veggie gardens. There was no escape for the girls. And, because Zéphirine like to think they were at least smart, they thought by completing the tasks quickly it would free them for the rest of the holidays: big mistake! Their mother would find some more fruits or veggies to prepare.

Zéphirine defied her mother by going to the garden dressed in a white suit and high heels to pick up potatoes. There was no excuse for their mother to let them off the hook unless maybe if you were on a death bed?

The girls also had to do the house chores as their mother despised cleaning and was an untidy person to make it worse. It was okay to give them chores, but Zéphirine couldn't understand the lack of respect their parents would show them. They would never make an effort to keep things cleaned. For instance, most of the floors in the house were timber. They would walk with wet feet and leave white footprints. And it did not help when one of the rooms was adjacent to the main bathroom. France, especially where they lived was not known for its sunny days.

"Your father and I work hard for what we have today." their mother would always say to the girls. And they got it, seriously, they got it. But how about a thank you for helping to keep the house clean? How about a reward or pocket money even? Zéphirine and her sister would never dare answering back to their parents, especially to their father who scared the hell out of them! Shutting up was better than a beating from either of them. Sometimes, some things were just not worth a beating.

Zéphirine hated school because she was bullied, but she loved school because it was her escape from home. She also found her escape through her neighbour, Vincent. They've always lived on the same street and been to the same school. He was an only child and his parents were running a successful business making them rich, well known, and liked by the community. So, he was one of those kids that everybody liked and wanted to be friend with.

Vincent was also cute, maybe she didn't know that at first, but what she knew and lived by: he was HER neighbour! And no one could ever take that away from her. Vincent and Zéphirine would walk to school together, they would play together every day, they knew each other's house inside out, and they had the friendship no one else had. They were the kind of kids parents on both sides thought: they will marry each other one day. Their love for each other was transparent.

As kids do, Zéphirine and Vincent would occasionally fight and not talk to each other for a few days, which would leave her devastated more than he could ever imagine. Or they had new kids –boys usually- coming into town for a short period of time who would try to break the friendship. But they would never stay apart for too long.

School holidays meant Zéphirine would go to vacation care, which she preferred opposed to her sister who chose to go to their Grandmother's farm. But vacation care proved to be a disaster for Zéphirine. Berthe Beaulieu was the daughter of the vacation care centre's director. So everybody sucked up to her. And for whatever reason, she hated Zéphirine and the sheep followed her because she was the daughter of the director.

Vacation care offered three days camping trips or one day outings. On that one camping trip all the girls were sleeping into one tent, the boys into another.

"I can smell piss!" Berthe said one morning and started in an over exaggerated manner smelling out every single bed, the whole twenty of them and of course Zéphirine's was by the door and the last one. And yes she had wet her bed, as usual.

No matter how many times Berthe would humiliate her, Zéphirine would still chose vacation care over staying at the farm. Even if sometimes she spent the whole day by herself as no one seemed to care, not even the adults. They went to a theme park, no one sat with her in the bus and no one wanted to go on the rides with her. No matter how much it hurt to be alone and mocked, she still went, hoping one day it would be different. It never was any different.

Occasionally Vincent would come on those camping trips and he would always stick by Zéphirine. He could have ruled the whole town. Hell, he could have created new rules. And he didn't even know it. He was a shy boy and oblivious to that kind of stuff. And Zéphirine loved him for that and for the person he was. Those rare priceless public moments with Vincent were well worth putting up with Berthe's crap.

Even though Zéphirine had loads of priceless moments she wouldn't want to exchange for anything, her hometown had left a big black mark, one that she tried to escape first by taking pills then by leaving and not looking back. It tainted her and left her wondering how she would ever survive in this world. "Snap out of it Zéphirine, you are in a new and better place now," she told herself. Was she really?

Marc was still buying juices but through his friends who came to the stall instead of him. Because they worked in the same place it was hard to avoid each other. Zéphirine accepted to go on a date with him three weeks later as they ran into each other while going upstairs.

Her mother had just sent her a new outfit: a pink mini skirt with matching no sleeve top. Zéphirine loved it. That was the only good thing she really appreciated from her mother, her ability to make the most exquisite outfit. Since she would never ever buy them brand clothes, she had to take advantage of her mother's skills. And she could not fault her mother for choosing what clothes to make her. She seemed to know exactly what Zéphirine wanted to wear and the perfect colours.

Zéphirine decided to wear the pink outfit on their first date. She chose the restaurant, a seafood place around the corner from her studio so she didn't have to rely on anyone to take her home.

Marc was an interesting character, a very smart and charming man. Even though he was French, he left France when he was 12 to go and live in New Caledonia with his grand-parents. At 18, he was sent to live with his father in Australia. Got married at 20 to an Australian woman and they had two children together. He came back to France to try and smooth his marriage. His wife was pregnant and gave birth to their daughter in Nice until she got enough of him and France, and flew back to Australia with the kids.

Zéphirine could talk about anything with Marc. Time flew and by 4am it was time to go home. He walked her home and asked if he could use her phone to call a taxi. So they went upstairs talked for another hour until it was really time for her to get some sleep.

"You could call a cab or I could stay here." Marc said, making no effort to hide his intentions.

She walked passed him to pick up the phone and dialled the number for the taxi. It arrived within 10 minutes and she walked him to the door.

"Goodbye!" she said and closed the door.

From that date, they saw each other every day. He invited her for lunch every day at the brasserie upstairs. They would also meet sometimes after work.

Physically, Marc was a pretty average guy. He was only a little taller than Zéphirine. He wasn't very muscular, but also wasn't fat. His blond hair and blue eyes just further added to his average appearance. What separated Marc from others was his charm and wit. In another life, he could have been a salesman. Zéphirine was convinced he could sell a freezer to an Eskimo. This intellect, and his ability to talk about anything, was what originally attracted Zéphirine to him.

It took her three weeks to succumb to his charm. And from that point of time, things spiralled.

Marc was bad news, very bad news indeed. But he gave her one thing: new-found confidence in herself.

CHAPTER 13: LOVE'S LOST DREAM

He'd phone me every Wednesday without fail, and would ride up from Portsmouth on his bike after work on a Friday. If I was on shift, he'd wait for me patiently in my room. It felt like this was what life was supposed to be. Allanah and Sean together. Sean immersed himself into the student lifestyle really easily, he was happy to drink the weekends away, and he loved being the older wiser member of our household. He had stories to tell, he'd been to the Caribbean, he was in the Territorial Army, and his dad had been in the army, so he'd lived in a million different places. The main thing I remember with clarity is that laugh, the loud speaker announcement that Sean was in the room and would like to be the focus of attention please.

Perhaps I'm being harsh, my emotions are still so raw, and the wounds deep that I can't take the good from what we had. I'm not religious, I can't forgive and heal myself. What doesn't kill us makes us stronger, but at what cost? Where has the woman I would have been? Where is the life I should have had? Down the drain because I'm weak, because I lack the courage of my convictions, lost forever. I can't even take solace in the life I have now, when you make mistakes as big as this you carry them with you wherever you go, you can't hide it in the cupboard with the other skeletons, and you can't tidy it up inside a box. You can only stare at it head on every time you look in your children's eyes and feel the void in their lives. All of the things they should have had, all of the things they could have been slipping away because the demon still pulls the strings. There never is an escape.

At the time, as a 19-year-old, I thought life was amazing, my nurse training was still going well, I loved working on the orthopaedic ward and felt like I had a place in the world. Tensions were beginning to build in the house, my friends saw Sean as being arrogant and I chose to defend him as he thought they were immature and shallow. We went out with them less and less, I hardly ever saw my housemates, and the atmosphere was beginning to get decidedly uncomfortable. Sean took my mind off it all by planning a holiday for us. We were going to tour Europe on his bike, he bought me my own set of leathers, and they were amazing. My own helmet confirmed my new identity, I was a biker girl. I loved the adrenaline of being on the bike and worked really hard at being a good pillion, I'd forward think and try to read the road, see what bends were approaching so I could reposition my weight. I imagined that I was weightless apart from when he needed me to help, and I fancied that we were a sight to behold racing down the country lanes.

One of my housemates was on a work placement year in Monaco, her being half French and a diplomat's daughter had given her first pick of the bunch and she'd opted for the glamourous. Sean decided that we should go and visit her and our tour became shaped around what felt like a once in a lifetime opportunity. We would be camping with stops through France before our stay in the glitz and glamour, then we'd head off to Italy before heading back through Germany so he could show me where he'd spent a lot of his childhood. We were armed with a road map of mainland Europe and a stash of cash courtesy of Sean. I had not a penny to my name, but he didn't seem to mind. We couldn't take much with us, once we'd rigged the tent and sleeping bags onto the bike we had room for a pair of shoes, a toothbrush, and not a lot else. I wasn't a vain person, I was clean and had my routines, but I would never spend time in front of a mirror or even wear makeup so I didn't need much.

The ferry crossing was from Portsmouth as that was his home town, we could load the bike up and just hop on, even though it meant the crossing was significantly longer, eight hours to get there. As soon as the boat began to slowly edge out of its docking, the sickness hit me. I became instantly disorientated, I felt like I was physically swaying and that everyone would be able to see that I couldn't stand up straight even though we were moving no more than five miles an hour. Of course Sean didn't flinch, he spent the first ten minutes trying to persuade me that it was my imagination as we weren't even moving. I wasn't fooled, I knew what I could feel, and of course he was amazing at sea because, after all, he was a dab hand at ferry crossings. He'd been there and done that, worked on a cruise ship, behind the bar as part of the entertainment crew, and sailed his way around the world. The thought of him being part of any entertainment crew is laughable, but again that's the bitterness talking, to the outside world he was always able to turn on the charm.

Calais was grey and windy, but that didn't matter, we were on the open road and that gave me such a feeling of freedom. The first destination was Orleans, north western France. I have no idea why that was our first destination, perhaps he thought it was a way of satisfying my obsession with New Orleans. When we arrived the sun was shining and the town was beautiful, we found a campsite that was close to the river and it felt like I was on holiday. I was eager to explore the world and taste what life had to offer, each new adventure made me feel alive, I couldn't get enough. There was an amazing cathedral in the town, and I was in love with the town. There was a giant mural over the side of some of the houses, a picture of someone painting houses, I really was in awe of the place. We sat at a café and Sean started to moan about the prices, saying that perhaps we'd need to find places off the beaten track in the future. He ordered his lunch, some sort of sausage and I had huge difficulties trying to decide what to have. I settled on chips, I love French fries, and it was the cheapest thing on the menu.

It turned out that his sausage was the parts of a pig that we wouldn't normally eat, wrapped up in what definitely looked like intestines to me. He ate every last morsel, much to my disgust and his own, he heaved at one point but refused to admit defeat, he even proudly declared that he would never eat that again. We spent the rest of the day pondering over the map and trying to decide what would be the best way of reaching Monaco as fast as possible to give us the most time there. Over the mountains was the shortest route, so the next day we set of on our Alpine adventure.

We were traveling in August, the height of summer, and Sean

had calculated that we'd be able to hit the south of France by the end of the day even though it would be a hard day's ride. He'd said that by going through the Alps we were cutting out at least a day's travel, and at this time of year the weather should be no problem. As we ventured further down the country our spirits were high, we nodded to every biker that we passed and received a foot wobble from them in return. At one point in our journey, the car drivers parted to the side of the road every time they saw a bike in their side mirrors, it was like Moses parting the sea, to make room for us to pass and we thought this was the best experience ever. We even sped past a police car, not seeing them parked up until it was too late, and they didn't pursue us.

Lunch that day was at a small café at a crossroads. The skies were beginning to cloud over and we definitely needed the pit stop. Sean tried to take the bike up on to the curb, aiming to park it neatly underneath the windows of the café as we had seen in other towns. I wasn't quite on the same wavelength as him and didn't foresee what his plan was. We reached the curb and he started saying something to me with the visor of his helmet still flipped down. I had no idea what he was trying to say to me, and then he stepped off the bike and let it fall to the ground.

He took his helmet off and turned to me with his blue eyes blazing angrily. I was still trying to disentangle myself from the bike too shocked to see how angry he was and still unable to hear what he was saying to me.

"I told you to GET OFF."

I know for a fact that I was in shock, I'd never seen him angry before and I certainly had no idea how he ever expected me to be able to just 'get off'. Being on the back of that bike when it was fully loaded and with panniers was a delicate operation. My thoughts were flitting between wondering if the bike was damaged to did he realise that he could have broken my leg? As it was only my foot was trapped under the bike and my boots had saved me from any damage, my pride was more hurt. At that moment I would have given anything to be able to ride off without him and disappear, to not have to face all of those people eating their lunch staring at the commotion happening right in front of them. Humiliation and embarrassment washed over me that was quickly replaced with fear. What would he do if the bike was damaged as he clearly thought the whole incident had been my fault.

Luckily there was no damage, barely even a scratch, so with my bruised pride I meekly sat down to have my lunch. This time Sean asked me to translate the menu for him and he steered clear of all unknown specialties. A brie baguette for me, cheap and simple. Steak and chips for him with a free lecture from him on how to cook steak properly. I wasn't really listening. We'd already been riding for hours that day, I felt exhausted, it was beginning to feel like less of an adventure that I wanted to be a part off. My ears were ringing from the noise of being on the road and my neck ached from holding my head against the wind. This was the farthest I'd ridden before, but the promise of the sunshine that waited for us in the South kept me going.

Perhaps Sean was feeling the same, I can remember him telling me that we'd know we were nearly there as the weather would start to get really warm. Revitalised we were ready for the road again, we said no more about the earlier mishap and I vowed to be more attentive for the rest of the journey.

The further we travelled, the worse the weather got. We came to a big town, I can't remember where it was, it may have been Grenoble but I'm not sure. The roads were really busy and we were faced with a choice. Again Sean was trying to talk to me through the helmets and I absolutely couldn't hear what he was saying, apart from the helmet hindering the sound, I had an incessant ringing and vibration in my ears that wouldn't go away. He pointed to the next major road sign we passed that showed the tourist route through the Alps, or the major route to the south of France, Nice. The rain was steadily flowing and there was a distinct chill in the air, but my discomfort wasn't what was important, he was the rider doing the hard work, so it was his choice, and somehow I managed to communicate that with him. There was a steady flow of traffic heading toward the mountains, so we thought it couldn't be that difficult to navigate through. There was not another motorbike in sight.

We were definitely climbing in altitude, the day was getting darker as we rode on, even though it was still early and the rain was freezing. My hands were wet through and numb with cold, my visor was steamed up so I had no choice but to open it, even when it was lifted a crack the fog wouldn't clear so I spent a lot of the time with it fully open. With my visor open, every time we changed speed I would bump helmets with Sean so that needed to stop immediately. I could feel the tension in him growing, we were sitting so close to each other and he felt like a tightly elastic band that was about to snap.

The road began to twist as we continued to climb higher, and there were visibility warning signs along with snow and ice on the side of the road. It was impossible to see how much farther we needed to travel, the weather was really set in, we were actually in the clouds and visibility was none existent. I knew we'd made a terrible mistake, this wasn't a journey for a motorbike, we were still ascending and the temperature was dropping rapidly. I couldn't stop myself from shivering despite my desperate pleas to myself, I was terrified of doing anything that would make the situation worse. There was nowhere to stop, there was only one thing we could do, carry on climbing the mountain and follow the road.

Finally, we had stopped climbing, and the miracle of it was we had beaten the clouds, they were below us still raining down their misery on the tourists that were heading for their mountainous holidays. We were frozen and drenched. There was no way we could continue traveling and thankfully a small village in the middle of the Alps appeared like a hidden oasis. I felt like we had travelled into another realm as this sunny and colourful place had no resemblance to the hell we'd just come from. There was even a hotel, where we wasted no time in deciding to check in to, despite the cost. I'm sure I would have died if we hadn't have found that hotel, I was too wet and too cold to think let alone survive the night in a tent.

The room price included a continental breakfast, I really was in heaven. I ate croissants and cheese until I was sure I would pop and the horror of yesterday was long forgotten. Our leathers were dry for the most part, only my flimsy used-to-be soft gloves reminded me of how wet I had been the day before, they were all crispy and unyielding when I put them on. The day was sunny and I was excited to resume our adventure, the map promised that the south of France was in fact just the other side of the mountain we were on, as soon as we started to descend we would be back on holiday.

An hour's ride from that alpine village brought us to a café that declared itself to be the highest of its kind in the Alps. Sean pulled into the car park and flipped his visor open, telling me that no wonder we had been cold the previous day, and surely we had to have a drink here to celebrate the occasion. I had a hot chocolate, fearing that there was more of what we'd ridden through yesterday to come before I'd feel the sun warming my soul.

It didn't take us long to find the road down from the mountains. We meandered for what felt like hours on really tight turns and twists as we felt the warmth of the air rejuvenate us. There were even other bikers appearing on the road, we had survived and were on our way to the coast. In fact, once we were down off that mountain I was too warm, sweltering in my black leathers, wishing there was a way I could take them off!

We arrived at Nice that evening, it was like no place I had ever seen before. There were sports cars everywhere and beautiful elegant women walking in summer dresses like it was a full time occupation. One in particular caught my eye; a young woman in a pink skirt with medium length hair in tight curls. She was walking with a man who held her arm possessively, but her grace outshone and I knew he would never manage to anchor her down. Her dark hair shone in the sunlight, her skin a perfect shade to match the depth of her eyes. I saw her look over at us and for a moment I wondered if she envied our apparent freedom.

My mind was blown, I wanted to soak up everything I was seeing and stay here forever. I was expecting Sean to pull over so we could run down to the beach and feel the sand in our toes. I longed for the freedom of the sea to wash away all that had happened on our holiday so far. When he didn't stop, I felt a huge disappointment and wondered why we couldn't even spare five minutes for the sea. We didn't stop at all in Nice, he ploughed on for Monaco, and even though it felt like it was a two-minute journey, I couldn't help but feel I had lost something by not staying there for even a small ice cream.

That's just the way it was with him. Sean's way or the highway.

CHAPTER 14: A VIEW FROM DOWN UNDER

Marc would always have a few drinks at the bar upstairs while waiting for Zéphirine to finish work. He was drunk almost every night. He also smoked weed every day. She didn't like any of his friends, not just because they smoked weed and did drugs, there was just something about them. *'Not the kind of people I would hang out with'* she thought.

She went to Marc's home once; a two-room apartment on the ground floor in the white collar class range of Nice, le Quartier Des Fleurs. The apartment was empty except for a fridge in the kitchen, a couch, and a TV set, a big ashtray brimming with cigarette butts on a marble coffee table. The closet in the hallway was full of dirty and mouldy clothes. "I don't have a washing machine so I just throw the clothes in there and I buy new ones." was Marc explanation. She tried to keep it together at the smell of it.

He told her he hadn't paid the rent since his wife had left with the kids about six months ago. Zéphirine was surprised he hadn't been kicked out. She was trying to process this new information about him. He didn't seem fazed by his situation. In fact, Marc was proud to tell her about the many eviction notices he was receiving.

This was the time to run, right? But she didn't. She believed when people needed help, she had to help if she could. Working on other people's problems made her less focus on her own. So instead of running, she offered her place, and Marc moved in.

When her lease was not put up for renewal, they decided to

look for a new place; a better place. The same real estate agent she had used for her studio found them new home; a more expensive condo which was smaller than her place. It was a much more modern apartment with a lift, a small glimpse of the sea from the balcony, and with a lock up garage. They had to invest in furniture and appliances. As Zéphirine had been employed for more than six months she was able to get a small loan to buy the basic furniture needed.

The place looked cozy. She particularly enjoyed the balcony and even though you could only see a little bit of the sea in between the two buildings in front of theirs, she thought it was grand. She enjoyed running downstairs at six in the morning to get some freshly baked chocolate croissants. She would have breakfast on the balcony, smoking a cigarette while admiring the view. The only inconvenience was having to take the bus to get to work. Well, there were actually two inconveniences; Marc was the second.

Life with Marc was far from easy. He was a charming man. They would talk for hours and they could talk about anything. He was fun to be around but he also had a bad temper which was not improving. He spent most of his free time at his friend's place and Zéphirine did not find them any more likable than before. He was a bad drunk and over emotional, clearly missing his grandfather and his son. He was also terribly jealous.

Zéphirine ended up having to quit her job because he said they could work together and he could provide for the both of them. But the real reason was that he couldn't stand her talking to customers, especially if they were men. To him men were ordering juices just to talk to her – because, you know, men don't have better things to do than coming to a shopping centre to have a fresh fruit juice made by a random young girl! They would argue about it and he would run to his friends, probably to do drugs.

Business wise, Marc always had these grand ideas, but nothing would ever come through. How he always managed to get money from the banks was incredible! He had the talk. People seemed to be mesmerized by him and they would just do as he said. Zéphirine also had to handle debt collectors' phone calls as he had managed to rack up some pretty hefty credit card bills. She would organise payment arrangements that he would never follow, always telling her not worry about it.

Zéphirine should have run, but who knows why, she didn't.

Then came the time Marc had to leave France. His Australian permanent visa was about to expire so he had to go back over there to renew it, and also to visit his children and family and sort out his divorce. He was due to come back within a couple of months.

There were issues with his visa or so he told her, subsequently one month turned into two, then three hence he told her to come to Australia. She was now into debts because she had quit her job and he wasn't here to provide for them as he had promised her. They had a bond on the apartment so it covered the rent for three months, but eventually she would get kicked out. Though she knew it would take months to get evicted, there was no way she could deal with eviction notices as calmly as Marc did.

So, she set out to sell everything they had in the apartment to buy her plane ticket. She had never thought about going to Australia, but why not? As she was short by $750, she took out the overdrawn balance she was allowed on her bank account, thinking she would pay it back when she came back. It was just a holiday; her visa allowed her to stay in Australia for three months at one time and was only valid for a year.

It wasn't in Zéphirine's nature to stop and think about the consequences. She was asked to go to Australia: *cool, let's go!* What about Marc? Their relationship was not the easiest. She liked him a lot. She loved him even. It wasn't the kind of love she had experienced with Luc though. But she had settled into a comfort zone and she loved that, the whole package. Was she ready for such a big move? What would she do there? What would she do when she would come back to France? This did not even cross her mind at all. She got her visa, paid for the ticket and left France, it was that easy.

***

Marc and Zéphirine hadn't seen each other in four months and she missed him. They had been living together for six months, and the apartment felt empty when he left. Zéphirine was looking forward to seeing him again.

It was a long trip, 24 hours in a plane with a one-hour stopover in Singapore. She was glad when the plane finally landed in Brisbane. The door opened and as soon as she disembarked, she was overwhelmed by the heat, and she loved it. It felt good to finally be walking on the ground and feeling the sun on her skin.

It was Wednesday afternoon and Marc was waiting for her at the arrival bay. She was happy to finally see his face, to kiss him and let him hold her.

"My family can't wait to meet you. We have to go to my grandfather first. He has to be the first one to meet you." he said.

On their way to his grandparents' house, Marc decided to stop by at an awful, low cost and malodorous motel, to have sex with Zéphirine; it was just sex. In and out, in and out... done. It made Zéphirine feel cheap. She worried about what people may have thought as they only stayed for about 30 minutes if that. Zéphirine was completely turned off and in that moment she knew she had made a terrible mistake. She knew they were not meant to be.

She could hear her mother telling her "I told you so!" Since the beginning of their relationship the warning signs had been constant. And in that instant she received confirmation of what she had known all along, she knew but she did nothing about it.

What could she have done really? She had just landed on the other side of the world, she had no money or possessions apart from what she had in her suitcase since she had sold everything to pay for her ticket. She made a choice and that was the consequence she had to live with. And she would have to make the best of the situation. It did not matter that deep down she was crying so hard. "You chose to come here, now live with it!" her goddess was yelling at her over and over!

Now, let the pretence begin...

His grandparents lived in a house that was so little it was referred to as the doll house. It was on an acreage owned by his aunt and uncle who lived on the other side of the acreage.

The house was squared and consisted of four rooms. The kitchen/dining room was cramped by a buffet on one side, the sink and some bench space with a window overlooking the road - which gave notice to any arrivals to the house - and a six seater-dining table in the middle which would take up most of the space. The bathroom was big enough for a bathtub and sink and with a bit of space to move around. The bedroom seemed to be the biggest room and probably full of treasures. Then there was the TV room with just enough space for the TV, a three-seater sofa and the grandfather's armchair with a marble coffee table in the middle.

There wasn't much space to move around in any room but the family managed to all fit when necessary. The doll house was the headquarters for the family; it was neutral ground.

The land was divided into two by some sort of wire fence which was mainly to keep the few horses on one side, so as to not destroy the grandfather's garden as he was a keen gardener. Baptiste and Lucie lived on this other side in a three-bedroom kit home, they had built themselves - they used to live in the dollhouse. They arrived in Australia back in the days they used to pay people to migrate. The house was nothing flashy and the furniture were bland. Obviously they were not into decorating or matching anything, but Zéphirine could detect they had a heart of gold. Baptiste looked like his father and surely following in the footstep to become the wise man of the family.

Another auntie arrived, Pierrette, and Zéphirine immediately liked her. They then had to visit yet another auntie, Yvette with whom they would be staying until further notice. Yvette seemed to dedicate her time telling Zéphirine why she should hate Marc's ex-wife, Stefania.

"She is crazy! One day, she took a broom and smashed his brand new Celica! She is crazy, I'm telling you! Do not talk to her." she had told Zéphirine a couple of times.

But Zéphirine didn't like being told what to do and she didn't like people who bad mouthed other people, especially those she did not know. In this case, Marc was the one to tell her what was up with his ex-wife. She didn't have to wonder about it for too long as on Friday morning before leaving for work he told her they had to pick his son for the weekend.

"And Stefania wants to meet you before she allows the children to go with us."

Fair enough Zéphirine thought. There were a few things that troubled her. She had landed in Australia just a few days earlier and already she had to put up with his kids and ex-wife? Marc had not even taken a day off for her! The only private time they had together was at that disgusting cheap motel. So she wasn't in the mood to meet the ex-wife and the kids just yet.

She also had the auntie on her case and even though she knew she was capable of making her own judgement, she didn't want to be in the bad books of anyone in Marc's family. She wasn't sure how long they would stay there, but she knew not to make enemies.

She didn't tell Marc what his aunt had told her about his ex-wife. She wondered if he knew about it. But if he did, he probably wouldn't care. She still raised the issue of not being ready to meet his ex-wife and kids but got her no results.

"She said if you're the one who's going to look after our children, she needs to meet you." he explained again.

Zéphirine paused, reining in her train of thoughts. She was going to look after his children like... a step-mother... because usually that was what this was called wasn't it? She had never thought about raising children. She could vaguely remember a few movies with step-parents and step-children and she went with the thought it might be fun to be a step-mother. Or wasn't the step-mother in movies always seen as the villain? She would have to find out and that time had come quicker than she had given it thoughts.

Stefania, lived in what seemed a small unit in an apartment complex in South Market with her new husband who barely spoke English as he was Sicilian; but his every word sent shivers down one's spine.

Zéphirine didn't like him at all. He gave her the creeps as he reminded her of the bad guys in the mafia type of movie. Stefania on the other hand was a lively, charismatic, and chatty woman that was going above and beyond to make sure you were comfortable. Zéphirine couldn't fault her and couldn't imagine her as the bitch Yvette had portrayed.

Marc's daughter, Arianna, was three and his son, Adrian, was eight. Stefania thought it was too soon for their daughter to come along this time. Only their son would join them for the weekend, and to Zéphirine that was plenty enough. Truth to be told, she wanted nothing more but to be alone with Marc which was not going to happen.

Zéphirine had never looked after children. Even though she was the eldest of all her cousins on her mother's side - she didn't really know the family on her father's side - she had never done any babysitting. Her sister was the one who did that and her little cousins always preferred her sister. Zéphirine apparently was too bossy and they didn't like that. When they played together in the attic at the farm, her sister always played the mother while Zéphirine always played the teacher. And that never bothered her, she liked to teach and lead others.

What bothered her now though was the lack of attention from her boyfriend. She was missing their relationship in France, well not all of it, but she missed their home and their privacy. Since she had arrived in Australia, they were always surrounded by his family and now his attention was only for his son. The kid was a spoiled brat. It was also apparent he meant a great deal to the grandparents. Adrian was the jewel of the Avernier Family and the grandparents would cover for his crimes if he ever committed any.

Adrian loved playing video games. Which was great because Zéphirine had a Gameboy with the latest Mario game to the envy of Adrian. He also liked to beat her at video games, but they got along fine. Besides playing video games with him Zéphirine wasn't sure what else she was supposed to do.

***

They were at Marc's grandparent's home sitting outside one evening, the climate still a great degree warmer. Adrian was perched on his dad's lap; his head, unwinding on his shoulder, Marc's arm around him. It was right then and there Zéphirine felt something she couldn't exactly clarify, sort of a clue of envy which was foolish in light of the fact that what she was taking a gander at her boyfriend with his child.

Be that as it may, to Zéphirine it was something new that stunned her. In her family you just don't do that, there is no physical bond between relatives. She had never seen her parents kissed one another except for the obliging kisses on the cheeks on New Year. She had never at any point seen them in a grasp or holding hands, not to mention giving her or her sister any sort of physical consideration other than reproving them with their hands.

Indeed, even with her sister, any physical contact felt weird and they would keep away from one another on New Year's day in light of the fact that it was the typical approach to welcome somebody (French kiss individuals on the cheeks, contingent upon the locale, one on every cheek or four times), it was better to do it with a stranger than her own sister who obviously felt the same way as Zéphirine. So watching Marc and Adrian do what showed up absolutely typical was stunning Zéphirine.

She was starring and Adrian saw her. And in that moment, he

knew he had her, he knew he would be her shortcoming. You could see it in his eyes; he was a brilliant child, a ruined little rascal whom from that day would verify her existence with his dad and it would be an intense one. She additionally knew right then that she, as of now, was not a need in Marc's life. She knew now for certain, she would never at any point be on his top rundown either.

She comprehended the children would be a need and that was ordinary. Or, possibly, she thought it should be what folks do regardless of the possibility that her parents never appeared to care. They just regarded them as slaves. She knew her relationship was damned, where it counted it re-avowed the inclination she had at the motel. She needed to prepare herself for what was coming to her. It was too late to run away.

CHAPTER 15: ALLANAH'S SUMMER OF SEAN

I'm fearful that you'll judge me as being the person to always lay the blame at someone else's feet. I know that Sean dropped the bike because he couldn't hold the weight as he tried to ride up the curb, that wasn't really his fault, but I don't think it was mine either. I know that he gave me the opportunity to say take the other road to the coast, and there really was no way he'd have known how awful that journey was actually going to be. Actually in hindsight he could have known, it was a fool's mission to ride to the peak of the Alp's on a motorbike, no matter what the time of year, with no weather protection or warm clothes. I never shied away from the blame, I always took it if there was a finger pointing. I could find a way of reasoning out why something had been my fault or how I could have stopped it from happening if only I had said or done that one thing. It was always about me; in a selfless way I was very self-centred. It was that mind-set that would be my own undoing, Sean didn't do it, and I did it to myself. I made my bed and told myself I had to lie in it.

Monaco was amazing, I soon forgot the loss of Nice. The weather was everything I'd hoped it would be, sunny, warm, and endless. We couldn't camp in Monaco itself so we headed through to the next town, Menton, where it was late in the afternoon by the time we'd set up camp. The fame and glamour would have to wait until tomorrow, which I didn't mind as where we were was so beautiful. The campsite was framed by the mountains and the air was positively tropical as far as I was concerned. Night time seemed to fall too fast, and with it came the insects that seemed to sing louder than the birds! Sean told me there and then that he wouldn't go camping with me again, I was too scared of everything and pathetic for his liking.

I had been looking forward to our holiday so much, going to places I had never been before, and seeing the world with young eager eyes. Now all I could do was feel hurt.

The night passed without any further damage, we'd spent the evening chatting to a local who liked to come to the site to meet with new people, a lot of wine flowed and in the morning I regretted having that last glass. The promise of the new day soon flushed away the anxieties and we were on our way. We would be meeting with Talitha later that day, but she had to work first so we needed to find a way to fill the time.

We had coffee in front of the casino, sitting inside to save from paying the premium for patio seating. We walked through the streets trying in our minds to recreate the Formula One race circuit. We looked at the marina from a distance and marvelled at the yachts. We found a café on a hill to eat our lunch, Sean thought that if we walked away from the centre the prices might be friendlier. He had an omelette and requested to speak to the chef, he then told him that it was the nicest omelette and demanded to know his secret. The chef humoured him and told him in a thick French accent, *it is the way you beat the eggs, you need a lot of air, always air*. I don't remember what I ate.

Sean's good humour was infectious, after the chef had been released back to his duties, a woman came to join us at our table, she was Scottish and said she was excited to be able to speak to someone in English as the locals normally didn't like to use it. We chatted away for a good hour, she told us that she'd moved to the area to retire but her husband still worked, that they lived in an apartment that overlooked the whole of Monaco and if we wanted to watch the Grand Prix we should stay with them as they had an amazing view. All we needed to do was come back to this café and we would find her, she lunched there every day.

It was time to head back down to meet Talitha. We passed a bar on the way that declared itself to be British, so we popped in for hydration. Sean nearly choked on his pint when he realised it had cost him £10. Then we headed back to the café de Paris, this time sitting outside.

We were all smiles and full of cheer when Talitha arrived, she looked like she belonged in Monaco, she was a free spirit with a kiss of bourgeois. Sean was in his element, he had someone to impress. We chatted for a while, the coffee was replaced with beer and in the sunshine it didn't take me long to feel like this was all some kind of amazing dream. We decided that we should all eat before we were too tipsy, and Talitha took us to a restaurant she had heard was fabulous. Sean ordered snails, we sat on the patio and money was absolutely no object. Talitha told us that were seated on part of the race circuit so I was so thrilled to be on part of the actual track. Daylight faded and the view was spectacular, the mountains, the ocean, the buzz, it was beautiful.

Happily drunk was probably a good description for us at that point. Talitha declared that it was time she gave us a tour, so off we went, pretending to be race cars and following part of the route my heroes take every year. Talitha suddenly became really animated and began laughing and clapping, 'Sean, you look like Jacque Villeneuve! We should pretend you are him and get invited onto the yachts!' I thought she was hilarious as there was no real likeness, but in that one moment it seemed like the most outrageous thing I'd ever done.

"*Regardez, c'est Jacque, c'est Jacque! Tout le monde, c'est Jacque*" she shouted as we ran giggling down the hill towards the marina. People did look, but not because there was a racing driver in their midst. This was a place of the highest sophistication, and for all of the bohemian joy Talitha brought with her, we certainly were not of a class that belonged there.

We did go to the marina, I marvelled at the yachts, even the security guards were in black tie suits. Talitha chatted with a few of them, I managed to follow part of the conversation. One of them had let her on to a boat party the previous weekend and she was asking him if he remembered her. Of course he did, he remembered all of the beautiful ladies he told her, Sean grew restless quickly and all of a sudden it was time for us to leave. We'd run out of money to spend there and the fun had stopped for him.

I fell in love with the Italian countryside, the groves built into the mountainsides, the healthy glow of the people there, the eternal sunshine. We moved swiftly on to Germany where Bratwerst and Curry Sauce became the height of excitement. We had a very drunken night in a town called Eiper, Ernie the bartender plied us with alcohol all night and then we didn't even pay before we stumbled back to where were staying. I think he did it for his own entertainment. I don't even know what we were drinking, but I'm sure at one point we were sharing a cocktail of every shot that was available in the entire place. He asked us if we had tattoos and showed us his, he lifted his right arm into the air, there was a pair of ladies legs, one on his chest the other on his arm with the arm pit in the middle of them where a lady's intimates would have been. I'd never seen anything like it before. Ernie was crazy, I remember that he disappeared at one point, cycling off on what was definitely a lady's bike and returning with a bag of white powder. He asked if I wanted some, but I had no idea what it was or what to do with it, so I politely declined.

Sean was hideous later that night. We were staying in a hostel and he was so drunk he tried to leave the room in his naked state. I woke up to find him crouched by the door with both hands on the handle fast asleep. I tried to bring him back to the bed but there was no moving him. When I woke up in the morning he was bright and breezy and had no idea what I was talking about. Before we'd made it back he'd become venomous and shouted at me, asking why I'd let him get that drunk when I knew he had to ride in the morning. We'd miss the ferry and it would be my fault, had I no sense. He went down to breakfast without me, I couldn't stomach breakfast or the garlic sausage that was on offer. I started to pack away our things when I discovered my passport. It was soaking wet. Sean had peed on it. It was definitely urine.

We did miss the ferry. We encountered the end of a hurricane, riding was virtually impossible. It had certainly been a holiday to remember and I vowed to never go camping with him again.

CHAPTER 16: TIL DEATH DO US PART

Marc and Zéphirine stayed at Berthe's house for four weeks until they got their own place. It was in the same area, about 10 minutes' drive from them and three minutes' walk to his cousin's house. Zéphirine was really excited because she had never rented a house before so this house felt like a palace: a three-bedroom house with a two-way bathroom. She had never even heard of a two-way bathroom, let alone seen a walk-in-robe! And it had an American kitchen with a breakfast bar, the type she had only seen in American movies. She was overflowing with joy and excitement! Except they didn't own anything so they had a big house with no furniture in it.

They borrowed an air mattress to sleep on from Pierrette. They got an outdoor table and chairs set for the kitchen from Marc's cousin. They used a cooler for a fridge: every morning Marc's grandfather would drop off some ice and sometimes some croissants probably because he felt sorry for Zéphirine. Marc was working with his uncle. When he dropped off Mark in the evening she would give him a basket full of their dirty clothes. The following morning when he came back to pick Marc up for work, he would give her back the basket filled with washed clothes ready to be hanged on the line. Marc's family would take turn to pick Zéphirine up during the day or she would walk to his cousin's house as she had nothing else to do.

After a week, someone in the family came up with the idea of renting what they needed.

"We can rent furniture?" Zéphirine asked surprised. And as it happened to be true she wondered why no one had suggested it before. They got a fridge, a washing machine, and a TV. And as they were out shopping she saw her dream bed: a four-poster timber bed with a privacy veil!

"This is it! This is our bed!" she cried out loud. This was how she learned about the lay-by plan. All they needed was a 20% deposit and it was all theirs as long as they paid it off within 8-12 weeks. She loved this country! No more aching back in the morning! Her intimate life would be better as well, or she hoped.

The house started to feel a bit more like a home but it was still a far cry from being cozy. The TV was on the floor and they still didn't have a couch. So they watched TV sitting on the carpeted floor trying to be comfortable with a few pillows.

Life seemed to stand still. Zéphirine was bored, time did not fly by.

Marc worked every single day and most of the time until late at night. She never asked why they never had any money left over and how they could never afford to buy anything else for the house. Though they could rent a gaming console and games every weekend for his son. And food. Grocery shopping was always a priority and they had a full trolley every week. Zéphirine blindly trusted Marc because he was eleven years older than her, had been married and had kids, surely that meant something?

Marc got this idea of starting his own business and rented out a factory in Brisbane North which he called Paris Marble & Granite. Subsequently they moved to Brisbane to be closer to his work and also closer to his kids. They would still be going to Pierrette's place at least once a week and to his grandparents'. Zéphirine was still bored but she was now spending more time with Marc's ex-wife. She was now a short bus ride away or they would meet up in a nearby shopping centre.

Having his own business didn't mean they had more money and they were still struggling to pay the rent some weeks. Zéphirine's first three months in Australia were coming to an end. She had to leave the country because of her tourist visa. Marc had no intention of going back to France. He didn't say it nor did she ask about it. She knew. His life was here. And if she wanted to be with him, her life had to be here too. He never asked her how she felt about staying here either. The money was tight but she refused to travel by herself. They travelled to New Zealand and stayed overnight at the cheapest hotel they could find.

Zéphirine was unhappy and bored out of her mind. She was living a day to day life without looking forward to the next day. Except for the nice weather, she couldn't tell much about Australia as they never did anything besides visiting his family. A couple of times they had driven up for picnics on the beautiful beaches of the Sunshine Coast with the kids. They also had taken them to the theme parks on the Gold Coast. That was as far as their outings would take them: one hour up the Sunshine Coast or one hour down to the Gold Coast.

Zéphirine didn't want to go back to France. It wouldn't be any better there. She'd have to start from scratch and most likely would need to stay with her parent's until she could get back on her feet. The thought of being under the same roof as her mother again made her stomach tie up in knots.

When six months came up, she went back to New Zealand overnight but by herself as they couldn't afford two tickets. On the way back, the custom officers were waiting for her.

"Please follow us." an officer said leading her to a back office. The room was small, almost claustrophobic. The cold, unnatural lighting and small table with two hard chairs only added to her discomfort. Another officer had brought in her suitcase and was going through her things on another table.

"This is the second time you left the country for approximately 24 hours. Care to explain why?" asked the officer that had brought her into the room.

I bet they think I'm a drug dealer Zéphirine thought.

"My boyfriend lives here." she replied.

"What is your boyfriend's name and is he here to pick you up?"

"Yes, he should be. His name is Marc Avernier."

The officer left the room for what felt like hours but in reality was probably only 20 minutes and came back with Marc.

"You have three months to get married and apply for a visa or leave the country. You are free to go now." the officer said.

Zéphirine shrugged. She was relieved and being told to get married did not quite register in her head.

Marriage. It wasn't something Zéphirine had ever thought about. Actually, marriage and kids were two things that had never crossed her mind. She remembered her friends in primary school talking about their dream wedding and having about ten kids. But she would never partake in those conversations. Marriage and kids were two words that had eluded her vocabulary.

And so Marc and Zéphirine decided to get married as if it was an event as casual as going out for coffee. His family didn't object to it nor were they surprised. Zéphirine called her mother to let her know about her impending wedding.

"Mum, I'm getting married!" she said in a kind of excited voice.

"You're getting married for the visa, aren't you?" her mother asked and not what Zéphirine expected her to say either. *Couldn't she at least pretend to be happy for me?* she thought. But that would be too much to ask of her mother. Her mother looked and acted unhappy and angry at all times. Maybe that is why Zéphirine never thought about having kids or getting married. It was just purely about living life for now.

So it was no surprise her mother would no show support on what was supposed to be a big day.

Zéphirine was getting along well with Pierrette's eldest daughter, Kelsey. The fact they were in the same age group may have had something to do with it on some level. But there was also kindness in her, she was not like most of her family. Kelsey also liked Stefania to the dismay of her mother.

Kelsey, Stefania, and Zéphirine spent a whole day shopping for a wedding dress. She got to check out some of those fabulous wedding dresses which she knew she couldn't afford. But it was fun to try them on and look like a princess, because in that moment she did feel like a princess and loved all those dresses. Due to their financial status, she settled for a simple but classy cream-colored evening dress that accentuated the curves of her waist and hips before opening up and spilling around her feet. On her head was a small, white fascinator with a lace veil.

Zéphirine organised a limousine to pick up Kelsey and her to drive them to Pierrette's house. The limousine would then take them to the Gold Coast for a night at the Sheraton. Marc had gone shopping at the last minute for the rings which ended up too small for Zéphirine's finger and had to be cut off her finger to be resized.

And so, on a sunny Saturday afternoon, by the pool at Pierrette's house, Marc and Zéphirine got married. Kelsey was the maid of honour while one of Marc's employees filled in as the best man. No large crowd of friends and family. No elegant reception afterwards. Just the bride and groom and their small group on a quiet afternoon.

If the wedding seemed like just another day, staying at the Sheraton was magical. Zéphirine had never stayed in a 5-star hotel before. It was not the honeymoon suite as they couldn't afford it of course, but the room was luxurious and had a spa in the bathroom. She had never been into one either and it was probably the best thing of this overnight stay. *The day we buy a house, it will have a spa*, Zéphirine thought.

The magic didn't last long, however. In fact, it ended as soon as they went to checkout of their room. Zéphirine wasn't surprised to be honest: Marc's cheque was rejected. They had to wait for one of his uncles to come to the rescue and pay for the room. Not exactly the honeymoon she had envisioned.

Now that Marc and Zéphirine were married they had to apply for the visa. The cost was a hefty $750 which at the time was a lot of money. And as always Marc said "Don't worry!" It was like his favourite sentence. Yet, it always left Zéphirine worried. And with reason, it never worked out. Marc was never worried. People would be knocking on the door chasing money for unpaid bills and Zéphirine would be hiding in the closet. She would keep the curtains closed and would never answer the phone because they always owed money.

And that day was no different. It was the last day for her to apply for her visa. Marc was late to take her to the embassy and when they got there, the office was closed. She was furious. Because as always, Marc never had the time, nothing about her was important enough.

"Don't worry, it will be fine." he said in his casual do-not-worry tone. They got to the visa department the next day.

"Are you aware your visa is expired?" the office woman asked.

Of course I am, she wanted to reply but chose to play dumb because she didn't know what else to do. "Really? I am so sorry. I thought I still had a few days." she instead replied.

The woman went ahead to process her application to Zéphirine's relief.

"See, nothing to worry about." said Marc with a smile. But Zéphirine felt like the urge to put her hands around his neck and squeeze hard. She had never been under so much pressure since she had met Marc.

Not only had she applied on an expired visa, the bank check Marc had written, bounced! It was no surprised when they received a letter telling Zéphirine her visa application had been denied. Her appealed was also denied. She had seven days to leave the country or be deported.

CHAPTER 17: ALLANAH'S FATE IS SEALED

I think I was beginning to have serious doubts about what I was doing in this relationship. Sean was a few years older than me, but nothing that would be frowned upon. He had lived a whole lifetime worth though. He had been to military boarding school, his dad had been in the Falklands war and posted in Ireland during the troubled times. He'd been married, in fact he still was married. He'd lived in Germany, he'd worked on the cruise ships, he'd been to the Caribbean, he'd been to Belize, he was in the Territorial Army, and whatever the topic of conversation was he knew all about it.

I wasn't sure there was room for the adventures that I envisioned for my life.

There wasn't time to think about it though, fate was bored again and using me for his own entertainment. Sean had a motorbike accident. Now before I run the risk of being over dramatic, it wasn't actually that bad. He was on his way to see me one Friday after work, riding through the devil's punchbowl his over confidence grabbed him by the throat and showed him what he was really made of. Luckily for him it was a few broken bones, scrapes and bruises along with a healthy dose of dented pride, oh and a bike that was lost forever.

The bit that I'm sure really made fate giggle was the very complete way those few broken bones completely debilitated him. Sean's right collar bone was broken, arm strapped up in a sling and out of action. His left thumb was broken through the base, requiring surgery to with an external pin to keep it back in place, rendering that arm out of action too. Or so the willing patient made out.

I received a phone call from the road side, a random passer-by with a shaky voice told me that he was sorry to have to be the one to break the news, but my boyfriend had been in an accident, the police were there but they were waiting for an ambulance, they couldn't say how badly injured he was at that time. The police were being cautious and made Sean lie on the floor with his helmet still on until the ambulance arrived. I was worried.

Sean's mum went to the hospital. I had no transport and no way of getting to Guilford. I made plans to go straight to Portsmouth to be at his house when he arrived back from hospital. In that one single moment, I made the worst mistake ever. There was no escaping fates cruel game from that moment on.

I was a student nurse; it was my job to care for people. When I saw Sean with both of his arms in slings and the sad look in his eye, I wanted to care for him, I wanted him to feel better. I told him I'd make sure he was ok.

It was a much bigger commitment than I had realised. He couldn't eat or drink without help. Even if there was a straw in his drink the pain in his shoulder meant he couldn't lean forward to drink alone. He couldn't wash or even go to the toilet without me being there to hold his hand. He was like a baby, he'd lean forward on the toilet and let me wipe his arse for him. How privileged was I? He tried to make me hold what passed for his manhood while he peed too, but that was one step too far, I made him sit down to have a tinkle, although I'm not sure why that offended me when wiping a full grown man's backside was acceptable!

In hind sight, it was ridiculous. It shouldn't have been me looking after him, I shouldn't have taken a step away from my life because he pushed his limits too far. I'd contacted my tutor at university and told her that I needed time out from my course. I remember her telling me that she respected my decision but that she felt I should reconsider, that it wasn't my responsibility to care for him. I thought it was, so I carried on wiping.

Sean wasn't a good patient. Never did he say thank you, I'm sorry, or this isn't your role. Instead, I was frowned at for not being able to angle the cup right for his slurping, called inconsiderate by his sister, who was living at the house too, for not doing the housework, and what was worse was his mother scowling at me whenever she visited.

In all fairness, the dynamics of the house were complicated. His sister had an 18-month old baby and she was living at the parental house while her husband was away doing his basic training for the RAF. His dad was in the middle of a midlife crisis. On Christmas Day, their family celebrations had been crudely interrupted by a hammering at the front door. An irate woman demanded to speak to their dad and declared that he was married to a cheater, that his wife had been having an affair with her husband for years and he needed to throw the trollop out of his house immediately. He went wild, no wife of his was allowed to cheat. So his mum no longer lived at the home, but she had a key, and would come and go as she pleased, sitting like the queen on the couch with a fake smile on her lips expecting the world to do her bidding.

Sean's dad reminded me of Groundskeeper Willie from The Simpsons, a loud and brash Scotsman who called a spade a spade. He was happy to spend the evening drinking whiskey and eating takeaways, and never talked about his life in the army. His biking days were a knee jerk reaction to the queen cheating on him, and he'd adopted the alchemy t-shirt look along with long key chains hanging from his jeans. I'm sure there was a leather waist coat worn one day too. He'd bought the fastest and biggest sports bike that was available on the market at that time, a Suzuki TL1000, and he was determined to feel alive again.

I think that the events of that Christmas had brought Sean closer to his dad, they'd taken their bike test together as a two fingered salute to the women that had spurned them. Apparently Sean's first wife had cheated on him too, she'd drunkenly kissed another man while on training camp with the TA. At the time, I thought that was a poor excuse for ending a marriage, she later divorced him on the grounds of unreasonable behaviour. There's always two sides to every story.

It was a month before I returned back to Oxford. I was behind on all of my work, I hadn't had the forethought to study while in Portsmouth. Sean lost his job, he was self-contracting in computer programming. He claimed that taking that time out meant that he was out of the game forever, the market would have moved on and he wouldn't understand the new systems in place. I believed everything he told me. He decided that his best plan was to move in with me in Oxford.

That did not go down well with my housemates. I'd been away for a whole month and now I was marching back in with my boyfriend. They began to dislike him a lot, there were arguments, shouting matches, and hurt feelings more and more often. I continued to defend him and tried to keep the peace with everyone, but my friends were slipping further and further away from me. I was also feeling the strain of supporting to adults on a student budget as Sean was earning no money and didn't know what he was going to do career wise.

He bought a bigger and faster bike on finance. He knew the guy in the dealership who told the finance company he'd seen evidence of income.

Still, I didn't run.

I didn't know how to run, he'd moved in with me, I hadn't asked him, we hadn't talked about our future, we hadn't declared our undying love for each other or mentioned how unbearable it would be to live apart again after that initial month. It just happened, on his terms, his decision.

Despite our distinct lack of income, we pretended we were normal people and had money to spend. We ate out a lot as that's what you did wasn't it? His favourite place to eat was the Jamaican restaurant that was a few doors around the corner. Sean had been to the Caribbean.

I shouldn't be so venomous, it was, and still is, his retirement dream. Sean's going to move to the Caribbean and open a bar, drink Red Stripe all day, and blend in with the locals because he's that laid back kind of guy.

There were some of the most colourful characters I had ever met in that one restaurant. The owner was a huge Rastafarian guy who seemed to have a chair permanently placed on the pavement just outside. He'd sit in that chair all day, smoking a pipe, and nodding the occasional greeting to passers-by. He'd always be really animated when we walked past so it enticed us in more and more often. The place was addictive, two houses that had been knocked through into one on the ground floor. Everywhere was so darkly lit that people blended into the corners. There was wood everywhere, shelves with green plants bursting from every wall, and a tiny one-man bar on the far side of the room, stacked high with rum. By the door there were stacks of crates that were full of exotic things like green coconuts and plantains. At the very back of the restaurant was a room stacked full of vinyl, shelves from floor to ceiling of reggae music and a player that only the master himself was allowed to ever touch. The speakers were absolutely huge and ran throughout the restaurant.

Once you set foot inside that door, you were transported to a world without boundaries. There was always a group of old men sitting at the far table smoking something that smelt sweet and sickly. There was no closing time, if people were buying then you could party until the sun came up. The music never stopped.

That restaurant seduced me and lured me into believing there was an adventure happening in my life. We spent more and more time there and one evening the place was packed to the rafters when we walked in.

'No man, you cannot come in tonight, we are too full, too full! You can eat if you help me', and with that I found myself serving tables for the evening while Sean tended the bar and dished out the rum. I couldn't quite believe it, and I worked hard that night. The evening was split into three parts. We'd wait until everyone was settled at their tables, the whole place, then take the dinner orders. The orders were given to the kitchen and our crazy Rastafarian would then bulk cook for the entire restaurant. 10 funky chickens, 15 Jerk chickens, and 5 goat curries all with rice and beans. Stage 2 was getting the food out to everyone while it was still hot. Stage 3 collect the plates and wash the dishes, in cold water, without washing up liquid. Apparently washing up liquid was a carcinogen, and hot water was too expensive so scrub those pots until all of the grease is gone!

The fabulous host would then walk around the tables, click his fingers at the barman, Sean, demanding more rum be brought to the table and collect everyone's money for the meals.

It was 4am when the last person left that day. I sat down at a table completely exhausted and convinced my toenails would fall off my toes as they felt so bruised. £75 was pushed at me, with a declaration of how fabulous we'd worked.

'Come live with me man, I have a flat upstairs just for the two of you, you work for me Thursday, Friday, and Saturday night, I pay your rent and give you £100'.

Given the situation with my housemates this seemed like the right thing to do. Sean and I were officially moving in together. A couple. Concrete.

CHAPTER 18: BACK TO SQUARE ONE

Zéphirine was back to the one place in this world she didn't want to be - home. Her parent's home. She had never looked back since the day she had left. Never missed it even. Regardless how difficult her situation had been. Now, she was a grown woman and married but she was back in the parental nest!

It wasn't that Zéphirine was extremely happy in Australia, but it was a far better place to be than here. There, at least she had her own house with an ensuite! Yes, she still couldn't get over the fact that the master bedroom had its own bathroom. They had moved to a bigger and better house in Brisbane. Instead of a two-way bathroom, the master bedroom came with its own bathroom and she thought it was the best invention in this whole wide world! She realised it didn't take much to satisfy her sometimes. Or maybe it was because of the lack of excitement or sense of purpose in her life that she settled on little details such as a bathroom.

Back to reality. She was here now, in France, with her parents and sister. Her sister had grown up and had a boyfriend of her own. Their parents made no effort to hide the fact that they disapproved. Zéphirine didn't care much. If her sister was happy, who was she to judge? She also realised her own track record with men disqualified her from judging her sister.

A few years had passed since she'd been home and she looked forward to meeting her old friends once she got over the jet lag. She fell asleep reminiscing about a Greek God she met once.

But she was married now and had no right to think about him. The past should stay in the past. Though when one of her friends arrived and they started to catch up on things, Zéphirine couldn't help it. They had talked about everybody and everything that had happened since she left town. She needed to know.

"So, whatever happened to Luc? Is he still around?" she asked.

"Of course he is. He moved out of his parents' place and lives somewhere between here and Semur and works in Montbard. He drives a four-wheel drive now." her friend replied. Zéphirine left it at that.

I am now married. Unhappily married, but married, she kept telling herself. Not many days passed without having at least a thought about him but she knew she had to let him go. She never understood what happened back then and now it was too late. *I am married*, she reminded herself with a big sigh. It was a small town and she opted to let fate do its thing. *If we are supposed to meet again, we will meet again.*

Her parents were getting on her nerves. Her mother was happy because she finally had a maid again - Zéphirine! Except she was an adult now. And even though she was still afraid of her parents, she didn't want them to take advantage of her. When she went downstairs for breakfast one morning after everyone had gone, she noticed the empty bowls and cutleries on the table. She left everything the way it was as it wasn't her mess. She cleaned up after herself though.

When her father came back from work at lunch time, the first thing he noticed of course was the messy dining table. He mumbled something Zéphirine couldn't understand. She decided to take a stand on the situation. She knew it wasn't much but it took a lot of strength for her to say it.

"I don't mind cleaning the table. But the least the both of you could do is put your dirty dishes in the sink. That takes less than ten seconds to do." Zéphirine blurted out. He muttered. Again, he was incomprehensible to her. But she spoke her mind and she felt good about it. The next morning, only one bowl remained on the table. Her father took the bait obviously but forgot to give the memo to her mother and she wasn't about to face her. Zéphirine feared them both but on different levels.

Another time, he mumbled his disgust about the rubbish bin. Her mother who was a tight ass liked to use grocery bags to put in the bin. Except those bags were not the right size for the bin and too small. The rubbish overflowed and the bottom of the bin was filthy and unhygienic. So Zéphirine took it upon herself to explain to her father - If they were using the right size bags for the bin, this would not happen. They wouldn't have to clean it even. 'It doesn't take a genius to understand that concept.' she muttered. A pack of 30 bags which is one a day at most for a month is about $2. Surely this wasn't that big of an expense to keep a bin clean or cleaner?

Once again her father ignored her comment and went to his office. To prove her point, she scrubbed the bin clean and went to the supermarket to buy proper rubbish bags. Nobody mentioned anything about it nor did she get a thank you.

Zéphirine called Marc every few days and they would talk for an hour or so. She did miss him in some ways. Or maybe she just missed her life in Australia. But was it really a life she had over there? Or maybe she just wanted to be far away from here. '*I would rather be unhappy in my own house with Marc than being unhappy at my parents' house*', she cried to herself. She had no idea how long it would take for the immigration department to approve her visa. She had to be patient and take each day as they came.

At least she had her friends. Even though it had only been three years, it felt as if she had left ten years ago. They changed. They were grown-ups! Two of them had their driver's license so now they were able to have coffee or lunch out of town. That was exciting for them to be able to finally do whatever they wanted because they were now adults. No more sneaking around or hitchhiking to get to places! Zéphirine realized how much she had missed her friends – all the mischief they got into, all the fun they had back in the days. They were her lifeline of her tortured home and school life.

On that particular day though, they decided to walk down to the lake like in the old days. It was a 20-minute walk, thirty if they walked very slow. They used to sit on the rail of the bridge, glancing at the river more than they would actually look at the lake. The river and the bridge had always been there but the lake was man-made and about six to eight years old.

It was a lovely sunny day with a light breeze but not enough to be too cold. The streets were so peaceful, it almost felt like a ghost town. It was lunch hour. Shops were closed. Everybody - as the norm in French society - were probably watching TV after having a heavy lunch.

As they were approaching the turn off to the street that would take them to the bridge, they heard a car approaching behind them, and you could tell it was speeding. A midnight blue Land Cruiser drove past them and quickly turned into the street to go to the lake. Zéphirine's knees turned to water. Even though she had never seen that car before, she knew who the driver was. There was only one person in this town that could take a turn that way. She tried to keep it together.

They crossed the main street carefully, making sure there was no other oncoming traffic, and started to walk down the Lake Street, silently. It was a short straight street. The four-wheel drive was at the end of it facing them. It started to move towards them slowly. Zéphirine's heartbeat started racing. The car stopped a few meters in front of them. And there he was - The Greek God. He came out of the car. And *oh my Gosh*, Zéphirine muttered. What a sight! He now had longer hair. Shoulder length that suited him perfectly. But physically, Luc had not changed. The same body, the same smile, the same voice.

Luc first acknowledged her friends and said hello by kissing them on the cheek as he was always polite, maybe a gentleman to some extent. Zéphirine had never faulted him. Well, actually he did cheat on his girlfriend with her. She never bothered asking about her. Every moment with him was golden. When he kissed or made love to her, no words could adequately describe her feelings.

Zéphirine had been in love with him since the first day she had laid eyes on him, and now she realised her feelings for him were as strong as they were back then. How was that even possible? This love thing. It was something she still could not grasp.

But the table had turned. Zéphirine was the one who wasn't single this time.

Luc finally came up to her. He kissed her on the cheeks to say hello and then stared with a broad smile on his face. She wanted to kiss him on the mouth. Breathe in his entire being.

Her friends had never asked her about him. Even when Zéphirine kept inquiring about him over the years, they never questioned her. Today, was no exception. They just walked away because they knew it was her time with the Greek God. They probably will never know how much Zéphirine appreciated them and their friendship.

"How are you?" he asked finally breaking the silence and freeing her from her train of thoughts.

"I'm good." she replied hesitantly, trying to figure out what was happening. Fate had put them together again. But why?

Awkward silence. He generally was not the type to not talk. He would always break up silences.

"I'm married!" she blurted out showing off her cheap ring on her finger and suddenly feeling like a moron.

"No way!"

"Yes way!" she protested asking herself *why the hell not*?

"Nope. It's just not you." he said.

Like hell it was not her! What was wrong with him? Not her? How would he know? Just because they had sex a few times did not mean he knew her! Of course, she would have much rather be married to Luc, maybe he felt the same way. All the same, his words bothered her. She remembered she had her handbag and therefore her wallet. She took out her Australian driver's license and handed it out to him.

"This is my ID in Australia. See the name on it? It says Mrs. Zéphirine Avernier, my husband's last name."

"Doesn't mean anything. Anyone can make a fake ID."

Why on Earth would she make a fake ID and pretend to be married? She was dumbfounded. If one person had to be happy for her, she thought it would be him out of all the people who knew her.

"Let's go for a ride. Get in!" he said as he was helping her into his car, which was quite high, and completely forgetting what just happened.

When Luc had his sports car, it wasn't to show off, though she suspected he was a bit proud. He was a male after all, and it was a nice achievement. But he mainly had a sport's car because he liked to drive fast and put all his driving skills to the test. With off road driving, the rules of the road meant absolutely nothing. Every impossible route just became possible. Zéphirine had gone four-wheel driving on Australia's magnificent beaches. They've had a few scares driving on the soft sand of Fraser Island, trying to escape the high tide. *There is nothing quite life cruising up a beach with windows down*. There were just trees, rocks, hills, and mountains where they were but it felt as liberating as driving on the beach.

After spending hours being bumped and tossed around, they finally arrived at the old granite mine. The light was almost gone. Time with a Greek God just flies. He stopped the car on a hilltop and like in the movies, they lay down on the front of the car watching the stars. It felt like just a few moments before it was time to go. Everything was speeding up around her. Her heart was beating fast. Zéphirine wished things would slow down like a movie scene. She wanted him to pull her into him and softly kiss her. She wanted to make passionate love under the stars.

"You haven't changed." he said.

"Yes I have! I wear less make up now. I am using earthy tones instead of the flashy blue and pink eye shadows." She had to stifle a laugh at the image she was painting in her head.

Luc shook his head and sighed, "You don't need makeup either way."

Zéphirine knew this was meant as a compliment but compliments always made her feel uncomfortable, so she didn't reply. Luc decided it was time to go home. His home.

A little two-bedroom house in one of the smallest villages. If you didn't know where to look, you would not even know it existed. The kind of place you would want to be if you wanted privacy. And Luc liked his privacy. This place suited him. It was warm and cozy. He decided to take a shower so she sat at the table, waiting for him. Her eyes and mind wandered around his house. She imagined living here with him.

Her jaw nearly dropped when he came out of the bathroom with just a towel around the waist. Water dripping off his hair and look at that body... was he doing it on purpose? Did he know the effect he had on her? Had her dreamy face been betraying her thoughts to him? She imagined she was dragging her fingers down his chest, her legs slowly moving up and down against his...

"Are you hungry?" His voice brought her back to reality.

"Yes." she answered quickly.

He moved to the kitchen and started to get things out of the fridge, in preparation of making dinner for the two of them. She continued her interrupted thoughts.

He had converted one of the bedrooms into a music room. They retired there after dinner. History repeated itself - the same scenario when they first spent time alone with each other. They were once again on top of each other, teasing, promising that neither would succumb.

She found herself in Luc's bedroom with him undressing her. Just like their similar encounter a few years ago, she didn't stop him.

Luc drove her back home the next morning, and she was terrified because she didn't know what to say to her parents. Sure she was 20 now, an adult, and a married woman. She felt as if she was sixteen again and had snuck out of the house. It shouldn't matter what she did now at whatever time. But she felt guilty. This felt so wrong. Yet, it felt so right at the same time. What had she done?

She was relieved when she realised no one was home, but she stayed off the radar that day, still trying to figure things out. Fate brought them back together again. Why?

Zéphirine went on a few more drives with Luc. On the days they didn't see each other, they would talk on the phone for hours. But they didn't sleep together again. Not even a single kiss. What happened was never mentioned and he never asked about her husband.

A week later when she called him, he told her they couldn't see each other and talk to each other anymore.

"Why?" she asked in disbelief.

"Because."

"Because what?"

"Because I met someone. I am in love with her. So we can't see each other."

"You met someone?" She laughed. "As if? When? When you are not at work you are talking to me so at what point in the past seven days did you meet someone and fell in love?"

"I did."

"What's her name?"

"I can't tell you and you don't know her anyway, goodbye."

Confused Zéphirine tried to make sense of things. She tried to make him tell her why they couldn't see each other again. He didn't betray any of his feelings to her other than he was in love with someone who wasn't her. She believed he was keeping the truth from her but he was adamant about not sharing it.

She hung up exhausted and disappointed.

She was a married woman. Married women only care about their husbands; not someone else they had not seen in years, she reasoned with herself.

Fate was in his favour this time: Zéphirine never saw the Greek God the nine months she stayed in France until her visa was finally approved.

CHAPTER 19: ALLANAH IN THE LION'S DEN

I was excited, we were moving in together and I was going to be all grown up, no more student living. The flat was a shambles, directly above the restaurant. We had a room at the front that was big, room for a bed and TV and all of our things, that weren't actually that much. There were some steps directly outside of our room with a hatch at the bottom step that let you look directly into the bar of the restaurant.

There was another room on that level but we weren't allowed to use that, the boys would appear in there to play when they were hiding from their mum and dad. The kitchen was large, with a table and chairs set up ready for use. Behind the table was a door that led to the adjoining house, and that's where the boys would come and go as they pleased.

There were ants crawling everywhere and whatever you touched was sticky with a thick layer of grease. There was no hot water. The bathroom had a bath and a sink, but bare floorboards on the floor so I hated being in there. There was a third floor to the house and that's where Gary lived, an alcoholic that we were to leave alone even though he frequently left a trail of faeces on the stairs and ate our food.

The music played every night, until late. I worked as a waitress every weekend until at least 3am each time. I was exhausted. I began to fail my university course and something was going to give. I dropped out of university. Sean told me that I had to do what made me happy, and as nursing wasn't what I came here to do in the first place, it made sense to leave. My mum was distraught, she stopped speaking to me after we had actual shouting matches over the phone. I was at a loss of how to make my life easier, I physically couldn't carry on with the way we were living, it never ever occurred to me to leave Sean.

We stayed at the Jamaican restaurant for a good six months. Leaving university didn't help with how I was feeling. I'd become the dutiful girlfriend with no prospects or direction in life. I'd started to feel uncomfortable in Sean's presence again, if I talked to another man he'd question me and tell me I had been flirting. It was my job to speak to the people in the restaurant and make them feel welcomed.

It was okay for him to talk to women at the bar though, and our first daughter is named after someone he met in that restaurant. He said he fell in love with at first sight as she was so beautiful inside and out. He was trying to get us to agree to a ménage-á-trois that night after a heavy helping of rum.

If I was drunk, he'd get cross with me and make me feel like I was being a silly girl, but it was absolutely okay for him to get so drunk, he didn't know where he was peeing at night. I started to regret leaving nursing, and when I told him that I was met with a barrage of reasons why I wouldn't succeed as a nurse, I didn't have the ability to hold down a career even if I did manage to pass the course. I listened to him and believed him.

I still worked as an auxiliary on my favourite ward to try and save some money for the life I wasn't quite ready to give up hope on. There was a part of me that thrived on that ward, I loved being part of a team, caring for people, and feeling needed. Sean hated me working there. He quite often met me at work if I was working late, I thought he was being my guardian, but one evening he drunkenly confessed that he was checking I was where I said I would be.

I came home after a shift one evening to an obviously angry Sean. He'd been drinking, but that wasn't unusual, and his eyes were like steel. My heart was thumping in my chest so hard I knew I was in trouble even though I couldn't think what I had possibly done wrong. My old diary from my college days was in his lap, he picked it up and threw it at me.

He shouted at me from across the room, *'why didn't you tell me? I have a right to know! You're not who I thought you were! Lies!'* I still had no idea what he was talking about, and as they always do the tears came before I could control them. I tried to ask him what I'd done, but all I could think to say was that I hadn't lied.

He'd read my diary while I'd been at work. It wasn't a diary filled with my personal thoughts and feelings so I didn't see any harm or what could have possibly made him so angry. He wasn't upset, he was absolutely livid. He'd seen the notes that I'd written to my friend, we'd declared ourselves the sexy bastard appreciation society and eternal lesbian lovers. That's what had infuriated him, he thought I was a lesbian.

Part of me wanted to laugh out loud, after all this was hysterical. When we went out together, we would dance like we didn't care and if we didn't like the men giving us attention then we would pretend to be girlfriends. While sitting watching those cool boys being all unobtainable at lunchtime we'd remind ourselves of the fun we'd had at Eddie's that weekend. It was harmless and innocent fun; it was normal stuff between two friends. Banter, plain and simple.

I tried to explain it all to Sean, but he seemed much happier to believe whatever sordid version of my life he dreamt up. I couldn't even understand what the problem was even if it had been true. He walked out and left me still crying, wondering what I'd actually done wrong and how the hell I was going to fix it.

He came back sometime later that night, he undressed silently and collapsed into a drunken sleep on the bed. Nothing was said about the whole thing ever again. He woke up, went to the Turkish delights to buy us lunch, and came back with a flourish of added olives by way of apology.

Too young. I was too young to be pretending I was ready to live this life. I wanted to see the world, ride my own motorbike, swim with dolphins, and be successful at whatever it was that I would be good at in my career.

The motorbike was the best thing in my world. We went to a local meeting every week and camping get-togethers throughout the summer where grown men hid from their lives and pretended they were full of youth and freedom.

Things began to change at the restaurant, I worked hard but Sean drank more than we earned. He also began to pick fights with the alcoholic who lived upstairs, that angered our huge Jamaican landlord. 'No man, you leave him alone, you leave him in peace or you leave'.

That seemed to kick Sean into touch. He found a job, selling medical supplies over the phone, full time basic wage with the promise of commission. He then said we needed to find somewhere else to live and applied to the council. We were given a two-bedroom flat in a tower block in Blackbird Leys. If there's ever a police chase on the television, it's always in Blackbird Leys. The car park in front of the flats had two burnt out shells of what used to be vehicles.

I couldn't help but be a little excited. Sean arranged everything, he signed the tenancy and collected the keys. There was a shed down a side alley that was just big enough to keep the love of his life in, his sport's bike. He would pivot it into place every night and struggle to squeeze it in without scratching her or knocking the racy red and black faring on the alley. I could watch him from the balcony in the flat, the care and attention he gave that machine was inspiring.

We had a sofa that my dad no longer needed and a dining table that helped break up the long thin room that was our living area. The kitchen was small but that was all we needed, the bathroom was horrible with a bath, no shower, and a huge cistern above the toilet with black casing and a pull chain hanging from it. To me it looked like it would have been more suited to a prison than a home. We did have two bedrooms and that made my nesting instincts kick in, I wanted that room to be filled, I wanted to have a purpose in life.

We didn't have any carpets in the flats, Sean said we didn't need them, the tiled floor that ran throughout would mean I could keep it cleaner. I mopped that floor every day and it never looked any cleaner, I was convinced there was an actual dust bunny working overtime to keep me frustrated. There were two storage heaters in the flat, one in the living room and one in the main bedroom, our only source of warmth. It was a shell. It took us two months to get round to painting the flats, it was something I really wanted to do, it felt so unclean and tainted. I'd found used syringes shoved in the airing cupboard when we first moved in, Sean said it was no big deal, but I didn't like it, and I was sure that those flecks, of what now looked brown, on the ceiling in the living room were further evidence of the seedy history of the flats.

It was sometime later that my suspicions were confirmed. I was taking the rubbish to the shoot in the communal hallway when one of the neighbours popped out to speak to me. I was a little surprised as we'd lived there for a few months by this time and I'd never seen or spoken to anyone who lived there. If I was honest, I was scared of everyone and everything. They invited me in for a cup of tea, I jumped at the chance, as my days were often long and lonely since I'd left university. I worked for agencies as a carer but it didn't give me full time hours, I didn't have transport, and the flats was too far away from the hospital now so my shifts there became fewer and further between.

I was mesmerized when I stepped inside their flat, it was an actual home, warm and cozy, and full top to bottom with memories of their life. Was it the carpet or the pictures that made it feel like home? I wasn't sure but I liked it.

When I went back to the flat, I felt determined to make the place feel more like our home. I cooked a stew hoping the aromas would fill the place and give it a cozy warmth. I changed all of the bed sheets, spruced the sofa and tried in vain to clean the floors. 6pm came and passed, no sign of Sean. I had no idea where he was or what time he'd be home, he finished work at 5pm and was normally home by half past. He had been late home more than once, staff training, a sale that promised commission but took longer than he thought, and a whole host of other trivial reasons that I couldn't deny or disprove.

I can't remember what time he actually did get home that night, but the stew was no longer worth eating and I absolutely wasn't hungry. He chewed away on the tough dry meat and pretended it was fabulous and that there was nothing wrong with it. I asked where he'd been and it was a lie but I accepted it. He had to stay late at the office to liaise with America, they were eight hours behind us time wise so he had to wait for their office to open before he could negotiate with them.

I thought that if I gave him a family to care about he'd want to come home. I told him I wanted a baby, he said it was a fabulous idea, and would definitely keep me occupied during the day. I fell pregnant straight away. He did come home on time every night after that, for a while at least.

We got married before our daughter was born. Sean didn't want to remarry, he said he'd been there and done the whole big wedding thing already and didn't want to do it again. In my hormonal state, I stamped my foot, he loved me enough to have a baby but not to get married? He lazily agreed that perhaps he could get married again, and I felt a huge relief, like there was some security and all of those little niggles that had poked at the back of my mind would disappear.

He announced our engagement to our biker friends over pizza, which came as a shock considering the last time we'd spoken about it was with me in tears wondering why he would have a baby with me but refused to marry me that ended with an acknowledgement and definitely no proposal. Where was the romance, the devotion, the love? Pizza and a promise that he'd go to *H Samuels* tomorrow to buy a ring.

I certainly wasn't swept of my feet and the fear returned in full force, what was I doing? It was too late now, I was pregnant, there was no choice, and there was no running away. This was after all what I had wanted.

The wedding was low key, a winter affair, on the steps of the registry office. I was the blushing bride. My dress cost £20 and was a Christmas sale special, the meal was in a restaurant next door to the registry office, the Mongolian Wok Bar. The drinks were in a bar that only his family stayed for. His dad's new girlfriend told me she had cancer, his uncle had just buried his wife, and the cousins were helping him forget that his wife might need some attention on this special day. There were no speeches, no dancing, no laughter, but plenty of regrets.

On our wedding night, my husband landed on our bed with a thud and stayed there fully clothed until the next day, while I slept in the nursery thinking of the bundle tightly wrapped up safe and sound, oblivious to the world around her.

CHAPTER 20: WHAT A WOMAN IS FOR

Marriage had never been on Zéphirine's list. Until she was issued with an ultimatum: get married or go home. Children had never been on her list either. In primary school, kids talked about how they would get married and have loads of kids! Zéphirine never partook in those conversations she thought were absolute non-sense. They never left her wondering about having children one day. All she cared was having friends who loved her for who she was and eventually, part of growing up as a young woman, she thought about boys. But it stopped there.

So when Marc told her on the phone, while she was still in France waiting for her visa, that his ex-wife was pregnant (from her new husband of course), it rang a cord. There was a touch of jealousy. Though she was not sure why. It had nothing to do with Marc either. Or maybe she was envious, or curious even? Curious about what? Nah, could not be curiosity. There was more to it but she could not pinpoint what she was feeling. Maybe it was more like a wake-up call: she was now married so the next logical step in a marriage is to have children. But whatever she was feeling, it left her unsettled and only one thing came up to mind:

"Well, I guess it is time for me to stop taking the pill then." she told Marc on the phone.

Marc could have said something like: "Let's talk about it." or more importantly "Let's think about this." But instead he didn't agree or disagree, he said nothing. So she stopped taking the pill as he was due to come to France for a few months. They hoped her visa would be approved by then and they would fly back to Australia together.

Zéphirine's visa was not approved when it was time for Marc to fly back, but she was definitely pregnant by then. She informed immigration about the change of situation and why she needed to be by her husband's side. This may have or not speed up her visa's approval.

After nine long months in France, she finally landed in Australia, already five months pregnant. She looked like a fat cow and would refer to herself as such. For someone who had been self-conscious her whole life and been on a very strict regime, seeing herself like that – *a fat cow* she called herself - was depressing.

On the other hand, Zéphirine never suffered any morning sickness. She felt exhausted all the time, maybe because of the hot weather or because she was just huge or maybe a bit of both. She had occasional cravings for strawberries and vanilla milkshakes from McDonalds. Other than that she was perfectly healthy and so was her daughter – the gynaecologist in France had told her from the scan it was definitely a girl, so she went with that.

Zéphirine could feel the baby move in her stomach. Not that it *moved* her much. Sometimes it was funny to see her stomach go distorted, sometimes it was painful. But people around her seemed to enjoy it and particularly liked to rub her tummy as if she was a Buddha. Even though Zéphirine was over half-way through her pregnancy, the whole situation seemed surreal; like it hadn't quite hit home.

She told the doctor to not tell her how much she weighted after putting on 27kg. Knowing she put on that much weight made her sick. She was fat, and being pregnant didn't make it a valid excuse. She couldn't bear the sight of herself at all and couldn't wait for this to be over.

When the due date was nearly there, they decided it was best for them to stay at Pierrette's place since she made the arrangements to go to a hospital in Brisbane. It was more practical for the family, closer for them, so they wouldn't have to travel too far to see the new addition in the family. When Marc moved to the Sunshine Coast, his family wasn't pleased about that. Although it was one to two hours at most away, for his family it was as if Zéphirine and Marc lived on the other side of the world. But

Zéphirine was not bothered, yet.

Zéphirine didn't have any friends. The only people she knew was Marc's bosses and their daughter, who had an obvious crush on Marc. Marc had even admitted they had gone a bit past kissing while Zéphirine was in France... which did not surprise her at all and she couldn't care less either.

The pain started late one night. It felt like period pain but it was almost constant and uncomfortable. Zéphirine barely slept. Pierrette thought it was best to go to the hospital that morning. Zéphirine knew nothing so she just went with the flow. But once she was at the hospital, in a small room, with the nurse telling her she was just about ready to give birth, she started to panic. This was not home. She wanted to go home. But the nurse told her she couldn't. Zéphirine got very confused, she could not figure out what she was doing here and why she had to stay. The nurse sensed her distress and tried to distract her with questions.

"What are you going to call your baby?" she asked.

"Allison."

"What if it's a boy, have you chosen a name?" she asked.

"It's not a boy, it's a girl and her name is Allison."

"You don't know that it is girl for sure."

"My doctor in France told me and showed me on the scan."

"Yes, but it is still not 100% guarantee." she carried on.

Zéphirine had now completely forgotten she wanted to go home because the nurse got on her nerves. Who the hell was she to tell her about her daughter?

"It is a girl and her name is Allison." she groaned.

At that moment, another nurse arrived and it was time to move Zéphirine to the delivery room.

The room was huge and sterile. Felt very cold and boring. It had a bed in the near middle. Next to the bed was an open shower with a chair in it. Zéphirine was in pain and since she didn't deal with pain easily they quickly offered gas which she gladly took. When that didn't seem to help her discomfort, the nurse showed her to shower were she sat in the pouring hot water. It felt good, especially with the added effect of the gas. But it was short lived.

The nurse moved her back to the bed and offered the needle. Zéphirine's fear of needles hadn't changed, but she was under no condition to fight it. She wanted the pain to stop, but after a few hours, the pain was more frequent and more painful. So they offered her the epidural which she didn't know much about it and Marc's Auntie who had been with her in the hospital all along, said: "Take it!" So she did.

After almost 10 hours and the dilatation had stopped in the last couple of hours, the doctor recommended a caesarean. They could wait another couple of hours but there was no reason to expect any changes and the baby showed signs of distress. Zéphirine just wanted the pain to end so she agreed. But when they asked if she wanted to watch them open her stomach, she was lucid enough to say "Absolutely not! Put me down!"

When Zéphirine woke up she was in excruciating pain, more than before when she had gotten here, or before they put her asleep. She heard a nurse say: "She is awake! She is awake!" And then a woman hovered over her, placing something over her breast, which Zéphirine came to realise it was a baby. But in her mind, she was in so much pain, and having just woken up, she could not deal with a baby. *Please leave me alone*, she was pleading in her mind.

The nurses got the message somehow or Zéphirine must have fallen back into sleep because the next time she opened her eyes she was in a different place. She was in bed, in a room, a drawn curtain on the left, a window with bright sunlight on the other side. It took a few minutes of adjustments to comprehend what had just happened. Marc and the family were surrounding her and the baby, her baby, Allison.

Zéphirine just had a baby. She was forced to breastfeed. Okay, well no one put a knife to her throat, but nobody offered any other option either. "Mothers breastfeed their child. That is how it is supposed to be." a nurse told her even though Zéphirine hadn't asked. Humans were funny like that sometimes, they could read your mind but never at the right time, go figure!

Zéphirine didn't like that breastfeeding business a bit. As if she wasn't in enough pain already from having her stomach opened, breastfeeding was the worst experience in her life too. The baby seemed to enjoy chewing her nipples while feeding which was very painful instead of enjoyable as she had seen on TV.

To make matters worse, she had to walk to the end of the hallway to get to the bathroom. Every move, every step she made, whether it was turning around in bed to find a somewhat comfortable position or walking, felt like her insides were coming out. It was the worst feeling ever, worse than getting a needle from the dentist.

In the evening, her breast had tripled in size and was so sore!

"My word!" a nun exclaimed as she entered the room. "You need to get that milk pumped out. You must terribly uncomfortable. I'll be right back." Zéphirine had no idea why a nun just randomly walked into her room, but she was thankful when she came back with a breast pump.

The nun showed Zéphirine how to extract her milk; it was such a relief! Her breast size went right down in size and did not feel as sore. She had extracted a few bottles with now the added inconvenience of having to walk to the kitchen to get them. There was no room service in this hospital.

But what Zéphirine really wanted, was to go home. This unfriendly environment didn't seem healthy for her. So she was glad to be finally released a few days later to go back to Pierrette's house.

The baby was the novelty of the family as there was no other at the time. There were enough hands to look after her and Zéphirine happily watched the people fussing over her baby. *"My baby."* It sounded strange. Zéphirine would watch the baby in her little coffin. She would extract the milk to feed her with a bottle or most of the time, Marc's grandparents wanted to do it or someone else in the family. Her maternal senses had not kicked in yet. Pierrette realised that and decided to show Zéphirine how to bathe her baby, hoping her maternal instincts would finally kick in.

Once bath time was over and Zéphirine had dressed the little bundle, Pierrette said: "You have to hold her, cuddle her, and kiss her. This is your daughter, not a doll." Zéphirine shrugged. It sounded simple. It sounded stupid. And to Zéphirine it was the most difficult thing to do. At first she felt awkward, unnatural. And it took a few more days for her to get it, a few encouragements from Pierrette, to learn something she had never experienced before: the precious, tender bond between a child and their mother, initiated by a simple touch. It was strange, but soothing.

After three weeks, Zéphirine was confident she could take care of her baby by herself. She wanted to be back in control of her life instead of having all those people around running her life for her. She was appreciative of their help but she wanted to be home, back into the familiarities of her things.

Back on the Coast, they lived in an old Queensland surrounded by a balcony from which you could watch the magnificent sunsets and sunrises over the Glasshouse Mountains. It was breath taking. An abundance of wildlife was coming in for feed and Marc's children enjoyed the entertainment.

"Put some bread and honey and the lorikeets will come for a feed." said Marc's grandmother. At first Zéphirine had left the plate at the back of the garden under the tree and would watch the birds from far away. For convenience, she decided to leave the plate on the far end of the balcony. Big mistake! The balcony was soon flooded by all sorts of parrots. It was fun at first, but a balcony covered by parrots is noisy and birds poo a lot!

The house was quite isolated. There were neighbours, of course she could have called in case of emergencies, but she had never met them or seen them even. There was no bus stop and Zéphirine still didn't have her driver's license. And now she had a baby, a pram to deploy, and a bag full of nappies and bottles and washers and stuff... way too much work to try to get out of the house. This baby business was a job in itself and Zéphirine was just not ready for it.

She was glad when the lease was not renewed and they moved back into civilization. Zéphirine loved their new house. Since Marc had the car, he was the one who had gone house hunting and found it: a brand new three-bedroom house on the canal and nestled in a cul-de-sac. She could easily walk with the pram to the shopping village within 10 minutes. A bus stop was also on the way if she really wanted to adventure herself a bit further. Life felt grand again.

One year had already passed since she had been back in Australia, and besides the family, Marc's colleague and her doctor, Zéphirine still had no friends. She spent her days indoors, looking after her baby girl, cleaning the house (which was spotless) and cooking food her husband liked to criticize, as it was never as good as his auntie's or his grandmother's. Not that she had ever admitted to be a chef in the kitchen. She cooked as a necessity, not because she enjoyed it. At least he could never complain about desserts as if she failed to cook him a proper dinner or to his satisfaction, she excelled with her baking and it was good enough for her and for him.

Zéphirine was not happy. Her life was dull. Marc didn't seem to care and was rarely home. Work was always a priority and with the amount of time he spent at the factory she thought they would be rich by now. But that wasn't the case, money was scarce and bills were always paid late. Zéphirine begged Marc to go to marriage counselling thinking it might help but who was she kidding? The counsellor just nodded to everything they said and that was that.

Her parents were finally coming to Australia to meet their grand-daughter for the first time. As the day of their arrival was fast approaching, Zéphirine began having second thoughts. Her mixed race heritage was coming back to haunt her. There were very few black people that lived in the area. She wasn't even sure that her daughter had even seen a black person. How would she react when she saw her grandfather for the first time? However, much to her relief and joy, when the day finally came, her daughter ran to embrace her grandfather, not caring one bit about his skin colour.

Even though she didn't have a job, Zéphirine was able to get her daughter into kindergarten twice a week. She thought it would be good for her to mix with other children since there was no other children in the family. And besides the family and work, they didn't have a social life either. Just because Zéphirine didn't have friends, she didn't want to rob her daughter of that same fate.

Zéphirine took Allison for a walk around the block for something new to do. Allison was about to turn two. A few houses down the street was a woman standing in her front yard holding a bowl. It looked like she was mixing a cake or something, overlooking two kids playing. When Allison saw the children, she got excited and ran up to them. The woman, in her early thirties, no makeup, dressed in jeans and a shirt, was smiling at Zéphirine and introduced herself as Kira North.

Kira's children were going to same kindergarten as Allison. Kira offered to drive them. Zéphirine had finally gotten her driver's license, but they only had one car, and Marc was using it to go to work. Usually, she would take a taxi to take Allison to kindergarten. Depending on the weather, she would walk back or take the bus.

Kira and Zéphirine were mostly extreme opposites. Zéphirine liked to dress up, Kira did not. Zéphirine always wore makeup, Kira did not. Zéphirine preferred a 5-star hotel, Kira preferred camping. Zéphirine wore high heels, Kira liked flats. Kira wasn't into technology, Zéphirine had to have the latest gadget. She bought the first 42" plasma TV for $8000, nowadays available for $500. The only loan Kira had was a mortgage, anything else had to be bought cash, and she hated credit cards. Zéphirine and Marc didn't have a mortgage but they had credit cards, a car loan, and debts from the business.

But Kira and Zéphirine got along so well they became almost inseparable. They had many things too in common, such as baking and going to the shops together, even though they liked different things. They also smoked like chimneys and enjoyed drinking wine. As the saying goes, 'opposites attract'.

Zéphirine admired Kira, she was a good mother, *unlike her* she thought. Kira knew what she was doing with the kids, Zéphirine was just going with the flow as she had always done with anything. Zéphirine knew she would never win the 'Mother of the Year Award' not that she aspired to that either. As long as her child had everything she needed, and as long as Zéphirine would not become like her own mother, were all she cared about. '*I am not like my mother and will never be*', was the mantra Zéphirine lived by and was constantly playing in the back of her mind.

Kira was 11 years older than Zéphirine, same year as Marc so she looked up to her. Even though she had considered Pierrette the closest thing she could have as a mother, Zéphirine spent more time with Kira. Kira was always there for her and Allisson. Pierrette and the rest of Marc's family for that matter, could not be bothered to drive up the Coast even though it was only an hour away. Having a friend, someone to talk to, to vent, to rant, to share secrets or jokes, made Zéphirine's life so much better.

Kira got to know Marc, as she often dropped by in the evening to have a cigarette and a glass of wine with them. Kira was a health freak but she had one vice: the cigarette, and her husband hated that. Zéphirine had given up the cigarette with great difficulties while she was pregnant but as soon she got out of the hospital she was back into smoking a pack a day. And having Kira around did not help slowing her down.

Marc and Zéphirine didn't have a social life because they were spending most of their time at his family. Marc didn't seem to have friends besides his colleagues and his ex-wife's husband. Marc was socially inept and did not like people besides his family. If he did not like a person within thirty seconds, he would never like that person. So it was difficult for Zéphirine to have friends, and friends she could bring home if Marc was around. But he liked Kira. Kira tolerated him.

Marc's birthday was fast approaching. Zéphirine had to put some thought into what to get him and opted for a PlayStation. He had hinted a few times he wanted one, and she thought they might gain some kind of family time. She bought him a racing game, *Need for Speed*, as she knew he liked car racing. The salesman advised her to get another bestseller called *Tomb Raider*.

Tomb Raider was a big hit for Marc and Zéphirine. They both loved the game and were excited about playing it together every night. They would take turns when one was dying or help out each other. Allison would fall asleep on their laps. Marc would usually stay up a bit longer and would be excited in the morning to tell Zéphirine what he did on the game and how he passed the level they were stuck on. Playing video games was now *their* quality time together or as good as it would ever get.

"We are going to a birthday party on Saturday afternoon." said Marc to Zéphirine who was surprised by the announcement. They were finally doing something else that did not involve his family or Kira!

It was a pool party for the daughter of a guy Marc was working with, Giovanni and his wife Dona. They lived on the other side of the canal so a five minutes' drive away from Marc and Zéphirine's house. Marc seemed to like Giovanni and Zéphirine got along well with Dona whom invited them for a BBQ the following weekend.

To keep busy, Zéphirine took on home studies on computerized bookkeeping. Marc was earning good money but they were always broke. So she thought she might be able to help her husband with his business. Zéphirine had always worked for someone so she didn't understand self-employment; her father was self-employed too but she was too young at the time to take interest. She also took a tax course to understand the Australian taxation system, where she met Nicole.

The course would give them a Certificate and the top three students would be guaranteed a job for the tax period. Zéphirine was interested in the job, but more importantly she wanted the knowledge. Nicole was a single mum with two kids and needed the job. She couldn't afford a printer and had no way to print some of the papers, so Zéphirine offered to them print them at her house. This small act of kindness led to another blossoming friendship.

Zéphirine now had three friends besides Marc's family and ex-wife; a monumental feat in and of itself since Marc never seemed to like anyone Zéphirine brought over. As an added bonus, Marc even accepted them into their home. On top of all these changes, Zéphirine was also pregnant with her second child.

CHAPTER 21: TWO BECOMES THREE

My daughter was a planned pregnancy, I wanted to be a family. Allanah the mother, the nurturer, the caregiver. My need to nurture is intense and has never left me. I wasn't a natural though, the sleep deprivation and overwhelming sense of responsibility nearly drove me insane. My mum stepped in, she came to stay for a week and installed some order back in to my life. Routine is important when you're lost and floundering, it lets you take one step at a time.

There was no doubt that I was depressed. I had wanted this life, to be married, to be a parent, and now that I'd got those things, I didn't know what to do with them. One evening, Sean was late home from work and my temper snapped. The unexplained absences were on the rise again and I felt it was completely unfair. He wouldn't answer his mobile phone and the office number had been directed to answering service, so his story about staying late was wearing thin. I had no idea what he was doing with his time and I didn't really waste energy trying to work out what he was doing, but that evening it was too much for my frazzled mind. I shouted at him, no how was your day, just straight headfirst into battle. I told him I was sick of it all, fed up of being a slave in that miserable flat, tired of not knowing where he was and absolutely done with never having a penny to spend. He calmly told me that I should get help, I clearly wasn't coping with being a mum and I should get it sorted before something bad happened. I took off my shoes and threw them at him. I missed and the one photo from our wedding day that I'd managed to hang in our scant home fell on the floor with a sickening crack. Sean seemed smug as his prediction came to life within a matter of seconds. I made him hold the baby while I cleared the broken glass up, all of the time screaming in my head that it would never have broken if he'd put carpet on the floor.

I wanted to leave, I wanted to go home to my mum and tell her what a terrible mistake I'd made, I wanted to start again with just me and my baby, but there was no room for me there. This was my life now.

I went to the doctor the next day, he told me that I needed marriage guidance counselling not anti-depressants. Sean disagreed and asked me to see another doctor, who did give me tablets. I do remember feeling suicidal, I thought I didn't deserve to be a mum and that I'd done a terrible thing bringing her into this life. My emotions were all over the place, so when Sean said he thought we should move I agreed with him. We could try and get a council house back in Redditch or his mum had a flat we could rent in Portsmouth. I wasn't feeling strong enough to deal with the skeletons in my closet, and my mum was already having enough problems in her life without my life disintegrating in her lap, so Portsmouth seemed the best option. It had to be better than the isolation I was living.

The flat was amazing, with carpets and heating. It felt a lot more like home. I found a job that allowed me to work from home and Sean tried his hand at selling disabled living equipment. Sometimes he'd take us to work with him, the shop was in Bournemouth, I loved the adventure and the old ladies loved playing with my blue eyed doll of a toddler, she was a beautiful girl and advanced too, she loved the attention and would melt their hearts. I loved being by the sea too, there's something liberating about standing before the open ocean and seeing it stretch on endlessly. I thought we'd made the right decision and that life would be ok. I weaned myself off the tablets and began to see the cracks again.

Initially, our biggest problem was money. There was never any and I failed to see why. We were both working, not fabulous jobs but a regular income nonetheless. We didn't live an extravagant lifestyle, we shopped sensibly for our weekly food and I tried to make things stretch as far as possible. We didn't go on holiday or buy designer clothes. We never had the money to go out on the town or explore our surroundings. In reality it was worse than that, we owed money seemingly to every man and his dog. There were times when I'd dread the phone ringing, it would always be someone demanding immediate payment for this bill or that loan. Like a fool I'd answer and try to arrange a payment plan, more often than not I'd end up in tears, partly born of frustration and sometimes due to their aggressive accusations. If I didn't pay they'd send the bailiffs, repossess my goods, take my car, and the threats ran on. I absolutely refused to answer the door: that was Sean's job.

There was absolutely no reason for us to be this much in debt, we had nothing to show for the endless bills and certainly no happy frivolous memories to account for the string of relentless phone calls. We started to have doorstep loans too, as soon as we finished paying one off the next one was taken out, it was the only way to afford anything, but again I wasn't sure where it went, £800 would be eaten within a week.

The first redundancy came as a shock, the company was in financial meltdown and the shop was closing with immediate effect. Luckily, I was able to increase my working hours and was promoted to a senior position which boosted my morale no end. Sean found another job quite quickly and it was a two-minute walk from the flat so, I felt sure we would be able to start getting on top of our finances. They threw a lavish Christmas party and spent the night plying us all with alcohol. It was the first time I'd been out for the night in Portsmouth and I danced the night away, thinking things would be okay, listening to the partners tell me how well Sean had settled in at work singing his praises.

I didn't know that I was already pregnant with my son. I was on the pill, and after a brief discussion about having more children Sean had made it very clear that he didn't want anymore. I felt a bit queasy at times, and suffered from vertigo, fell asleep early in the evenings but had no other signs until my new bundle kicked me hard to announce his presence. I emailed Sean at work to tell him we needed to talk and then left for an early lunch break that consisted of a trip to the chemist and then a visit to the ladies room. It was a positive, and I was four months pregnant.

Things definitely did not go to plan from there, two weeks later Sean was made redundant again, or so he told me. It caused friction as I was outraged that they could lie to me, telling me how fabulous his future was at their company only a few months previously to be leaving a family without an income after they find out there's a new addition on the way. He was mostly silent while I raged on about the injustice of the world. I phoned the car finance company and told them to collect the car as I could no longer afford the repayments. She tried to convince me that it was a mistake, I should simply stop paying the monthly instalments which would lead to a default on the agreement, the car would be repossessed and no further action would be taken. With hormones running riot within my system I told her through sobs that I hadn't held off the bailiffs for the last year to have my credit history scored with a repossession now and that I would end the contract legally in the correct way. The car was collected and a bill for £2000 landed through the letterbox as a settlement figure for early termination of the agreement. I should have defaulted, she was right.

The unexplained absences began to increase again, and I found myself not caring where he was. I wanted to go home, I wanted my mum. I even packed my bag and bundled my sleepy daughter in the car one evening. I drove to the top of the hill overlooking Portsmouth and wondered what I was doing with my life. I had a husband who clearly didn't want to be home, and definitely didn't want this baby. He had no job for the third time since we'd been together and money seemed to pass through our fingers faster than air. I already loved the baby growing inside my belly, but there was no way I wanted to bring him into a world where he wasn't wanted. At least if I went home, we would all be loved and accepted.

I waited for my mobile to ring, the one my work supplied, but it didn't. I knew that I had just enough money left in the bank to fill the car up with petrol to take me home to my mum. All I needed to do was phone her to tell her I needed to come home. That seemed like an impossible task, to admit defeat, to acknowledge how I had failed as a wife. I went back to the flat, he was in bed sound asleep and snoring. It was like he had been waiting for me to leave him and that it was what he wanted. I was filled with hurt and shame, what was so wrong with me that my husband didn't want to be with me. I asked him why he didn't phone, I tried to tell him I wanted to feel the passion, wanted to know he cared, why he couldn't even bring himself to ask me to come back. He simply told me that he thought I'd made up my mind.

I discreetly nurtured my growing baby, I loved him with all my strength and willed him to feel it. I tried not to talk about him with Sean, just to act like a new baby in our life would be as normal as the day before. He didn't speak about our plans for the future, or share his vision of what life for us would become. Instead, he bought himself a brand new computer with the last of his severance pay and proceeded to clock up a large phone bill with his visits to the internet. I let him do it, as it gave me time to prepare for the changes that were about to happen. In my mind, if he was on the internet he was looking at pornography, and if that meant he wasn't out on the streets spending our money on prostitutes then all the better for my children. It was the only explanation I could find for his secrecy and time spent away at night. I'd even found a driving offence ticket that he'd tried to hide from me, scrunched up in the corner of a shelf, why hadn't he told me? I was becoming more and more convinced that prostitutes were the explanation for everything. It didn't bother me, I was too busy making my baby and daughter feel loved to care what he got up to. Our sex life was not explosive, always had been, I didn't instigate or welcome any attention, our marriage was a sham.

We moved again, Sean declared us as being homeless to ensure we'd get homed with the council, he said there was no way I could manage in the flat with two small children. As normal, I let him have the control. We went to view our one and only offer of accommodation. I cried. My belly was as big as a whale and my daughter was in my arms, clinging to me for reassurance, as we walked around the empty shell that was so much like the flat I had hated in Oxford. This time we were on the top floor, the eleventh floor. I fumbled for words, trying to make myself understood, this wasn't a place for children to thrive. I was distraught and defeated, the woman from the council looked at me with not an ounce of pity or soul and calmly said 'well if you're going to be homeless this will be like a palace compared to living nowhere'.

Sean promised me he'd make it feel like home and that I wasn't to worry about a thing. I had no choice but to leave it all up to him.

CHAPTER 22: DARKEST BEFORE THE DAWN

If Zéphirine thought birth was painful with Allison, it was absolutely nothing compared to the pain that woke her up at 2:00 am. After two hours of painful contractions, she begged Marc to drive her to the hospital. By the time they got there, the pain was so excruciating that she could barely walk. Why on Earth had she let Pierrette and Kira convince her to give birth naturally instead of another caesarean?

Because they had health insurance this time around, Zéphirine had determined that they weren't repeating the experience of her first pregnancy. She planned to have a water birth this time around. She also wanted to have her own room at the hospital, with a private bathroom.

The nurses guided Zéphirine towards what looked like a huge spa bath. Kira was there too to massage Zéphirine's back with some special oils they had bought together, supposedly to help with the pain. It did not help.

The pain was intense! So intense, in fact, that Zéphirine couldn't even talk. When she wasn't screaming in agony, she lay there silently cursing those around her.

Marc, obviously anxious, was pacing around anywhere the hospital staff would let him go. He would wander out of the room only to come right back in a few minutes later.

"Are you okay honey?" he asked.

"Do I look fine to you?" Zéphirine replied in her mind. Why

couldn't he go and watch porn or something! As if he could not see the pain she was in, he asked for Nicole's phone number who was looking after Allison. Surely he could ask Kira. Surely it was written somewhere. But he was insistent and obviously couldn't see a better way to get the number.

"5!!!!" Zéphirine yelled.

"4!!!!!"

"3!!!" Talking was excruciating. She surprised herself that she could even recall the phone number. She was also pissed off that Marc was making her say it. It was a shame her hands were firmly attached to the edge of the bathtub as she imagined them around his throat right then. Why on earth did she wanted another child for? Was this pain ever going to end?

The only position she could handle the pain was to sit on her knees. But the doctor couldn't monitor the baby's heart so he decided it was best to get Zéphirine out of the bath. The nurses guided her on the floor on all four as it was still the only way she could handle the pain, on a bean bag.

Zéphirine wondered again why she had listened to anyone to go for a natural birth and wished she had gone with a caesarean birth. *"Where is the gas? Where is the needle, drugs even? Please give me anything, I'll take it."* But no words were coming out of her mouth. She was begging for people milling around to read her mind, dammit! Surely they could see she was in pain, no?

Keeping a dialogue with herself in her mind, believe it or not, actually helped. If she had never even bothered to wonder about childbirth, again, this time she had no choice. Zéphirine couldn't quite fathom how a baby would actually come out from down there. Being in pain was one thing, but a baby coming out was an entirely different thing. She was being asked to push in between contractions and so she was following orders still wondering how this was even possible and begging for it to end.

Then she knew. Just like that, the baby was finally ready to come out.

"Pierrette! He is coming!" she was able to say.

"No, he is not!" she replied.

Seriously? Pierrette chose that time to doubt Zéphirine? As if she would not know when her own son was ready for this world? He was! And so his head popped out just like that. It was the most incredible thing! His head was out. But Zéphirine couldn't feel anything anymore. She internally started to panic. The contractions stopped, there was no pain anymore. She was exhausted and wondered how the hell she was going to get the baby out completely. Until she felt the urge to push again and that was it, Adrian was born. It only took four hours and two big pushes. Zéphirine was amazed. She did it!

The delivery was so excruciatingly painful that Zéphirine never wanted to go through that again. Nevertheless, she was glad to have given birth naturally. It was truly the most amazing experience she ever had; one that you must go through to fully understand it. Even years later, she would still remember it as if it happened the day before. She did it without gas and drugs, she was so proud.

She successfully breastfed Adrian and enjoyed it. It didn't hurt like it had with Allison. Adrian knew how to suck a nipple, Allison didn't! But as big as her breasts were, and she had put as much weight on as with her first pregnancy, she still didn't have enough milk. But breastfeeding was a nice experience this time around. She appreciated not having to get up in the middle of the night to get a bottle. Zéphirine's sister explained how her husband would get up in the middle of the night to make the bottle and then even change the baby:

"Are you serious? Marc can't even change a nappy unless it's just pee and I still have to beg him to do it!"

Marc was married to his work. Bringing another child in this world did not improve the relationship whatsoever between Marc and Zéphirine. Not that children are supposed to be a miracle cure for a troubled marriage. He was always at work, they were always broke, and Marc was the most careless human being walking this Earth. The day she came out of the hospital, they had to move out from their house on the canal. She hadn't even seen their new home as it all happened while she was in hospital. And there was still some, no, not some, all of the packing left to do!

Kira and Nicole came to help. Surprisingly, even some of Marc's family came to help too, but Zéphirine knew that it was mainly because of the baby she just had. She would later find out that it would be the only time her in-laws would care for the children's welfare. Pierrette did show a little bit of compassion for Zéphirine by fussing over her carrying anything heavy so shortly after giving birth, but she had no choice. This needed to get done. They had to be out of this house.

Kira was also moving out. She and her husband had decided to put their house on the market and to rent for a while until they found a block of land to buy. Zéphirine and Kira had gone house hunting together before she gave birth. It was heart-breaking as they were no longer going to be neighbours. It was only a 40 minutes' drive but it would never be the same. There wouldn't be any dropping by for sugar or a video. No more chatting and sipping wine seated at the table outside overlooking the canal.

Marc's choice of housing was as good as it can be to suit his taste. It was out of town, which worried Zéphirine a little bit, but the house, even though it was old, was very spacious. It had a fireplace, a pool, a tennis court, and overlooking a golf course. It didn't take long to get used to it. The kids were not able to enjoy the pool much because it was winter, and with Mt Coolum looming over the house, it was humid and colder than usual. The water in the pool never seemed to get warmer even though it was sunny most of the time. But everyone seemed to enjoy their new home.

Zéphirine loved the fireplace. Although they wouldn't have cold winters in this part of Australia, it was still a comfort she enjoyed from her time in France and in the UK. Zéphirine kept it running all winter. It was like bringing a piece of her old home with her. After six months, unfortunately the owner decided to move back into the house so they had to move again. This was the part Zéphirine hated about Australia. Unless you bought your own home, there was never any guarantee you would stay more than six months to one year in a house. The initial lease was six months, kind of a trial period then you would get one-year lease. They did well with the house on the canal as they stayed there nearly three and half years, the longest they would ever stay in one home.

The house was out of town and a bit far from everyone, but they had getting accustomed to the area which had magnificent beaches. So they looked for a house in the same area. Zéphirine did the house hunting this time since they now had two cars. The only requirement was the house had to have four bedrooms and a pool. But a rental with a pool in a nice area was not easy to find. Unless you wanted a mansion at an exorbitant price, and there was plenty of those around. The only suitable house she found had no pool. But as she got talking to the owner directly, he agreed on raising the rent to build a pool. It was perfect!

Zéphirine's parents decided to come to Australia for Adrian's first birthday. They didn't like how Marc was raising the children of course. He was too soft, too lenient with everything, and they couldn't stand that. Every time they stopped at a petrol station Allison would cry for a drink and Marc would run to buy her one – a behaviour not acceptable for Zéphirine's parents. Zéphirine spent her time hovering over her children and trying to keep peace, as she didn't trust her mother. She worried her mother would try to reprimand them with her loose hand, something Zéphirine would not tolerate from her, and she knew her mother's hand was itching too often.

If Zéphirine's parents didn't like how Marc was raising the children, they hated even more how he was running his business. Marc was talented and he excelled in his trade but keeping the business afloat was a different story. Zéphirine was doing the accounts but she had no say over anything. For a start, all their employees were overpaid and jobs were under-priced. There was never enough money to pay the expenses such as leases or taxes. Zéphirine had already taken the fall with his first business by going bankrupt in order to be able to start all over again.

Her parents knew what they were talking about since they were themselves successful business owners and financially stable, though a few inheritances had also helped. They both did work hard. Zéphirine's mother hated spending money. Her father was careful but liked to indulge from time to time and he did it so well. He was a very sociable person and would be out at events quite a lot. Her father, whom also enjoyed getting drunk at parties, would also enjoy many bottles of champagne to the dismay of her mother. These were vivid memories Zéphirine had from her childhood.

But they knew how to conduct business and you could not fault them on that. And Zéphirine was grateful for them to be spending time with Marc trying to teach him some basics. They even helped him financially. Well, technically it was Zéphirine's money; a $10,000 savings account she accidentally found out about when she went back to France for her visa. She was allowed to cash it in at 18 but her parents only decided to give it to her now. But at the root of it all, money was never the issue why Marc couldn't run a successful business.

Zéphirine and her mother were busy in the kitchen preparing

lunch for Adrian's birthday party. It was a French affair and Zéphirine was glad her mother was there to help. There was a lot of expectations and standards when cooking for her husband's family which she never quite met. Lunch was a full four-meal course: an entrée, main meal, cheese plate and dessert accompanied by the proper wines. If Zéphirine excelled at baking, cooking anything else was still not her forte. And the more Marc criticised her cooking skills the less she felt like trying to do anything better.

After sweating and fretting in the kitchen all morning, it was time for them to get ready before the guests arrived. Zéphirine opted to wear a skirt her mother had given her. It was a light blue skirt, the same colour as the sky, and it fluttered around her ankles. Printed on the skirt were large white flowers. Her mother still knew exactly what she would wear, what would suit her and she was spot on with sizes too. Zéphirine loved that skirt and she had only worn it once before that day.

"Go and change. I don't want you to wear that skirt." Marc ordered Zéphirine.

"Why?" she asked.

"It is see-through." he replied.

Her mother just laughed.

"It is not." Zéphirine told him.

"I want you to remove that skirt now!" he insisted.

"Don't you even dare!" Zéphirine's mother stepped in. "Your father would not let me wear anything that would be inappropriate! This is just ridiculous!"

Zéphirine was torn. Does she listen to her mother or her husband? She loved that skirt! Zéphirine was particular with her clothes. She loved simple but classy clothes. And once she loved a piece she would keep it for life, or for as long as she could. And that skirt suited her so well she thought.

Marc was a jealous man, Zéphirine knew that, but he had never commented on her clothes before. Though she now rarely wore mini-skirts, she mostly hid her body with maxi skirts. Her style had change over the years. Not only because there were not many shops around there which had nice clothes, but she outgrown the mini-skirt style. Although she wasn't that old, she didn't feel young either. At 26, she was married to a man who acted like a child, she was a mother of two, a step-mother of two, and surrounded by

166

bunch of very demanding in-laws. How could she not feel old?

She looked at herself in the mirror and decided to stick with the skirt. When Marc saw her coming out of the room, he watched her with an annoyed look. Actually, Marc was pissed off. If her parents hadn't been there, he wouldn't have given her a choice. He gave them a hard look and decided to back off. But he wasn't happy.

Kira arrived with her two kids, her husband wasn't the social type either, well especially not with a whole bunch of French people. Giovanni and Dona showed up with their daughter. Nicole also joined them with her two kids. Those were the only people Marc had accepted in their circle and were allowed to mix up with his family. But it didn't mean he liked them.

As his family arrived, Marc barely acknowledged their presence. He refused to talk to anyone and just nodded at them. He was sitting at the far end of the table sipping his wine. Of course, this kind of attitude was not going unnoticed and raised questions. The whole situation unfolded so quickly Zéphirine was unprepared. Her parents were just acting as if nothing happened. If asked, she answered: "Marc is upset because he thinks the skirt I am wearing is see-through."

And now everyone was trying to figure out if Zéphirine's skirt was indeed transparent which got Marc even more pissed off. He stayed at the table eating and drinking, a few words here and there, but he wasn't going to get over it. He never got over it. Every time she wore that skirt, they would get into arguments. Her mother had even replaced the lining with a darker and denser material. He would not have it. In the end, it was just too much drama for just a skirt, so Zéphirine gave it away.

Marc and Zéphirine's relationship was over and had been for a long time. It was probably over the day he left France. But she was not a quitter. She was married and a mother of two. She was going to try and save her marriage! Where to start though? How do you do it? Zéphirine was far from an expert when it came to relationships!

She tried to get the spark going again by buying the latest *Tomb Raider* video game, hoping he would play with her, but he didn't care. Marc only came home to eat and sleep, and he would be lucky to even get sex as she would usually be asleep or pretending to be. And yes she also used the headache or her menstrual excuses, sex had become a chore and she avoided it like a disease.

The business was still doing poorly. They were making enough money to pay the wages but that was it. Until a French business man approached Marc for a possible partnership. The business man needed to invest in an Australian business for him to get a visa. After several meeting they signed a contract.

Zéphirine welcomed the idea, but she did not trust the guy. There was something about him. The same way she never liked Stefania's husband. And the feeling was mutual. She told Marc who kept reminding her it was just a business arrangement and the deal was going to make everything better. And so she believed him. Because in the end, all she ever wanted was for everything to be better and for them to be happy. Well, she also wanted to get rid of the debt collectors.

But debt collectors and overdrawn bank accounts was nothing compared to the bomb that one day was dropped on them: Marc's grand-father was diagnosed with cancer and had at most three months to live. It was a shock for the family and seeing him deteriorating every day was heart-breaking. Marc's grandfather was the pedestal of this family and he was like a father to Marc.

Marc and Zéphirine were barely talking to each other so she had no idea how he was feeling, though she knew he was distraught. She decided to let him come to her when he would need to talk. Somehow, she thought they still had that connection somewhere. How could she have known he had found another shoulder to cry?

Marc's grandfather was in the last stage of his cancer and got his one wish: the whole family was there and talking to each other. Even his daughter he had not seen in over ten years had flown from France to see him. Aiden, the spoil brat, was outstanding. The selfish boy Zéphirine knew was no longer selfish. He did everything he could for his great-grandfather including bathing him.

They were expecting him to just pass away at any time as there was nothing left of him. They all went to his bedside one by one, one last time. When Zéphirine held his hand, she was not even sure he knew who she was. She looked at him lying on his bed, withered; a hollow shell of the vibrant man that he once was. Marc's grandparents were the only people that had always been there for her and Marc. When everybody else used to say *'you live too far away for us to come and visit'*, they drove all the way to see them. And at their age, it was admirable. He passed away that night.

When they got back from the funeral, Marc and Zéphirine went outside and sit in silence smoking.

"I think we should separate." he said, although it sounded a little firmer than just a suggestion.

Even though it took Zéphirine by surprise, she knew he was right. Their lease was over, they had to move anyway and their relationship had not improved the least. It was not like she hadn't tried to make things work. They started to look for separate places.

CHAPTER 23: ALLANAH'S TRUTH

It took Sean a month to decorate the new flat. I kept telling him I was going to come with him as it was taking so long, plus I wanted to be a part of it. He told me it wasn't safe for the baby with all of the fumes and our daughter would be bored, so I was best to stay at home. I didn't believe him, there was no way it was taking that long to decorate and when he finally declared it ready for us to move in I lost all patience and confronted him directly. I told him I didn't believe him, that I thought he was seeing other women and that if it they were prostitutes I'd rather not know, but that I couldn't carry on with the lies, the blatant lies.

He left us at the new flat and drove to his Nan's. He didn't come home that night.

The next day his mum came to see me, she pretended to look around the new place with admiration, saying what a good job her wonderful son had done with the decorating, declaring the new stripy second hand sofa much better than the one my dad had given us. I disagreed with everything she had to say, I had no idea who had sat on the disgusting gaudy sofa before me, whether they'd smoked or taken drugs on the thing and I couldn't understand why Sean had insisted on having it replace the clean black one that had never been a problem before. As for the décor, bright yellow was fabulous to help light the hallway but orange wallpaper in the lounge? All I could offer was polite nods and a sharp bite of the tongue.

Finally, she cut to the chase. "I know he didn't come home last night, he's been with his Nan in tears. He doesn't know how to tell you that he's an addict. We all thought he was over it but apparently he's not."

My heart was thumping, there really was a problem, and it wasn't all in my imagination or any of my fault. My mind raced, an addict, he always seemed in complete control of his senses, he never smelt of alcohol after his extended trips to the shops, he really didn't seem to have ever taken drugs while we'd been together so I couldn't imagine what he was addicted to.

"He's addicted to fruit machines, he spends hours pouring money into them and can't walk away until he's lost everything."

It all fell into place with a loud click. His mum carried on talking to me, explaining how he'd had problems before but they thought it had all been sorted, how it wasn't her fault and she blamed his aunt for letting him play on the 2p machines when he was a child. I wasn't listening. How dare he, how dare he take my money and throw it away. That money was for our family, for my daughter, for the baby on his way. We lived on the edge of nothing just so that he could look at a machine with flashing lights and couldn't even face me himself.

I told her to tell him to come home, to stop being so childish and face his responsibilities, the baby would be here any day and he needed to be ready.

He came home, he got a new job, and started planning his life. He wanted to be a paramedic. It was the first time I'd seen any enthusiasm in him, I wholeheartedly encouraged it, and I thought everything would be ok.

It wasn't long before he was well on his way to achieving his dreams, he started working for the ambulance service and became an ambulance technician in no time. He was away for eight weeks and in that time I found my own place in the world. I engaged with the community, found out I was fab at helping to support other mums around me who were finding life just as hard as I was. I strived to help them succeed as parents, to enjoy their children and to never feel like they were alone. I began to prepare for going back to university to finish my degree and to finally train as a midwife.

Sean started drinking every night, if he wasn't on a night shift he'd drink at least four cans of lager. I started drinking too, why should he have all of the fun? The children were young and impressionable and I'm ashamed of how selfish I was in my behaviour then. I'd give them my all during the day, but as soon as it was 7pm it was my time. That was also partly due to Sean's nature, he didn't want the children making noise in the evenings, so with every ounce of my being I willed them to be sleepy by 6:45pm. After dinner I'd make sure we all played together, I rolled around on the floor with them and let them clamber all over me to wear them out. I'd then enforce cuddles on the sofa so they'd know they were loved, and then led them to the safety of their room to sleep and dream of fluffy clouds while I drank a bottle of wine to forget my own pain.

For a while it seemed to be a functional way to live. I filled my days with children and volunteering, and the nights with alcohol that seemed to bring on laughter. We even mingled with our neighbour, propping our doors open and blocking the corridor we felt safe to take it in turns to provide the alcohol and entertainment. We'd be up until past midnight most of the time, talking about how weird everyone else in the world was and sharing our lives with that neighbour. Her son's father was her best friend who she loved hopelessly, but he would never commit to her. We saw a lot of him and his teenage son liked to dress up as an animal, apparently there was a group of them that met on the web to discuss fetishes and how best to hack Microsoft in equal measure.

That neighbour often gave me reason to worry about her and her child. I would often walk past in the day and hear her screaming at her toddler. If I was going to knock and ask her if she wanted coffee, it normally made me retreat and head out to the park instead. I tried not to judge her, there were more than the odd times that I found myself shouting at my own toddler, but this seemed different. She'd asked me if I would look after her son for a week so that I could teach him to talk, all he would do was sing along to music videos that she would play to him endlessly, all day, every day, but he would never speak to her, only scream in her face. That boy was diagnosed as being autistic, but I'll never know if he was born with the problem or if his circumstances dictated the outcome.

I was told by a neighbour that she had heard shouting coming from her flat with noise coming from the window, she was watching out of her own window when she saw something flying past. She looked at the ground and saw a pet rat crawling away on the ground, dragging its rear legs behind it, obviously wounded from its journey down eleven stories. There was no way that could have been her rat, she loved that animal although she had told me she was uncertain if she would be able to keep him for one reason or another. I asked her directly if she'd got rid of the rat, she freely admitted that she'd thrown him out of the window, apparently he'd been fighting with the female who had killed him, so not knowing what to do with the dead pet she lobbed it out of the window. I was scared at how close our lives were when she was so obviously unhinged.

The internet became a massive part of our lives as I tried to keep my front door closed of an evening. Sean and I found a chat room on Yahoo where we could spend the evening talking to other people and answering quiz questions without ever leaving the home, it was almost as good as a social life.

It wasn't long after my son was born that Sean started to imply his sexual needs were not being met. I didn't consider myself to be very experienced in the bedroom and the birth of my children had left me a little introverted especially where sex was concerned. Sean bought a web camera and set the computer up in our bedroom and began to explore other chat rooms in the evenings. He bought me gaudy underwear from Ann Summers, not the kind that made you feel sexy and feminine but the cheap seedy red laced all in one. When I was shy in wearing them he'd put them on instead. The more wine I drank the more normal it felt, even if the web cam was pointed in our direction. He befriended a lesbian couple in America and tried to make me agree to meet up with them. I stopped going into the bedroom at night and left him to his own devices on the computer.

He would chat to women in private and I'll never know the full extent of what went on, but the one evening when I logged on I forgot to change the settings and it was his account that logged on instead of mine. As soon as I was online Gretchen started chatting in my box, I also chatted with her so there was nothing unusual there, but the tone was very different than when she'd talk to me. I let her type away, asking if Sean was going to put his camera on for her tonight again and how much she'd missed him, and how she loved what they shared together and had been waiting for him to log on. I left the chat box open, I didn't reply to her, I think she realised her mistake and when Sean saw that I knew about what they had been doing he told me it wasn't cheating, internet sex was allowed.

If you can't beat them join them. I made him buy me my own computer, I found my own friends to chat with and I grew ever more determined to succeed in creating my own life and career.

That was when Sean told me we were moving again, leaving Portsmouth. He couldn't progress in his career here, he needed to move to a trust that would train him as a paramedic. That was the beginning of the end for us. Part of me wanted to believe that we could have a new start ourselves, cut out the drinking, live like a real family, find a way forwards with each other. We moved to Stoke, I made friends where we lived and gained some independence. Both of the children were now at school, so off to work I went. I found a job that let me nurture and acknowledged the skills I had to offer. I worked with paralysed children and became their arms and legs, I earned the best wage that I was likely to ever achieve without a formal qualification. Sean hated me working there, said I would never be able to handle the job emotionally or physically. I was determined to prove him wrong.

On the one hand I'd never had so much in life, we were finally living in a family three bedded house, with a garden that I grew strawberries in. I'd made friends where we lived, a whole heap of friends that I really treasured and loved immersing myself in their families. I'd cook for their children all of the time, loving the sound of our house being full. I revelled in the thought that I was liked and people wanted to spend time with me. Our families were really intertwined and I loved it, Sean seemed to like it too, even if he was stern with the children. His mantra was 'my house, my rules' but thankfully there didn't seem to be many times that he felt the need to flex his muscles.

When we were on our own in the evenings, we didn't speak or hold a conversation. I craved a way to engage with him and to find something that would make me feel like our marriage was worth holding on to. He always wanted the latest mod cons even if we didn't have the money to pay for them, we had a ridiculously sized TV in the front room courtesy of the catalogue. As soon as the PlayStation 3 was released he had to have it with a complete set of games. We hadn't even been away on a family holiday together but it was okay to thrift everything we had away on things that I simply didn't see the attraction in. In fact, I hated that machine, I became convinced that the PlayStation had been conceived by a Divorce Lawyer, he spent so much time staring at the TV and pretending to evade the orcs that I could have been sat naked next to him and he would never have noticed.

You can guess what I did to fill my evenings, the old friend, my bottle that soon became two, of wine. We were in a bad spiral, we would drink to escape each other, to pretend everything was okay and to great excess. Whatever we bought we would drink as fast as possible, and if it was before 10pm I'd stumble across the road, desperately trying to seem sober and sensible, and buy another bottle of wine for me and four lagers for him. To end the evening, he would more often than not order a kebab to be delivered, we must have been their best customers, and that was after our family evening meal. The whole time my cherubs were tucked up safely in their beds dreaming the innocent sleep.

The computer habit escalated too, our cupboard under the stairs was converted into an internet chat room. We had a computer each, again technology we couldn't afford, complete with webcams and swivel chairs.

I tried to tell Sean that I was unhappy with our marriage, that things needed to change, that it was unfair to carry on feeling this empty when life should have been full of vitality. He sent me back to the doctors. I started taking the tablets again, except this time I knew it wasn't me. I was certain that it wasn't wrong to want to feel loved, to want more than an alcoholic existence to survive life. His internet explorations went well beyond my comfort zone, he asked me to look at pictures with him, lady boys from Thailand. I told him I didn't like it.

The day that my mind was finally closed to him forever was the day he came downstairs wearing my clothes, my favourite bohemian gypsy skirt with the sequins on, my white gypsy summer top and I could see he had my favourite black balconette bra on underneath. It was the only bra that I had ever found that fit me, my boobs are so small it's difficult to find something that doesn't mock me. He was not a trim man; he was ruining my clothes. What came next was even more disturbing.

"What do you think? Am I sexy? I want you to fuck me and tell me what a naughty girl I am."

I opened another bottle of wine, I was absolutely mortified. I needed to find a way out.

CHAPTER 24: MÉNAGE À TROIS

Zéphirine signed the lease for a house around the corner from theirs. Moving to a house so close was not any easier. The amount of work was still the same, even though there was not much distance to travel back and forth between the two houses. Marc was careless as usual, letting her handle everything. She no longer had a car because the finance had repossessed her Ford Explorer when she went bankrupt.

Marc relied on her for packing the whole house, as calling a moving company was out of the equation. Marc didn't care. Work was always more important even when it didn't seem to bring any income. And he was more careless than usual as they were now going separate ways.

Zéphirine was packing her desk. It was her favourite corner, her solace. The desk was a massive corner piece with a hutch positioned so she had privacy for the lack of having a room for it. She looked at her hand. Her wedding ring was hurting. *Swollen fingers, must be stress* she thought as she removed the ring and put it on one of the shelves. It was a never ending task putting everything they owned in boxes. And then would come the cleaning, she was not looking forward to that part either.

The landlord was furious because they weren't moved out in time and who could blame him? But that did not grant him the right to insult Zéphirine in the middle of the street for everyone to hear! Zéphirine called Marc crying. She was upset. Within 30 minutes, he was at the house with one of his employees to help out and finish the move. He had a few words with the landlord and they were now acting like best mates! Who cared that the prick had insulted his wife, right?!

At this point, she resented Marc more than ever. Zéphirine had tried everything humanly possible to save her marriage. She accepted everything that he and his family threw at her which sometimes or most of the times weren't in line with her moralities. But she took it all no matter what. Right now though, she couldn't wait for him to be out of her life which would take a little while longer as he was still looking for a place.

The two weeks Marc had to spend in HER house until his new home was ready, all they did was arguing. It reminded her of her parents. Was it what marriage was all about? Arguing all the time and being unhappy? She wished she had given it more thought before getting married. But thinking before acting was not in Zéphirine's DNA. And it was too late now. Regrets were a waste of time and she could only move forward now.

When Marc finally moved out of her house, Zéphirine was so relieved. She resented him. She was angry at him! He would pick up the kids on the weekends and they wouldn't say a word to each other.

Zéphirine watched his ex-wife over the years arguing and blackmailing Marc with the children like most divorcees do. Not that she could blame her, she had plenty of reasons. But she didn't want to do that with Marc. And knowing how he was with money, she wasn't expecting much on the financial side either. So she just let him pick up the kids whenever he felt like it and the kids could go whenever they felt like it. Marc picked them up every Friday night to Sunday night without fail with the occasional pick up on Saturday morning instead because he had to work.

The first two weeks they were apart, Zéphirine didn't have time to give her new life much thoughts. She was simply too busy unpacking, organizing, taking care of the children, and arranging the new house. Once everything had settled down, she felt more at ease. Slowly, but surely, she and Marc started to talk to each other again like civilized people. They got along so well that they started dating each other again. He would sometimes spend the night at her place but would leave before the children got up and whenever he had the kids she would sneak in to his place after he called to let her know the kids had fallen asleep. She would leave before they got up. It was fun and exciting! It gave a new meaning to their marriage.

Marc loved his apartment and had become a little obsessive about keeping it clean. Usually he expected Zéphirine to keep the house spotless and Marc was such an untidy person it made her job much harder. Marc never cleaned up after himself. You could trail him through the house. He would cut a piece of cheese and a slice of bread on the bench, breadcrumbs everywhere. He would make a tea, even though the bin was an arm extension away, the tea bag would remain on the bench. He sat down on the couch to watch TV, removed his socks and left them right there on the floor. When going for a shower, he left his clothes on the floor. Zéphirine bought a laundry basket and placed it next to the shower. But that was too much work for Marc to lift the cover so let's put the clothes on top of it!

But what had annoyed Zéphirine the most over the years was the smoking weed in the house. She had accepted the fact he was smoking but did not want it around the children so smoking weed in the house was off limit. They had agreed to it. But Marc would still smoke, in the toilets. Every couple of days Zéphirine would find a stash of weed and flush it and throw the bong in the bin. He would argue and she would remind him of their agreement: no smoking weed in the house.

Marc spent most of his time at the factory so the few hours he spent home he could refrain himself from smoking weed, Zéphirine thought. They would argue about it over and over. She would explain her point of view over and over. He would agree over and over. And then he would again smoke in the toilets. So tough luck. She gave him plenty of warnings. Weed found in the house get flush down the toilets. But that never stopped him from smoking.

Now that Marc had to feed the kids when they were staying at his place, he realised the cost of living was expensive amongst other things. Kids were expensive and hard work! As a father of four, it was a bit ironic he only realised it now.

"I don't know how you do it. I bought Adrian the drinks he wanted and when we got home he said he didn't want them anymore! And food is so expensive!" he said.

"Wait until you have all 4 of them under your roof." Zéphirine told him laughing.

Even though they had separate lives, Marc was still jealous and she wasn't allowed to see anyone. Not that she intended to, it didn't even cross her mind. And how could she? Marc was always on the phone, at her house, or she was always at his apartment. She was also working at the factory until he found himself a new secretary. Basically Marc and Zéphirine were still a couple, they just didn't live together. And it seemed to work fine.

When Zéphirine stopped working at the factory, she was still dropping by to check up on the office, or simply to say hi and have a quick coffee with Marc.

"By the way, I forgot to tell you I have a friend who is going to stay at my place for a while." Marc said.

Zéphirine knew her husband well. So she immediately sensed there was more to the story. For a start, the friend had to be a female otherwise he wouldn't have said anything or would have mentioned a name in the sentence. And the friend was probably someone she knew. But she let it played out because that was how Marc's mind worked.

"Awesome! And I care why?" Zéphirine asked innocently.

"My friend is a woman." he shrugged.

She knew it!

"Do I know her?"

"Yvonne."

Zéphirine had never met Yvonne Cédolin. She was Marc's ex-girlfriend from when he was seventeen and living in New Caledonia. Zéphirine had heard stories from Marc, his grandmother, his auntie Pierrette and his ex-wife.

"He had all these beautiful women at his feet and he chose her? No way! She did something to him, a spell as they often do over there." said his grandmother. She was referring to a love spell: a woman would take her menstrual blood and use a few drops in a drink to make a man fall in love with her. There was more to it but that was the gist of it and Zéphirine didn't want to know more.

"My mother sent Marc from Australia saying he had to be with his father. The truth is: she didn't want him to be with Yvonne." said Pierrette.

"She came to our house once. I was pregnant with Aiden. I pretended I had to go to the shops but instead I hid by the window and listened to what they were saying. She told him she knew she could not have him – since he was a married man, obviously - but just wanted him to give her a child! Seriously? I was six months pregnant with our son! The first thing she would have noticed was my big belly! That woman is crazy!" said Stefania.

Zéphirine also recalled when they were living in the house on the canal, Marc came home and said:

"Guess who called me today?"

"I don't know, who?"

"Yvonne! She's in Sydney. She explained her frequent travels to Australia because of her job so my auntie gave her my number."

"Well, you can always invite her here if you want to catch up with her." Zéphirine did not see any threats at the time about an ex-girlfriend traveling to Australia.

Call her naïve, but Zéphirine still didn't see Yvonne as a threat to her. The way Marc had humiliated Yvonne back in the days, she did not think the woman would try to get back with him even though it happened twenty years ago! Zéphirine expected Marc to go and sleep with other women because she believed it was his nature to do so but she could not see it happening with Yvonne.

When Zéphirine implied as a joke Yvonne might try to seduce him he said "no way" with a disgusted gesture.

"Come on, even if she comes out in some sexy lingerie?" she joked.

"There is nothing sexy about that woman." Case closed.

That was enough for Zéphirine to conclude she was not a threat. But no one else saw it her way. Besides, Marc and Zéphirine were spending lots of time together. They were getting along so well like they had never been before since they had settled in Australia.

Dr. Norton had been more of a therapist and friend over the years to Zéphirine. She was seeing him on a regular basis and felt he kept her sane. He knew every inch of her body being her doctor since she had come back to Australia pregnant. He'd also seen her in her every mood and knew every details about her life with Marc.

"Come on Zéphirine! A woman in a man's apartment? Don't be a fool!" Dr. Norton snorted at her. "Look, I love my cousin. But a woman in his apartment? It does not matter who she is, fat or ugly... he is sleeping with her!" said Kelsey when Zéphirine called her for an opinion about the situation.

Was she the only one who had faith in Marc? Stefania took her side. She couldn'tt see it happening either. She knew Yvonne and she knew how Marc felt about her.

But when Marc had informed Zéphirine about Yvonne's stay, she was not expecting her to be there so soon. He had not told her when she was coming, just that she was coming. So when the next day Zéphirine tried him on his landline because she could not reach him on his mobile, she got a shock when a woman answered! She hung up without saying a word. Zéphirine knew who had answered the phone.

"She is already there? That is sneaky." she thought. But Zéphirine still trusted Marc and thought nothing more of it.

****

On that weekend Marc was due to have all his kids. Zéphirine drove to Brisbane to pick them up on Friday night. Marc would bring them back. On Sunday night, Stefania called Zéphirine.

"They should be at your place in an hour. It was a mad house here." said Stefania.

"And? Did you talk to her?"

"I invited them for coffee. She was polite to me. I was chatting with Marc most of the time and I knew she was staring at me, but it didn't bother me. She told Marc to call you to let you know when the kids would be home. So I told her not to worry, Zéphirine knows the kids are in safe hands with me."

"What do you think? Is there something going on between the two?"

"Nah! No sparks! Do not worry, there is nothing going on, they are just friends. Or if there was anything between them that would make them the best actors ever!"

Stefania and Zéphirine had their differences. They had gone through ups and downs along the years but they remained friends to the surprise of many, the family especially.

"How can you be friend with your husband's ex-wife?" people often asked Zéphirine.

Being friends made life easier for everyone and most importantly the kids. Both women knew Marc well and they both knew how crazy his family could be. Sticking together was the best way to go. And when they needed each other, one was always there for the other.

If Zéphirine had any doubt, there were gone now. Life resumed. And a few days later nothing unusual had happened. The phone rang. Zéphirine picked up.

"I have to talk to you." said Marc.

"Yes, sure. When?" she asked.

"I'll come over for lunch tomorrow."

Marc's tone of voice was cold; something was wrong. "There's no need to speculate." Kira said, trying to reassure Zéphirine. "You'll just have to wait and see." But Zéphirine knew that something was not right.

"Can't make it for lunch. I'll pick up the kids from school and we can talk then." he told her the next day on the phone. Once again, Marc's tone of voice was not right.

The kids were over excited to have their father around.

"Can you make some coffee?" he asked Zéphirine. Her stomach contracted at his tone and the look on his face.

She nodded and walked to the kitchen to prepare coffee. She was observing him while doing so. He was settling the kids in front of the TV then headed outside. Zéphirine waited for the coffee to finish, poured two cups then headed outside too. She lit a smoke hoping it would calm her down. Marc looked stern, and when Zéphirine met his gaze, he looked down to his cup of coffee. He took a drag of his cigarette, watched the smoke escape from his mouth and said, "It's over between us."

Marc's revelation was met with a stunned silent.

"Did you sleep with her?" Zéphirine asked with a shaky voice.

"Yes." he replied.

She closed her eyes for a moment trying not to be sick imagining her husband with that woman.

"I want you out of my house. Now." Zéphirine managed to say in a calm voice.

"We can talk about this."

"There is nothing to say. Just go!" she yelled.

"I don't want to hurt you. I had to be honest with you. I respect you."

The word 'respect' kept echoing through her head, over and over. She snapped back to the present. Zéphirine hated swear words but right now, she could not care less about being polite.

"Get the fuck out of my house!" She suddenly exploded. "How fucking dare you, you fucking piece of shit?" Zéphirine was now screaming and pushing him out to the door. Part of her wanted to kick him.

The yelling alarmed the children who were now between both parents, confused, crying wondering what was happening. Zéphirine was trying to get them back inside the house while pushing Marc away and ordering him to leave them alone at once. But the children did not what to let go of their father and hanging to his legs, in tears!

"Fine, take your kids and go away! Fuck you and go to hell Marc!" Zéphirine implored. It was more than she could handle. She needed time to think. She needed to retreat. She needed... fuck! Well, she didn't know what she needed. How could he do that to her and with the kids around?

She locked the door behind them and walked to her bedroom thinking about what just happened. Zéphirine perched at the edge of her bed and looked at herself in the mirror. She wondered why she hadn't seen this coming. Or maybe she knew but didn't want to see the truth. She sank to the carpet and started crying uncontrollably. After all she did for that man, to maintain their marriage, the sacrifices. And she thought they were back on track, that they would be happy when all along he was maintaining a relationship and having sex with his ex-girlfriend and her!

****

For three days straight she cried, smoked too many cigarettes and drank too much coffee. Loud music playing, it was a wonder the neighbours had not complained. But she didn't care. She replayed the past couple of months. She remembered the few days here and there he disappeared and stayed off grid. He gave no explanations for those absences. When he was not sleeping with her, he was sleeping with his ex-girlfriend. She felt worthless and degraded. She was twenty-nine and she had failed again. She looked back and tried to understand where she had gone wrong. She did everything she could to save her marriage. What the hell was she supposed to do now?

Kira and Dona had dropped by trying to comfort her, trying to feed her to no avail. She was skin and bone and inconsolable. But they also had lives and family to look after. And Zéphirine wanted to be alone. She suddenly felt completely exhausted. It was as if all life was draining out of her. She reached for the dresser and pulled out her sleeping pills. She stumbled wearily to the couch in the living room. There was nothing she could accomplish now. She picked up the bottle of vodka and drank from it as she swallowed a tablet, then another one, until she finished them all and the bottle.

Zéphirine flung herself down upon the couch, resting her head against one of the pillows, slowly closing her eyes. She was drifting off when the phone rang. She scrambled to reach the cordless phone on the coffee table and heard a voice when she mechanically picked up.

"Zéphirine? Hello? Are you there?" Kira asked. Zéphirine tried to speak but found she had no voice. She had fallen into a deep sleep.

CHAPTER 25: ALLANAH LIVING THE LIE

I told no one about how I was feeling, not even my best friend. I spent all of my spare time with Vicki, she was an inspiration to me. She had two children the same as me and a home that was always full of love, even her crazy dog would try to love you. There were times when she was frazzled by it all, but I loved the way she was so selfless, always putting her family first. I knew she was a much better person than me. I'd first noticed her in the playground at school as I stood by myself nervously wondering if I would ever feel like a part of this community like I had back in Portsmouth. She seemed so confident and assured as she talked with a woman with short blonde hair and a multitude of children were constantly running up to them to ask questions or share something exciting while we waited for the bell to ring. I wanted to approach her, I wanted to be her friend, and she always crouched down to their level to speak to them, softly and carefully listening to what they had to say.

My daughter became friends with her eldest and we did begin to speak to each other, she was actually in the same position as me, new to the area after having moved hundreds of miles in pursuit of a better life. This small town on the edge of the moors had offered us all a promise of richness of family life, a fulfilment of our aspirations. It turned out the other woman she spoke to in the playground was her sister, and I was the only person in the world who hadn't picked up on the family resemblance. To this day, I still don't think they look alike, but they are frequently mistaken for one another. She wasn't the female version of the pied piper either, her sister had four children too, which explained the constant flow of little voices.

At her daughter's birthday party, she appeared with a new addition to the family, Vicki had acquired a baby. Her family were there, all cooing over the baby and I couldn't work out how I'd failed to notice she was pregnant. At that time, we weren't firm friends yet, but we did speak in the playground every day and I was perplexed.

She asked me if I wanted a cuddle, of course I did, I never gave up the opportunity to have a baby snuggle and I realised how much I'd missed not being in the hub of activity like I had been back in Portsmouth. I still couldn't bring myself to ask why I hadn't noticed. I was too scared to look so ignorant, I'd spent a good 2 years working with pregnant mums and here was a baby in her arms.

A few weeks after the party Vicki and I were chatting in the playground. I started to notice that the baby had olive skin and curly black hair. There was also a swelling to her tummy that I could see now, and again I chided myself for having not ever noticed she was pregnant! I knew that there was no way her husband was the father of this baby, but there was no way this beautiful woman was ashamed of the baby or hiding her away from the world. I was too polite to comment or ask her about it, if she wanted to tell me she would I told myself. That morning she asked if I wanted to go back to her house for coffee if I was free, she was going stir crazy being cooped up with the baby all day. I was so excited to be invited that I probably came across as scarily eager. I couldn't believe she had asked me, I was so ready to be her friend, all I had ever seen from her was a display of love and kindness, I wanted to be more like her.

I was so excited to be sitting in her house, cuddling the baby, who by now was obviously not looking like either one of her parents, and revelling in the mess that was her home. There was washing everywhere, a hulking dog following you wherever you moved ready to lay his head in your lap as soon as you sat down, toys and crayons across the floor, and a general sense of chaos that lapped around the edges. My coffee was too strong, but I loved every drop of it, after 6 lonely months of being in a new town I finally had someone to talk to, who knew absolutely nothing about the horror that was my marriage.

Of course the baby wasn't theirs, it was her husband's cousin's, who was declared unfit to parent and already had a stream of children in care. Social Services had asked family members if they were willing and prepared to take on the baby or she'd be put up for adoption with strangers. Vicki's heart is kind and full of love, they took the baby and raised her as their own, even though her belly was swelling with a new baby of their own. Her life would never be simple, easy or quiet, but it was something I saw she needed, to be surrounded and to nurture. I completely understood that need, and Vicki seemed to provide the love and care that everyone needed so easily and effortlessly. She was unconditional, she would give without ever needing back. I needed back, I needed to be wanted, to be loved, to be valued, and to be worthwhile. She was a better person than me I had no doubt of that.

We became inseparable. I made her laugh and helped her to discover her mischievous side. She hardly ever drank so she was the best influence on me, an evening together would be tame with a bottle shared between us instead of my usual two to myself. She hated technology so we would watch TV together, a girly film or a gripping series that we'd like the look of, there was no seedy internet or lewd suggestion. She listened to what I had to say, whatever it was that was on my mind and she'd help me find a solution to my own thoughts. She made me feel like I was a good woman, a good mother, and a good friend. She would tell me how frazzled she was with the house and we'd plan an evening away from it all, a body shop party or a picnic in the park.

Even Sean seemed to enjoy my new friendship, he became friends with her husband, and her sister's husband, and the three families seemed immersed in good times. Sean was acting like a man in the day time, engaging and seemingly adjusted. We would arrange evening get-togethers as often as possible, if we were all together then the perversions couldn't come out to play. I think Sean knew what I was doing and he made friends of his own that he met in the school playground. He had a self-destruct button that he simply couldn't help but play with, if life was going well and as it should he'd have to find a way to break it. His new friends certainly weren't the bomb, but they were the fuse.

I hated his friends, there wasn't a redeeming feature that I did like about them, and I tried. I don't like feeling like a bad person, I try to see the best in every person I meet, try to find a reason why they'd behave badly or not to my expectations, but with this couple I just couldn't see a reason or find any part in my heart for them.

Ben and Shirley were dirty, in appearance and in their home, yes Vicki's house was chaos but it felt safe and clean. If I managed to make it to the kitchen in Ben and Shirley's house, my feet would stick to the patchy Lino on the floor where there was untold spillages and god knows what else. The kitchen sides were piled high with unwashed pots and pans, and there were crumbs and dried half eaten meals left on the side. It was even impossible to get to the kettle. Ben was disabled, an ex-squaddy, so Sean felt some kind of kinship with him instantly. He'd been discharged on medical grounds after falling onto his back during a training exercise. There was no official spinal injury but he'd been in chronic pain since the event and walked with the aid of a stick. The only thing that relieved his suffering was cannabis, to which he indulged himself freely and frequently throughout the day. He would unashamedly roll a spliff, light it, and smoke it in my presence, and if I was there so were my two impressionable and innocent young children. I hated the smell, I hated the thought, and I hated the fact that Sean was so comfortable about it all. If we were there in the evenings he'd always join in, which was fine by me, the perfect excuse to gather up my children and head home for the night.

The pair of them were self-proclaimed Wiccans, to which I would often personally dispute, but there was no previous experience in my life to compare them too. I suppose it's the eternal dreamer in me that wants to be a child of the Earth, a pagan spirit in touch with the Goddess and all of that mystical nonsense. My vision didn't include an angry man that waved his stick at the kids to threaten them every time they made noise and a smelly woman that had nylon purple dreads braided into her hair.

Shirley asked if my cherubs would help her with her hair the one evening, she said it was time for her to change her dreads, as she liked to call them. I wasn't really sure what this entailed and after she told me that her two loved doing it I thought I'd be making them miss out if I'd have said no or made up an excuse. I wasn't with them when them when they did it but the story my daughter told me afterwards made me cry. Shirley had head lice, they had to spend two hours unwrapping the join of each synthetic braid to untangle her nest so that she could wash her hair and get rid of the lice. I don't think I need to say that my two came home with their own critters in their hair. I chided myself constantly for being a snob, and Sean frequently told me the same, but Ben and Shirley never gave me any reason to think otherwise.

Sean worked shifts so when they said they were celebrating the summer solstice I eagerly tried to engage with them as he would be on a night shift, the free spirit in me was always on the lookout for new and liberating experiences. I was invited to theirs that evening for their solstice party. The party consisted of a tent in their back garden and a jar of scrumpy cider. I was thankful to my forethought of bringing a steady supply of lager as I willed the sun to rise as soon as it could to end my misery. As usual, the children were excited as they got on really well with their two girls, even though it was blatant they each had their own issues. The eldest wore nappies at night time, at the age of 12, and left the used ones lying all over the landing so every time I braved their bathroom I was confronted by used pull ups. My cherubs were there, playing in amongst that dirt and grime, I hated it to the point of despair. I swear that every minute I spent in that house took a whole year off of whatever time was left of my marriage.

One of my most awful memories of that place was when the children were all playing together upstairs. They got themselves into mischief by drawing on the walls, and all of them were certainly old enough to know better. The girls panicked and did what any child in fear would do, they blamed my son. Sean went wild, stormed up the stairs like the angry giant in Jack in the Beanstalk, definitely after blood. He was shouting, my son must have been terrified. He dragged him down the stairs and smacked him hard on the bottom.

"How you dare deface someone else's property, you are a guest here, what the hell did you think you were doing? I should beat you senseless for this, I've never been so angry."

My world crashed down around my ears, tiny shards of my soul scampered away in fear, anger and regret. My son was terrified, sobbing his heart out unable to even defend himself of the crime he'd been charged with. I flew off the disgusting excuse of a couch and swept my son up out of the reach of his dad. I yelled for our daughter to come downstairs straight away as I cradled my boy, grabbing my coat in my trembling hands and heading to the front door as fast as my shaking legs would carry me.

"I'm sorry my son drew on the wall, I'll send him over to clean it off at a more appropriate time, Sean stay as long as you like, you obviously need to chill out." and I never set foot inside that house again. How dare he! Just how dare he! That house was the single most unkempt place I had ever set foot in, how dare he punish our baby for doing what they had all been doing and in front of his friends. That girl pissed her own bed every single night because she was too lazy to get up and use the shit streaked toilet, but my son wasn't allowed to be goaded into childlike behaviour without being beaten?

It was official, I now hated Sean with every ounce of my being. There was no love, and now I was convinced that I had doomed my children to a life of hell too.

Sean still spent all of his spare time with his friends, getting stoned, getting drunk, and gambling. He chided me constantly for begrudging him the chance to be himself. I stopped caring. I did care that he sold all of my DVDs to Ben though, the CSI collection that was a present to me from Sean in a feeble attempt to find common ground and spend time together. His reasoning was that DVDs were obsolete, we needed blue ray now, and I didn't watch anything anyway, so he may as well get the cash for them while he could. How would Sean know what I did or didn't watch? I came home from work one day and they were simply gone.

When Sean told me he'd booked us a holiday I was excited, then of course, he had to invite Ben and Shirley to come with us, they deserved a break after all. Our relationship was dead, I knew it, I was very surprised that no one else could see it.

My two cherubs had loved going over there though, it gave them a freedom that they'd never experienced before. At the bottom of Ben and Shirley's garden, they had open access to a field that let them play unhindered for hours. I would excuse myself from staying at their house as often as I could, knowing Sean would be talking endlessly about games, Mafia Wars, Poker, and whatever else I couldn't bring myself to be enthusiastic about. We'd just purchased a puppy, a gorgeous slate blue border collie, my birthday present, and a consolation to try and hold our family together. Sean would stay in that smoke infested house while the children climbed trees, and I would let the puppy play in the field trying to train him and keeping a close eye on the children without them knowing about it. My dog was the best trained dog I'd ever known, perhaps I have Ben and Shirley to thank for that, I spent the whole of that summer letting him chase the Frisbee and coming back to me for a sausage treat when I let him off the lead.

That puppy healed our family a little. He brought us all back together and gave us something to love equally, to build memories and teach us all to laugh. It was about time we had an animal in the family that Sean could accept and love. This was our sixth attempt at a pet, and cats were a no go as far as I was concerned, one rejected ginger tabby and two dead kittens was enough for a lifetime. He insisted on a dog though, he tried rescuing first, one direct from someone's home in Derby, and again she was another thing who just wasn't there when I got home from work one day. He told me that it was obvious the dog had been abused in her previous home and he couldn't take the risk of having her in the house with the children. He told me he took her to the local shelter, where they'd told him they had met this particular dog before after a member of the public had raised a concern about its welfare. I believed him.

The next dog was a male mongrel pup, Neo, (my favourite film of the time was The Matrix), he lasted no more than a week, and what was a perfectly chirpy dog was returned to the shelter, a quivering defensive snarling wreck. Sean took an instant dislike to him, thought he was pathetic because he would submit to him too easily and so kept him locked in a cage whenever he was home. There was a truly nasty side to Sean that felt like it was ready to pounce, it would seep out of the edges and let you know it was there but never truly display itself long enough for you to capture it.

With my life starting to show itself as being successful Sean seemed to realise that he needed to step up. It was time to start paying attention to me before my wings grew too wide, after all there was no point in letting me soar high on my own. He bought himself a new motorbike, for once financially we seemed stable. My job doubled our household income and our rent was really low. I told him I wanted a car of my own, we'd always gone from one clapped out old banger to another, and it was always me that was driving it when it took its last breath. I wanted a toy to play with, if he had a bike then I was allowed fun too! He found an Escort Cabriolet, turquoise, and it worked its magic on me. It was a classic! A really big and heavy car to drive that made me feel king of the road, I could get behind the wheel and feel like I was having fun, and on those rare moments the sun shone the roof would be down and I was free, almost as free as the birds I would watch circling high above me on the thermals. I didn't care that it drank more fuel than a tank or that the roof leaked when it rained.

We brought my puppy home in that car. I wanted something to love, I wanted to prove to my children that we could have a pet in the family that would be all of the things I hoped for without the anger and hatred that had come before. I took charge, I found the puppy, I bought the puppy, I nurtured him, trained him, and kept him. The day we picked him up, we had the roof down and Sean said he would drive as I obviously had the pup in my arms. He was so tiny curled up on my lap hiding his head not understanding what was going on. I promised him I'd keep him safe, he seemed to understand as he looked in my eyes. Sean was distracted by me talking to the pup and promptly reversed my lovely car into a parked car behind him. It was a sickening crunch and the owner of the car heard it, he raced out of his house to confront Sean. I don't remember what happened. I was too angry; how can you reverse without looking behind you? He'd kill me if that was his bike, there goes my no claims bonus on the insurance, and how perfectly typical. Something had to happen to mar my day with my new pup.

I loved that dog like he was my own child. He represented my first victory over Sean. He tried to ruin our bond, tried to be angry with that dog, tried to take him to a field and leave him there, but I wouldn't allow it. I was finding my own voice, feeling the strength of my will and becoming powerful in my soul. If he could be that cruel to an animal, he could do the same to my children. I needed to find the strength to change my life and escape.

He sold my car, the insurance became too expensive on our renewal quote. I let him win that battle. It was time to learn which ones to fight.

CHAPTER 26: NICE

Marc was seventeen when he started to date Yvonne. He described her as nice, pure and simple. She was an innocent girl; the type you take home to meet your parents. She had long brown hair and a sweet smile that seemed to be infectious to those around her. Their favourite dates were grabbing some coffee at the local café and walking out under the stars. Every now and then, they would walk to the beach and just listen to the sounds of the city off in the distance mix with the sounds of the ocean waves lapping against the sand.

One night, Marc decided to take Yvonne to a club in Noumea. Yvonne, being out of her element, was anxious the entire night and finally made the excuse of having a headache to go home. She pleaded with Marc to take her home but he stubbornly refused; an obvious change in his personality due to the alcohol. Yvonne finally decided to hail a taxi and left. No sooner had she left when a swarm of girls began chatting with Marc. Angry that Yvonne left, he went home with one of the girls. Much to his surprise, the incident never got back to Yvonne. In small towns, word typically travels fast. This quickly became a common occurrence and Marc began regularly taking home random women from the clubs.

On his last night before leaving for Australia, he went out with Yvonne to their favourite café. One of the girls Marc had been hitting on at the club was there and struck up a conversation with Marc. Yvonne, confused as to how Marc knew her, began questioning him as to what was going on. That's when Marc's secret life was revealed. Yvonne left in tears and Marc left with the other girl. This would be the last time he saw her before he left the country for good.

Zéphirine woke up in the hospital bed feeling weak and groggy. What had happened? How did she get here? The last thing she remembered was laying down on the couch crying and...why had she been crying? She had been crying...because of...HIM.

It all came back to her in a rush; the revelation of his ex-girlfriend being back in his life, the fight, the kids crying, the three days of abuse she put herself through afterwards. It all came flooding back. She shut her eyes but all she saw was her husband with HER.

Zéphirine later found out that it was Kira that had called the ambulance to her house after she couldn't get a response from Zéphirine on the phone. Probably a good thing that she did. There's no telling how long she would have laid there before someone decided to check up on her. It took seven days for Zéphirine to regain her strength and feel ready to go back home. The doctors, wanting to ensure she was indeed all right, kept her for an additional day.

Marc and Zéphirine decided to work out their issues and give their marriage another try which did not impress Yvonne. And Marc didn't want to handle it. So when Yvonne faxed him a letter, Marc gave it to Zéphirine to read and deal with it. As she scrolled through the message, she could feel her face turn red and her fingers began to tremble. Zéphirine wrote her back:

'Dear Yvonne,

He did not humiliate you enough that you chose to come back into his life and believe all his lies. It goes to show how well you know the man. He liked you, yes, no doubt about that. And he never meant to hurt you, because yes we did talk about you in the early days we got together. The one thing he said to me though was that he was glad to never have given you a child, which at least was one thing he had done right. And not just because of you but because he has his hands full with four of them and could not deal with another one. But you wouldn't have a clue, would you?

To think you actually want to raise my children because you have deemed me an unfit mother made me laugh out loud. Who the hell are you that makes you the expert in motherhood or better than me even? Are you a mother? No. Oh, but because you are an auntie to ONE child that makes you the expert? Right... of course it does.

You dated Marc for a year or so when he was a teenager. Now you think you can tag along, change him, and make him a better man? How? His ex-wife and I have lived with the man for over ten years combined and bear his children, JUST four of them. We have endured his family, his temper, and many of his other less than savoury traits. We can honestly say we know the man pretty well. But you, what do you know exactly? Please go back to wherever you came from and stay away from us. Regards, Zéphirine.'

Zéphirine hit the send button on the fax machine and thought it would be the last time they would hear from that woman. But the next day, they got a response. Yvonne had sent the fax back with a note: *This is what I find coming back from the hospital.*

Zéphirine was deep in thoughts and smiling. Why send the fax back? Did she think Marc was unaware of the letter Zéphirine had written? *"Handle it"* had said Marc firmly to Zéphirine. And she considered replying to make her reel in her shoes. But Zéphirine thought the woman had suffered enough. Marc was the one who tricked her into coming back to him with his emotional blackmail. He hadn't meant to her hurt again and he truly never did. But his mind worked differently. He had to see it for himself that she was still in love with him and she was!

***

But Zéphirine and Marc were never meant to be. He had moved to Zéphirine's house but their relationship spiralled. His first born was on drugs. Marc decided the best way to help his son was to do drugs with him.

Town of Seaside, where they lived, was a particularly beautiful estate. There was a double garage on the back overlooking the beach, with a separate studio that was rented out. When the studio in the house next door became available, Marc decided to rent it for Aiden. He also decided to hire him at the factory and, as if that wasn't enough responsibility, he also hired Aiden's cousin who happened to be also a drug addict that ran away from home.

Christmas seemed to just sneak up on them. Zéphirine kept eyeing Adrian in the back who seemed on edge and glued to his mobile phone. Even though she had always supported Marc's first two kids and was always there for them, Zéphirine and Adrian barely got along enough to be in the same room. Zéphirine drove every weekend to pick them up. Every time they needed something, usually money, she would drive and bring it to Stefania. She was the one who found excuses every time Adrian would call to talk his father who wasn't home or didn't want to talk to his kids because he was too tired or too high. She never treated them any differently than she would for her own children.

Zéphirine was not big into the whole family reunion idea, especially with Marc's family, since they had separated. They had not cared about it. No one even bothered to come and visit, or even call, when she was in hospital. They did not even check on the kids. Kira was the one who made sure the kids were safe as she didn't know Yvonne from a bar of soap.

"Done it once, done it twice, and he might do it again, so just move on." Pierrette told Zéphirine when she found out about Yvonne. Since the grandfather had passed away, things had changed and Zéphirine no longer cared about them and made no attempt to be part of his family. She was not their blood after all.

As usual, per the French tradition, there was a big Christmas Eve celebration, with the largest table in the house loaded up with way too much food and piles of neatly wrapped presents underneath a gigantic tree.

It turns out Zéphirine was not the only one who wasn't in the Christmas spirit. Aiden had stayed at the table glued to the phone, barely talking to anyone the entire time they were there. Both Marc and Adrian had changed since the passing of their Grandfather, though no one ever mentioned him. Zéphirine knew something was not quite right with Aiden, but she just could not figure out what it was.

When midnight finally arrived and all the presents were opened, Marc motioned for them to leave. Aiden was more than eager to leave, which was very surprising, but not so surprising when she was told the reason.

Zéphirine was beside herself when she found out Aiden had left a friend, under aged, at the studio who might be overdosing. That was the reason behind the constant texting on his phone. Zéphirine was furious.

"Why on earth didn't you tell me about it? We should have checked up on the kid before we left! Can you imagine if that kid dies in there? What were you both thinking?" Zéphirine queried.

She tried to remain calm and kept her eyes on the road while scolded Aiden.

"*Salope!*" he told her, with a defiant look she could not ignore. Aiden spoke French fluently and he had just insulted her by calling her a slut. She took it ten time worse than if he had said it in English. French was her mother tongue after all. She indicated, parked the car on the side of the motorway, and got out of the car. There was no plan, she was upset and started to walk away.

Marc came after her.

"What the hell are you doing?"

"I'm not driving with your drugged out son in my car calling me names! Are you even going to tell him off for that?"

"Get back in the car!" Marc ordered her.

"Nope."

"Please, you are the only one sober and of age to drive."

"Then I'll drive you back to your family."

The family was not too impressed about their return. Only Zéphirine had been oblivious by the fact that Aiden was on drugs and it was obvious they didn't want to deal with the situation.

"You should calm down, go home, and sleep it off. It will be okay tomorrow." one of his aunties said.

"Marc, you should not let your son insult your wife. You cannot be your son's friend. You are his father and should be acting as such." said his uncle.

Everything revolved around Aiden. The business was in financial difficulties as usual. Marc got a $10,000 credit card which was supposed to be used for cash flow but instead he went and bought new furniture for his son's new apartment. They only spend about $6,000. And they could not go to the cheapest store of course. Were four leather chairs at $250 each really necessary?

Aiden and his cousin were not even working while getting a full-time wage. Since Zéphirine was running the office, she was trying to keep the workers satisfied. She didn't want them to find out that the son and cousin were getting paid the same amount as those who were experienced stonemasons and actually doing their job. It was a constant battle.

Zéphirine was paying for her groceries when her bank card got declined. She knew she had money. She picked up her mobile and dialled Marc's number.

"If you're going to empty our joint bank account, you should let me know!" Zéphirine told Marc angry.

"What the fuck are you talking about? I didn't use the account!" he replied.

"Well if you didn't use it, somebody did because my card just got declined for insufficient funds. And I know there was money in this account." she snapped at him.

She got a bank statement and saw that $500 had been withdrawn from their bank account over the past few days little by little until the last cent in Brisbane. Marc had not gone to Brisbane in at least a week as far as she knew. Zéphirine went to the bank to report the card stolen. She told the banker she suspected her step-son had stolen the card and asked them what she should do about it.

"You could report him. This is a crime though. Once you report him you cannot go back and it could affect his future." the banker explained.

"Okay, I'll talk to Aiden." said Marc, who was not convinced his son would do such a thing. However, nothing came from it. He admitted spending the money but did not apologise for his actions. Zéphirine just took out money out of his pay until it was repaid. And that was that.

Zéphirine finally had enough. Having to handle a deadbeat druggie for a husband was one thing, but then adding in a step-son and cousin was simply too much. Financially, the business was a disaster. His business partner left as soon as his visa was denied. There was simply nothing left for her. She had finally given up on Marc's family who obviously did not give a damn about them anyway.

Marc at least had his grandmother who was still attempting to make contact with him. Zéphirine, seeing how troubled Marc had been and knowing there was nothing she could do for him, begged him to go and see her. She was the only mother he had ever known. And so, after much pleading and discussion, he went to go see her.

She was so happy to see Marc that she immediately began

cooking him dinner. While they were eating, he showed her pictures of the kids Zéphirine had given him. The next morning, she did not come out of her room. She had passed during the night. Zéphirine was genuinely surprised she had survived her husband that long. They were the kind of couple who were inseparable throughout their marriage with a kind of love that never dies.

CHAPTER 27: ALLANAH'S AWAKENING

For all intents and purposes we were the perfect family. Both of us upstanding members of the community with jobs to be proud of. We did both work shift work, so there were times I'd have to leave the children overnight, but I didn't start my shift until 8pm, plenty of time to get them settled and asleep before I left. What Sean got up to when I wasn't there was none of my concern. I'd switched off.

I'd finally managed to tell my mom how bad things were. I didn't tell her the sordid truth, but she knew how deeply unhappy I was in my marriage. She told me to leave him and come home, that she'd help me with the children and we could start again, free of him. My mom had always hated Sean, and hated is the truth. She thought he was arrogant, rude and totally unlikeable. She'd even banned him from visiting her house as he caused chaos whenever he visited.

My mom had watched me for years fall further and deeper into the clutches of him. At one point, I was so thin she was forced to voice her concern. I wasn't really aware of what was happening, but Sean told her to keep her nose out of his business, there was nothing wrong with me other than the damage caused by my parents. It took my mom a long time to be able to talk to me without that hint of hurt in her voice, and years before she was able to tell me exactly what he'd said to her. After she left her third husband for being too controlling she found her voice and told

Sean he was not welcome in her house. He'd overstepped the line one too many times.

For me, it felt like an impossible situation for a few years. My mom was being distant and I hated the marriage that I definitely felt trapped in. I was a grown adult with huge responsibilities, I had to deal with the mistakes I'd made and follow them through. To hear her say she would help me leave felt like a huge weight had been lifted from my shoulders. It was at that point that the fear started to really build. There was no way this was going to be easy. I'd built a life everywhere he'd dragged me and now I was going to be running back home, to the place I'd run away from to begin with. I also knew he wouldn't let me go. I was mistaken if I thought I had a choice in all of this.

I talked for hours with my mom, how was best to leave, make him think it was his decision to let us go so that monster that was growing inside of him wouldn't be released. We were playing the long game. I was leaving him but it may take years for it to actually happen.

Of course, Sean knew I was pulling away so he tried to claw me back. Off to the doctors for more anti-depressants. This time they worked against him, my inhibitions were lost, my mind had already been made up, the medication made me bold and rash.

I visited home more often, sometimes driving down for the day when my mom didn't already have plans, other times for a long weekend. Sean began to object and told me how dangerous it was for me to drive on the motorway when I worked shifts. He suspected that I was drifting away.

Our vehicle troubles had become an issue again after the latest wreck he'd afforded me seized up on the busiest roundabout in Stoke after I'd filled the petrol tank fully ready for the week. After spending a good ten minutes assuring the RAC that I hadn't filled it with the wrong fuel I was towed home. Sean saw an opportunity to tie me to him, I took out a lease car through my work that meant I was obligated to stay with them for three years.

I wanted a VW Golf, to me that represented freedom, he demanded we had an Audi A3 and when that car turned up, I fell in love with it. My brand new car. I'd earned it, it was my job that allowed me to drive it and pay for it. That car did become my freedom, there was no stopping me, and I could zoom up and down the motorway to my heart's content in that gorgeous car.

I hadn't made any firm plans to leave, I knew it would happen, but how and when was still unknown. Our relationship was none existent, all intimacy gone and any attempt he made would make me physically repulsed. I didn't want to be a part of his perversions anymore. He blamed the stress of my work and the tablets for my disinterest in him.

My alcohol consumption continued to rise, and when he was on a night shift, I'd spend the night on the internet flirting with my friends and drinking up to three bottles of wine. There was a morning that I woke up bleary eyed on the couch with all of my clothes strewn across the room. I had no idea what I'd been up to and who had seen but the webcam had been on. I managed to hide all of the evidence and stumble into bed before he came home from shift and nobody from the online group ever passed comment, so I still don't know what went on.

One morning, we were on a quick turnaround with our shift patterns, he'd been on a night and I was due on an early. He was late home and needed to take the children to school, I was ready to go and pacing, undecided as to whether to phone work and alert them that I'd be late. It was unavoidable and my boss knew that Sean's work came first, he couldn't just leave a patient if they needed him.

Unfortunately, that's exactly what he did do. He left a child at home to wait for an ambulance so he could get home on time.

I was mortified. A complaint was lodged against him by the GP who had initially requested ambulance assistance. He was suspended pending investigation and called before the council to answer to the complaint.

Sean's attitude about it all was appalling. In the weeks leading up to this one incident, things at work had been escalating. He was a solo paramedic responder in a car, he thought this would give him the more exciting jobs, he could be there faster and maybe it would help him to achieve his dream of working on the air ambulance. In reality, it meant he was often stuck in people's houses waiting with poorly patients until an ambulance arrived to take them to hospital. With an overstretched A & E he was a stop gap when the hospital was busy and backlogged. This offended him and his overstretched ego, while he was babysitting he couldn't be out there saving lives. What he didn't see was that it was his job, he was a servant to the people and had a duty of care. He clearly didn't care and took it out on his colleagues, his students, and his boss. A handful of complaints about his attitude had already been logged against him that culminated in an actual shouting match with his boss. As soon as the GP lodged her complaint, his fate was sealed.

I was furious with him. The day before we'd had an argument about his attitude at work. It was one of the rare moments that I'd raised my voice and stood my ground with him.

"This is your job, it's what you have to do! You go where you are sent and you treat who is there, you can't pick and choose your patients according to the grand glory scale of Sean. You listen to your boss, you nod and smile, you work in the NHS not a building site, you can't bawl at him when you get pissed off. This is your life, you lose this job I'm gone, you can't put your family at risk like this because you don't like the way someone speaks to you over the radio!"

He blamed me, if I hadn't of needed to go to work he wouldn't have left the child. There was no way this was my fault, he had a mobile phone, he could have told me the situation, I tried to phone him but he'd switched it off on purpose. He knew exactly what he'd done.

After a short suspension, he returned to work on an ambulance, part of a two-man crew so that he could be reeled in and tamed. We waited for the paperwork to come through detailing exactly what would happen when he was summoned to London and what hoops he'd need to jump through to keep his job.

Part of me thought it was the perfect time to jump ship, another part thought I would break him and no matter what I thought about him the children deserved to have a dad. I don't believe that anymore.

Life was beginning to spiral and my bubble was bursting even though I already knew it was a mirage. I'd met someone who I could escape the turmoil with. He stole my heart in an instant and not because he tried, but because he was so vibrant in a world that was rapidly being swamped in grey.

I should have played the role of the doting supporting wife, Sean was going through hell with work, but I couldn't find it in myself. He'd brought the whole mess crashing around his own ears and I was gone already in heart and soul, I'm sure he knew.

My flirting with him online became a meeting that I didn't ever think I'd actually follow through with. There's no excusing my own behaviour, I was married with children for all intents and purposes. I don't know what made me agree to meet him let alone follow through with it, other than a new found boldness that came with having completely given up on ever being happy with Sean. I wanted so desperately to be happy, I'd done everything I could to try and be the good wife and mother. I'd lost my life making everyone else happy. Here was an adventure I couldn't resist.

I'd met him a few times before, the first time I'd ever laid eyes on him I was with Sean, and I knew that I was physically attracted to him. He was a lot younger than me, still in full flow of his youthful attitude towards life. He'd just walked 20 miles back from a nightclub because he'd lost his wallet and couldn't get a taxi. His sister was his first port of call in a bid to get back to his flat. That was his story and I believed it. He was dangerous and reckless in an exciting way. I felt the pang of my lost life more than ever in that moment.

Our paths crossed again briefly when I'd gone to collect my car from Vicki's house one Sunday morning. She wasn't home but my flame was there looking after the dog, he invited me and the children in for a cup of tea. I knew at that moment that I shouldn't, because there was a part of me that wanted nothing more than to be in his company. I felt alive just being in the same room as him. I've never been so dismayed to get to the end of a cup of tea, there was no reason to stay any longer, my dreary reality was summoning me back. My son managed to wedge himself in the cat-flap in Vicki's house that day. Something happened that would change me forever when I heard him laughing and talking to my son like he was a normal mischievous child.

I didn't hear from him again for a long time. I found myself waiting for him to be dropped into conversation by Vicki, desperately trying not to look to eager or interested. He'd moved back to Luton so that's why he hadn't been around but was moving in with her sister in a few weeks as he had a job close by. My heart leapt, while trying not to show it, I'd get to see him!

I did see him, we would go to BBQs and he'd be there and every time I saw him I was more enamoured. Not only was he extremely good looking, but he was so sexy, and clever. Whenever Sean would try and force his superior intellect on us all he was there ready to challenge it, he had such a unique way of thinking and

205

understanding the world around him.

At no point did I think my crush on him was dangerous. Both of his sister's told me how much of a wild child he was, an untamed spirit. He'd travelled Australia and rode a motorbike with abandonment, left a stream of broken hearts up and down the country and was a lad of the highest proportion. There was no way I'd ever attract the attention of this man.

I was at home one evening, mesmerised with my laptop while Sean lost himself to the PlayStation. The chat box pinged at me from Vicki with our usual how's things type of conversation. I immediately proclaimed my displeasure at being a widow to a computer game and that was it, my life was changed for ever.

It wasn't Vicki chatting to me, it was her brother, and when she saw that he was on her account chatting to me she promptly slapped him and pushed him off her computer. Five minutes later his cheeky face popped up on my screen with a friend request and we carried on chatting. This time, I knew it was him and he knew I was unhappy with my home life. He probably didn't realise how desperate I was for an escape, I needed colour in my life and as the words flashed on my screen I lured him in to my life. He showered me with compliments and told me how he wouldn't ignore me if I was sat next to him on the couch and I told him to prove it. That was when we arranged to meet. It was the best mistake I've ever made.

CHAPTER 28: JORDAN, DEAN, AND ZÉPHIRINE

There she was in Sydney by herself. Zéphirine had unwisely chosen an ill-timed season to travel to this part of the world. It was wintertime, so it was very bleak, stark, and frigid. She had spent most of her life living in a semi-tropical environment where for the most part folks were friendly, smiled at you for no obvious reason, and greeted you like the warm sun on your back. So she was highly out of her element which added to the dreary feeling she had.

Repressed thoughts buried long ago in her mind flooded back like a tidal wave of negativity. Bitter memories about the cold weather went right along hand in hand with life in the big city where people attitudes were as foreboding and icy as the arctic air that would whip the life out of you on the street. Everything was fast-paced in Sydney. She felt like a lost puppy in search of its nurturing mother. She decided to stay at a Motel where she had Internet access so she could look for a job although being in a highly emotional funk that was the last thing on her mind.

She browsed the Internet and came across a social network by the name of 'Plurk'. She decided to sign up and created a profile. Almost immediately it drew numerous friend's requests, primarily males. The discussions for some reason remained limited to a group of five guys, albeit anybody else could add to it.

Her life outside of the virtual social network was in shambles and luckily she had the internet to fall back upon. She discovered micro-blogging and quickly began to communicate with people all over the world. Micro-blogging was different than other ways of communicating via the internet because you could only type a certain number of characters in each post. The term '*Micro*' meant *limitation in character communication* for each post. Similar to chatting, anyone could see what you were typing, and join the thread unless the profile was set to private. Micro-blogging was a cyber-collage of all forms of communication available on the internet which included blogging, chatting, forum posting, and MySpace. And, at the time, it was the rage on the internet to micro-blog.

Although the cold of Sydney soured her big time, she started to feel alive again. She started to enjoy being by herself, not having to worry about anyone else but herself. She enjoyed not having someone to complain she was on the Internet all day. The cherry to her ice cream sundae of internet solitude was created by her chatting away with her internet buddies about everything under the sun except dating. No longer did she have to put up with her ill-tempered daughter or hide from my ex-husband's never-ending torments. No longer did she feel stressed out or worried about anything. She felt a peace inside her that was a long time coming.

During that time, she met Dean and Jordan.

Jordan was to become her platonic love. It was a love that although felt real she knew would never go any further than the internet. They would never meet and one day it would come to an end. But he made her feel like she was special again. He made her feel like she was much more than just a sex object.

One day, Dean sent her a private message apologizing for writing something he thought might have offended her. Being that she could not recall what it was she assured him that she wasn't offended. What they talked about was all in good fun. That particular chat became the defining moment and birth of an amazingly incredible friendship.

Dean and Zéphirine enjoyed picking on each other and they both loved to disagree on everything. That quickly escalated to their becoming an online item. Although it was love at first click, it would be months before they realized and admitted what happened between them. Their connection with their comparable misery ridden past along with the way they both broke free meant that they were kindred souls. At times in this road called *LIFE* they often seek out those who have travelled along the same battered emotional landscape as themselves. Dean was *that* person. He was the one Zéphirine connected with her need for emotional bonding.

Zéphirine's cousin met Dean and her for lunch in New York and asked them how they had met. When she told him they had met online and instantly became best friends he replied,

"How can two people who have never met become best friends? A best friend is someone real that you can touch." He then proceeded to touch his best friend in front of them to show what he meant.

Zéphirine replied, "Why the same way you met your best friend of course!"

But like most people he failed to understand.

The online world, although virtual, was still the real world. Whilst they connected socially online their feelings were still the same. They developed connections with people that can turn into friendships. They joked around, played tricks on each other, and behaved like goofballs on the norm. Drama too was a big component of their social network. In one case Zéphirine found herself arguing with another woman and because it was for the most part women in the thread, the thread was referred to as a cyberspace cat fight.

Zéphirine was living a normal life but, since most people could not relate to her online social activities, she felt she was highly misunderstood.

A friend of hers tried online dating after being single for a while, and was not getting anywhere with meeting guys in the real world. "Their profiles sound good and they seem nice while reading their email, but as soon as I meet them, they are completely different from what I had imagined." she complained to Zéphirine.

Zéphirine had been on dates with guys she had met through online dating and the impression she got from their profiles or email was no different from when she actually met them. So she had a hard time to relate to her friend.

However, Zéphirine was used to meeting online people without any expectations, which set her apart from the rest of the crowd. Her friend joined a site expecting to find a certain type of person, and yes it was a valid reason to join online dating, to find a good match, but an online profile was usually written to be read and make the person look good, although some failed miserably. A profile didn't make a person perfect for you or anyone in particular, and Zéphirine found that out the hard way. She had been online for so many years and because of her Internet marketing skills and the numbers of blogs she had, along with the customer support she had to offer, she grew accustomed to meeting people online and see things that others could not see.

It was no big deal to her, just another aspect of life that she was now used to and was even fond of in some way. And maybe she was opened to the idea of having online friends knowing that she would never meet them. Being online meant that you could be anyone you wanted to be, and that idea excited her, although she would like to think she was as honest as she could be online. Her personality didn't really change, but it could have if she had wanted it and no one would be the wiser.

There was no real way for anyone to know if the person you were chatting with was for real or not; if it was a man or a woman. You just had to trust your gut instinct. Zéphirine had many friends whom still chose to remain anonymous and would never reveal their real names, but somehow they still trusted each other and she was sure that if she ever met that person it would be who she thought he or she was. She would know them in person the same way she knew them when they communicated by email or chat.

The fact that Zéphirine liked to be online didn't make her any different from anyone who preferred to venture out to clubs and bars.

One week after meeting Dean online, who really put her at ease mentally, as they were chatting through Plurk, he challenged her to call him. She laughed to herself, as it was such an easy challenge to fulfil. So she went along with it. He sent her his phone number through a private message.

Zéphirine thought Dean would have given her a random phone number, as he loved a good joke, but no, it was him and it was a delightful surprise to hear his voice for the first time. Dean was shocked, as he didn't think she would actually call him. He was also worried about the cost of the phone call. No matter how many times she insisted it would be next to nothing, he kept saying he would pay for it. They talked for about 40 minutes, which in the end was simply not enough time for her. He was truly happy to talk to her; she could hear it and feel it in his voice. From that day, Dean and Zéphirine spoke to each other on a daily basis.

As they were talking she posted a message on the website

saying she was on the phone with Dean, right at that moment. Jordan sent her a private message saying he was jealous that Dean had heard her voice and could talk to her. She playfully countered back with: "Jordan, if you want to call me, all you have to do is ask for my number."

"Really?" he asked surprised.

Zéphirine lived in Australia and those guys lived in different countries, on the other side of her world, so she didn't mind giving out her mobile number. Somehow though, she knew she could trust those two. Worst-case scenario, she would change her number if any issues were to arise from giving it away to two strangers. It was no big deal.

So, Jordan called her right away and oh my goodness, in some ways she fell in love with him just by hearing his voice. It was no secret Zéphirine loved the British accent and she loved Hugh Grant just for that. Hearing Jordan's voice, actually being able to talk to each other sure strengthened whatever they had going on between them. He also started to text her every morning before going to work, during his breaks and anytime he felt like it.

Jordan's good morning messages were just the most amazing thing she had ever read. He made her feel as if she was a goddess. He made her feel special that every single day she would impatiently wait for his message. And if it happened friends surrounded her and he wasn't being too overly erotic, as he would most of the time, she would show the message off. Everybody knew about Jordan; they just didn't know the whole story. Jordan was never short for words. She always wondered how on earth he came up with all that. Not one single text message was ever the same.

"Jordan, how come you have such a wild imagination all the time?" Zéphirine asked him and he replied with four text messages:

"You inspire me...x,"

"You entrance me...x,"

"You beguile me...x,"

"You excite me...x,"

Every morning he never failed to send her a text message: "Good morning delicious, divine, delectable darling...xxx" These texts always made her smile and made her day. Zéphirine could never get enough of his messages.

She was buoyant as Dean and Jordan made her world go round.

She felt content which was something she hadn't felt in a very long time. It was not perfect, but they made a difference in her life and she could not ignore that fact.

Until one day something caught her eyes on Jordan's timeline: he mentioned *his son*! Jordan and her spent a lot of time chatting and texting each other but not once did he ever mention children and not once did she even thought about asking. She squeezed her eyes shut not sure of what to do next, torn between anguish and fear. She went to his profile to investigate some more, stalking him even, and as she read through his whole timeline again and again she realized there was no mention of any children or even a wife.

'He is probably divorced' she thought or maybe she was hoping he would be as everybody was a divorcee nowadays

She had to know. She knew she had to ask him eventually but she didn't want to. She was afraid of the answer. And for good reason: yes, he was divorced, but he was also remarried and had two young children. Her illusions were shattered, hopes disintegrating, but it was too late, she couldn't let him go. There was just something about Jordan, and even though she had Dean with whom she was spending a lot of time, and even though she knew how wrong it was to be involved with a married man, she wanted Jordan.

Zéphirine asked Jordan to call her once about something she was upset about. She was crying on the phone to him and he would just listen to her cry with the occasional *"aww honey,"* then he would say something to make her laugh; everything was all forgotten and she would feel happy again. Jordan would listen, Dean would not.

CHAPTER 29: THE SUNSHINE IS GONE

I always feel better when the sun is shining. The warmth gently caresses my soul and soothes my demons. I knew I was playing a dangerous game but my soul needed that warmth, and my mind needed that danger. I was alive, and I was allowed to feel.

I never wanted anyone to get hurt, or be disappointed. I suppose it's always an inevitability, but I'm not proud of what I did. It was easy to find time to sneak away, leave half an hour early for my shift, an extra night shift that never happened, home late after a get together with the girl's from work that I was never actually invited to. I no longer felt isolated in my life, I was making my own adventure, and I was feeling again. I was healing myself, making myself feel valued and strong enough to break free of my chains. I was moving forwards, gaining momentum, getting ready to brave the storm.

My sunshine left me, I was heartbroken, but I didn't blame him. I was under no illusion that we could ever be a 'real' couple. We'd been sneaking around secretly behind everyone's back for too long to ever tell the truth and he was young, he deserved to be free of my tangled web. He moved back south and before long was living with another girl, he'd obviously been keeping his options open for a long time, and I couldn't blame him. After all, that's probably what he thought I was doing. I didn't ever tell him I was leaving Sean; I didn't want him to see it as his fault or his responsibility. I wanted him to be happy in life, that's what happens when you love someone. I was in love. It had been a long time since my heart had clouded my head in poor judgement like this. I couldn't stop crying; I would never see my sunshine again. I'd dread being around his sister's in case they mentioned him or how happy he was in his new life. I kept my distance from them and him. I tried not to text him, I tried to leave him alone and gradually the pain slowed down long enough for me to start rebuilding my future, one that was away from Sean.

It was nearly Christmas and the children were more excited than usual, it was snowing and laying on the ground in big thick drifts. We built a huge snowman in the front garden and tried to go sledding but Sean in his usual arrogance got chased off the horses' field with a very angry 'this is private land' dismissal. The thing about that, apart from my white knuckles of fear as we were driving up the rickety road, was that I kept telling him we were on someone's private drive, we needed to turn around and find somewhere else. To make matters worse, the owners of that snow-steeped downhill field had to help push us out of the snow as we got stuck in a drift turning the car around in their drive! For a man that allegedly has an IQ in the top ten of this country, he can be stupid.

I'd made Vicki and her sister gift bundles for Christmas. I missed their company and wanted them to know I cared a lot about them even though I'd been distant recently. We'd arranged to get together for Christmas drinks that evening and a general excuse to be girly. Enough time had passed that I felt safe in their presence and wouldn't care if they spoke about their brother.

Vicki messaged me to say she wasn't feeling up to it, she had a headache and was a bit down in the dumps. I was really upset as this was the last evening I had off leading up to Christmas. I begged her to change her mind and said we didn't have to go out, we could just stay in together and I wouldn't keep her up late. She relinquished and agreed to see us all at her house. I went armed with a bottle of Portuguese Rose and goodie bags and let Sean drop me off so I wouldn't need to worry about picking the car up in the morning.

I remember that evening so well, I was wearing an old tie dye mini skirt that I'd bought from Birmingham when I was 16. I hadn't worn it for years, but I was exuding a new found confidence. I wanted to be the free spirit I had wanted to be as a teenager. The night was silent when Sean dropped me off, the snow creating its own blanket of peace upon the world. Everyone was tucked up safely in their homes, exactly where they should be.

We had a brilliant girly night. Vicki was quiet and withdrawn to start with but I put that down to her normal grumbles about the house being chaos. It wasn't long before she was upbeat and joining in. She'd bought me a miniature bottle of Baileys with some chocolates, perfect. It was still quite early, around 10pm, when we all decided to leave, after all she was nursing a headache. Her sister said her goodbyes and left after offering me a lift home. I declined as it was only a ten-minute walk, plus she had far enough to travel along country lanes to get home without me changing her journey route, I knew if she took me home she'd have to go down a one-way track that was probably thick with snow by now.

Vicki seemed reluctant for me to leave after her sister had gone, almost like she wanted to tell me something but was unsure of how to say it. I remember it so well because I wanted to tell her everything in that single moment. How unhappy I was with Sean, what had happened with her brother, and how I was planning to start my life again, which would mean moving away and losing her as my friend. I couldn't find the right words to start, and the moment was gone when her husband came back home.

I have no idea where he'd been, and looking back we didn't ask where he was at the time either. He wasn't a drinker and didn't have a large circle of friends so there was no reason for him to have not been at home that evening. The atmosphere became tense and I sensed that this was the reason Vicki had originally cancelled our evening together, and me in my pig-headedness had forced her to still see me when there was something going on. I felt stupid and insensitive and really regretted not having seen it earlier. I quickly made my excuses and got ready for my brief but cold trek home. Her husband offered me a lift and I politely refused, I was looking forward to the walk home, I needed the exercise, it wasn't far, I'd already intruded on their evening enough for one night.

He wouldn't take no for an answer and I started to feel a little uncomfortable. In an attempt to ease Vicki's growing discomfort I agreed to let him drive me home. I was starting to feel that I had been the cause of whatever disagreement had happened that day.

Life can change so quickly, one blink and your pathway changes.

The cards are dealt and laid on the table and you have no choice but to play them. He drove me part of the way home. The town was deserted. He reversed into the social club carpark and switched the car off.

I began to panic, was he going to shout at me, tell me what I'd done to upset him? Tell me how much of a useless friend I was having kept my distance for so long? Had my children upset one of his?

He turned to me and put his hand on my leg.

I couldn't breathe, was this happening? What was he doing?

"You've worn a skirt for me, my Christmas present."

His hand moved up my skirt and before my mind could even comprehend what was happening his hand was inside my knickers and his fingers probing inside of me. My scrambled brain started to scream silently, tried to turn it into sound but before it could escape his other hand pushed me back into the seat and his mouth locked firmly on mine, his tongue forced past my lips and savagely whipped around the inside of my mouth.

My heart thumped in fury, my body shrank away into another world, one where this wasn't happening.

Someone passed the path at the end of the car park and alerted him to his senses. I told him this couldn't happen; it wasn't right or fair on Vicki.

"You're right, someone might see us."

He started the car and pulled back onto the road. My heart was hurting, it thumped so hard and fast in my chest I thought it would burst free and abandon me. We drove past my house and he didn't stop. I froze, he hadn't finished with me yet, he wanted something more from me and I had no means to escape.

He stopped at an abandoned pub car park on the edge of the town.

"No one will see us here."

He started to kiss me again and I asked myself over and over what I had done to make him think I wanted any of this. I wasn't a flirt, I treated him the same as anyone else, with grace and courtesy. I didn't wear revealing clothes, my skirt was a first and accompanied with thick black tights. His wife was my best friend.

I submitted to him, shamefully there was no fight in me. I was petrified. His hands on me were warning enough that he was stronger. What was to be achieved by trying to push him away or fight him? A feeling of self-worth that's what.

I think he wanted a fight, expected more from me, because the kiss lasted no more than a minute and there were no more violations. He took me home with the parting words of 'Go home and fuck your husband'.

I begged him not to tell his wife, like it was my fault, doing or idea. He told me not to worry and that it was not something he'd share. He thanked me again for his Christmas present and wheel spun the car off into the night.

As soon as I got in the house I burst into tears. Thankfully Sean was asleep upstairs. I drank the Baileys straight from the bottle and sent a text message to my sunshine, my ray of light and the one who had given me hope. I told him that Vicki's husband had just kissed me and no matter what he might say I hadn't kissed him back. I don't know why I did that, I didn't want him to think I was a whore and sleeping my way around his family, but I also didn't want him to be involved. I wanted it to have never happened, for no one to ever know.

He didn't reply to my message, but the damage was done. He knew and when one person knows it means it's a secret straining to be heard. I could never have foreseen the ripples that stone cast would eventually make. The pain and anguish that followed weren't my fault, but I wish I'd never told anyone. Not even my sunshine.

CHAPTER 30: BEING LED ON

Dawson was a flirt, not hard core but still obvious. He was a nice guy and Zéphirine enjoyed talking to him. If it wasn't for Dawson, she would have cancelled her trip to the USA. He so wanted to meet her that he came up with the idea of a 'Plurk tour' to meet other Plurkers around the USA.

Dawson planned Zéphirine's trip, but the idea started with André in Dallas. He was also from Plurk and they had spent a lot of time corresponding to the point they decided to meet. At first, André wanted to visit her in Australia. He had some family who worked for a flight centre which entitled him to cheap flights. When he found out his discount was just for North America's flights, Zéphirine gave it some thoughts. She had always wanted to go the USA. She needed a break from her life. And so she booked a plane ticket.

Jordan and Dawson did not Like André much, but they tolerated him and since he was Zéphirine's friend, they didn't have much of a say. But Dean could not stand André. It was a clash of egos, a rivalry between the men, although none of them would admit it.

"You are going to America and stay with complete strangers, people you only know from the Internet? This is crazy, they might be murderers for all you know!" a worried friend implored of Zéphirine.

"Well, we all have to die one day, so I'll take my chances but I'm pretty sure I'll be all right." she replied laughing. Most people were not enthusiastic with her idea. But Zéphirine was so enthralled by this adventure she could not care less about what others thought.

***

André treated Zéphirine well and they did a lot of things while in Dallas like visiting museums; they drove down the road JFK was shot, and she ate authentic Mexican food for the first time. Zéphirine thought it was the best thing she had ever tasted. She wanted to visit the set of the TV show Dallas, but André told her it was highly overrated and expensive for what it really was.

His best friend was gay and they went out mostly to gay bars. Not that Zéphirine minded but she still thought it was a bit strange. He had kissed her when she first arrived but that was it. In fact, she was under the impression he couldn't wait for her to leave.

André dropped her off at the hotel on her last night as Dawson was on her way to her. André didn't bother to check up on the room or even asked how long it would be before Dawson would arrive. A kiss on the cheek, a quick *"be safe"*, and he was gone in no time.

Zéphirine was terribly confused. She had been dropping not so subtle hints the entire time they were together, but André never reciprocated. Suddenly it hit her; going out with André's friend to gay bars, lack of interest in Zéphirine, his fabulous fashion sense. André was in the closet! Zéphirine giggled at how she didn't see it sooner. André must be interested in his best friend that they hung out with!

Dawson was driving all the way down to Dallas from Chicago. In the last hour, Zéphirine was talking to him on the phone to keep him awake. When he finally made it to the hotel she rushed downstairs to meet him. When he saw her, he hugged her so tight she could barely breathe.

"Sorry," he said, "but I am so happy to finally meet you!"

And so was she. They had spent so many hours talking about that trip and planning it. They had now sixteen days to travel all around the USA and meet a different person in each city. Let the fun began!

Their first stop was the next day to meet another *Plurker* from Dallas, Sally, before taking off for New Orleans. Dawson was not the technology orientated guy. He relied on maps instead of a GPS.

So they got lost. It was night. They were hungry and they couldn't see any signs of where they were or even signs of life. Until they finally reached a diner.

For a moment, Zéphirine thought she was in a movie. The black and white checker tiled floor of the diner and the jukebox in the corner only added to the surreal feeling that they were in an old detective movie. The fat cook with a missing tooth flashed them a smile as they walked in, but didn't say anything. When they got seated an old, thin waitress holding a notepad and pen came by to take their order.

After ordering their meal they walked over to a couple of cops, who were having a late dinner at the end of shift, to ask for directions. They were friendly enough and when they found out they were tourists, they offered to take their picture as well as introduce them to their favourite diner cuisine, grits. Zéphirine chose to have the grits with sugar instead of salt; not what she was used to but still delicious.

They met Julia in New Orleans. If Julia was a personality on *Plurk*, she was even more so in real life. Due to her distaste for fat people, her no nonsense demeanour, and her liberal peppering of the word '*fuck*' into her posts, she chose to stay anonymous online. She went by so many different names, it was hard to ever pin her down. When they finally met her in person, they were shocked at who she really was. She was a fit beautiful and exotic petite Asian woman who looked like she couldn't hurt a fly... until she opened her mouth and let a flurry of words fly with plenty of '*fucks*' laced in there for good measure.

From New Orleans they drove to Chicago where they met another *Plurker*, Madame Maracas who was also a *Second Lifer*. She was an ex-cab driver who seemed to know the story of every building in Chicago. She showed them a few restaurants where you could write messages on the tables and chairs. Dawson and Zéphirine couldn't think of anything to say so they simply wrote "*Zéphirine and Dawson were here.*" It was miserably cold in Chicago during Zéphirine's visit there, but it didn't seem to faze Madame Maracas as they made their way through the city on their site seeing adventure.

Next stop was New York. Zéphirine flew there on her own. She would meet with Dawson again in Las Vegas a few days later. Dean was picking her up at JFK airport. She was really excited to finally meet the person who had been her best friend for the past six months.

She was walking towards the exit at the airport and noticed him from far away. He was everything she expected him to be but the minute they hugged each other she realized he also was everything she was not expecting him to be... he was tall, handsome, and charming.

"You're taller than I thought." said Dean.

"I'm wearing high heels you goof ball!" she replied

"Even with your high heels, you are still taller than I imagined."

"Is that a problem?"

"Nope. Let's go."

Dean had booked a room at a hotel nearby. The receptionist apologised because the only room available only had one bed. Dean looked at Zéphirine. She shrugged.

"That's fine." Dean said to the receptionist. He paid for the room and took the key card. They spent the rest of the day, doing her laundry, on their laptops plurking, tweeting, chatting, laughing, and joking until they fell asleep, spooning.

The following night, they had to go to Manhattan to meet another online friend, Lavender. Dean had already met her with another group of *Plurkers* some weeks before. They both knew Lavender had a crush on Dean. So when Dean booked a hotel down in Manhattan he made sure there were two beds just in case Lavender decided to stick with them.

Lavender's crush on Dean could not be more obvious. She tried every trick in the books to get Dean closer to her. But Dean only had eyes for Zéphirine. Lavender was so eager to please Dean she forked out the $400 tab. It was time to go when the staff thought they all had enough drinks. As they started to walk towards the hotel, Lavender pretended to be drunker than she actually was. Dean eyed Zéphirine: they both knew Lavender was obviously going to stay with them the night.

Lavender was walking ahead of them.

"I am sleeping in your bed." Zéphirine whispered to Dean.

"There is no way I am sleeping with her anyway. I told you I do not like her in that way at all."

"That's fine, but you know she wants you and she is going to try..."

Dean shrugged. When they got to the lobby Zéphirine decided

to check her emails and to report on *Plurk* leaving Dean to deal with Lavender. She had to use the hotel's computer since they had dropped their laptops at Dean's parents' house.

When Zéphirine went back to the room, Lavender had gone home.

"I went to bed, told her I was tired and had too many drinks I didn't feel wel. I pretended to sleep and started to snore so she went home."

"That easy? Good one!"

But something else was bothering him. Dean had an iPhone which was the latest gadget at the time. The iPhone allowed him access to the internet 24/7 and he could check on *Plurk* anytime. Dean was upset about Zéphirine's latest status' update: *Dean and Lavender are in the hotel room by themselves...*

"It is supposed to be a joke Dean, don't be a party pooper!" Zéphirine said.

"I don't want my name to be associated with her."

"It is a joke and everyone will see it that way."

"I don't like it at all."

"Deleting it now will make it look worse. Can you please stop worrying? This is silly."

By then Zéphirine was sitting on top of Dean in bed. Because that was what friends did, wasn't it or was it?

"What do you want from me Dean?"

He looked at her for a short while then pulled her to him to give her a lingering kiss. He released her and apologized, but then kissed her again, and again, and again... their very first intimate night together and the start of something they had not yet imagined starting.

Dean and Zéphirine spent four days together. She was flying to Las Vegas to meet up with Dawson and Dean was flying to Dallas. Coincidently their flights were at approximately the same time so they stayed together as long as they could. There were both trying to hold back the tears.

Dawson and Zéphirine stayed in Las Vegas for a few days. She didn't tell him what happened between her and Dean in New York, mainly because she wasn't sure what it meant. Dawson rented out a car and they drove to San Diego to meet a couple who had met each other on *Second Life*. The last stop was to be Los Angeles. Too much driving, not enough sleep, 21 days later and it was the best trip she ever had! This break was really what she needed. She left Los Angeles feeling reinvigorated about life and ready to take on the world when she got back home. She had proven to everyone, even herself, that she could do something as big as explore an entire country without the help of her family and friends.

Dean and Zéphirine never talked about what happened between them, but they made plans for her to fly to New York for Christmas. Out of the blue, as Christmas was fast approaching, Dean confessed to Zéphirine in an email:

"I am not saying any of this is my fault. I just figured I would start off by saying that. Face it and think about what I am about to say here. It's all I ask.

1) I am a 35-year-old male who is divorced and has a child support payment larger than most people can afford.

2) I live with my darn parents. Don't get me wrong I am aware there is nothing wrong with this.

But it just bothers me like you would never believe. I want out of here so bad it is not even funny. There are so many reasons I say this to you. I will try my best to explain. I need my privacy - I hate that no matter what it is I am doing my parents are there. My father goes through my stuff which is annoying alone. Even if I were to take the time to meet someone, where do I take them? Home where my parents are? Forget about it. I am beyond embarrassed. I had to take you here. It does not say much about a man these days. I just want to be on my own. I know I would be happier even putting aside meeting people. I have lived away from home since I was 17. It really sucked coming back here. I just had no choice.

3) My job is freaking annoying and killing me. I go to work hating that I even work there. The problem is this: the money is good and the benefits are fantastic. I won't find a secure job like this one making what I make anywhere else. I just feel as though my life is going downhill when after divorcing I was fighting to make it better. It is just getting so old.

Now something I never talked to you about before. This is going to kill me to even tell you. I just have no choice but to say it now because I hate the fact I kept it from you.

I am in love with a woman who lives far away from me. I fell for this woman after my divorce. I met her online and have been spending days and nights with her on the phone and online since then. Let's leave it at that. There is no reason to go into full details.

All I know is this... It is a long process. The problem is I am a man who knows nothing about making love and spending that time with a woman I enjoy being with, like for instance with you. I have very strong feelings for you. I loved every moment we spent together. I just do not know where I want to be in my life and it is killing me. Slowly, but still killing me."

He is in love with another woman and he is only telling her now after sleeping with her? She didn't know what to reply to him. Zéphirine read the email many times. How did she not see that coming though there was no way she could have predicted that.

"Hard to believe you kept something like that hidden so well."

"I know you would not understand because you won't listen and I don't feel like talking about it."

"I would not understand? I am the first person who would understand! And I do listen! We spent so much time together talking about everything and nothing!"

"You're right, we do. And during the time I met you, she was no longer in my life. One of the reasons I joined social network sites even."

"You said you started to talk to her again a few months before I came over. We have been talking since June so we've known each other for over six months."

"That is correct."

"And not once you felt the need to mention it? It's not like we have never talked about your ex-girlfriends before!"

"It was not something I wanted to talk about."

"I can't always read between the lines Dean. Why didn't you want to talk about it?"

"There was nothing for you to read in between. As I said before, my intention was not to hurt you. I want to be single for a while. I mean that. You're a beautiful woman and I am extremely attracted to you. It is not even the other woman or women that make me feel the need to be single."

"What is it then?"

"Just what I want at the moment."

"Can you please elaborate because for over the past six months, you spent most of your free time with me? Then you slept with me. It's not like I twisted your arm to do so! So I'm having a hard time trying to understand what is happening here!"

"I met her online three years ago. I was married, just not

224

happily married. She was engaged to be married. She started falling in love with me and called off the wedding. Since then we have been talking like 24/7. About a year ago she was diagnosed with breast cancer. That nearly killed me because an ex-girlfriend died in my arms from breast cancer. It actually scared me away. The breast cancer thing is very scary, so I started to withdraw my feelings but was unable to completely. She had a partial breast removal and since she has been going for chemo treatments. It is taking a toll on her and it started to cause issues between us so we decided we would take it day by day. Well that wasn't working for me. I wanted more. It started to cause more problems between us. We decided to chill. We stopped talking for a long period of time. Till just recently. During the time I was socializing online and meeting other people, she and I were not an item. We just started talking again and want to try to get things back to normal. Although I do not know it will work. She is still having her treatments and she is praying it may be all over by February although she sort of doubts it. Afterwards she will have her reconstructive surgery to make it look normal again. So I don't know what will transpire from all this. This is the truth. I was not hiding it from anyone. I just chose not to speak of it."

"And where does that leave me?"

"I have no clue. I am honest about that. I can't say where that leaves you. As I said before, I really like you, a lot. I just need to see what happens with her and I. That is important to me. If nothing happens, oh well, I still want to stay away from the dating scene for a while. I have been in it for way too long. I need a break. I figured I'd have some fun and no, fun does not include using people. Besides, had I known you were having this kind of feelings for me I would have most likely talked to you about the situation earlier. Perhaps not about her but what myself was looking to do and how I wanted it to be."

"Don't kid yourself! I didn't have any feeling for you until the day we met and then slept together. But right now, I don't think we can stay friends."

"I am sorry to hear that and I think that's wrong. But whatever you wish."

"Why is it wrong Dean? Because I have feelings for you and you can't handle them? You want to be with someone whom you havn't even met. What am I supposed to do? Pretend that everything is fine? You lead me on Dean and THAT is wrong."

"I never led you on. How does a person lead one on not knowing what they felt?"

"You slept with me when apparently you were in love with somebody else! How is that not leading someone on?" she typed right before slamming the laptop shut.

CHAPTER 31: ALLANAH'S BREAKING POINT

At the time, I made too much of the whole situation. No one had been hurt, just my soul and that didn't matter. I should never have let the whole damn thing get so big and out of control. Hunter was furious as it was his sister that was being hurt. I could see his impossible position, there was nothing he could do even if we were allowed to legitimately speak to one another. Sean had no idea what was going on but it didn't take long for him to find out.

The next day Vicki's husband sent me a text message and said that she was out doing the Christmas shopping, could I pop round and help him look after the kids. I sent Sean.

After Christmas, we all had one of our gatherings, we had been planning on hosting a pre-New Year's party for all ages and I couldn't see how to get out of it. Hunter was there too, we were both furious about the situation, and I could see the anger building as Vicki's husband found reason after reason and excuse after excuse to be near me or touch me. I thought I was being paranoid but I wasn't. The night ended but the damage was done. Sean sensed there was something going on, he outright there and then asked me if I was having an affair. I told him what happened with Vicki's husband the week before.

I shouldn't have.

He was furious. He phoned him and told him he knew what had happened, that he had 48 hours to tell Vicki or he would tell her. All hell broke loose.

He told Vicki that I had instigated it, that it was mutual, and that he thought I wanted to see him again.

The family was divided in a second. The other sister said she didn't believe him, that he groped her more times than she could remember, but she hadn't dare speak out for fear of losing her sister.

I spent days crying. My gentle hearted Vicki, whose very being was so delicate and precious had been torn apart by my inability to keep quiet. She thought I was ganging up on her and turning her sister against her.

I fell apart emotionally. Sean was so angry, threatening all of the things he'd do to the 'cheating little bastard'.

I was a cheat.

After a week of limbo, I made a leap. I decided I was moving back home. I applied for a job and wrote my letter of resignation. I told Sean. He said he thought it was a brilliant idea and he started looking for a house straight away.

He didn't get it, I wanted to move on my own, with the children. Without him. I got swept along with his new found enthusiasm for a while, he transferred ambulance departments, said it was exactly what he'd needed after being placed on special measures for a year by the paramedic council. Then I found my courage. What was the point of the heartache and pain I'd caused if I just ran away to Redditch and pretended everything was okay? Where was my backbone? I'd already let my shame hurt my best friend, how long was I going to let my life be ruled by the desire of others?

I told Sean I didn't love him anymore, that our relationship was over. He calmly agreed. In his mind he blamed Vicki's husband, but he must have realised we'd been wrong for far too long now. He begged me to give him a month after we moved, just to confirm it wasn't Stoke that was wrong. I agreed.

We moved in January. My boss refused to accept my resignation. She rearranged my shifts so that I only needed to work three days a week to cover my hours and used my annual leave to cover any shortfall. She was amazing, and it meant I got to keep my car.

February 21st, I told Sean that our marriage was officially over. I didn't like living a lie, I would move my things to the spare room and he could decide what he would do from there.

What started calmly became a thing of hate. He pretended to

be okay but in his mind, I was suffering the after effects of what had happened and would return to my senses any moment.

I was busy for three months working full time in Stoke and part time in Redditch. I separated our bank accounts and told him we were financially independent. We did the sums, I paid half of the rent and bills, and he paid the other half. I transferred £460 a month into his bank account to pay back the stupid things he had wanted to make himself feel more of a successful man and the bank loan we'd taken out to rid ourselves from our ever increasing overdraft. My two jobs let me begin to save some money, I was going to be able to move into my own place as he was obviously going nowhere.

As time went on Sean became frustrated as he realised I wasn't going through a phase. He started to throw a few insults my way, I was just like my mother, I'd never be happy, and I'd dragged him to Redditch just to ruin his life.

It all washed over me, I was doing the right thing, I was my own woman, and I had a right to be free. I was still so saddened by what had happened with Vicki. Her eyes begging me to tell her I'd made it all up. Her sister had also started sending me nasty emails. I was a liar, I'd made it all up to cover the wreck of my own marriage, if I ever messed with her family again she'd personally see to it that I didn't get to walk away, how could I even think to try and destroy Vicki like I had. I blocked them all. I didn't need her projecting her own demons onto me, there were enough of my own tormenting me as it was.

Hunter kept in touch, he encouraged me to find my own feet. We didn't promise each other anything, but he knew how important it was that I get my life together. I was drawn to him like a moth to a flame and his messages became the only thing that kept me going in my life.

As much as I had grown to resent Sean, I didn't want him to be hurt more than was necessary. That was another thing I got wrong. In hindsight it was always going to be a disaster. There was a monster inside of Sean that was waiting for an excuse to be released. I gave him that excuse. He took my phone from where I'd carelessly left it on the sofa and read my messages. I was telling Hunter how I wanted to see the world, how I dreamed of walking on the sandy beaches in Australia.

Sean went wild, again. He demanded to know who I was

messaging, even though it really was actually none of his business. We had been officially separated for four months. I should have been free to message who I wanted, dream what I wanted. He thought differently. He refused to give me my phone back. He stormed outside into the garden and stamped on my phone before launching it into the woods.

I was angry too. How dare he? I knew in my heart this arrangement wouldn't work for ever but I wanted to have had longer to save money. He demanded to know who it was so in my anger I told him. I was fed up of not being free even though I'd made the decision to be exactly that. I was tired of pussy footing around trying not to upset him, here have the truth. I don't love you and I hate living here with you. My skin crawls when I think about you, I can't stand the smell of you, and I can't wait to be free of you.

He started to shout, to demand to know every tiny detail. He began to threaten me, he would tape me to the bonnet of my car with my eyes pinned open so that I could watch him chop of Hunter's dick before setting fire to my car and watching me burn.

I laughed at him, I told him how pathetic he sounded. I told him I was going and I walked out of the door.

It was my way of keeping everyone safe. I knew he was serious. I knew he could hurt someone. If I left him with the children, he couldn't go anywhere. He'd have to stay in the house and calm down.

He phoned my mom and told her she'd better go and look for her slut of a daughter as I was officially homeless. She found me as I was on the way to her house. She was fuming. I explained why I'd left him with the children and she agreed it was best for now. She didn't judge me. She knew that as bad as the storm that was brewing was, I was finally really free.

CHAPTER 32: SECOND LIFE

Zéphirine felt betrayed and foolish. How could she have been so wrong? How did she not see it? She was looking for clues and queues… She tried recalling all the time they had spent together, Dean had done a great job to omit that part of his life.

But Dean and Zéphirine were online figures and neither one of them was prepared to give that up. If it was relatively easy to stop talking to each other; it was hard to avoid seeing what the other was doing on *Plurk*.

When she saw he replied to one of her online status updates, Zéphirine sent Dean a private message asking why he would bother.

"I was thinking you may have calmed down and perhaps a response in an update would get you to talk to me again. Wishful thinking perhaps, I don't know."

"I miss you Dean."

"I miss you too, Zéphy."

"I don't understand why you want me to talk to you knowing how I feel."

"That's your feelings not mine. I didn't want to stop talking with you."

"I wonder sometime if you even care."

"How do you figure? You're the one who stopped talking to me, not me, you! You really do hate me! Of all the people you wait till now to hold grudges." he said sadly.

"I don't hold grudges nor do I hate you, far from it. But you hurt me and betrayed me. I hope you do realize that?"

"Look Zéphy, let's be honest here. I am not upset with you at all. I wish you were not upset with me either. Of all the people out there, I find a woman I can share all my thoughts with and feel I can talk of anything I chose to. That person is you. I am sorry I had no other person I felt comfortable with as I did with you. I do know this though: I never wanted to lose you as a friend. I love you Zéphirine. I honestly do. You became a best friend to me. I know I should have perhaps done things a bit different. We all make mistakes. Trust me, you were not a mistake. One of the reasons I turned to you was because I truly trusted you. I am very happy I had the chance to share that alone time with you, something I will never ever regret. I am sorry you felt used. I honestly did not think that would have happened. Had I known that Zéphirine, I would have never, and I mean never, chose to do what we did. I know I am a mess at the moment, undecided of what I want in life for one thing. All I know is this: since the divorce, I just knew I needed a break. I did not want to be tied down to another woman for a long while. I needed to trust someone. I trusted you. I wanted you like you would not believe. You are the first woman I slept with in a very long time. I am sorry for the fact I am only a man. A beautiful woman beside me, wanting what I wanted... I couldn't have just turned you away. I really miss you Zéphirine. I do not know what else to say."

"I don't regret it Dean. Just taken aback by the fact you omitted that part of your life."

They tried to move on like nothing happened, but it couldn't be helped. Zéphirine just couldn't completely get over what Dean had told her. She tried to keep her mind occupied by spending most of her time on Second Life, much to the dismay of Dean.

On Christmas Eve, Dean video-called Zéphirine as usual.

"What are you doing?" He asked.

"Nothing much." she vaguely replied. "What are you up to?" she said trying to change the subject.

"You are on Second Life again, aren't you? That's it! I am joining now!"

And so he did. So what was *Second Life*?

Second Life (SL) was a social virtual world. Zéphirine first joined back in 2006, when it was frequently mentioned in Online

Marketing campaigns as something you had to be in it. She joined, but honestly didn't understand the concept of it after spending a few hours on there. Dawson was the one who lured her back into *Second Life*. And Dawson knew everything about it, taught her, showed her around, and she became fascinated, if not addicted, to this virtual world.

People on *Second life* usually tried to reinvent themselves. You could do on SL what you would never do in real life or you became what you were not in real life. Some tried to remain true to themselves through their avatar like Zéphirine and Dawson, then later on Dean and other friends.

A lot of *Second Lifers* were on *Plurk*. And a lot of women had tried to get Dean to join *Second Life*. But he kept saying it was the one thing he would NEVER ever join. And he had told Zéphirine the same thing hundreds of times. So she was quite shocked when he decided to join and even to let HER create his avatar, the avatar that women adored and would be fighting over for his attention.

On *Second Life,* you pretty much did whatever you were doing in real life but it was in a virtual world. You could work, go shopping and buy the wildest clothes. Friends, relationships, marriage, and sex were big matters in *Second Life*. Communications happened through private messages, group chat, public chat and voice calls. There Zéphirine was renting a house and co-owned a nightclub with a real life friend who had decided to see what the fuss was all about from what she had read on *Plurk*.

Zéphirine and Dean were now spending most of their free time on *Second Life*.

"If I ever get married again, I will not have internet." Dean said laughing.

"Why? Would you cheat?"

"No, I wouldn't and by not having internet nor would my wife, at least not in my home!" He laughed again.

"I could not have both: one partner in real life and a different partner in Second Life." Zéphirine said.

Dean shrugged, "I could see it happening if it was a non-working marriage, but not in a good marriage. Then you should be faithful."

"You should be faithful regardless if it is good or bad." said Zéphirine icily. But who was she to judge?

Fifty percent of the people they knew on *Second Life* were married or had a relationship in real life, while having a virtual affair in *Second Life*. Half of those fifty percent claimed they were in a bad relationship and the other fifty had no particular reason, it was something to do and something not real, so it didn't matter and couldn't be referred to as cheating in their opinion.

Zéphirine was in love with Dean in real life as much as she was in love with him in *Second Life*. The closest relationship Dean and she could have, was a virtual one for now.

One of the main attractions to Second Life was going to clubs to meet and dance with other people. Dancing was the equivalent of flirting in the real world. While dancing, couples would chat, share personal information, and have suggestive conversations about what they would do if they met in real life. Zéphirine always hated it when Dean danced with other people and this usually led to arguments, both inside and outside of the digital world. Dean didn't see anything wrong with it since, according to him, it was *'just a bunch of pixels'*.

One day, while their avatars were entangled on the dance floor, Dean said, "Something tells me you and I will get married in SL."

"Why?" she asked surprised.

"Because we are a drama couple." he responded laughing.

"We are so not!"

"I am not interested in anyone else. How's that? Good enough reason, no? You were the first." he continued.

"I'd rather you marry me just because you love me Dean."

"They say the first is always the best. I do love you Zéphirine. You know that. It is so plain to see."

"I don't think it is so plain to see."

"I love you but I do not know what will happen in real life. I do know this: I want people here to know that my love is for you."

"Ok." she said, unsure how to respond.

"Ok, never mind. I am not good at explaining myself."

Dean flip-flopped between booking Zéphirine a ticket for her to come with him on his Christmas vacation. By the time he made a decision, it was too late for them to get another ticket and he was regretting it.

"I wish you came this week I will admit it. I am kicking myself in the ass."

"Now you're telling me!"

"I just did not want to hurt you any longer. I hate that I fell in love with that other woman whom by the way has been dying for some time. For some stupid reason, my heart tells me to wait for her. I know nothing will happen between her and I though, and I hate to say it, but I almost do not mind."

Zéphirine was exasperated. "Dean, you're not making any sense! Do you want me or do you want her? I never understood what was going on between you and this other girl, but I'm tired of the back and forth." She felt drained. Something always seem strange between Dean and this girl but she couldn't quite put her finger on it.

Silence.

"Did I say something wrong?" he asked.

"No, I am just reading what you wrote." she lied.

"Do you understand though?"

"I do." she lied again.

"It hurts, doesn't it? I'm sorry."

"Dean, I honestly don't know what to say."

"Saying something is better than nothing. The truth helps too. Perhaps I am too honest. I don't know. We have been such great friends and we spend so much time together, I don't think I even knew really. There is a big difference between being online and actually meeting. Sometimes two people will get along well online, but in real life it is a different story."

"But we get along so well online and offline."

"Yes and when we met it was just like I had known you all my life."

"I agree. It was the same for me. I really needed that time with you. It was fabulous and so much fun. I wished we had more time instead of rushing and me being so tired with all that traveling."

"Me too, but I expected that, you did a lot of running around."

"But that's okay, we can do that again. Next time you get a week off, I'll come back. One of my friends was hoping I could come around April because she is supposed to be in New York."

"Will be a long time from now through," he said, "but I'll see what I can do."

"How come you're still awake?"

"Spending time with you, my love. In a few days, I'll be back at work."

A month later Zéphirine took ten days off work to go back to the USA.

If she had been on cloud nine for the past ten days, it was not so when she came back home to an eviction notice because of graffiti in one of the bedrooms. The house was at least thirty years old. They also knew the house, just like all of the other houses on that side of the street, were due to be demolished within two years as part of the shopping centre expansion project.

Zéphirine had always lived well by her husband's side even though it was not easy and they were in debts most of the time. But her husband had managed to always make sure she and the kids always had a roof over their head. Their last house was a two-story, three-bathroom mansion with a pool on a prestigious part of Kawana Island. She fell in love with the house when Marc had shown it to her.

The house was brand new and had served as a home display. The kitchen was fancy with the latest appliances. There was a media room which became the video games room. Upstairs were four bedrooms and she was in love with the master bedroom. The ensuite had two sinks and a spa. There was a large walk-in-robe in which she would sometimes stare at thinking she no longer wanted to see a man's clothes in her closet. The master bedroom itself was so spacious.

Marc had said he would buy the house so she wouldn't have to worry about moving the children all the time. In Australia, you were a very lucky person if your lease was renewed after a year. Landlords would sell the houses, owners would want to move back in, sometimes landlords wouldn't like kids there, and a whole host of other reasons. It didn't matter if you were a good tenant, a long term rental was never a guarantee.

Of course, she should have known Marc buying the house would never happen. Marc was short tempered. Every job he did always ended with arguments and no money for weeks, or months even. Her weekly wage was slightly more than the rent so she was forced to downsize. That is when the company she was working for offered her that old house.

It was a downgrade. Even the kids didn't want to move there. It was an old three-bedroom house, one bathroom and no walk-in-robe. It had old wallpaper which was stained, and one had to wonder about some of the stains. Allison who had a creative mind thought it was quite cool to draw on the wall. And to be honest, it added charm to the room. But Zéphirine knew the true reason they wanted her out was because she was no longer working for that company and the time for demolishing those houses was approaching.

But it wasn't just the house that made her life difficult. Allison was at the age of rebellion when she was always right and could do whatever she wanted. She was defiant and Zéphirine gladly admitted she preferred avoiding her own daughter as her mood swings were too much to handle. Even Adrian avoided his own sister. She would cry to Dean who would hear all the arguments as they were on Skype most of the time.

It wasn't enough that Marc wasn't a father figure to the kids, they knew how to play her and their father against each other. Adrian would call his father saying there was no food in the house. Marc would bring down bags of grocery, mostly junk food, and would verbally abuse her saying she was an unfit mother for not feeding the kids. The kids were far from unhealthy and definitely not starving. When Zéphirine said no to the kids, Marc would say yes. The kids knew it, used it and abused it.

Zéphirine had enough. She wanted the father to step in once and for all. She just could not do this anymore. So Dean offered for her to stay with him and she gladly accepted. She made a deal with Marc.

"Now is your chance. Since you seem to think I am such a bad mother, you can have the kids and the house while I will be in the USA for three months. And we shall see if you can do a better job than me."

Her friends didn't like the idea of her abandoning her children.

"Abandoning your children is when you leave without saying a word and with no intention of coming back. I'm going away for three months then I'll be back home. We also have this thing called the internet to stay in touch. I need a break. If I don't do this now, I will shoot myself, then you can say I abandoned my kids." Maybe it was a bit over the top. But Zéphirine meant it: die or live. And that was enough to shut them up. She hated when people were making assumptions not knowing what was really happening behind the curtains. Sure Zéphirine always smiled, she would not dare show the slightest sadness in her. Pretending to be happy was a difficult job, but she knew how to do well.

Dean was looking for an apartment even though Zéphirine had told him it wasn't necessary; she was happy staying at his parents. Besides she didn't want Dean to go all out with the expense knowing she would have no income for the next three months. But Dean insisted he could afford it.

It was a small but big enough for two, one-bedroom apartment. He had gotten the keys just a few days before her arrival, so he only had brought in his bed, desk and computer, the TV set and gaming consoles. Not that he had any other possessions to bring.

"We need to go shopping for kitchen stuff, a dining table, and a couch" Dean said.

For Zéphirine, this kind of relationship was totally new. With Marc, she was the one going shopping, making the decision about what to buy and she even had to learn how to put furniture together. If it had taken them one hour to set up their bed the first time, Zéphirine could now do it on her own in fifteen minutes!

With Dean, they made decisions together and they would do everything together. They would cook, clean and do the laundry together. If Dean didn't feel like cleaning the table, he would ask if it was okay for Zéphirine to do it. She would get up in the morning fifteen minutes earlier so he could sleep the extra time while she was getting his lunch box and coffee ready. Because his job consisted of mainly driving, they would be on the phone most of the day until he got home. Dean gave Zéphirine a whole new meaning to what it was to be in a relationship. She no longer felt depressed or miserable. Around Dean, she could be herself.

The ninety days she was allowed to stay in the USA came really fast. It was time to fly back to Australia. The goodbye at the airport was especially tough this time around. Zéphirine fought to hold back tears, but she could feel her lower lip quivering. As she hugged Dean goodbye, she had the uneasy feeling this would be the last time she would see him.

Within just a few weeks of being back in Australia, Dean wanted her on the first plane back to him no matter the price! Dean had also proposed to her on *Second Life* and wanted them to plan their virtual wedding.

"We need to write our vows." Zéphirine told him.

She was surprised to find his vows in her inbox the next morning:

I promise to give you the best of myself and to ask of you no more than you can give.

I promise to respect you as your own person and to realize that your interests, desires and needs are no less important than my own.

I promise to share with you my time and my attention and to bring joy, strength, and imagination to our relationship.

I promise to keep myself open to you, to let you see through the window of my world into my innermost fears and feelings, secrets and dreams.

I promise to grow along with you, to be willing to face changes in order to keep our relationship alive and exciting.

I promise to love you in good times and bad, with all I have to give and all I feel inside in the only way I know how.

Completely and forever.

Dean

CHAPTER 33: A BREAK FROM SEAN

Early the next morning, my mom took me back to the house. All was quiet, everyone was still asleep. On the drive, my clothes lay strewn in piles where they had fallen from the bedroom window. There were cigarette burns in all of them and he'd done me the favour of leaving the butts crushed into them. There was a pair of my boots, sodden, I later found out they were soaked in his urine, and my ornaments lay scattered and broken where he'd lobbed them from the front door. There was nothing left for me to pack, so I scooped it all up into the trunk of my car and went inside to get the children.

Once they were safely gathered, I confronted Sean.

"I hope you're happy with your night's work. I'm taking the children to my mom's. Clear your head, sort yourself out, and don't ever threaten me again."

The children pretended that they hadn't heard any of the previous night's shenanigans, but they were both extremely subdued. I later found out that he had woken them both up after I'd left the previous night and had told them their mommy was a whore, that she had gone now so they didn't need to worry. Unforgivable.

All three of us cozied up in the spare room at my ma's. We took it in turns to sleep in the bed and I actually think it was the safest all of us had felt for a long time. The children adjusted so well. I tried not to talk to them about what was happening. I didn't know what to say to them and I felt completely responsible for the way it had blown up. I should have handled it all differently. I should have left him years ago.

We were on the waiting list for a council house, I was unable to find anywhere to rent that was in my budget. I managed to keep working and found a way to make sure the children were always looked after without their dad being able to interfere. He hated it. He hated how easily I'd strolled out of his life. I survived. I managed. In fact, I thrived without him.

My next mistake was accepting a replacement phone from him. He bought it so he knew the number. I didn't realise what it meant at the time, but that phone should have been crushed and launched as far away as possible. It gave him some measure of control back. He didn't know where the children were after school and he knew better than to try and visit my mom's house. So he only had one option left. He signed himself off sick from work and drove to Stoke. He spent his days sitting just out of view of Hunter's house and his sister's.

I had no idea what was happening to begin with. Vicki's sister thought she had seen him sitting across the road at one point, but thought no more of it. She had no way of contacting me to ask either, so Sean was pretty much free to do as he wished.

When we moved to Redditch, Sean had refused to take my dog with us, the one last thing that held our family together. He was trying to sell him but I couldn't stand the thought of our baby being given so coldly to complete strangers. I begged Hunter to take him, I told him that he was the only person I trusted with my dog, and thankfully the two became best friends.

Sean started to get braver, and broke into the house where Hunter was living. He left him a note with his watch on his bedside table.

'You've taken my wife and my dog, you may as well have my watch.'

When Hunter got home from work that day, he discovered the unwelcome gift and went straight outside to look for the intruder. Sean was sitting in his car over the road, with a can of lighter fluid in one hand and flicking a lighter in the other. Hunter started to walk over to him, Sean started his car and drove off immediately. He wasn't seen outside their house again.

When I heard what had happened, I phoned Sean. I made sure

he knew that this was his final warning. I would phone the police. I would have an injunction made against him. I would make sure the paramedic council knew how unhinged he was. I would make sure that the children were safe from him forever.

He started crying down the phone, telling me he needed help, that he wasn't sane, that he couldn't live like this anymore.

My heart was cold; I didn't believe him or trust him. I told him he wasn't my problem anymore, I'd been asking his family for help for years, and now it was his turn to ask them for help. I ended the call and felt no regret.

Later that day, Sean was admitted into a psychiatric unit as a voluntary patient. He had told them he could no longer cope because his wife had left him. I visited him at that unit, I wanted them to know exactly how unhinged he was and the threats he had made. They wouldn't let me speak to anyone about it, a breach of patient confidentiality, and Sean refused to confess what was really going on. The whole thing was an exercise in manipulation, to make me feel guilty, to try and make me go back to him. Pathetic.

After his three-day assessment, he was released with no further intervention required. He demanded to see the children, which he was entitled to. I told him he was unsafe to care for them, if he was fragile enough to be admitted onto a psychiatric unit, then he needed to prove he was ready to care for two children. He hissed at me, it was a voluntary admission, they were taking no further action and he needed no treatment. I hissed back, that's because you lied and didn't tell them everything you've been doing, stalking my old friends, and breaking in to houses. I needed to know my children would be safe, that he wouldn't use them as a weapon against me. I was petrified that I would never see them again if he took them. He'd do that to punish me, I felt sick with the fear. I tried so hard to shelter them from what was going on, but they knew he phoned me at least seven or eight times a day. That I would end up shouting at him down the phone. My mom would get angry with me answering the phone, but I didn't want him escalating things if I didn't, if I spoke to him he would stay where he was and vent his poison. If I ignored him, he'd find another way to spread it.

In August, Sean decided he was going away for a few weeks to clear his head. I actively encouraged it. It would give me chance to go through the house and see if there was anything I could salvage from my possessions. He asked me to go to the airport with him before he flew to Gatwick, and said that he had booked a hotel room for me and the children to stay in as his flight was late at night. I agreed to drive him there as it would mean I knew he had definitely gone and that he wasn't using it as an excuse to plan anything else.

We arrived at the hotel much earlier than we needed, but it had lovely gardens so I took the children outside to explore. The hotel was fashioned in dark wood everywhere that gave it a sense of Victorian elegance and opulence. Sean headed straight to the bar and got exceptionally drunk. In the space of two hours, he had drank so much he could hardly stand and was slurring his words. He started to make a scene in the lobby so I told him we should go upstairs to the room so he could sober up before his flight. There was no way they would let him board the plane in that state and I was determined to see him go.

One thing led to another, and in full view of the children he started pushing me around. Calling me a fucking whore because I refused to let him sleep with me 'one last time'. I told him he needed to calm down. He grabbed my arm and dragged me to the door of the room, opened it with his free hand and pushed me out of the door. I could hear the children crying, they were scared and helpless. Sean still had a hold of my arm and was pushing me with his other hand kicking my bag out of the door. My handbag with my purse and car keys scuttled down the corridor and I left them there as I clawed at the doorframe to get a grip. There was no way I was letting him lock me out of the room, my babies were in there. I managed to get a hold of the frame and remember my nails ripping as I grabbed with every ounce of strength I had. He had lifted me off my feet and still kept on pushing until my daughter hit him from behind and cried 'no daddy'. That was all I needed to be able to break his hold. I ran back in the room and pushed him out hard, I pounded his chest and screamed at him. I told him to leave, to not come back, that he should stay in Germany, that I hated him. I slammed the door and collapsed in a sobbing heap on the floor. My children were there in a second, holding me tight, telling me it would be ok. I'd failed to shelter them from it all.

Ten minutes, after he'd left the room there was a knock at the door. I was a bundle of nerves and too scared to open the door. The man's voice from the other side told me that he'd received a complaint from neighbouring rooms about the noise, if there were any more complaints he'd be forced to ask me to leave. He also asked me if that was my bag in the hallway. I answered yes through my tears and asked him to leave it on the door handle. He did and left me in peace. I finally summoned up the courage to open the door and retrieved my bag. I closed the door quickly and went back to the children who had thankfully fallen asleep, probably through emotional exhaustion.

About two hours later, I heard a noise at the window. I couldn't believe it; Sean was in the garden throwing stones at the window. How had he known which one was our room? I opened the window, not because I wanted to speak to him but from fear of him making a scene that would lead to our eviction. He said he was sorry. I didn't care. I told him he needed to make sure he was on that flight and I threw his bag down to him, with his passport and his ticket. He left without a fuss.

CHAPTER 34: ZÉPHIRINE AND DEAN

Zéphirine,

I want to start this letter by saying that you are a truly an amazing woman in my eyes. I knew there was a connection between us the moment we started talking back in June last year. Immediately, I felt I had known you forever. I found myself opening up to you in ways I have never opened up before. From relationships to financial issues, I shared things with you I thought I would never share in a million years as they were some of my inner most secrets. Right from the start, I had noticed a want for you, a want like never before. The want became needs and the more we would talk the more I would fall. After hearing about your love for Jordan, I realized that you would not be available for me if I were to have let you in. Then I finally got to meet you. I was amazed at how beautiful you were. I just knew it would be hard to have a week with you and I wanted you in a way I felt I never wanted another. I felt it would be difficult and almost unbearable.

Then you opened up to me as well which left us both vulnerable to sharing one another with each other. For me that was amazing. Never thought I would do that. I am not really the type of guy that easily opens his arms and heart for a person. I do blame it mostly on my past though. I have found no love in any of the women I have spent my time with. Such long relationships really ruined me as a person. I hate that I bring these issues to you more than anything in the world. It has made me a person I am not even comfortable being. I feel I have become a nothing, a failure, and find myself lost in hurt and shame. I do not know if they ever even loved me but I knew I would be loyal an honest throughout the relationships.

I know I send you mixed feelings based on the things I say to you at times. I am a hopeless romantic, confused with what it is I want in life and in a woman, if I were to allow one in at all. I feel we all have been hurt one way or another, although in different ways of course. I tried explaining to you the other night what it was about you that hurt me the most. I mean it when I said you seemed desperate and I believe you tend to fall for guys no matter if the person you let in. I have been trying to figure that all out for some time. I know you better than you think. For some reason, I have this crazy ability to read people. I will admit with you it can be tough at times but I see things and think things. Scary thing is some are true. I believe there are others in your life you love as well. I know you say no, and will say no, but honestly, look at the trends and you would understand why I say all this. I am not saying it's bad either. I do know this though: I never wanted a relationship with a woman like yourself who shares so much about their lives and pictures and stuff online. To me that is scary. I want a woman who will be for me, and us, as a couple. Someone I can trust with anything we share or have together. Some women know so many men and still allow themselves to love others. I am not sure you understand what I mean. I just hope in a sense you do.

Just so you know, I mean no harm by the things I said up there. Just explaining things is all. I want to say this to you: I love you like nothing I ever loved before. We have such great times together. I know we don't do much when you're here but I enjoy it one way or another. I know you feel bad that you are unable to help me with rent and all that but I want you to know that if it were up to me, I would not take a dime from you no matter the situation. We have to deal with what we can have with the laws and visa. Until then we will just have to take it day by day. I still wish I was in a better situation with my life to be honest, just trying to take it day by day as well.

I love you

Dean

"I'm tired of Dean's little secrets. I have been here over two weeks not even once has he mentioned my name on *Plurk*. I asked him why and he said that he doesn't like to talk about his private life. Then I realized the one person he talks to on a nearly every day basis doesn't know I'm here with him, but knows I was being evicted from my house. That was a personal matter only a few close friends knew about. But that's okay for him to go and tell about my private life but not okay to say we're re living together? Haley told me to take it slow with Dean, you know, little steps, but it pisses me off now." Zéphirine ranted to Jordan. They had not talked in a while so there was a lot to fill him on with.

"It sounds like you two need to have a good long talk. Do you think he's a bit overwhelmed by you being there?" asked Jordan.

"HE invited me. HE wanted me to be here. Dean does not want to let me go, I have him crying on the webcam every time I tried to break it off. His excuse: he does not know what he wants to do with his life."

"So if you were trying to break it off before - why did you go back?"

"Last year he explained he'd always been in long relationships. So he was never really single and wanted to stay single for a while. Which I can understand, but single guys or newly divorcees would just go out most nights and have a few flings right? Dean spent all his spare time with me on Skype. I was the one to push him to go out and when he was out he would call me! He used to ring me to check if what he was wearing was okay. I thought we would work it out."

"So are you sure you really have fallen for him - don't you want someone with a REAL life who can woo you and take you out? You deserve to live life to the fullest. You are a beautiful person who needs to live life."

"I love Dean very much, no doubt about it and I can truly understand the fear of commitment, but I thought by asking me to be here everything would change. Dean has no experience in the '*woo a woman*' department. Not everybody is like Jordan..." She smiled.

"I guess you'll have to teach him then! Every woman deserves to be treated like a princess, especially you! What is with this '*other*' woman thing? We all need a gentle nudge now and then!"

"He '*met*' her online while he was still married, and from what I gathered, it was a comfort thing which is understanding when being in a bad relationship. But they never met her in real life. And she has been battling breast cancer. I don't know too much because I don't want to know really. But she still calls and am pretty sure he was talking to her on the phone last night."

"So more of a virtual friend thing really?

"Yes, but he said he was in love with her. Though it sounds more like a rebound thing. Two years I think, and they never met. She is in Florida. I am in Australia and been here to see him three times already. I wish I could live closer."

"I can see how that would be difficult. I think he needs to learn how to woo you."

"I don't see her as a threat, but I don't like how he talks to her about what WE bought for the kitchen! How does he learn, do I get him some DVDs?

"Have you talked to him about her? Are you jealous? Perhaps if he knew that it would make a difference?"

"It is not jealousy, I just feel like I am this big secret, nobody knows we are officially in a relationship, why the secrecy about it?"

"Perhaps he's afraid of hurting her feelings? But I think he should be thinking about your feelings!"

"I know he feels sorry for her, I mean who wouldn't? But I am here. We live together!"

"I could teach him a thing or two about pushing the right buttons - Zéphirine style!" Zéphirine burst out laughing. "It probably wouldn't go down too well!" Jordan added.

"I wish he would learn 'the Jordan's style'!"

"That sounded a bit saucy!"

"I don't want you to disappear again like you did before, Jordan."

"OK. I promise! So do you have good sex with him?"

"Jordan!"

"So with the money thing, that must be difficult, feeling like you have to rely on him?"

"He took this apartment knowing he couldn't afford it. Took out a loan for it, and uses his credit cards when I told him I was fine with staying at his parents' house."

"See how I changed the subject?!"

"I can understand living with parents is hard, but putting yourself into debts? Dean went back to his parents after him and his ex-wife sold their house. The sale just covered the mortgage. She took everything. At first, we were supposed to stay at his parents'. But he decided to take an apartment."

"Can you not get a job?"

"Not allowed, I don't have a visa. Dean knows it could take years to get one, unless we get married. He knows all that because we talked about it before I came here."

"So are you going to get married? Just so you can get a job and not have to rely on him, you would get married?"

"NO! I didn't say I would get married just for that. Dean... I love him. But he's never going to ask. A *Second Life* wedding is all I will ever get from him."

"Why don't you ask him?"

"Ask him what?"

"To marry you."

"Are you insane?! I will never ask a man to marry me. That's a man's job!"

"It's the 21st Century, it is quite acceptable now!"

"I don't care, I still think it is a man's thing and I want it that way."

"Got to go sweetheart. I've missed you and still think you are abso-fucking-lutely fan-fucking-tastically gorgeous. I looked at your blog, pics, and videos a lot in my absence and they have provided me with '*great pleasure*'. Nothing beats the real you though."

"I love you."

"I love you too, you crazy insane beauty!" Exclaimed Jordan. Zéphirine playfully tossed back her hair and bit the tip of her finger, striking her seductive pose. This sent Jordan into an even bigger tizzy. "Now I have a HARD ON!" She disconnected the video call.

As the 90-day allowance to stay in the USA drew to an end again, time seemed to speed up no matter how much Zéphirine willed it to stop. She already knew the separation this time around would be unbearable. She couldn't bring herself to let go of him as they reluctantly trudged through the airport. She finally broke down when she looked over and saw the tears in his eyes. She wanted to say something to comfort him, but couldn't. What was there she could say? Even though she had a few issues with Dean, and they seemed to fight all the time, she loved him. She really wanted to fix things with Dean, but ultimately she wasn't sure she could. It was time to leave.

Zéphirine,

I love you. Thank you so much for all your help and all you are doing with my website. I am sorry I tend to frustrate you. Just know that I appreciate all you do for me. Just another reason added to the already growing feelings I have for you. I miss you and I am counting down the days till we can finally say we made it. Only then will I be fully satisfied knowing you wouldn't ever have to leave me again. To know you is to love you. To have you to call my own, my wife, my lover, and friend, I know we will be in a relationship that will be unbreakable. That alone means so much to me. I am to have met such a perfect woman. I will forever cherish every moment we share. I love you Zéphirine. Always and forever.

Dean

CHAPTER 35: FIRE

My cherubs and I were starting a new adventure; we were moving into a flat. It was small with two bedrooms, but that was all I needed, and there was ivy growing across the front wall that spread around the windows that made it seem enchanting and magical to me. When the clouds cleared the sun filled that flat with life. It was an amazing feeling. My children flourished, they were so resilient. I felt like I was being a good mom, caring for them and building a life for us to move forward.

Hunter had gone to Australia. He was spending three months over there with someone named Marc to give us the room to breathe, to build a life that may or may not have room for him in it. For me there was never any doubt, but for him it gave him the space to assess the situation without the endless harassment from Sean.

Sean sent countless messages to him via email, text, answerphone, and Facebook proclaiming what an arsehole Hunter was and how he'd never live happily with me, that he'd never set foot in the same house as his children, that I'd rip out his heart and leave him destroyed. If I ever told him I loved him I was lying, I was incapable of telling the truth, and once the glory of our honeymoon had worn off I'd leave him like I'd done with Sean.

I'm not sure how Hunter felt about it all. He stayed calm and accepted the wrath aimed at him. He didn't want to be a home wrecker, and each time he tried to talk about it, I would get upset and frustrated. My marriage breakup was nothing to do with him, it had been dead for years, and it was my lack of courage that had led to him ever being embroiled in the whole sorry mess. There were times when I tried to let him go, I felt that the baggage was just too much for him to carry, that he deserved more than I could ever offer. What I failed to realise was that wasn't my decision to make, it was his. Now I know you fight for what you love.

Sean wasn't fighting for love. He was fighting for what he thought was his right. He thought I was his possession to own. He wanted me to be the wife that made him fulfil his social expectations. By night, he dressed as a woman and looked at porn that satisfied his desires, by day he was a paramedic, with a wife and two children. I had blown that illusion out of the water, I didn't want to play that game anymore.

Things had calmed down considerably since his departure to Germany. I only received one phone call from him, he'd told me he'd phoned to say goodbye, and he was feeling sleepy now as he'd injected himself with insulin. He wasn't diabetic. I told him how dare he phone me and I ended the call. I phoned his sister and told her to sort it out. She started to shout at me, with a torrent of abuse. I stopped her dead in her tracks. I had been pushed around one too many times. If she ever wanted to see my children again, she would learn to treat their mother with respect. I had asked her for help years ago and they had ignored me, this was the consequence, and she now needed to take responsibility for her brother whose behaviour was escalating way out of control. That was the last time we spoke.

Sean returned to Redditch. The phone calls started again. I knew I had to answer them or he'd turn up at the flat. The scene at the hotel haunted me and there was no way I was prepared to have another physical confrontation with him. He told me he'd failed as a husband and a father, and that he didn't want to see the children anymore as they were a constant reminder of everything he had lost. I spent hours telling him he had to step up, he couldn't just deny their existence, and that they needed a dad in their lives. Why was I bothering? I genuinely thought that they needed their dad in their lives, that they couldn't be deprived because of my own selfish life choices. I wish I'd let him walk away from us all, but that was probably never a real threat anyway, just another way to try and draw me back into his life.

We had been in the flat for a month or so, the phone calls had become an expected hindrance in my life. At home, at work, in the middle of the night, first thing in the morning, there was no escape. Sean had agreed he wanted to look after the children for a weekend and we arranged a date, it was going to be a trial for a way forward, he would look after them when he was not on shift and we would try to give them a normal life.

Vicki had been back in touch with me. She told me how much she had missed me and she forgave me for everything that had happened. She wanted to come and see me and her sister wanted to be a part of it too. I think they had some inkling of the hassle Sean was giving me and wanted to show some support. I'm guessing Hunter had something to do with smoothing the way over with his family too. I was thrilled, I so wanted to be accepted for who I was. The forgiven sentiment irritated me a little as I wasn't sure what she was referring to, the way I hid my relationship with her brother from her or for what had happened with her husband. If it was the latter I would ignore it, she deserved to be happy and none of this had ever been her doing.

We arranged a girl's night at my new flat for the weekend that Sean was going to look after the children. It was more convenient to let everyone stay over, and we'd have the room since the children wouldn't be there.

Sean found out, I'm not sure how. I had a suspicion that he had been hacking my Facebook account as messages that I hadn't read were marked as open, but I couldn't see how it could be possible. His knowledge of my 'party' made me really believe he had gained access so I changed my password. I chided myself on my paranoia and wrote a long email to Hunter telling him how happy I was that his sisters' were coming to see me, and that we were all finding our feet in our new home. I also told him how I was going to phone the insurance company next week to have him named as an additional driver on the Audi to help me with my commute to Stoke when he returned. I hoped he was enjoying his time in Australia but I missed him loads.

The children went to their dad's. They were excited and I was gripped with fear. I knew I had to let them go, but I was terrified he would hurt them, or himself, while they were with him. They were supposed to be staying three nights, but on the Saturday morning he phoned me to tell me my son was ill and wanted to come back home. He told me I'd have to cancel my plans for the evening as there wouldn't be room for everyone. I was unsure as to what he meant. I thought maybe he was insinuating that I was going to have a party because I was free and single without the children. I couldn't see how he would know about Vicki and her sister coming to stay. I ignored his comments and waited for the children to come home. My son was suffering a reaction to something he had eaten, it was something that had happened a lot when he was younger but we hadn't seen it for a few years at that point. He told me he hadn't eaten anything unusual so there was nothing I could do but nurse him back to health. As soon as he was with me, his sickness left and he started to feel much better. My paranoia was telling me Sean had made him ill on purpose but I stopped myself in my tracks. Sean was annoying but there was no evidence to prove he was actually crazy enough to poison our own child.

The girls arrived, we had wine which had now become a rare treat for me, and the Wii. We danced the night away and laughed as the people in the flat opposite were watching us as we danced. I hadn't managed to get curtains yet, having furniture and carpets in the flat was a massive achievement, I hadn't seen the need for curtains. Vicki's sister asked me what car Sean had, and when I asked her why, she told me she thought she had seen him parked on the corner, over the road. Fear surged through me, but when I went to the window I couldn't see him. He wasn't supposed to know where my flat was, I took the children to him.

He was soon forgotten as we carried on with our catch up. It was like nothing bad had ever happened. I had my best friend by my side. It was 2am before we all crashed and admitted defeat. Vicki slept in the children's room and her sister stayed on the sofa where she had fallen asleep earlier. We covered her over and all went to sleep.

I woke up trying to break through a haze. I could hear commotion and see that all of the lights were switched on in the flat. The children! I jumped up and ran into the hallway, in full panic that something had happened to them. I could hear a car alarm going off outside and my senses were fully alert. Something was very wrong. That was my car alarm. Where were the children? They were still in their bed, my daughter was just opening her eyes as she was sensing the growing confusion in the flat.

Vicki's sister was shouting. 'There's a fire, there's a fire! We need to get out'. A sudden realisation hit me. The car was on fire. My car was on fire! I scooped up my children, covered them in their dressing gowns, and grabbed their coats, we ran out of the flat and out of the back door to get away from the fire. While I was grabbing my coat, my son ran to the window to see what was going on. I could see the reflection of the flames on his face, the fire was fierce and in full flow. He doesn't remember ever seeing the fire. Again, I'd failed to shelter them.

We huddled outside, chaos had erupted all around me. The neighbours were all awake and running around excitedly. Whose car was it? Was it arson? Siren's squealed into the close and even from behind the flats we could see the blue lights flashing in the night sky. I could hear people asking what was going on, who did they think had started it. I was numb with shock. That was my car. That was how I got to work. That was my life.

A loud boom echoed across the quadrant and I gasped in shock. It was followed by pop after pop as more of my car exploded and succumbed to the heat of the fire. A tap on the shoulder brought me back to the reality of the moment as a firefighter asked me if that was my car. I told him it was and he asked me to go with him. I didn't want to see it, I didn't want to face the horror. It wasn't the fact that I had lost a car, that didn't matter, it was that it was so close to my home, where my children slept.

The fire was now under control, or so the fireman was explaining to me, the loud bang had been the petrol tank cracking under the pressure of the heat and the pops had been the nitrogen in the tires. I asked if he was sure it was under control as the flames were still consuming my car. He replied that there was nothing else left to burn, it would soon die out. I was gobsmacked. He asked me when the last time I had drove it, and how much fuel had been in the car. I told him that it had been around 10am the previous morning after I'd collected the children and that I needed to refuel as I had decided to wait until the Sunday evening before getting ready for shift on the Monday.

He told me that decision had possibly saved our lives, that if the tank had been full the car would have exploded with the force of it sending it crashing into our flat. He told me he had phoned the police as there was no doubt in his mind what had happened: this was arson. He asked me if I had any idea who would want to cause me harm, I said my ex-husband. He nodded and left my side. The police arrived. They took my name and address. They asked if anyone held a grudge against me. I told them my ex hated me. They said they couldn't speak to him without being presented with any evidence and someone would be in touch. They walked away and left me standing there in the dark. That's when I saw the glove lying on the floor. Right next to my petrol tank. A purple latex free glove. Just like the ones supplied on the back of an ambulance. That glove waved at me but no one else could see it. It still lay there the next day when the recovery vehicle dragged the moaning metal across the floor and out of my life forever.

The phone calls stopped. There was no more harassment. He'd done what he'd set out to do. It was finally over.

CHAPTER 36: DECISIONS

After travelling back and forth from Brisbane to Newark several times, Dean thought Zéphirine should go back to France.

"Go and make peace with your parents, you only have one set of them." he said.

Zéphirine had not talked to her parents in a few years. She had not even bothered informing them about her divorce though she knew her mother would be happy about that. "I don't believe in divorce, but in your case it is necessary." her mother had told her on the phone once.

Life with Dean was extreme in comparison to life with Marc. Despite Dean's secrecy on some things, she enjoyed their relationship. They had the occasional fights. Sometimes it seemed absurd, it was like they had to fight just to prove they were human beings and could work it out, because they always did work out their differences. Dean and Zéphirine were seen as the perfect couple, the couple every one envied. But you just never knew what was going on behind closed doors.

One of their arguments was about Facebook. Zéphirine was upset Dean still had his status set as single. Practically everyone knew including his family so why keep it secret? It made Zéphirine feel as if Dean was ashamed of her; or perhaps keeping it under the radar for unknown reasons to her.

"Nobody cares; nobody reads those things on Facebook. Besides I have you as my partner on *Plurk* and *Second Life*," was

Dean's argument.

"Everybody cares, especially all those females after you Dean! That is the first thing they will check about you! And it is just what humans do instinctively anyway: they have to know if you are single or not!" she argued.

Most people on *Plurk* and *Second Life* were anonymous unlike Facebook, which was why he didn't mind adding her on there. The fact he had never mentioned on any social networks they were living together worried Zéphirine.

Zéphirine had sent him the request. She gave him a couple of weeks to respond. When he did not, she removed him as a friend on Facebook.

"Don't expect me to add you back." was all he said. And so they never mentioned Facebook again. Zéphirine knew it was silly, childish even, but she wanted to make a point: even if it did not matter to him, he should at least consider her feelings and do it for her. How hard could that be?

For the few months Zéphirine and Dean were apart, they kept their relationship going through *Skype* and *Second Life*. Flirting on *Second Life* was the closest thing they could get to intimacy. Not many people understood that of course, and that's why she didn't bother mentioning Dean to her mother. She sent a picture collage of herself and the kids which included one of her and Dean, so it wasn't exactly breaking news. They looked good together; happy. Most people who knew them described them as the couple that you just have to look at to know how much they were in love. But even with all that going for them, something still wasn't quite right between Dean and Zéphirine.

Zéphirine's son was going to be in France, spending time with his grandparents and meeting the family, so she thought this would be a good time to visit her parents too. She'd also get the opportunity to see her sister and her kids. It was strange. Zéphirine was officially an aunt, but didn't feel like one. What do aunts do? She was close to her friend's children and would do anything for them, but for her own sister's kids, she wasn't sure what to do.

Her sister had moved to South of France, which had left Zéphirine surprised. If there was a group of people that would never move from their hometown, she was certain her sister would have been one of them. She and her husband had done well and built their home. Their mother seemed to be pleased: at least she had one child who had done the right thing with what it seemed the perfect household: a house, well trained kids, and a husband with a secure job.

They were going to spend the Christmas Holidays at her sister's house and with her in-laws. Zéphirine was glad to have her son by her side, a familiar face, because she felt like a stranger within her own family. And with her son she enjoyed speaking English because nobody understood a word of what they were saying. It was grand.

At least while they were staying at her sister's, Zéphirine could talk to Dean. Her parents didn't have internet and the only Internet café in town opened occasionally and for short hours. So staying at her parents' had a lot of disadvantages. She wasn't sure what making peace with her parents would achieve. It was clear they had nothing in common and they would never be close.

Zéphirine wondered about Luc. She hadn't thought of him since Dean had walked into her life. But she was now in her hometown and wondered if she was going to run into him. She decided to look for a job in Paris. There was nothing to be gained in this town and it felt as if she was walking backward. Luc was the past. This was the town she had left when she was seventeen not looking back and the best move Zéphirine had ever made.

Zéphirine got a job in Paris as a secretary in a start-up which mainly hired her because she was bilingual. Within a week she hated her job. But it came through just at the right time to avoid her mother who was starting to get on her nerves. To top it all off, with no internet and a poor phone reception, there was nothing much to do. Paris was not next door, two hours and half away to be exact, but it was worth the sacrifices to not have to put up with her mother.

Zéphirine,
I repeat: DO NOT OPEN TILL ON THE TRAIN!!!!
Ha-ha! I wanted you to wait till on the train to give you something to do. I am hoping when I send this off to you it doesn't wake you either. Either way, I trust you will wait till morning.
I first off want to tell you how happy I am that you have found a job. I know it meant so much to you to start making some money. I am also happy because it will now give you something to do while we wait painfully for the visa. I felt horrible you went back to France and nothing good came out of it. I was truly hoping you and

your family would make amends this time. I suppose I should have trusted you telling me nothing would change. I am sorry for that. I feel really bad as I feel as though I forced you. Anyway, enough of that for now. I am a bit disappointed and worried about your long days though. I worry about your safety and health very much. Five hours of train rides and a full working day is a bit crazy in my opinion. I trust you know what it is you're doing and getting yourself into. I hope someone from your family in Paris will take you in to make this new job a bit more tolerable. I can't imagine just how bored you must be at your parents' home. Thankfully your son is there in a sense. I do hope the job works out for you though. Sure you could have probably done better as far as money goes but that too may change in time. I am really looking forward to hearing about your first day at work and also any complaints, if needed. If you do not mind, please send me an email with the time you get out of work when you can and approximately what time you would be arriving back home. Hopefully we will have a chance for me to call when you get in so you can tell me all about it. I am truly excited for you. I hope you will make some new friends as well. It's good to have human friends over all these online basket cases. I wish you the best of luck for your first day baby. Show them what you got (not your privates) and make me proud.

Well, we started step two of the fiancé visa. I want you to know I am truly excited in what we are choosing to do. I honestly cannot wait to you see again. I miss you so badly it hurts. Just the thought of missing you as I do, brings tears to my eyes. I must say this. I have never in my life missed anyone like I miss you. So this too is new to me. You better believe I am really looking forward to the day I can be near you again. I am really sorry the Christmas trip didn't fell through. But now it's not so bad seeing how you will be working. Besides we probably wouldn't get to spend much time together anyhow. In the meantime, and till we can meet again be strong as it is all we have going for us at the moment. See, I am trying to keep the positive attitude you have been throwing at me over and over.

Well anyway, I won't bore you to death. Have a safe trip and a great day. I will say my usual good morning when I wake. Keep your phone on vibrate and answer whenever you can. Good luck and enjoy! I love you!! Xoxo

Dean

After missing the train one night as there was only one, Zéphirine had to spend the night at one of her mother's friends in the Banlieue Parisienne. It was then decided she would stay there. It was still a bit of a commute, but better than the two-and-a-half-hour train ride back to her parents' house. And at least she had internet access and could therefore chat with Dean more often as well.

Zéphirine actually enjoyed her commute to work. The train station was only fifteen minutes away so she typically just walked there. She always passed two patisseries with the most delectable scents wafting from their doors; scents that were unique to France. It was usually too much to resist and she would wind up buying a fresh croissant to eat on the subway. Where she had lived in Australia, they did not have nearly as many homeless people as her new commute and it was depressing to see. The thought of the cold Paris winter made her feel even more sombre at times. As soon as she opened the door to the office, any good feelings she had disappeared. She was grateful for the view of the Eiffel Tower, it cheered her up a little.

Zéphirine was accustomed to the friendliness of people on the Sunshine Coast. She's had several jobs and always had enjoyed the atmosphere and was getting along with her colleagues. In this office, whether it was typical French, she wasn't sure because she hadn't worked that much in France and she was young at the time. The two managers were plain rude to her, especially one of them who thought he was some kind of hot shot director. The sales team also thought they were better than her. Not once did she ever got invited to lunch with them, she was just *the secretary*. She couldn't wait for the day to end the minute she sat down at her desk. She hated her new job.

While in Paris, Zéphirine had bought herself an iPhone 3GS. It was for sure the best thing she had ever bought and made it so much easier to keep in touch with Dean. She wished she had believed him sooner when he was begging her to get an iPhone. But then again, she couldn't afford it back then. She loved the fact they could talk on Skype or send instant messages at any time or wherever she was.

After a long day at work, all Zéphirine wanted to do was to chat and spend time with her boyfriend and occasionally with her friends overseas. It was tough being away from them and was feeling nostalgic. She always looked forward to hopping onto *Second Life* to catch up with Dean and other SL friends. Until one night she caught Dean's avatar flirting with another woman. Well, actually the woman was flirting with him. Zéphirine was following the chat and it was so obvious. And rude it was of the woman knowing that his *Second Life* partner and real life girlfriend was around. But then again she knew that some women would stopped at nothing to get Dean's attention. But when Dean agreed to a dance with the woman, Zéphirine had to charge.

She knew Dean was an attention whore but he had pushed her buttons one too many times, and today she was not going to have it. So they argued, through instant messages. Dean denied he was flirting or that he was aware she was flirting with him. She didn't believe him, causing him to close up and become distant.

Zéphirine thought she was losing him. She needed to see him. She had to see him. Payday was still a few weeks away. So she did the one thing she never thought she could do and she called her father to borrow money. He said yes but then her mother took over the phone and said she couldn't have the money because she didn't trust her as she was an irresponsible person especially when it concerned money. They argued for forty minutes. It was the talk Zéphirine had played in her mind a hundred times but knew it would never go further out of her mind as she was too fearful of her mother. She ripped into her mother as much as she did.

"As far as I am concerned, you are dead to me." Zéphirine told her mother who laughed in reply.

"I promise you you'll be talking to me again within a year like you always do." Zéphirine's mother carried on.

"Are you challenging me? Let's see how it will turn out this time." The phone clicked. Zéphirine was done. *Peace will not be happening after all* she thought to herself. But she didn't feel sorry. Her peace was made by telling her mother how she felt for once in her life. And since her father didn't even bother to take her side, she wasn't going to talk to him either. And she was fine with that too.

Zéphirine waited to get paid and planned a surprise weekend to see Dean. While she waited, she collected all their pictures together and special messages and organized them into a book.

She mailed it out to him on a day she was certain he would receive it just before she arrived. She arranged for Dean's father to pick her up at the airport and to drive her to the apartment.

Zéphirine wasn't sure what to expect when she would see Dean as he was still upset about that incident on SL. But when he opened the door, a smile of joy and satisfaction lit up his face. It looked like his eyes were getting misty. She had made sure he wasn't working and he didn't have his son on that weekend. He thanked her for the book he had received as planned the day before. "It made me cry. I love you so much!" he said holding her and kissing her hard on the lips.

That weekend went too fast. She didn't want to leave; he didn't want her to leave. In fact, she nearly missed her plane because of some roadwork on the highway. They didn't have much time to say goodbye and maybe it was for the best as it seemed it was harder to leave than it had ever been. As soon as she was back at her place in Paris, Dean begged her to come back. He didn't want her to leave anymore.

Her son came to stay for a few days with his grandparents and while in the same house, she managed to not see her parents at all and just enjoyed the company of her son. Thought she was disappointed they had taken him to the Eiffel Tower. She wanted to do that, she wanted the cliché picture in front of the Eiffel Tower with her son. But she wasn't going to give her mother the satisfaction of her being upset. Zéphirine took him to Disneyland, not as epic, but it was still something.

The family in Paris, on her father's side, was also happy to finally meet her son. They wished they could have had more time with him, but since her parents had paid for his plane ticket, her mother kind of thought she could do whatever with him and therefore not take him to a family she didn't like. Although there were some bridges between the two sides, it was still very much a race war between the two families and Zéphirine didn't want to be a part of any battles between the two. After all, that's why she lived on the other side of the world and it had taken her so long to accept her mixed heritage.

No matter how much she tried, Zéphirine couldn't come to like her job. This was unlike other jobs she's ever had before and she hated it! Finally, one morning, she woke up, booked her ticket, packed her belongings, and left to go back to Dean.

CHAPTER 37: ALLANAH'S LOOSE ENDS

With everything that had been thrown at my feet I didn't give up. There were those hell bent on destroying me, but in equal measure there were those with a heart of gold. After the car had gone, I almost despaired, if I had no transport then I had no work.

I won't lie, I cried for hours once the girls had left. I sent Zéphirine a message as I had no other way to get hold of Hunter. There was one thing I wanted more than anything in the whole universe: to feel his strong arms around me telling me it would be ok, that it didn't matter, the car was a replaceable meaningless object and the only thing that mattered was our safety.

That was a big step for me, Hunter loved Zéphirine and her family like they were his own. He had a loyalty to them that I sometimes found hard to understand or accept. There were parts of his life that he still hadn't shared with me and this was one of them. I had never been to Australia, yet that was the place that had enchanted his soul. I'd never met Zéphirine's family and Marc, but Hunter longed to be with them and had chosen to be there with them rather than helping me. I understood the reasons why, I needed to prove to him what I wanted in life, he had to see I was serious. He gave me the space to become independent and free myself from the shackles. He also left me to deal with the non-stop torrent of abuse over the phone from Sean. Actually, that was something I hadn't realised until that moment. When the flames were doused so was Sean's anger, I hadn't heard from him at all, there was a blessed silence.

Zéphirine had visited England in the winter before. Winter is the worst time to visit England, the days are short and the nights draw into a long depression of dampness. The snow makes things pretty, but never lasts for more than a week, and we all know that snow brings its own sadness. In short, if you want to see the best of England and its people, only come in the summer. The sunshine restores the spirits and refuels the zest for life. That's one of my excuses for being such a moody cow when I met Zéphirine.

I was jealous too. She probably knew Hunter better than I did. He had lived with her for longer than I had known him, she had shared memories with him that I would never be privy to and I just couldn't help being that green eyed monster. I wanted him all to myself, I wanted to immerse myself in his very being so badly. I convinced myself that Zéphirine and I had nothing in common, and that she didn't even like me. How could I ever measure up as the one who had captured Hunter's imagination when life in Australia was so vibrant? I tried to find common ground, but for the most time I was so self-absorbed with my ongoing battle with Sean that I withdrew myself from her. Her time in England must have been as miserable as the damp streets outside. For that I was sorry.

Now, I needed her help. I didn't know if she would read my message, why would she? My hands shook as I told the story of what had happened and as the tale unfolded I was convinced that I would never hear from Hunter again. He would stay in Australia, happy and safe, without endless complications. Hunter was only accessing the internet through the café in the mall every other day at best and I was desperate for him to tell me everything would be ok.

I huddled in the corner of my tiny kitchen. This was the furthest place away from where the charred remains of last nights' pyrotechnics were. There was a sense of denial whilst I sat there, I could make the calls I needed and try to make sense of what I would do next. I contacted work, I told them what had happened, that the car was not going to be replaced by the company as it was a total loss, ending my contract of service with them. My boss was amazing, she told me not to panic, that she would sort something out.

Within a day everyone had rallied around me. A hire car was being delivered courtesy of work, it gave me two weeks to raise funds for a new vehicle. My dad was searching for a car for me and would buy it, letting me pay him back in manageable instalments. Maybe he did really care and I just couldn't see it. My ma messaged me every hour checking I was ok, did I need anything, were the children ok, did I want to stay with her, had I got the curtains up in the lounge window yet? She was my constant, but the fact that she was worried told me this was a big thing.

My phone rang with a number that I didn't recognise. My heart raced as I realised it was an international number. Hunter had got my message, Zéphirine didn't hate me after all, and for her being able to give me that lifeline I would always be eternally grateful. It felt like I had been given a second chance with her, a way to show her I wasn't a moody bitch after all.

The call only lasted ten minutes, but it was hours in my heart. He told me not to worry, the car wasn't important, that I needed to stay safe, did the police know? I told him of course and that they had promised to refer me to victim support. I reassured him my ma was on hand, the children were ok and that we didn't need anything. He told me he'd be home soon, that he'd look after me. That was everything I needed. He didn't blame me, he didn't want to run away, and he was coming home soon. It was better than I could have imagined, he'd booked his flight home.

There's the rainbow. When all else seems lost and you have no idea what path to follow next, the sun peers around the edge of the clouds, the rainbow appears and you know everything will be just fine. For every bad thing that happens, the universe will balance itself out eventually, it has to be that way otherwise I'd have given up a long time ago. When the rainbow is hard to find there are those in our lives that will step in and step up. Our friends, our heroes, our lovers, our hopes and always our dreams. Without that night, with the flames licking high into the frozen night sky, my Hunter would never have seen how much I really did want him in my life. My Zéphirine would never have known how much I wanted to reach out to her, be a part of her world, see her land, feel her dreams.

Without that night breaking me free from the hate of others I would never have been able to move forward and embrace the rainbow.

CHAPTER 38: BREAKING OFF

Another three months in the USA had passed and Zéphirine was back in Australia. Marc and the kids had moved to a new house after the old house was finally scheduled for demolition. Troy who had befriended Marc, became a housemate. The kids had made him their uncle; he was part of the family now. They all liked to refer to Marc and Troy as the odd couple. They were not gay, but their friendship was so unlikely.

Staying with Marc reminded Zéphirine why they were divorced, so she was happy when Hunter announced his arrival. Hunter and Troy were accustomed to Zéphirine and Marc's disagreements, to put it mildly. They were the only two people who would always stay neutral between her and Marc because they were friends didn't want to pick a side.

However, Marc had his moments and could turn from being nice to a total jerk: "I'm tired of seeing your fucking face, I can't wait for you to leave." he once said when a small disagreement about his choice in friends unexpectedly escalated into a full-scale fight. Another time at the dinner table with Troy, Hunter, and the kids, Marc said out of the blue, "You know kids, your mother is only here because she needs a place to stay but as soon as she has the money she will leave so don't think she's here for you." Those were the times she hated him. There was no need for that kind of emotional abuse. She thought they had an agreement. He had never looked after his first two kids or their kids, so surely looking after them every few months wasn't too much to ask.

Marc's attitude mainly changed from nice to nasty every time he saw Zéphirine bonding with the kids. Zéphirine had the connection with the children he never had with them. Marc thought this bond would break over time. But Zéphirine and Adrian shared a passion for video gaming and while overseas they would play co-op games online. With Allison, it was a simple mother and daughter relationship. Marc had said many times he didn't know what to do with the girls. Zéphirine and the kids loved watching TV soaps that Marc thought were girly or lame. No matter what, Zéphirine knew she could never win the 'Mother of the Year' award, but she loved her children and would always be there for them. She came back for the kids as well as having to work to pay for her next plane ticket. In her mind, it was a win-win situation. She also couldn't let Dean carry all the costs every time. It was a life she had chosen to live. It wasn't like she had left without saying goodbye. They had discussed altogether how it was going to be for a while before she left the first time.

Zéphirine received a text message from Dean asking her to go on Skype immediately. She picked up at the first ringtone. Dean was crying.

"I'm sorry to call you like this but there is no one else I'd rather talk to."

"That's okay, Dean, you know you can talk to me and it's not like I've never seen you cry before. What's happening?"

"I lost my job."

"What?! How did that happen?"

"They caught me."

Once a month, Dean had to work seven days in a row and he hated it, even though the following week would be a short week since he would be off Monday, Tuesday, and then work on Wednesday, Thursday and Friday then off for the weekend. Most of the time on his working weekends, he would do his rounds and always do his job. But he would leave earlier than he was supposed to. His boss caught him doing it for thirteen weeks so he was watching him for a while. He gave him a choice to quit or get fired.

Dean quit. Zéphirine thought the company had been harsh on Dean as he had been working there for eleven years. Why wait thirteen weeks and not give him a warning instead?

Dean had good benefits and the overtime hours, even though not many, were highly paid. If he could stick there for twenty years, he would get other advantages for his pension. But as long as Zéphirine had known Dean, he had told her how much he hated his job almost every day. "So boring." he used to say. When Dean was at work, he would always call her and they would talk for hours. He would always have his laptop and most of the time he was on *Second Life*. Zéphirine never had a full-time job that gave as much freedom as Dean had since he was unsupervised most of the time. She thought it was great and she would have used that time to do something else like read books or even do some studies. Dean preferred to complain about it especially when he couldn't get a good internet reception. In a way, he got exactly what he asked for.

Only now he realised how good he had it. Finding a good job with a good salary and good benefits was not easy. He was also not entitled to any unemployment benefits since he chose to quit. Dean was not a happy man. His cousin got him a job where he was working but Dean decided he couldn't handle it and quit after a few weeks.

"I worked 12 to14 hours a day, six days a week and I don't even earn what I used to earn. I have blisters on my feet. Look." Dean said while sending her a picture.

"I seriously don't need to see your blisters, Dean." Zéphirine tried to comfort him as much as she could under the circumstances of being on the other side of the world.

But the thing was, Zéphirine thought, sometimes you had to suck it up. She was doing some professional cleaning to pay for her ticket and to buy a new laptop. Cleaning was far from being a glamourous job but it was money and because of her constant traveling it was the easiest job to get. The truth was: Dean always had a negative attitude on top of being lazy. *But when you love someone, you take them for everything that they are, the good and the bad*, she would tell herself.

The only time Adrian was leaving his room now was to go to school. When he was not at school, he was playing video games online. Marc now hated gaming or anything that had to do with the internet. He blamed Zéphirine for their son's gaming addiction. She never let their son played 24/7. Even though she spent a lot of time online, she didn't play 24/7 either. He was their father. All he had to do was to be firm with Adrian, to say no and make sure he followed the rules. At dinner time, instead of making Adrian come and eat at the dinner table, he would bring him a plate in his bedroom!

Zéphirine was not about to blame herself for what was happening. She brought up the kids on her own. Marc was never around and his family didn't give a damn about any of them. Adrian barely knew them as he was only a few years old when they first separated. And since that day, the family had decided to step out of their life for good, not even a birthday card or Christmas card. Zéphirine didn't understood why and had raised the issue several times with Marc who chose to ignore it, saying there was nothing he could do about it.

Zéphirine didn't want to be like her parents and always made sure the kids had everything they needed or wanted. But she also had rules, strong moral and values that she tried to instil into their minds. Marc was always against her. She said black, he said white. The teachers at Allison's preschool had warned her back then.

"We are two teachers in this classroom. The children know if they ask one teacher and she says no, they can't run to the other teacher because she is going to say no too. Parenting is exactly the same. You have to be on the same page otherwise it just cannot work."

Zéphirine knew that but Marc did not. Marc and Zéphirine were like antipodes while she and Dean completed each other in many ways. When Dean's son came to the apartment, he was allowed to play video games but when it was time to have dinner or to do something else, he would do as he was told. Sometimes they had to tell him more than once; he was a kid after all. But the kid followed their rules. In Marc's world, the kids made the rules and if Marc said anything, Adrian would call him names and abuse him with no consequences. It wasn't okay for Adrian to play video games all day long and Marc going in his room to smash the Xbox on the floor was not a solution either. Every time something would not go Marc's way, he would break something.

When Zéphirine asked Marc to get more involved in their kids' lives, she had hoped it would give them more stability; that he would teach them morals and values and why they should respect the rules that were in place for them. Instead, it seemed Marc only wanted to walk all over them and impose his will on the kids.

Dean survived off his credit cards and by cashing in his pension. He also had to be out of the apartment. Zéphirine thought he was going to go back to live with his parents.

"Are you crazy? I'd rather live in my car!" he said.

He had her a bit worried for a while, so she called his father and asked him what he thought and reassured her that Dean had already organized to move back in with them.

"Why don't you come up in September and then you can help me move out?" asked Dean.

"You know I would love to be there with you and help you any way I can. I would love to have you 24/7 for once as you are always working when I'm there. But you would be depressed and complaining about not having money to spend. Beside, to come in September would cost me an extra $700 that I'd rather have in my pocket for us to spend. As much as I really want to see you, we have to wait a bit."

"Yeah, I know you're right, I just miss you."

"I miss you too Dean."

Zéphirine booked her ticket for early November and decided she would arrive as a surprise. So she let his father know who for some reason didn't keep it to himself this time around. Dean called.

"You cannot come in November."

"Why not?"

"First, my father can't pick you up because he and my mother have a wedding to attend that weekend. Secondly, what is the point of coming since I am working six days a week? I come home around 8-9pm and Sundays are the only days I can actually relax."

"I just want to see you Dean as it will be six months we have not seen each other. I don't care that you are working, you've always worked when I was there with you. I just want to be there when you wake up and I want to fall asleep by your side."

"Well you just can't show up whenever you feel like to!"

"I'm your girlfriend Dean, so I think I can! I just want to see you." Zéphirine pleaded.

"I don't think it is a good idea."

"Whatever."

That was the last word Zéphirine heard from Dean.

CHAPTER 39: PLEASANTVILLE

Zéphirine's plane ticket was non-refundable. Dawson offered her to come and stay at his place in Green Bay, Illinois. She only had to buy an extra ticket to fly to Chicago where he would pick her up. In doing so, she had to spend one night in New York as there was no flights in the middle of the night. She couldn't afford a hotel for the night, but truth to be told she was hoping for Dean to pick her up.

Dean and Zéphirine were still not talking but he would know she was travelling because of her social check-ins. And that didn't fail: as soon as she landed in L.A. he messaged her.

"What are you doing in L.A? Partying?"

"Nope." she simply replied.

"Are you going to Dawson?"

How perceptive of him, Zéphirine thought and replied with a "Yes."

She managed to slip in the short conversation she was staying overnight in New York because her corresponding flight was in the morning. But he didn't question it and said he had to go before saying "By the way, I quit my new job." Trying to not be too hopeful while waiting for her next flight, she checked her emails. One said she had a comment on her personal blog. When she read the email, she got a little bit of a shock:

"Stop writing lies about Dean being your boyfriend. He hates you with a passion if you only knew. If I were you, I would also

remove all those pictures you have of you and he. You are sick and sad."

She quickly logged in to her blog to unpublish the comment and changed the settings to *'all comments have to be approved before being published'*.

She sent an instant message to Dean with a copy of the message asking him what was that about. But in the meantime, she received a few more comments:

"This Dean was my fiancé and he does live in New Jersey and you are not traveling back and forth there to see him. Stop dreaming." The woman carried on with a copy and paste of the exact message Zéphirine had sent to Dean: *Please tell your woman to stop harassing me. If you want to hate me, that's fine by me. I don't need to hear her crap. I feel humiliated enough, I can be mean too if somebody pushes me.*

"Zéphirine, Dean does not dictate to me what to do or when to do it. I am not being mean... I merely stated true facts."

And her last comment was:

"You are a lying tramp and Dean is getting an attorney. You had better remove all those lies and photos you have on your sites."

What annoyed Zéphirine the most at first, was that Dean copied and pasted her message meant to him to the woman. She didn't want that woman to think she felt humiliated by her. This message was meant for Dean and the woman took it out of context.

Zéphirine tried to understand what the woman's problem was. What did she mean by *'merely stated true facts'*? Dean and Zéphirine had a whole history together that was not very hard to prove: the pictures were real, the stamps on her passport, Dean's family taking her in, they had common friends. So who the hell was she to say Zéphirine had not been in a relationship with Dean?

But the fact that Dean didn't take a stand at all got to Zéphirine. "It has nothing to do with me, I was just caught in the middle of it and I don't want to hear about it. I warned you both." was his explanation.

"Wow!" Zéphirine said out loud to herself after reading his message for the tenth time. *Nothing to do with him? Seriously?* What happened to the guy who used to call her 24/7? What happened to the guy who could not wait for her to come back, the guy who used to cry at the airport, the guy who tried to make her miss her plane or handed her his credit card for her to book her plane ticket? Was that really the same guy who had just sent her this message? It was hard to conceive and believe he had forgotten their almost three years together.

But Dean never liked conflicts and refused to deal with them. It was as easy as to say to that woman: "Yes Zéphirine was my girlfriend and you knew about her since you used to call me at the apartment when she was there. She came to visit me many times and I took the apartment so we could be on our own instead of staying with my parents who did not mind having her there. And I am dickhead for letting her go and letting you trash her like that." Okay maybe the last part was a bit too much. But how hard was it to state one simple truth?

But it was then and there, she just knew Dean would not come to the airport and try to save their relationship. She knew this fairy tale was about to end. Dean and Zéphirine were over.

Going to Dawson ended up being a bad idea. They had a few good times, but mostly they were both depressed as his girlfriend had just broken up with him. But if Zéphirine spent most of her days crying in bed, Dawson was stalking his ex on every social networks. At least they shared passwords. Dean kept his computer and iPhone locked. When she was not crying she would find solace on *Second Life*, though it was never the same without Dean. She had gotten back in touch with Jordan because he always knew how to make her feel good.

She caught up with a friend on *Second Life* she hadn't talked to in a while and he was in a mood to listen to her vent.

"I'm having a hard time trying to get past everything. *Second Life* was a turning point, so many memories. I guess it must be different for you because you have your real life separate from your second life." She spilled to her friend.

"Well actually that separation is something I don't do well. Separation is part of how the relationship unwound."

"Any separation would be hard, *Second Life* or real life, I suppose."

"What I mean when I say that is the separation between RL and SL, relationships here or in any medium are not generally flights of fantasy to augment a dull RL, at least that is what I think. Those people who can do it that way are takers, sucking up emotional energy from the givers. I guess if two can set rules, it may be possible, but I don't know how yet. Pick the letter before the 'L' -

you have only one heart to break."

"I don't understand how people can be emotionally involved with two people. I have another friend here who is married and has been in a long time relationship with a woman on *Second Life*. We often talk about it. He always says he's happy with his real life. So, I don't know, I don't understand it." She sighed.

"The dirty secret is that one emotional tie is broken."

"I would say it is cheating but you know what, relationships suck anyway so now I don't care. I was never good at it and should have stick to staying single."

"Well Zéphirine, intimacy is a basic need, which is not to be confused with sex. I think you were better at it than you think. I think that every encounter makes us richer or poorer but don't get me started! It will take a lot of time!"

"You know, it's not something I am proud of, but before Dean I was involved with that guy online. I didn't know he was married at first. When I found out, I was hurt but I was too emotionally involved to back down. I knew we would never meet anyway. And we were such good friends too, still are. He made me feel like I was a goddess! Until it was too much for him, he couldn't stop thinking about me. It was affecting his real life so he let go of me and then I met Dean so it was good timing in a way." Zéphirine said.

"Well trust me. That starts because intimacy is broken. Hard to recapture but relationships last for a long time for a lot of reasons. When my folks divorced I was twenty and they had just celebrated their twenty fifth wedding anniversary."

"I never asked him because it was a bit hard to believe whether it was true that he was having issues with his wife. It's a classic excuse I've noticed."

"Have you seen the movie Pleasantville?"

"No, I don't think so."

"Oh go get it!"

"Ok."

"Tonight!"

"Yes, I am searching for it right now!"

"Real life becomes Pleasantville, picket fence, black and white, some become accustomed to it and value it. It is set in the 50's which is a cultural phenomenon that idealizes something we can't understand. But our parents do and some of us have it drilled into us too. So for your guy before Dean, he lived in Pleasantville. You felt like a goddess because you were the outlet for everything he actually valued."

"I used to tell him that his wife was a lucky woman."

"Nah, you are the lucky one."

"Why?"

"She doesn't know the version of him you did."

"So he wouldn't be like that in real life?"

"She may have worked daily to kill that version of him. Let me make this idea personal. I am a motorcyclist, risk taker, adventurer, and drummer. All these things were intriguing twenty years ago to my wife. She lived vicariously and dreamed of saving me from myself and I guess I liked the idea of being saved. Are you with me so far?"

"Yes."

"But in the end, I'm forty, I am still that person and I want to reconnect with him because I feel alive when I do. So the rift is not dysfunction in a working relationship. It works pretty well in many ways. I bought an Audi TT and have to drive it alone to be connected to that guy. Imagine if I could have a passenger that enjoyed it, many metaphors but the roadster is real. I am convinced this is everywhere. Opposites attract and then as the relationship matures they just become opposites."

"I don't think opposites attract."

"Back to your question, yes, he would be like he is in real life but it takes lots of empowerment because it has been beaten out of him for a long time. Opposites attract less as we get more life experience. You need to educate your view."

"He did tell me once I was making him feel good about himself though from what I knew of him I thought he was a pretty confident guy."

"Do I strike you as confident?"

"Yes, though I don't know that well so I could be wrong."

"I am, and I do things in my work and life that are amazing. But that does not change the need for affirmation of the silly part of us. Deep down I think most people crave one thing: to be really deeply known, and loved. But to be deeply known is a risk most won't take."

"And appreciated."

"Yes. We attach conservative morality to emotion instead of action."

"I never had a true relationship before Dean so I had no idea how a couple worked. Life is too complicated."

"Untrue. You will mourn a long time for Dean I think. And that is probably a good thing as it will turn into a view of the impact he had on who you become and you will conclude you are richer."

Zéphirine sent a message to Hunter letting him know she would be in the UK on the eighteenth of January, to be ready to pick her up.

CHAPTER 40: NOT GOOD ENOUGH

When Dawson had invited Zéphirine, he had all those grand business ideas to work on. But none of it happened because Dawson spent most of his time locked in his bedroom. By the time Zéphirine's stay was nearly over, much to her relief, he had finally gotten out of his self-centred, depressed mood. But it was too late to start any business ideas together.

Now, she was back in the UK, after all these years and it felt surreal. It was time to start a new life and meet new people. Zéphirine was looking forward to seeing Hunter again and finally meet the woman he had been raving about when he was in Australia last, Allanah.

Zéphirine believed Dean was her soulmate. So in the past three months she had hoped a little Dean would turn around and say '*Let's give it another go.*' But it did not happen. They barely talked to each other since the breakup. He was the one initiating the chat each time though, but always about things like "how do I update this on my blog" or "can you check this or that". It was never about them. She never engaged with him and kept any chat short and to the point.

Hunter lived in Stoke. Zéphirine finally got to meet Allanah. At first, the two women didn't click, but they did get along well enough. Zéphirine was under the impression Allanah didn't like her much.

In comparison, they couldn't be more different. Allanah was a pale woman with a thin frame. She had mentioned that she'd like to get a boob job one day, although Zéphirine wasn't sure if she was serious or not. She also had quite a few tattoos. They did have two things in common, however: wine and writing, which they had quite a few conversations over.

Zéphirine was hurt and still mourning her relationship with Dean. After nearly three years of ups and downs, with more ups as even with his secrets they were happy and in love. She was riddled with pain and guilt. She withdrew into herself and felt like giving up on life again. Luc came into mind. It was ancient history but she still remembered how heartbroken she felt when she left her hometown. She had hoped so many times that one day they might be together. Then she met Dean and now it was over too.

When Marc and Zéphirine broke up, they were on and off for a few years before the final strike. It did hurt, but it was nothing like what she had been feeling for the past few months. It seemed as if a knife of pain was stabbing her through the heart. She thought Dean was *the* one. How could she go on without him?

Zéphirine had mental scars that wouldn't heal. Desperate, she decided to call a helpline before the pain suffocated her any further. However, it didn't help. Years ago, she had wanted to become a counsellor to help people who struggle to accept themselves like she did. She had enrolled with Lifeline Australia and knew all the guidelines that they had to stick to. The call was pointless as she knew the entire script before the counsellor even opened her mouth. She hung up feeling even more miserable.

The household seemed happy. They all had a life. Hunter was with Allanah. They would go to work in the morning, come back at night, planned dinner, and did things together that did not involve her. It felt like everyone else was moving on with their lives while Zéphirine was stuck in a hole that she couldn't climb out of. She felt alone. She was alone. She was sick of feeling sad, lonely, and unwanted. She couldn't cry because she didn't want anyone to hear her cries. So she went for long walks at night, because it was easier to conceal the tears in the darkness.

She thought of Stoke as a very sad town, cold and grey; the perfect town to be in if you wanted to feel even more depressed. Zéphirine found herself standing on that line again between giving up and seeing how much more she could take. Every time she walked over the bridge, she wondered why she couldn't find the strength to jump. Then again, with her luck she probably would survive the jump. Her dark thoughts were back and she desperately wanted out. *'Let's find some pills'*. In movies, there was always a container full of fatal pills in the bathroom cabinets. In reality, there was not much of anything in terms of dangerous medications in a house. Not that she knew much of what could hurt her and what was available over the counter in the UK. She went to the chemist and bought some over the counter sleeping aids and a bottle of vodka. Overpowered by grief, she swallowed all the pills and drank herself into oblivion.

Morning was a bit painful but she was still amongst the living. She looked around and listened. The house was silent. Everybody had gone to work. *Nobody would notice if she wasn't there anymore* she thought. She packed her bags and set off without knowing where to go. She got to the train station where she bought a one-way ticket to London.

A few hours later, the train arrived at Kings Cross Station. "What next?" she asked herself. She walked to an empty bench against a kiosk in the middle of the station and sat there. She sat there for hours, looking around, her mind blank, thinking but not thinking.

Zéphirine's gaze shifted to a man in a uniform walking towards her. He had a *'Jason Stratham'* presence, except he was much taller, that's why she noticed him. "Hi," he said in a tentative voice. He then proceeded with too many questions such as "are you okay?" "are you waiting for someone?" "are you lost?" She looked up and saw the time on the clock, 9.30pm. She couldn't remember what time she had gotten there, but it was early afternoon.

Zéphirine wandered the streets of London during the day and slept in the waiting room of the train station at night. Until it was time to wake up and face reality. She sank to the floor and completely broke down. She cried until every single tear was spent. It wasn't the end of the world. She had to let go. She had to move on.

She made use of the free Internet at the library. A guy came up to talk to her. His intentions were flirtatious but there was no way she was in the mood for any relationships. Because he was English and she had told him a bit of her situation, he was able to explain a few things to her. She had entitlements since she had worked in the UK before and was holding a French passport. He also recommended her to stay in a hostel and pointed out some cheap ones.

She went from hostel to hostel until she found one that accepted longer stays in Bayswater. She shared a dorm in the basement with seven other girls. Most were only there for a night or two, but a couple were there on a semi-permanent basis. There were people in the hostel from all over the world. Quite a few had interesting stories to tell about their travels. Some not so much.

Zéphirine was mesmerized by the fact some of the guests had been living in this hostel for five to seven years. For now, it would do but she could not see herself living in such poor conditions more than three months and that was a stretch. There was a rat in their room. The girls asked the management to do something about it. The manager kept saying he would take care of it, but nothing was done. One of the girls ended up buying a trap and caught the rat leaving it to the cleaners to take the corpse away.

Some of the girls had no respect. One came back to the room in the middle of the night and turned on the light instead of using her mobile phone like the others would do. She also decided 1am was a good time to make a phone call. There were also the occasional fights about the shower as this room had its own bathroom unlike other floors where they had to share bathrooms and toilets between all of them.

Most of the time the toilets were so filthy Zéphirine had to use the ones in the closest shopping centre as they were kept clean. She decided to avoid the toilets in the hostel altogether unless there was no other option. But in general she tried to stay at the hostel only to sleep, shower and occasionally cook some food. Since she was a five-minute's walk to Hyde Park, she decided to get back into shape and would go for a jog in the morning. She then headed off to the nearest Starbucks to enjoy the free Wi-Fi and the free coffee refill.

She befriended a French girl who told her there was a position available at the hotel where she was working. Zéphirine got the job as a receptionist and it was a ten minutes' walk from the hostel. The working conditions and the pay were low. But she was working with fabulous people and that made her job enjoyable. Working as a receptionist was challenging though. There was a lot to complain about the hotel, but she was just an employee trying to make the guests feel comfortable. She quickly learned that abuse from the guests came as part of the job.

At the hostel, Zéphirine had moved to smaller dorm of four but after six months of being there, she decided it was time to move out. London was a very expensive city to live in. She had befriended a Russian guy in the hostel with whom she decided to share a room in Notting Hill. It was still walking distance to her job. The room was just big enough to fit a kitchenette, two single beds, a wardrobe and a table with two chairs. For the electricity they had to use gold coins like a parking meter. There was a shared bathroom every two floors, which were barely any cleaner than the hostel. At least it was a LITTLE cleaner. Not having to share a kitchen was also a plus as they didn't have to worry about people stealing their utensils if they turned their back for a moment. Some of the long term residents had lock up cupboards in the kitchen, but Zéphirine never had the intention of being there that long. Six months was long enough.

The guy that she had chosen to move in with left a lot to be desired. He would leave his dirty dishes in the sink for days, if they actually made it that far. In a big house, it wasn't as big of a deal, but in an area this small, it was a problem. There's wasn't much space to move around and the dirty dishes attracted bugs. As if all that wasn't enough, he'd also eat her food when she wasn't around.

In the morning when she got up, she would find tobacco left on the table where he had rolled his cigarettes. He was not making any effort of keeping the place clean and Zéphirine was not his cleaner. Besides, she had a full-time job and he barely worked. So the tension between the two started building up. At first it was little arguments here and there. Until one day it blew out of proportion. He was yelling at her with a thick Russian accent in a threatening way. She panicked and ran to the hotel crying. Jay tried consoling her the best he could, not knowing what had happened that shook her up so badly.

Her shifts were from 3pm till 10pm and that night she didn't feel like going home. So when one of the guests at the hotel, Rufus, a regular who would always flirt with her, asked her out for dinner she thought anywhere else was better. They met up at Nando's after her shift. He had brought her a little present: a FUKC bottle of perfume. She thought he was sweet.

He was shorter than her, so not the type of guys she would date but he was good company and fun. And fun was what she needed right now because besides working, eating, and sleeping there was not much else she was doing with her life. They started dating. He said he was working for a Football club and was going to meetings all around the UK. He seemed to love shopping as he always had loads of shopping bags and was always coming back late to the hotel because he had to go and exchange this or that in a shopping centre. Since she finished at 10pm six days a week, it fitted her schedule.

One night as they were walking back to the hotel he gave her a £20 voucher and asked her to buy a bottle of water. The bottle of water cost around £1 so she got the change and gave it to him. He did the same though he bought a few more things. When they got out, he asked her to do it again. She said no as she was not feeling comfortable with doing such thing. It was obvious he wanted the change out of the vouchers. Seeing a look of suspicion on her face, he explained he was getting shopping vouchers as benefits from his job and it was the only way to cash them. It was odd, Zéphirine thought. She was not completely sold on the explanation but decided to let it go for now.

They saw each other for a couple of months until she had another argument with her roommate. This time however, when it was time to pay the rent, he left a note saying he thought she would be moving out so he had already spent his half of the rent. There was no way she was going to pay the full rent, especially with him already owing her money from previous months. In those types of places, there is no lenience for late payments so she was forced to give their notice to leave. Fortunately, they had paid a bond which allowed them to stay another two weeks, just enough time to make other arrangements.

At work, it had become incredibly difficult. The owners of the hotel were despicable people to work with. Everything in the hotel was going against her morals and values. There were no ethics in that place. All they cared about was to make money. She was working six days a week, sometimes 10-12 hours shifts, had worked 21 days in a row once and she never got a thank you from her boss.

Zéphirine thought about going back home to Australia. Dick didn't like the idea. He wanted her to stay and said he would help find a new place or they could live together. So they started looking at places together. As work became unbearable she resigned. The truth was, she really wanted to go home. She missed Australia and she missed her children whom she had not seen for almost two years.

Dick had just moved in to a new place of his own and wanted her to stay with him for a while. Since she had to move out anyway, nowhere else to go and was going to be out of a job too, she agreed.

Where Dick lived, it seemed to be at the end of the world. They had to take a train, then a bus, and then a long walk or it seemed long because they had so much stuff to carry. But the place was nice. It was a small one-bedroom apartment but no bathroom to share with others, a proper sized kitchen and separate living room. It actually felt like a small piece of heaven compared to what she had been living in so far. They set out to go shopping to buy furniture and kitchenware. He bought everything with vouchers and returned credits. Again, she had an uneasy feeling and thought it was odd.

Dick had to go to Manchester for a meeting. But there was issue with his pay check so he asked to borrow money promising he would pay her back very soon. They went to Manchester and she racked up a £350 bill for a two nights stay. Then he said he had to go to court in London but was very vague on the details.

He left her with their suitcases at a coffee shop nearby the court. She waited for two hours then she received a text message from him: "I've been remanded. I'm sorry. I love you. Call my lawyer."

Zéphirine was left with no choice to book her ticket home. She had called the lawyer with the number he had given her. The lawyer told Zéphirine she was not allowed to discuss her client's affairs but explained how to visit him in jail.

Zéphirine had always thought that if there was one person she would ever visit in jail, it would be her ex-husband, not some random guy she had just met. Yet, instead of enjoying her last day in London with her friends, she spent it trying to visit a man in jail she barely knew.

Visiting someone in jail was not a simple affair. She waited and waited. Then she was placed into another room and was listening other women casually discussing who they were visiting like it was an everyday thing to do. Zéphirine felt completely out of place and wanted to run away. When she finally got into the communal room, he was crying, begging her not to go back to Australia. He had no idea how long he would be there. She had no place to stay and no job. And most importantly he was still very vague about why he was in jail.

Before rushing to the airport, Dick asked her to do one more thing for him: go to the post office to buy a notepad, envelopes, and stamps for Australia and mail it to the jail so he could write to her. On her side, she had to open an account online and fund it with £5. She was allowed to send unlimited amount of emails which costs 20p per 700 words.

She couldn't get her stuff back from his place because she had no idea how to get there, or even how to get in, and could not afford it either. Between helping him out and her plane ticket, she was penny less.

Dick got a one-year sentence. He wrote about one letter a month to her. No matter how many time she asked, he never said once what he had done, but repeated over and over how he had always been honest with her and could not wait to see her again. Lucky, there was that thing called the internet and she found out the truth.

Dick stole his grandparents' identity and ran up a debt worth tens of thousands of pounds to fund his gambling addiction. He admitted to ten charges of fraud and false representation, two wallet thefts, and two charges of intercepting post belonging to the Royal Mail without lawful excuse. He wrote more than 200 cheques worth up to £15,000 to a number of companies including Tesco, Sainsbury's, and South West Trains, which he knew would bounce as he had insufficient funds. His bank account transactions fraudulently reached £10,000. He and another guy were arrested at Royal Ascot on suspicion of handling fake currency during the biggest week of horse racing. Dick had denied sixteen charges of fraud and was released on conditional bail. The day she was waiting for him at the coffee shop, he was returning to face trial at the Crown Court.

She never once let on that she knew all he had done. She kept asking for an explanation but he never once admitted to anything. She kept writing because she felt sorry for the guy, after all, spending one year in jail could not possibly be fun. She also found out he had access to those vouchers through connections. He would buy stuff in one town and would get a refund in another town, that was why he had those so-called meetings. Dick had

285

indeed work for a football club but had been fired a long time ago.

EPILOGUE: NEVER LOSE HOPE

It had been three years – they had gone by in a flash.

Wishing to begin building a new life together, Allanah and Hunter had crammed their belongings into as few boxes as possible, packed up the two children, drove across the country, and found the best lodging that they could afford on a shoestring budget – enough to live in, but it was by no means the Biltmore. In this house, a proposal, and then a son eventually arrived.

Zéphirine was sincerely shocked by this, as Hunter had talked about it with her and he was adamant – he didn't need, and didn't want, any children. But Zéphirine knew he would be an excellent father, as she had seen him with her own children – their favourite uncle, Uncle Hunter, even more loved than their real uncles.

Despite the always-present flowers in a vase on the kitchen counter, life was not rosy. With life together came the typical hurdles of raising two teenagers alongside a toddler – iPhones and Thomas the Tank Engine, crying over partners and crying over saying no to another cookie. The fact that Hunter had face-planted leaping over the hurdles of starting a business was not of help either, Allanah could see that they were red, despite the fact that "Rome wasn't built in a day," according to Hunter. When it wasn't talking about the business, it was Hunter's fascination, one that would consider morbid-obsessive, of Australia. This was especially present when the topic of money came up, him insisting that moving to Australia would help to absolve their debts. Allanah saw it as running. Memories and dreams of fruity drinks and sandy beaches would last no longer than five minutes when arriving there.

"I wish I had put a bit more of an effort to get to know you when you were here." Allanah said to Zéphirine one day. Over that time, they had become much closer, soul sisters, practically. This had grown even stronger due to the fact that Zéphirine was now Hunter's employee set to the task of maintaining his website. When things felt terribly black, a conversation could change the outlook to only a tinge of grey, not better, but navigable.

Zéphirine confided in Allanah always, despite the difference in that Allanah had always been a hopeless romantic and firmly believed that Zéphirine would find her own fairy tale (or close enough to one) soon. Zéphirine envied Allanah in that constant positivity of hers. She had managed to find her dream man. The distance, with Allanah in the UK and she being in Australia, had never hurt their friendship.

Zéphirine had introduced Julia to Allanah, online. Allanah and Julia were extremely different in their character, one being overly shy and an introvert and Julia being totally out there, and Zéphirine in the middle with a bit of both, shy but also a social butterfly at times. Their circle of three was eclectic, but, it worked. The women truly cared for each other.

Zéphirine tossed and turned in her bed, sheets twisted around her. She was still pining for Oliver. When she closed her eyes she could still feel his hands roaming her body while they danced. She remembered her own hands caressing his chest and feeling his abs. How she wanted to just rip his shirt off and put her hands on his chest! Whenever she had thoughts about him, she could feel her heart beat faster and her breath quicken. Every nerve in her body would go into overdrive. Trying to tear herself from her fantasies, she realized she had never wanted a man as much as she had wanted Oliver.

"You are so seriously stupid Zéphirine!" she told herself. Oliver and Zéphirine had met once, just once, for a few hours, six hours at most. How was she still thinking about him a year later was beyond all comprehension. As others had stipulated, he probably had a wife and could not care less about her. She became sick with concern, knowing how little she actually knew about him.

Her heart was not letting him go. In the dark, she tried to reach for her iPad on the bedside table, wishing that she would have to reach over him to grab it. As she fumbled, a clink and plunk sounded in the darkness, her sleeping pills. She considered taking them again. She shook herself to reality and grabbed the iPad, leaving the pills on the floor. She gave herself a few moments to think about it. Allanah was right, Zéphirine had to know. She adjusted herself and opened her email, almost mindlessly. She knew what she wanted to say, instinctively. She started to type. The email was titled: "What do you think of when you hear the term 'executioner'?"

She smiled: *'if that did not catch his attention nothing else would'* she thought to herself. The email's subject did not really mean anything. Zéphirine was just looking for something catchy, a strong headline to 'get your emails opened' as she had been taught in marketing. It was not that she thought Oliver would not read her email, because she knew he would. Whether he was going to answer it, was a different matter.

***

There is no moral to this story as it is life's great irony - or perhaps it is the sad reality of life. And so we start chasing rainbows as we constantly plan for the future, we desperately seek love; we envision what our lives are supposed to be like but the biggest discovery is that nothing goes the way we anticipate. As their journey was filled with hardship and pain, Allanah and Zéphirine strived to make sense of their experiences to conquer love, life and happiness. One had succeeded by finding her soul mate and the other had not, but they had found each other and with that came the gift of true friendship.

A true friend is someone who knows you better than you know yourself, who challenges you and supports an indescribable bond. Neither one of them would be alone to fight their own battles anymore, whether it was to vent about managing a busy household, bitch about the neighbour or crying over a date gone wrong. It did not matter that they were separated by an ocean and thousands of miles, Allanah and Zéphirine were right alongside each other and ready to tackle whatever life's hurdle would be thrown at them.

ABOUT THE AUTHOR

Prisqua Camiul has always longed to tell a story; to have her words heard and understood.

Originally from France, now settled in Australia, she is embarking on a new journey in life: studying Writing and Communications courses, publishing her first women's fiction novel, working on a sequel, and writing short stories.

Writing is a form of therapy for Prisqua; the sound of the keys tapping away enables a story to be told.

Writing has been part of her life for a long time with Prisqua keeping a diary from her teenage years and now keeping copious notes from her life encounters on her laptop, iPad, and iPhone.

A cup of coffee and a walk on the beach are essential along with keeping active, healthy, and of course, hunting and shooting Aliens on her Xbox a few hours every day.

Website: http://chasingrainbows.xyz/

www.ingramcontent.com/pod-product-compliance
Lightning Source LLC
Chambersburg PA
CBHW071859020726
47502CB00003B/815